Outstanding praise for
THE LAST SECRET

"An extraordinarily powerful novel cinematically weaving one gripping layer into the next. From the frozen hellscape of Eastern Europe during WWII to the lush green of Salt Spring Island in Canada, *The Last Secret* delivers a thrilling story of survival and love that held me spellbound throughout."
—Genevieve Graham, #1 bestselling
author of *The Forgotten Home Child*

"A tense and thrilling ride of a story."
—Janie Chang, bestselling author of
The Porcelain Moon and *The Library of Legends*

"With *The Last Secret*, Maia Caron firmly establishes herself as one of the most powerful, truthful, and poetic voices in Canadian historical fiction."
—Natalie Jenner, bestselling author of
The Jane Austen Society and *Bloomsbury Girls*

"Sweeping from hardship to heartache, *The Last Secret* is a timely reminder of the bonds forged, broken, and recast on WWII's Eastern Front. Here, revenge is served tundra-cold, but with a dash of sea salt and fire."
—Shelley Wood, internationally bestselling
author of *The Quintland Sisters*

"*The Last Secret* is a masterfully crafted historical thriller, a riveting tale that sweeps across decades and continents. The intertwined stories of a Ukrainian woman ruthlessly pursued by the Russian secret police and a scarred young artist at the mercy of her nurse's sinister machinations converge in a climactic, heart-stopping showdown on a remote island in the pacific northwest. Maia Caron has irresistibly woven historical drama, mystery, and romance in a gripping tribute to women's resistance and resilience."
—Lilian Nattel, author of *Only Sisters*

The
LAST
SECRET

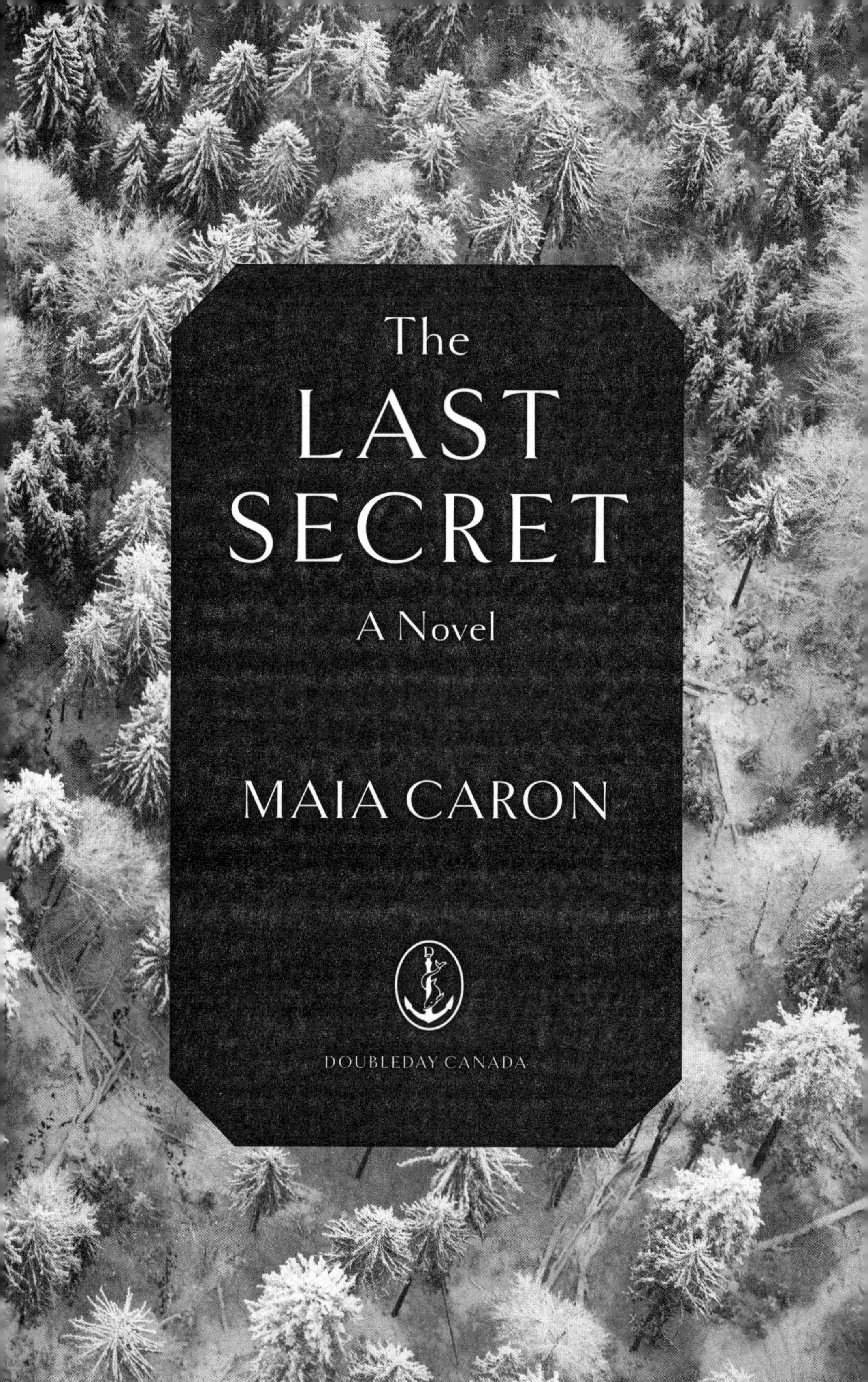
The
LAST
SECRET
A Novel
MAIA CARON
DOUBLEDAY CANADA

Doubleday Canada and colophon are registered trademarks of Penguin Random House Canada Limited

Library and Archives Canada Cataloguing in Publication

Title: The last secret: a novel / Maia Caron.
Names: Caron, Maia, author.
Identifiers: Canadiana (print) 20240322525 | Canadiana (ebook) 20240322533 | ISBN 9780385688826 (softcover) | ISBN 9780385688833 (EPUB)
Subjects: LCGFT: Novels.
Classification: LCC PS8605.A764 L37 2024 | DDC C813/.6—dc23

This book is a work of fiction. Names, characters, places and incidents are products of the author's imagination or are used fictitiously. Any resemblance to actual events or locales or persons, living or dead, is entirely coincidental.

Cover and interior design: Kelly Hill
Cover images: (coat) Anna Gorin, (trees) OliverLeicher, (braid) Cavan Images, all Getty Images; (frame) pingebat, (coat collar) Galina, both Adobe Stock
Interior image: Bernhard Lang/Getty Images
Typesetting: Sean Tai

*The author wishes to acknowledge the support
of the Canada Council for the Arts*

Printed in the USA

Published in Canada by Doubleday Canada,
a division of Penguin Random House Canada Limited

www.penguinrandomhouse.ca

1st Printing

For the Daughters of Ukraine, past and present
. . . and Shasta, my beautiful girl

======

They reckon ill who leave me out;
When me they fly, I am the wings;
I am the doubter and the doubt,
And I the hymn the Brahmin sings.

RALPH WALDO EMERSON, "Brahma"

PROLOGUE

Rimini, Italy
JUNE 1946

THE CAGE IS NARROW and humid as a steam bath, with just enough space for Nikolai Belyakov to execute a slow circle around the prisoner. A single bead of sweat trails down the Ukrainian's cheek, and Belyakov takes out his handkerchief to tenderly dab it away.

Marko Ivanets leaps to his feet, only to be jerked back by the handcuffs around his wrists, attached by a chain to the table. He turns his head and spits on the floor. "*Moskal'*."

"You disappoint me," Belyakov says, bringing the handkerchief to his nose. He inhales a last, thrilling smell of ocean, sun, and sweat, before tucking it into the pocket of his field tunic for later. "A Ukrainian who fought in Hitler's Waffen-SS should show respect to his Soviet superior. Do you forget who won the war?"

Ivanets lunges at him, like a mad dog testing the length of its chain, and the Soviet agent itches to sink his fingers into the prisoner's short blonde hair, force his head back and expose his jugular. But it's necessary to handle this affair delicately. Marko Ivanets is Belyakov's only ticket back to Moscow, a return to what he does best.

"I expected to find you sickly and overworked," he adds with a smile, "but look at you—tanned and fit. Is it true you sing in the Rimini prison choir?" The former Ukrainian underground commander says nothing, only eases his bulk back into the chair and fixes a blue-eyed glare on his interrogator, who can't help but admire his profile, noble as any Cossack hetman. Unsettled, the Soviet removes his cap, running a hand over his dark brilliantined hair and wishing he could drown himself in a bathtub of vodka. Or something stronger. But none can be found in this *blyadskiy* POW camp on the Adriatic, still recovering from the war.

Belyakov had expected a proper interrogation room, not this cage with its thick steel wire walls, cramped as an isolation cell in the Gulag, assembled in haste at the back of a flimsy prefab hut on a disused airport runway. A single bare light bulb hanging from its cord stirs in a breath of humid air from the open window high above them, too far from the ocean here for a trifling breeze that might cool the room. How he would like to have the former Waffen-Sturmbannführer in the basement execution chamber of Lubyanka prison in Moscow, in the room he designed for interrogations such as this, with a sloped cement floor and the black hose hung neatly on its hook. In that room he always won a confession; he always knew how to make them cry.

And beg for him to stop.

Until the day five years ago when NKVD guards knocked down the door of that interrogation room and discovered him at the point of no return. Nikolai Belyakov, star NKVD interrogator, as he was rushed, his arms pinned back. Then the indignation of arrest and the burn of his own brutal interrogator's final words.

"Do you understand how far you have fallen? I'm disgusted to look at you . . . a monster, a filthy person, a pervert . . ."

He blinks away the memory and considers the prisoner. "State your rank and birthplace."

"Rank: corporal," Ivanets says in Ukrainian. "Birthplace: Ukraine."

Belyakov flinches at the sound of Ukrainian, a language forbidden in Soviet Ukraine since 1764 by Catherine the Great. He glances at the British private, his back rigid with attention on the other side of the cage, a lowly soldier the camp commander has sent to ensure this remains an interview, not an interrogation. The private cannot possibly understand Ukrainian or Russian. This conversation will remain confidential. Still, he longs to use other tactics. "You are not a corporal but a major," he tells the prisoner in precise Russian. "A fascist Waffen-Sturmbannführer, no less. If you return with me, you will be treated like royalty." How unnatural it is for him, this polite exchange.

"Some of my men were manipulated into leaving with your earlier delegations," Marko says, beads of sweat gathering on his forehead. "They were shot in the back of the head before the train left Italy."

Belyakov inwardly curses the sloppy work of the operatives who preceded him, too eager to shoot these traitors and fling their dead bodies out of train cars, where the emotionally overwrought Italians had found them. "We will provide you and your wife and son a luxury apartment in Moscow," he lies, dangling the ultimate reward.

"You will not speak of my wife and son!" Marko shouts, a scar on his cheek turning livid red.

"And *you* will adopt a tone of respect—" Belyakov is cut off by sudden shouts that drift through the window, a ball game of some sort going on outside. He closes his eyes to breathe in the delicious sweat of so many muscled bodies cramped together in this shamefully hedonistic prisoner of war camp. After being denounced and demoted by the NKVD, given only two men when he once commanded hundreds, Belyakov had traveled a long, hard road during the last two years of the war, a pariah relegated to hunting Ukrainian underground bandits behind Nazi front lines. He had remained in Soviet Ukraine, secretly building a small network of his own spies. But in the end an NKVD operative had found him and his two men camped on the bitter slopes of the Carpathians and handed him direct orders from the Kremlin.

Stalin needs you! You must do what your comrades could not— persuade the British imperialists to hand over 8,000 Soviet Ukrainians of the Fourteenth Waffen-SS in reparation for crimes against the Motherland!

Belyakov and his men had scrambled their way to Italy—a three-day train journey to Rome, then dusty motorcycles up and across the boot, anticipating success and a way back to decent Moscow apartments, drinkable vodka, and respect. Yesterday, under a relentless sun, Belyakov had stalked into the Rimini camp, hoping to find a wilted pansy in command, one who would quail in terror at the real man Moscow had sent to finally get the job done, the closer. To his outrage, Brigadier Block was decidedly not a wilted pansy, but a British war hero who cunningly installed the three-man Soviet delegation in a foul army tent beside the camp mess hall. Belyakov's wool uniform stank of fish and cabbage. Simmering with resentment, he stands over Ivanets unable to stop thinking of Block's horse face as he sat behind his desk, war medals gleaming.

"I will have the list," Belyakov had quietly demanded in stilted English. Without invitation he had settled himself in the single chair across from the brigadier and lit a cigarette, ignoring an ancient fan that wheezed in a corner, churning dank air across the room. He took a different approach than that of earlier Soviet delegations. Why bother attempting to persuade the British commander to hand over traitors when Belyakov could simply hunt them down individually? Arduous and time consuming, yes, but perhaps the only way forward.

"The Rimini camp list?" the brigadier asked, rubbing an awkward finger over his chin, as if wiping the egg off his face. When earlier Soviet delegations had persuaded him to hand over some of the Fourteenth Division prisoners, Eleanor Roosevelt and the Pope had intervened on their behalf. Now the British considered the Ukrainians *surrendered enemy personnel* and not the traitors they really were. "I'm afraid that is quite impossible," Block said. "Moscow would then have the names and birthplaces of every one of the men in this camp." He looked up, pointedly. "Which is why the list is classified."

"Classified?" Belyakov wavered on the knife edge of fury and imagined Brigadier Block in the Lubyanka interrogation room, begging for his mother. "The international military tribunal found the Waffen-SS a criminal organization," he reminded the man, who'd become suddenly fascinated by a paper clip on his desk.

"As I understand it, ancestors of these Ukrainians resisted Soviet oppression for centuries," the commander said, his voice wavering under the strain of imperialist propaganda. "Does it not stand to reason that their sons and grandsons joined SS divisions to fight communism when Germany gave them the chance?"

"You do not understand ungrateful peasants." Belyakov sat back in his chair, blowing smoke at the ceiling before placing his right hand, palm down, on the brigadier's desk. "These *traitors* join fascist pigs to bite the hand that feeds them for centuries."

Block raised an eyebrow. "Didn't Stalin starve millions of Ukrainians to death in the 1930s?"

Not enough of them, Belyakov thought, but he said nothing. His fingers clenched and unclenched on the desk, attracting the Brigadier's anxious eyes. "Stalin himself sends me. As a Soviet ally you are obligated by the Yalta agreement. Turn these men over to me." He knew this effort was futile, but there was one other prize he might secure. Belyakov let his pause lengthen, until the blood had drained out of the brigadier's face. Then, forcing a reluctant tone of respect for the commander he said, "What of Marko Ivanets, underground codename: Roman? Only Ukrainian man promoted to Waffen-Sturmbannführer."

"I will afford you the same opportunity as other Moscow delegations," the brigadier said, fidgeting in his seat, "and let you speak to the major. But you cannot have him."

Now, in the cage, Marko Ivanets is proving to be stubborn and uncooperative, even lying about his rank. *Corporal.* What luck to find him here, the underground commander Belyakov had hunted three years ago, in Ukraine, and thought lost to the war. He makes another slow circuit of the interrogation room, pausing at the cage door where the British guard stands, close enough to smell the musk scent of youth, close enough to unnerve him.

When he turns slowly toward his prisoner, the man does not pale or falter, as he should. "On the night of May 8, 1945, as the Red Army approached Graz," the Soviet agent begins, "you were Brigadeführer Fritz Freitag's highest ranking Ukrainian officer. Freitag had the right idea— shoot himself to avoid capture by the Red Army. Did you and your men think we wouldn't notice when you changed the name of the Fourteenth Waffen-SS Division to Ukrainian National Army and surrendered to the British? You believed they would protect you." He leans toward the prisoner. "How did you think you would escape *me?*"

He waits for a response, for an admission of guilt, but the prisoner remains silent. The heat in this room is suddenly too painful to bear and Belyakov toys with the top gold buttons of his wool tunic, longing to tear it off. The prisoner appears maddeningly oblivious despite the sheen of sweat visible on his chest and the thudding pulse at his throat. Belyakov admires, with a short man's envy, the elemental force of Marko Ivanets in his hand-me-down version of the British army's summer prison uniform of khaki shirt and short pants.

From behind, he lowers his hands to the prisoner's shoulders, elec- trified by the feel of hard muscle beneath the shirt before Ivanets jerks away. "What happened to your SS uniform, hmm?" Belyakov smiles. "And the Nazi weapons you carried. You were commander of an artil- lery division, an officer who gave orders."

"Only German officers issued orders."

Belyakov itches to slap this lie off the prisoner's face. He refuses to let Marko Ivanets slip away under an umbrella of protection from the British. He closes his eyes briefly to compose himself, feeling raw and exposed, his self-control drifting away like smoke. Slipping a hand into his pocket, he runs trembling fingers over the case that contains his little white pills and over the stark comfort of his sterling silver flask. "If you cooperate, Moscow will welcome you as a hero of the motherland," he says, suddenly weary, his aching head reflecting what this lie has cost him.

"I have never been a citizen of *mother bloody Russia*," Ivanets says, then turns his head to look him up and down. "*Korotyshka.*"

Belyakov leaps to face the prisoner, employing an old interrogation technique. He forces a strangled sound from his throat—the sound of a man being hanged—then holds up his hands in Marko Ivanets' face. Belyakov speaks into the sky-blue irises, into the frank hatred of a *hohol* peasant: "I am small, yes, but these are hands of steel. These are the hands of Stalin."

In the silence that follows this pronouncement, the British private shifts on his feet outside the cage. Has he registered a threat, despite the fact these words were delivered in Russian? Let him. Belyakov has not broken the agreement he made with Brigadier Block, nor damaged the prisoner. A smile plays at Marko's lips, as if aware that he's forced a check against Belyakov's king, but the NKVD agent has other moves on the chessboard. He places Stalin's hands on the table and looms over his prize. "Stop lying—you are a bandit, a terrorist, and a traitor."

"*Idi na khuy,*" Ivanets mutters under his breath.

Belyakov wets his lips, enraged and aroused in equal measure. The British guard knows nothing of his past, that Moscow considers him an outcast, a pervert. "If we were alone in this room," he says, letting himself loose, "I would vigorously oblige you." He savors the look of shock and alarm on Marko Ivanets' face. "You would throw your head back to cry out in pleasure, and then"—he makes a slicing motion across his own throat. "Quick, fast—a beautiful way to die."

Now there is a flicker of curiosity, maybe fear, in the Ukrainian's eyes. Belyakov paces the room, waiting for his pulse to slow. He pauses for a moment before the prisoner. "Perhaps you have heard we are breaking the underground in Soviet Ukraine. Those we haven't shot in their holes have crawled away to the villages to hide, like cockroaches. We are actively searching for your parents, your grandparents. They will be arrested and sent to Siberia."

"Search the graveyard." Marko's hands are clenched so tightly upon the table his knuckles have turned white. "Stalin starved them to death in '32."

Belyakov quietly curses. If Stalin had foresight, he would have kept enough Ukrainians alive to provide the NKVD with bartering chips. He leans close to whisper in the prisoner's ear. "What of your wife? Your son?" The gratification Belyakov feels at what he does *not* say, what he holds back, is almost orgasmic. He's tempted to give Marko one small hint, a worm to crawl in his brain, a threat so vaguely terrifying he might guess it has already come to pass.

"Do you think I would trade my wife and son for eight thousand Ukrainian men?" Marko laughs in his face. "They are safe and no longer in Ukraine. You have nothing."

Belyakov thinks of the Rimini List. How can he not? British intelligence will move these Ukrainian traitors to England, and the list will be locked up by MI-6, never to be seen again. He studies Marko's smugly entitled face and allows himself a private smile. "Your British commandant has refused to share the camp roster list of your men," he says, measuring his words. "But it will soon come into my possession. Each one of you will be hunted down and executed, your families sent to Siberia."

Marko laughs again, yet his expression betrays a brief flash of concern. "You will never get your hands on that list."

For a moment, Belyakov imagines himself standing in the Lubyanka interrogation room, wearing his long leather apron and rubber boots, but he banishes the memory and reminds himself: *there are other methods.* He has planted a seed, now he must wait for it grow.

Hitler underestimated Soviet power; the West underestimated Soviet power. But neither would underestimate Nikolai Belyakov. Still, he knows there is no other choice but to give up. For now. This fish will slip back into the sea, and Belyakov is playing the long game. He will wait and watch, rely on *her* to do her job and *him* to remain safely tucked away. At some point in the future, Marko Ivanets will crawl across a room like this on his knees and offer the list to him in supplication.

He turns to leave, but Ivanets looks too assured, too confident that he's escaped his fate. Belyakov pauses at the door.

"Do not mistake it," he says. "One day, my hands will find your throat."

SAVKA

Deremnytsia, Reichskommissariat Ukraine
FEBRUARY 25, 1944

THE MUD BENEATH Savka Ivanets' knees vibrated with the shell strikes of Nazi and Soviet artillery and the buzz of Russian planes strafing Wehrmacht troops at the front lines, only five kilometers to the east. She knelt at the river's edge, so close to her mother and her sister, Lilia, their foreheads almost touched. Nazis still held this part of Ukraine, but the Red Army was grinding closer every day.

"If I eat another stinking chestnut root, I'll *die*," Lilia said, glancing over her shoulder at the forest that carpeted the mountain behind their village. "I'm going to the woods," she threatened. "Early *shchavel* will be sprouting under the trees."

"You're not going anywhere," Savka said. She exchanged a look with her mother, whose weary eyes flicked between her two daughters. Mama, who trembled at the first sign of discord and whose layers of tattered clothing broke Savka's heart.

Warming temperatures had melted most of the winter's snow, leaving half-frozen puddles and turning mud on the banks of the river into a kind of quicksand that sucked at their knees. This ground had been fought over for centuries by Vikings and Russian empresses, Polish princes and Mongol khans. But now it was threatened by another, perhaps more formidable foe. "The forest is a guerrilla war zone," Savka warned Lilia. "Do you want your throat slit by a Soviet partisan—"

The words were torn from her mouth by the blast of three Messerschmitts roaring overhead on their way to the front. Savka's nostrils filled with the primeval smell of frigid river water and water chestnut plants that had died off with the coming of winter. Wind scoured the damp skin of her cheeks, and the spectral sun was dimmed suddenly by a thunderhead rolling down the slopes of the mountain, sending shadows across the river. Though she didn't know it, the war would soon sweep Savka up and carry her down a river like this one. She did not yet know there were deeper levels of despair than fearing her husband was dead and searching vainly for food with a stomach empty as a gourd. She looked up at Lilia, who was impatiently waiting for her to take the bait. Was it possible to stop her rebellious sister from getting herself killed? "If it's danger you seek, you'll soon get it when the Russians come," she said, through gritted teeth. "They'll rape and murder every Nazi collaborator." Mama's hand flew to her mouth, and Savka immediately regretted her words.

Lilia threw down the stick she'd been using to dig out chestnut tubers. "So advises my dear older sister, wife of a Waffen-SS officer, still carrying the medic bag she stole from the back of a Nazi ambulance. I'd rather take my chances with partisans than spend more time with *you*."

Savka bit her lip. She was not a rebel like Lilia, but everyone had been forced to take chances during this war. When Savka had answered the call from the Ukrainian Red Cross years ago, her husband, Marko, and the underground had expected her to steal and hoard a cache of medical supplies to treat insurgents. But it was like torture for a woman like her, who would rather be doing anything else than watch for lax Nazi medics to leave their ambulances unattended in the village whenever they passed through. Each time she managed to snatch a kit or supplies she feared the cold steel of a Luger at the back of her neck.

"Stop your bickering," Mama said, rubbing her temple with mud-died fingers. "The Germans have stolen everything from us—*Tato*, Andriy . . ."

Savka looked away, striving to bear the impossible. When the Germans had invaded Ukraine in 1941, they'd taken every scrap of food for their armies—bushels of buckwheat, cabbage, and beetroots—leaving her village with only a few goats. To support the family, her father and brother had volunteered for the labor program in Germany. Her *tato* and Andriy had planned to send their wages, but there'd been no letters home. Savka had heard tales of starvation, armed guards in the factories, and no access to shelter during the British bombing raids. A veritable death sentence.

"I'm going to the woods." Lilia scrambled to her feet. "See if you can resist a bowl of borshch when I find *shchavel*."

Savka gave up. "Try not to get yourself killed," she muttered darkly, getting up off her knees to scrub a beet-shaped tuber in the cold river. She tucked it into her pocket. Beneath her coat, the sleeves of her sweater were pulled down over her trembling hands, the fingernails rimmed black with mud. She glanced back at the farmer's field, still covered in a mantle of thawing snow, and into the forest, not three hundred meters away, the leafless trees consuming whatever light remained of the day. Once every villager's childhood playground, the heavily wooded slopes of the mountain had become an escalating battleground between two kinds of guerrilla fighters: Ukrainian underground insurgents and Soviet partisan gangs of outlaws who had been parachuted behind the front lines.

Lilia was stomping off through the reeds at the river's edge when Savka shouted after her. "Wait." A shrouded figure had emerged from the forest. It paused a moment before seeing the three women at the river and struck out across the field toward them.

"A partisan?" Mama said, her voice a tremor. "Out in broad daylight."

"It's just a refugee who's wandered from the main road," Savka called to Lilia, if only to calm her mother's fears. "But he might be hungry enough to fight you for chestnut roots." Somehow the burden had fallen to Savka, eldest daughter, to bring her family through the war unscathed, a task that had become increasingly difficult as the front closed in on them. She sank to her knees again and crawled toward another square inch of mud that had yet to be turned over, ruthlessly sinking her stick, and feeling the bark vibrate against her hand to the pounding of Nazi howitzers.

From the corner of Savka's eye, she could see Lilia watching the strange figure cross the field with an expression of curiosity and unease. "Gerhard will not allow any harm to come to us," Lilia said, as if her Nazi tank commander lover could somehow protect them. "The Germans will be victorious."

A burst of rattling fire came from the Soviet machine gun nests at the front, which had become a kind of background symphony, the repetitive boom of antiaircraft guns like a thundering timpani drum in a Wagner opera.

"That sound you hear," Savka said, "is the Germans being destroyed by the Red Army."

Lilia blundered back through the reeds, yelping when a gust of wind lashed at the Victory roll she'd teased and pinned into her hair that morning. Her husband, Vasyl, had served in a Schuma battalion but had been killed last year in a battle with partisans in Belarus. Shortly after they'd learned of his death, Gerhard had come into their lives, when the village had become a base for the Fifth SS Panzer Division and every family was forced to billet its officers. Despite Savka's and Mama's efforts to prevent it, Lilia had fallen in love with the Nazi tank commander—who'd come to conquer, starve, and enslave them. She'd cut her braids and curled her hair to mimic a picture of Betty Grable in a battered *Photoplay* magazine he'd brought her.

"I wouldn't expect *you* to take a risk," Lilia said, her face lit up by tracer flares and artillery that blazed the clouds orange and red above the tree line. The sisters shared dark blonde hair, but Lilia had blue eyes to Savka's brown, and—on the rare occasion she chose to unleash it—their mama's gap-toothed smile. "Perhaps your SS husband has had *his* throat slit by a partisan," Lilia sulked.

Savka froze in the act of yanking out a particularly difficult root. She'd sworn to herself she wouldn't brood over Marko's fate. But Lilia wasn't making it easy. The first flakes of snow swirled around their heads, and she drew the frayed ends of her shawl over her nose to keep out the smell of bog, chimney smoke, and fear that her husband might very well be dead.

Marko had expressed frustration in his last letter, complaining that partisans were organizing themselves in villages and forest strongholds, blowing up Nazi-held bridges and supply depots, and causing so much damage to the German army that his Waffen-SS division of ten thousand Ukrainian men had been kept back from the front with orders to destroy them. Savka had longed for a little more personal information. "Dead men do not write to their wives," she said to Lilia, unable to keep the sarcasm from her voice.

"That letter came three months ago," Lilia, said, always with the last word. "The firefight we're hearing might be *his* unit getting slaughtered."

It began to snow in earnest—cottony, wet flakes drifting out of the clouded sky. Savka shook her head to dispel the image of her husband, a bullet in his chest, left to bleed out in the woods, another Ukrainian warrior murdered by Stalin's partisans. She hadn't seen Marko in over a year, and though she might insist to her family that her husband was still alive, she'd already steeled herself for a letter from the German high command and spending the rest of her years as a widow.

The big guns at the front were silent for a blessed moment, which somehow made the Red Army seem that much closer. "I think it's worth the risk to get *shchavel*," Lilia persisted, staring at the forest, as if she were already there, foraging among the trees for her precious sorrel shoots. And ignoring the ominous threat that hung over them in the brittle air, an imposed silence that swooped down like the mute wings of an owl. "Our children are starving."

Savka's eyes were drawn once more to the refugee, who was almost halfway across the field, draped in layers of coats and scarves, head down, intent on reaching them. At the sudden percussive thud of an infantry mortar from the front, the figure stumbled and fell, then awkwardly hauled himself to standing. Fear rose like poison in her throat. Was it possible that Mama had been right, and this really was a Soviet partisan? If one had ventured out of the forest, there would be others. And Lilia's daughter, Sofiy, and Taras were alone in the house. "We must get back," she said, rubbing mud off her hands. "Warm ourselves at the fire, boil these roots, and drown out the incessant noise of men trying to kill each other."

Mama slipped a comforting arm around her shoulders. "Taras is safe," she murmured in her ear, and Savka felt those worries ease in her mother's embrace. "You will not be separated from your son," Mama soothed, almost rocking her. "Remember before the war, when you were in the garden past sundown and Taras would come out with a candle and a book—always with his nose in a book?"

Savka blinked back tears. Yes, she remembered. Her son was smart. There were hopes for his future, university in Kyiv, the life of a scholar. "I didn't bring him up to carry a rifle for Stalin," she said, forcing brightness. "At thirteen." Mama patted her shoulder and Savka bent again to grub the root she'd been working out of the mud. Why did Marko not send another letter? She said to Lilia, "The war will soon be over. We will stick together and survive it." How tired she was of uttering such platitudes, when she could do nothing to protect Marko, and their son was at risk.

The wind had picked up and snow was falling heavily now in a cloaked, silent curtain of white. Savka watched snowflakes melt before her in the marsh mud, one after the other. Something so beautiful, destroyed by the cruel earth. What Lilia had threatened was true: With her lover in a tank battalion, and Savka's husband in the Waffen-SS, the Soviets would consider the entire family Nazi collaborators. Before the front rolled through their village, they would become fugitives, forced to leave Mama's house, which had been in the family for generations, forced to leave this village and perhaps Ukraine, forever.

"WHICH ONE OF YOU is Waffen-Sturmbannführer Ivanets's wife?"

Savka jumped to her feet, the mud sucking at her boot soles. She turned to find the mysterious figure—a woman—had arrived without them noticing and was now standing among the reeds on the riverbank, sketched shadow-like against the gray light. Behind her, Mama let out a gasp, her hand shooting out to take Savka's.

Lilia took her other arm. "It's a courier from the German high command," she whispered in Savka's ear. "She's come to tell you Marko is dead."

Feeling all her hope snuffed out, like the snowflakes on the ground, Savka leaned into her family, tears hovering on her eyelashes. "How did my husband die?" she asked, bracing herself for details she did not want to hear.

The woman made a sound of exasperation and slashed her way through the reeds, soon standing before them, her desiccated boots sinking in the mud. "How should I know if he's dead or alive? *Slava Ukraini*," she said, tapping a fist to her chest in greeting. "Natalka, from Kuzak's bunker." She paused. "I'm only interested in his medic wife."

"*Heroiam Slava*," Savka replied, letting out the breath she'd been holding. Hunger and fear had already brought her close to the breaking point. Confirmation of Marko's death would have sent her over the edge. Somewhere out there, in this dirty war, her husband might still be alive. "You're a *banderivka*?" she asked, staring into Natalka's dark, startling eyes. Women insurgents who followed Stepan Bandera, leader

of the Organization of Ukrainian Nationalists, did not live with men in
the bunkers. Natalka was several years younger than Savka, eyes hazed
with suffering, wearing a coat and trousers that were too big for her. An
old leather holster around her waist held a Korovin pistol, and a skunk
smell of body odor emanated from within her layers of ragged scarves.

"Yes, I'm a *banderivka*." Natalka scowled, looking down her nose
at them. "This is what you village women do to support the underground? Root like pigs in the mud?"

"We're digging water chestnut roots for soup," Mama offered, her
hand still in Savka's, gripping it tight.

Natalka made a face. "We eat better on the mountain," she claimed,
her cheeks hollow with obvious hunger, her thin body marked by a
winter spent in an underground bunker.

If one looked past the grim determination and grating attitude,
Natalka was pretty. Savka couldn't help but feel grudging admiration
for a woman who loved her country so much she'd live with men in a
glorified cellar, fighting for a free and independent Ukraine. She'd never
been in such a place but envisioned a damp, claustrophobic hole with
just enough room to walk past the narrow sleeping benches lining the
walls. She shivered violently. Below the muddied hem of her skirt, she'd
reinforced her stockinged legs with long strips of flannel torn from an
old sheet. But the temperature was dipping and cold air on the wet
and muddy strips had frozen them into ice-caked armor. "You aren't
supposed to leave your bunker in the winter," Savka reminded her.

"You don't say," Natalka said. "Who else is going to keep the partisans from descending on your village and stealing your sons?"

Partisans. There was only one reason an insurgent from Kuzak's
bunker had emerged from the forest, asking for Marko Ivanets's medic
wife. "What's happened?"

"I need you to come with me," Natalka said, ignoring her question.
Savka shrank back. "Not to the forest."

"Where else?"

At the sudden staccato rip of machine gun fire, the four women looked up as two planes roared over the mountain—a Soviet Yak chasing a Messerschmitt that climbed in evasive maneuvers and did a slow roll, the black swastika on its tail flashing as it attempted to elude the enemy pilot.

Lilia clasped her hands in mock prayer. "Destroy the Soviet," she muttered, "*please*," as though Gerhard himself were in the cockpit. But the Russian plane was faster and emptied its machine guns at the Messerschmitt, finally scoring a direct hit. Smoke rose from the German plane's wing, and it spiraled, quickly losing altitude.

The Messerschmitt careened over the river, too fast to give the pilot time to bail out. The engine stalled and it disappeared behind a hill, exploding in a fireball in the forest.

Numb now to this common occurrence, the women drew scarves over their noses when the sudden cloud of diesel fumes drifted to them on air. Natalka shrugged. "One less German to steal your food. One more Soviet to rape your daughters."

Lilia flinched as if she'd been kicked. When the Russian plane banked and roared over their heads, returning to the front, she followed it with a pointed finger. "Gerhard has taught me to shoot," she said ruthlessly.

Savka lost patience with her idiot sister. "He's playing with you, Lilia—he can't take you back to Berlin."

Lilia stalked off a short distance, smashing half-frozen puddles with her boots. There was a smear of mud on her cheek. She looked too much like the little girl Savka had fought with in childhood just as bitterly as she did today.

"You're jealous," Lilia said over her shoulder. "Marko is dead, and you have no prospects."

Savka's eyes smarted with tears. It was one thing to imagine Marko dead, another to hear it from the lips of someone she loved just as much. She tried to ignore Natalka, who watched this sisterly squabble with her arms crossed. If Marko had been killed, how would Savka save Taras from the encroaching Red Army? A widow and her children suffered if they did not have a man to protect them.

Mama placed a gentle hand on her shoulder. "Lilia is lonely and needs a father for her daughter." She sighed heavily, gripping the handle of her walking stick.

"I'm lonely, too," Savka cried, finally breaking.

"This is all rather touching," Natalka took Savka by the arm, "but I need you to come with me," she ordered. "Now."

"My son is expecting us back," Savka said, trying to pull her arm away.

But Natalka didn't listen, dragging Savka from the protective embrace of her mother and sister.

2

JEANIE

Gallery Nouveau, Vancouver
FEBRUARY 1966

I'M MORTIFIED THAT ONLY four people are milling about this vast, open gallery like they're in an Agatha Christie novel, plotting murder. Cue the disgruntled waitress, a sullen bartender, my caregiver, Pat—who's nursing a whiskey, her face a brooding study of *I told you so*—and the intensely curious gallery owner.

I watch her sail toward me, glass of wine held in front of her like she's going to battle. When she called several months ago to ask if Jeanie Esterhazy had enough landscapes for a show, I was elated and disappeared into my studio, painting like a fiend. But she's sidled up too close to me, the trembling artist, dressed in a navy skirt suit that makes me look like I should be directing passengers to their seats on an airplane, not headlining a gallery opening. I've been reclusive, hiding from every single person besides Pat for years now; this proximity to someone with an Etch A Sketch smile is insufferable.

"Behold," the gallerist says, gesturing to the big, rain-battered front windows. As if she's summoned them by witchcraft, a swarm of people have appeared on the sidewalk, jostling to be let in. The door opens and deposits them in the entryway, drenched wet as otters, shaking damp off their coats and bewildered at the sudden light and warmth. "They're here to see *your* work."

Now I'm paralyzed with nerves and a vague, niggling worry.

Something's not right. I thought I was here on my artistic merits. Is she capitalizing on my recklessly tragic past?

She sneaks furtive glances at me, frowning in that vague, insipid way people have when they've read daily newspaper accounts about you and are imagining what it must have felt like to suffer that much damage, that much hurt. Her eyes are too bright, too glowy, and the truth hits me like a sucker punch: *This is a pity party.* I pluck a deviled egg from the passing waitress's tray and regard the new arrivals with dread. Here be wolves. A few of them crane their necks, searching the rabble, passing over the waif in a hand-me-down suit, tragically stuck in another fashion decade.

"Come see Jeanie Esterhazy," I say, sotto voce, "the sideshow freak."

"Nonsense. They want to meet you." The gallerist gives me a playful shove. "*Socialize.*"

I swallow my deviled egg and try to smile—a slow rictus, really. "The last time I socialized, I found myself knocked up and tripping down an aisle in a wedding dress."

She trills a laugh—as if she thinks I'm joking—and swoops across the room, leaving a cloud of perfume in her wake. I consider escape, consider flinging myself out the door or shrinking into a corner, when a miniskirted blonde approaches, legs clad in blinding psychedelic tights. Her hunched shoulders are swathed in a cape, which is terribly brave of her. Gliding past, she bumps my elbow, and turns to look me over. Her expression sours at the sight of my skinny legs poking out beneath the knee-length skirt, and my long hair, wrestled by Pat into a bun that more closely resembles a bird's nest perched on top of my head.

"Oh," I say, because the blonde is pretty and hip in all the ways I'll never be. The gallery lights beat down on me like another sun, and I start to sweat in my prickly suit. Unbearable. *Take me out to die like a dog in the woods.* Pat assured me she would remain at my side this evening and divert prying humans, but of course she's otherwise occupied, sending disturbing come-hither looks to a poor man she's trapped near the bar. The blonde is gazing at me expectantly and I force my sensibly pump-shod feet to hobble forward. I close my eyes, waiting for the first awkwardly blunt question, *What did it feel like* . . .

"Waitress," she says. "Can I have a glass of champagne?"

My eyes snap open, a furious blush speeding up my neck, shame and relief coexisting, burning like a brand. Wordlessly, I point her in the general direction of the bar, and she flashes a peace sign.

"Sorry we started without you," I profess, as she melts away.

Where have they all come from, quaffing wine or beer, making cultured remarks? The air smells of wet sheep, Swedish meatballs, and cheap perfume. And the din is incredible, a chorus of starlings desperate to out-chirp each other. Smoke hangs in a cloud near the ceiling, lifting from dozens of cigarettes dangling from dozens of hands. What is it they say? Where there's smoke there's fire.

I bolt across the room, my pulse racing. Pat and the man she's cornered are giggling over the naughtiest thing they've ever done in public. Not a common Pat topic, but her face has turned a lovely, bloated crimson, and she seems willing to go in any conversational direction if it means she can make this guy laugh.

I range up behind Pat, close enough to smell her unwashed hair. "Get me the hell out of here," I whisper. "Someone almost recognized me."

Pat regards me with that wolf-disturbed-at-a-carcass look she saves for our lesser moments. I can hear her breathing. "Almost recognized you? You'd think you were *famous*." She says this with unnecessary emphasis, perhaps for the benefit of her newfound friend, who reminds me of a hamster I had when I was a child, all twitching whiskers, stubby legs, and pert-eyed inquisitiveness. "Even I can see these are rubberneckers," Pat says, "curious to meet the monster."

The elevator drops ten floors inside me at the stony expression on my caregiver's face. *Monster.* How dare she?

Pat licks her fingers like a cat and slicks down a hank of hair that's dared escape her *Rosemary's Baby* pixie cut. Her dark eyes are inspiring, like leather buttons, I think, or two nubbins of coal that someone, a miner presumably, might have chipped out with his axe. Set deep in that floury face—full lips, wide-planed cheekbones, the kind Vermeer or Rembrandt might have loved to paint—the effect is disconcerting, even when you don't know what she's capable of.

Muscles twitching in her jaw, Pat grabs me, her fingers wringing the tender flesh of my upper arm like a dishrag. "Don't go anywhere," she cheerily warns her conquest before steering me away. She fetches a child-sized glass of wine from the bar, then deposits me behind a low partition near the gallerist's desk. "We'll just have to cart these paint-ings back," she gripes. "Where they'll molder to dust in your studio." When she leaves, I crouch thankfully beneath my toadstool, finally safe to drink, brood, and brace myself for withering comments from those who must destroy the faeries.

"Her detail is remarkable," floats over the wall. "I feel like I'm there."

"Puts me in mind of Albert Bierstadt."

"Or William Morris Hunt."

William Morris Hunt? How awful. I toss back the wine and make my way back to the bar.

But the comments aren't *withering.* I order a stiff gin and tonic and pulse with a little hard-won glory. Maybe all these rubberneckers really have come to see my art. As I slink back to my rabbit hole, glass in hand, I slow to give someone the royal wave, when I'm blinded by a flashbulb going off in my face.

"Just one picture, Mrs. Esterhazy," a reporter exclaims, lowering the camera. I feel dizzy and nauseous. Despite blazing overhead track lights, the gallery suddenly seems a shadowy maze and me a mouse trapped in it, with no avenue of escape. Because I'm presently famous for only one thing, I gulp down air, bolting for the partition—and ano-nymity—wiping my sweaty palms on the suit Pat forced me to wear. But it's impossible to outrun my notoriously tragic past.

"Mrs. Esterhazy!" the reporter shouts.

"It's *Ms.*," I growl.

"Why did Michael leave you after the accident?"

I skid to a stop in the center of the room, flustered and ashamed. In the years since I was discharged from the hospital and Pat became my caregiver, she's often cruelly reminded me why Michael did a runner.

He never could stomach damaged goods.

The din subsides as people turn to stare. If they hadn't recognized me before, they do now. Some coughing. A few ripples of discontent. The deviled egg sits like a rock in my stomach.

"Why, she's lovely," a woman says, as if she expected the creature from the black lagoon. "You can't even see the scars."

I'm frozen in place, my heart doing the flamenco in my chest, listening to rubberneckers talk about me like I'm not even here.

"Terrible what happened to her," another woman remarks.

"Her mother and aunt died, too, not a year later," the man beside her agrees. "Poor thing, all alone in the world."

After a few more cryptic murmurs from the gray masses—mentions of God and curses and burdens some of us are given to bear—I sag with relief when Pat launches herself across the room. She catches the journalist by his elbow, jostling him and his camera toward the door, giving me an all too familiar *you will pay* look. I resume a dignified clip back to my hiding place, out of the firing range of stares from women who've suffered nothing worse than knee scrapes or the odd dose of chlamydia—women with husbands, babies, and children. Women who are loved.

I can see Pat through the bank of windows, on the sidewalk. The rain has stopped and she's sharing a smoke with the newspaperman, her head thrown back in laughter, probably having a good snort over what she has to put up with as my nurse. If only he knew the truth.

My heart has settled into a thin, even drumbeat. I've been told some of what happened on that fateful night, but my memories were obliterated by severe trauma, coma, and a selection of very good drugs. I can't remember details—a blessing, my vigil nurses Pat and Kay said at the time. *You don't want to remember.* They protected me from the many newspaper articles, and from reporters like this one—prying journalists who asked devastating questions. Protected me from those who might remind me of what really happened that night. To this day, Pat keeps journalists at bay and hides any articles speculating as to my whereabouts. The hard kernel of rage I've harbored toward Michael Esterhazy has sustained me, encouraged by my nurses and Aunt Suze, even my own heartless mother. *Michael did this to you. He ruined your life.* An image of him looms in my mind alongside the elaborate fantasies I've had, of getting him fired, stealing his first born, evening the score.

But then a real memory rears up from the recesses of my mind, a hideous Italianate wedding cake and Michael standing beside me as we cut into it, his smile strangely vacant. The noise and chatter in the gallery fall away and I look down, watching helplessly as the embroidered French lace of my wedding dress and its full ballet tulle skirt crumble away like leaves blown from a tree by a sudden wind. I lift my hand to touch my bare stomach and the small, round, precious bump when Michael grabs me and astoundingly, we've cycled back four months before the wedding, to summer camp. He's leading me into the dark wood behind the cabins, glancing back with a seductive smile.

I have memories of the night Michael and I went into that forest. I have memories of him standing at the altar, but not his ghostlike form looming over me as people screamed and sirens wailed.

If only you hadn't been so fucking careless, Jeanie.

Stunned, I stumble backward, tripping over the gallerist's chair. The forbidden gin and tonic surges through my system, mixing dangerously with my pain medications. How has this one poisonous memory of Michael somehow exploded from my brain? I shake my head and swallow hard. I don't want to remember more of this nightmare.

But Michael's words echo in my ears. If he said I was careless, I must have been. *What happened that night?* What did Pat, Kay, Aunt Suze, and my own mother not tell me?

Pat arrives in a fug of Jack Daniels and cigarettes, accompanied by a balding man in a corduroy sport coat. She glances down at the gallerist's desk and her eyes calcify as she takes in the two empty glasses. "You're drunk."

"I had a memory . . ." I trail off, feeling lightheaded.

Pat lifts a hand to check her side part and glances at the man in the corduroy coat as if to say, *Please excuse the lunatic.* She slides one arm around his shoulders and hooks her other arm to pull me close, pouring an acid whisper into my ear that's just loud enough for the man to hear, if he wants to. "This dweeb has bought one of your little paintings. Just one, mind you, so don't get too big for your britches."

"But I remember," I say helplessly, sending a grateful smile to the man, who thankfully appears not to have registered Pat's rude comment.

"Impossible," she proclaims. Now her hand on my shoulder feels more like an eagle's claw than anything remotely human. "You don't have memories of that time, Jeanie—too unsettling."

I draw an unsteady breath. "The accident . . ." I trail off, then look into her eyes. "Pat, I didn't cause it, did I?" Even though I whisper the words, saying them out loud makes me feel like a horribly pathetic disaster.

There's an expression on Pat's face that I haven't seen before. Perhaps it's uncertainty, or relief. "You should *not* be allowed in public," she says from between clenched teeth.

She hasn't answered my question, and I know she never will. The two of us will crawl back to Salt Spring Island and forget any of this ever happened. I lean my head on her shoulder and pretend that it belongs to Aunt Suze; that she's alive and somehow still loves me.

Pat stiffens. I've gone against protocol. Besides the fleeting hug we exchange at Christmas, our physical interaction is null. No one has touched me in years. I suddenly realize how lonely I am, how hungry for contact—even if it's this brief connection with one of my least favorite people.

She clears her throat, loathing this sort of emotional display, and I know I'm testing her patience. "I'll adjust your medications," she says, blinking rapidly. "You'll never have to remember anything bad again." She finally releases me from her iron grip, but not before dropping a parting shot: "You may think you can get away with this hysterical show here, but when we're home . . ."

Unfortunately, I fully grasp her meaning. I'm ensnared like a fly in the web of a spider on our little island in the Pacific.

I cannot unhear Michael's cold words, and I feel the hard kernel of rage—the anger that once kept me going, the rage at him for abandoning me to this life—turning inward on myself. Unmoored, I wonder if Pat has been right all along.

I am a monster.

3

SAVKA

Deremnytsia, Reichskommissariat Ukraine
FEBRUARY 25, 1944

STUMBLING UP THE RIVERBANK, Savka glanced back at Lilia and Mama who clutched at each other as they watched her reluctantly follow Natalka. The *banderivka* struck off across the farmer's field, her long dark hair unbound and streaming from beneath a leather aviator's cap she'd most likely picked up from a downed Soviet aircraft. Puddles that had just refrozen shattered under their weight and echoed like gunshots in the air; ice water soaked Savka's boots and her flannel-wrapped feet, already numb with cold.

Snow fell from the leaden sky, almost obliterating the thickly treed slopes of the mountain, its peak blanketed in clouds. Savka kept her head down, focusing on Natalka's battered leather boots. Surely, the *banderivka* wouldn't force her into that forest.

Natalka stopped to light a cigarette and snuffed out the burning match with her fingers. Savka caught up with her. "What happened?" she asked, out of breath.

"Two days ago, I was out tending my trapline when I ran across a band of Soviet partisans in the forest," Natalka said, stashing the spent match in her pocket. "Kuzak turned out our entire bunker of seven to hunt them down. Hand-to-hand combat—and Bohdan got the worst of it when a partisan lunged at him with a knife. Kuzak called a retreat. Bohdan couldn't walk, so I stayed behind. The bloody partisans surrounded us. But they left this morning in a hurry." She laughed bitterly. "Probably new orders from Moscow."

Savka stepped closer, eyeing Natalka's holstered Korovin pistol, which had obviously been stolen from partisans. She knew it was prized, but for two entirely different reasons: use the gun to kill the bastards, but if they corner you—kill yourself to avoid capture. When Natalka let out an involuntary groan and clutched at her side, Savka reached for her medic bag. "Let me look at *your* wound first."

Natalka motioned her away. "It's nothing—just a scratch." The *banderivka*'s hand drifted over the grip of her pistol, a vain attempt at resistance. It was hopeless, of course—as Hitler had come to learn after Stalin defeated him again and again on the front—the Soviet hammer and sickle threw long shadows.

"How badly is Bohdan wounded?" Savka asked.

"Bad enough." Natalka straightened, pulled her cap lower over her forehead and struck out again, cigarette smoke trailing after her. They were heading for the forest and the thickly treed slopes of the mountain looming high above.

Duty drove Savka forward. Her breath came in shallow exhalations as she muttered a prayer to somehow become the brave medic Natalka believed her to be. *Banderivtsi* stayed in their bunkers in winter, but fought partisans in the summer, often bringing wounded insurgents for treatment at her kitchen table in the village. Savka had never been asked to go into the forest. Yet she'd heard that women who'd previously served the Ukrainian Nationalists in the villages by supplying food and clothing, or medical aid, were being asked to take on more dangerous roles as the front drew nearer and subsumed villages on its way. They were leaving the safety of their homes and families to courier battle plans between bunkers or to serve as medics in the mountains.

With Natalka's arrival, Savka realized that women were also joining bunkers—once the domain of men—and learning to use guns stolen from the Soviets. Though the thought terrified her, she understood why females were being chosen for these treacherous jobs: What partisan would see a woman out for a forest walk and suspect that a coded missive of underground battle plans was stitched into the hem of her skirt? But Savka also knew these women were being captured by the NKVD, who then tortured and mutilated them. Some had even been burned alive—anything to break them and force them to give up enemy information or reveal bunker locations.

The ninth commandment in the OUN handbook had been drilled into her head: *Neither pleading nor threats, torture or death will force you to reveal secrets . . .* She was sure Natalka would stoically endure having her fingernails pulled out, and not scream when sprinkled with gasoline and set on fire. *But me?* Savka thought. *I might manufacture a bunker location, just to avoid torture.*

There was no way to tell how late it was in the afternoon—perhaps two or three o'clock. Dusk would come soon. And curfew. Natalka stopped at the edge of the forest. A cold fog had descended, blurring the smooth gray trunks, as though some dark thing had awoken and hung still and silent in the air around them. Savka looked to the east and thought of her husband trapped by partisans, fighting them elbow-to-elbow with the Germans.

Write to your wife, Marko, she prayed. *Tell me you've not been killed or captured.* She ventured a glance into the dark trees. *Captured.* A very real possibility if they entered this guerrilla war zone.

Natalka rampaged through a creeping row of Cossack junipers just inside the tree line. She thrashed through bush after bush like a mad witch, unleashing a string of bawdy Russian curses.

"What are you looking for?" Savka ventured, her voice small. Did she really want to know?

"We might run into Medvedev himself," Natalka replied. "Stalin's favorite partisan. They say Moscow air dropped a Hero of the Soviet Union medal into that bastard's little stronghold. Along with more Tokarev TT-33's . . . and good vodka."

Savka clutched her medic satchel, fighting to get her panic under control. The sky seemed oppressively low, the air raw with the smell of pine sap and snow. Her eyes crept to the beech trees lined up like soldiers, expecting to see a flicker of brown or black at any moment, partisans dressed as Ukrainian farmers, skulking through the woods, eager to shoot underground insurgents and bothering any Wehrmacht unit that might be passing through on its way to the front.

"I can't go in there," she reluctantly admitted to Natalka. "It's a war zone." She felt her face turn red with shame.

Natalka straightened, frowning. "I've just come from that *war zone*. Risking my life in the struggle for an independent Ukraine."

"I have a husband and son," Savka stuttered, hoping to avoid another confrontation. "There's more to lose."

Natalka pointed at her medic bag. "Where did you get the kit?"

"A Nazi ambulance . . . but now they're too well guarded to steal more." Savka prayed that Bohdan's wound wouldn't exhaust her dwindling supplies.

"I thought you'd be brave," the *banderivka* muttered, almost ripping another juniper from its roots. "Wife of the great Marko Ivanets, codename Roman," she mocked. "Too important now to remember he was once Commander Major of the Military District of Lysonja."

Savka looked away, embarrassed to be spoken to like a child afraid of her own shadow. "If you had a husband, a son, you would not be so eager to risk your life."

"I would have had Roman, if you hadn't taken him first." Natalka beat at a bush. "Where is it?"

Savka bristled. "How dare you." Perhaps this was a rough sort of humor, the manner in which men in the bunker might rib each other about women, but Natalka had nerve, thinking she could have a chance with Marko!

"Simmer down," Natalka said with a laugh.

Savka made a concerted effort to calm her breathing. She wasn't made for the insurgent's life—the cruel jokes and struggle, the hardship, and the cold. "If partisans catch us, they'll shoot us on the spot."

"They won't have a chance when I'm firing back with a PPSh-41." Natalka pulled out a submachine gun she'd hidden in a bush, cupping the round drum magazine with affection. "Twelve hundred rounds per minute. Know what the Soviets call it?" She laughed. "*Papasha.*"

Savka's stomach flipped to see the same kind of long-barreled weapon that Gerhard had taken off a dead Red Army soldier at the front. Laughing, he'd patiently explained to Taras in their kitchen, "The name of this gun in Russian translates to *Daddy,*" before showing her fascinated son how he meant to convert the weapon to use German ammunition. The irony was not lost on Savka. If the two women were overwhelmed by a platoon of Soviet partisans, Natalka wouldn't hesitate to shoot Savka with a Russian gun before killing herself.

The *banderivka* took Savka by the arm, dragging her toward the trees. The forest cloaked them in twilight darkness, and they climbed in the silence of the woods, Natalka wildly aiming her *Papasha* into the shadows while the hair stood up on Savka's head. The beech branches were frosted with ice, some of last autumn's red leaves still visible among the sparse covering of snow on the ground. The trail the women were following was well-trodden. *By whose feet?* Savka wondered, imagining large groups of partisans moving in stealth through the woods. A flash of something in the corner of her eye, figures flitting from tree to tree. No, just the fog, breeding phantoms. Something touched her, like the tip of a claw, rousing the frightened bird inside her, its wings beating against the bones of her chest.

4

JEANIE

Salt Spring Island
DECEMBER 4, 1972

I SMELL SMOKE.

Swimming out of a dead sleep, I lie petrified beneath the weight of blankets, a curious, charred smell assaulting my senses. Wayward thoughts leap out of me like sparks.

Is there a fire?

I need to get out.

Where am I?

I sit upright in bed and stare into the dark room. The familiar sound of rain on the roof convinces me that I'm safe in my house on Salt Spring. But it's been years since I've awoken in the middle of the night, thanks to the drug cocktail Pat administers before bed. I'm normally comatose until she wakes me in the morning.

I rub my eyes and blink to clear my head. The phone is ringing downstairs. Suddenly, I hear Pat in the hallway, roused from her bear-like slumber, hand creeping along the wall and her careful tread on the stairs. She either trips or stubs her toe and swears under her breath, and I throw back the covers and limp to the door, chronic pain fizzing and igniting the network of scars across my body. Blinking to clear my head, I reach for the handle, but it fails to turn. I jiggle the knob, sure I'm hallucinating. She's locked me in.

I stand motionless, pure, hot adrenaline coursing through my blood, but I force myself to take one long breath, trying to slow my heart rate so I don't spiral into a meltdown. *A candle. It must be a candle I smell.* I forbid candle burning and Pat positively hates that "hippy dippy shit," but she must've lit one tonight. Maybe to torture me, to punish me for the mysterious crime I've dared commit. She knows it's the smell of death to me.

My first impulse is to pound on the door and scream at her to let me out. On the verge of tears, I clutch at my flannel nightgown, the perfect kindling for a flame that would surely race up my body, searing my flesh, setting alight the bedclothes, the macramé plant hangers, my frilled Priscilla curtains at the window.

I close my eyes against the image of my body transformed into a burning pyre and whisper reassurances to myself, "There is no fire . . . there is no fire."

The phone is still ringing, but Pat finally snatches it up in the downstairs hall. "Whatthehell, it's *two in the morning.*"

Slowing my frantic breath, I press my ear to the door and listen. Pat pauses, then annoyingly lowers her voice. "Who is this?" She's no longer angry Pat or surprised Pat, jarred out of sleep by a telephone call in the middle of the night. Here is the Pat I know too well—eerily calculating and as shrewd as a used car salesman.

Her voice drifts up the stairs, louder again. "Is that right?" she taunts the caller. "What makes you think you can call this late?" She listens for a moment. "It's not my job to wait by the phone all day for some stranger to call!"

I transfer my weight from one bare foot to the other, wishing I could project myself into the downstairs hall to hear every word. Who's she talking to?

"Why?" Now Pat's voice is suddenly sharp with disbelief, maybe even shock. "Never heard of him." A familiar thumping noise tells me she's struggling with the hall table drawer, possibly looking for paper and a pen. "Like I said, I've never heard of him," she repeats, frustration lacing her voice. "What's your name?" I can picture the look of outrage on Pat's face as she wedges the receiver between her ear and shoulder. "Out of the question," she blurts. "Jeanie suffers from debilitating pain. She's fragile and can't be bothered." The sound of my name brings bile to my throat, and a blooming panic. What does this late-night call have to do with me?

She listens again. "I will *not* give you our address," she says firmly. I dare to take a breath. Years ago, international newspaper men and curiosity seekers sometimes called at night, naively impervious to Pacific Standard time, but Pat put an end to that with an unlisted number, even though she felt it was "a rip off." My mind races. Could it be someone related to Michael? If so, how did he find us and what does he want?

I'm so caught up in my thoughts that I don't hear Pat climb the stairs. But suddenly a floorboard creaks in the hallway.

She's breathing against the door. "Jeanie," she says in a slow whisper. "Jeanie."

A pulse throbs at my temples and I freeze in place. She must have heard me rattle my cage door.

Her voice vibrates low and threatening. "I don't think you'd want anyone poking around, would you? Not after what you did."

I hover for a bone-chilling moment, waiting until Pat finally moves away from the door and returns to her room. What did I do that was so terrible that even she finds it abhorrent? Tiptoeing silently toward the bed, my feet cold on the wood floor, I ease myself under the covers.

I've not had another memory of my wedding since my art show when I heard Michael's words in my ear. *If only you hadn't been so fucking careless, Jeanie.* Despite the time that's passed since that night, despite the fact that I haven't recalled another thing, I'm steeped in guilt. What if I was responsible for my accident and for what happened to my marriage?

My mind wanders back to the phone call. The person on the other end wanted to speak to me, wanted to come out *here*. What did this mystery caller want, exactly? I shake my head. It doesn't matter, because Pat wouldn't give him, or her, our address. I've buried the feeling until now, but is it possible that I've done something terribly wrong?

I fear that somehow, I have. Pat isn't just my caregiver. I stare into the darkness, and a feeling of profound loneliness floods my heart. She's my jailer.

Pat is here to protect me from myself.

5

SAVKA

Deremnytsia, Reichskommissariat Ukraine
FEBRUARY 25, 1944

"THE WOUND HAS GONE septic," Savka said the moment she saw Bohdan. Natalka had left him hidden on the hillside, behind a group of ancient boulders that had been deposited when a glacier scoured the mountainside in the last ice age. There was more snow at this elevation, and when she knelt beside the patient, her bare legs felt numb with cold beneath her frozen flannel wrappings.

Bohdan turned his head in voiceless agony, gripping a hunting knife as Savka continued to monitor his pulse, his white knuckles betraying just how badly he was injured.

The sounds from the front were muted here, but suddenly a percussive boom of a big shell hitting its target floated over the trees and Natalka spun to face an invisible enemy, her breathing ragged, spooked. "Soon, the Red Army will be crawling like rats through these woods," she muttered, brandishing her *Papasha* and glancing at Savka. "When will the great Roman desert the SS and bring us weapons and men to kill them—" Her last words were drowned out by a thunderclap of mortar fire from the front that shook the ground beneath their feet.

"I haven't heard from him in months," Savka admitted. Her hands trembled as she unbuckled Bohdan's crude leather holster that held yet another Soviet-made pistol. It still made her flinch, hearing the words

Marko and *SS* in the same sentence. Her husband had left the underground last year and joined the Fourteenth Division on orders of Mykola Lebed, de facto leader of the Ukrainian underground. After the German army was defeated in Stalingrad, Hitler, fearing the loss of more shining Aryan sons to Soviet tanks, had put aside his hatred of the Slavs and reluctantly formed a Waffen-SS division in Ukraine. Marko had entered officers' training and was assigned a battalion, and his men were issued German submachine guns and Lugers. For the underground, it was a strategic choice: infiltrate the SS and, at the right time, take over the division with military training and weapons that would form the basis of a Ukrainian liberation army strong enough to prevent both Germans and Soviets from invading their beloved Ukraine ever again.

Savka cut into Bohdan's rough woolen trousers at the thigh to expose his wound. As she sterilized a pair of tweezers with iodine, he barked a low, worrisome cough. Carefully, she picked dirt from the deep gash in his leg, and a freshet of blood oozed from his injury. Bohdan stifled a cry, his head flung back, as Savka sprinkled yellow sulfa powder over his wound. He was hot to the touch and delirious, wincing and tightening his hold on the knife. It was like treating a wild animal caught in a snare.

Natalka took out a pair of binoculars to scan the forest. As she lowered them, she sent Savka a dark look. "Do you have food?" Savka obediently turned out her pockets, and the water chestnut roots tumbled across the snow. Natalka looked down at them with an expression of disgust. "You billet a German officer and bring us these?" Glaring at Savka as if she were hoarding rock candy and chocolate, Natalka began gathering the roots, stashing them in her own coat pocket.

Savka turned back to the banderite. His wound now clean, she placed a gauze bandage over the gash in his thigh and pinned it in place. He stabbed at the air with his knife, delirious. "You were close to losing this leg," she said. *Then what good would you be to the struggle?*

Savka rummaged blindly in her medic bag until her fingers finally closed over her precious supply of opium tablets. She opened the tin. *Only three left.*

"What's that?" Natalka demanded.

"Something for the pain." Savka pressed a tablet into Bohdan's mouth, snatching her fingers away, in case he bit them. Suddenly, Natalka appeared at her side and pried the tin out of her hands, stowing it in her pocket with the roots.

"You can't take my supplies!" Savka sputtered.

"Coward," Natalka spat defiantly. "If you don't supply the underground, you're a traitor to the cause."

Yes, I'm a fraud, a coward, Savka wanted to shout. *You are the* true *banderivka.* She kept her head down, her breath shallow in her chest at the thought of a confrontation with the brave Natalka, who was like a rabid dog, waiting for its prey to meet her eyes before launching an attack.

"If you haven't heard from Roman, he's dead," Natalka persisted. "Can't you see?" She picked up her gun and nudged Savka with the barrel, seizing the medic bag and throwing it over her own shoulder.

Savka resisted the urge to grab the *banderivka*'s machine gun and shoot her between the eyes. "Give it back."

When Natalka ignored her, Savka resigned herself to losing the supplies. Shadows had lengthened in the forest, and her thoughts went to her return journey, although pride wouldn't allow her to suggest that Natalka escort her to the edge of the wood. She'd make the walk alone. "If I'm not home by dusk, my ration card will be confiscated," she announced without thinking.

"Did you hear that?" Natalka said to Bohdan, imitating Savka's voice. "Her ration card will be confiscated." The *banderivka* kicked at the bark of a tree. "Steal another Nazi medic bag. Replenish your supplies."

Savka ground her teeth to stop herself from screaming. "What if I'm caught?"

"You will kill yourself," Natalka said without pause. She lifted her chin. "Shouting *Slava Ukraini* in their faces. It is the only correct way to end your life."

Savka knew that such an imperative came directly from the underground handbook—*You will not hesitate to commit even the greatest crime, if the good of the cause demands it.*

Natalka grabbed Savka by the arm. "Maybe you and your sister share Gerhard between you."

Natalka held her in a death grip, and Savka tried to pull away. "I'd crawl through Stalingrad on my knees before taking up with a miserable German," she cried.

Bohdan stirred and Natalka released her, springing to him like a cat. Using a long stick to haul himself to standing, the two freedom fighters turned, and Savka watched them disappear into the trees.

As she retraced their path down the mountain, Savka's body still buzzed with adrenaline. The dim light from high above had faded, and her breath was like a sonic boom in her ears. Without the *banderivka*, the forest seemed haunted; as though there were a partisan behind every tree, ready to pounce on her. Savka felt exposed, vulnerable, and thought of Taras. The children had been left alone in the house for too long. Were Mama and Lilia still kneeling in the mud or had they returned to ensure Taras and Sofiy were safe? She was almost running now, frantic to see her beloved son—always sunny, filled with a happiness that had eluded her since the war began.

The trail ended abruptly, and she turned in a fright. Had she missed a turn somewhere? In '41, when the SS discovered that Soviet partisans were using the forests, they'd cut crude roads to accommodate their armed units, and Savka had stumbled on one of those roads now, the muddied snow raked with fresh wheel tracks. She shook her head to get the distant echo of men's shouts out of her ear and the acrid smell of cooking fires from her nose. It was only fear, manufacturing imaginary enemies. Her breath rose like steam in the frigid air as she started back up the way she'd come, but she'd hardly taken a step before halting. Voices. Her body anxious to bolt, she cocked her ear, listening for Ukrainian inflections, which would mean this was a Schuma battalion on a forced transport raid. But there was something about the frenzied shouts that made her turn, the guttural sounds of a language she'd become too familiar with the last few years. She crept closer through the tall pines, close enough to confirm that a German patrol was camped in the forest.

Savka set her back against a tree. Despite the Germans brutally butchering Deremnytsia's Jews at the start of the occupation, the underground and the remaining people of the village had forged an uneasy alliance with the Nazis over their mutual enemy. The presence of the SS in the forest tonight meant she no longer had to fear partisans. Risking a quick glance around the tree, she saw soldiers clapping each other on the back and roaring with drunken laughter, intent on downing enough liquid courage for the job they must do tomorrow—hunting partisans. But these were strange men, rough Nazi soldiers in occupied Ukraine. Who knew what they would want to do with a lone Ukrainian woman who had lost her way.

She spotted a few sentries pacing in the distance, wearing the distinctive field-gray uniform of the SS, and an army ambulance parked on the old road.

Natalka's words rang in her ears.

Steal another Nazi medic bag. Replenish your supplies.

Savka took a deep breath to bolster her courage and ran forward in a crouch, hiding behind the fender of a staff car, her skin crawling with anxiety and an icy blast of terror. The light of cooking fires flickered through the trees, and late winter snow fell in fat, wet flakes through the tree branches already drooping under the weight of other storms.

Silently she counted the phantom forms of Nazis, estimating numbers and firepower, analyzing risk. Not a unit but a full battalion. The ambulance was out in the open and too heavily guarded. Savka reconsidered and carefully withdrew, melting back into the forest.

She found the right trail again, and within half an hour she'd gratefully emerged from the woods and joined a rag-tag cluster of refugees on the road to the village, escaping the Red Army advance. The sky seemed oppressively low, cold air biting at her cheeks in the gloom of twilight. A group of women and children had gathered in the square around a fire burning in a metal drum. Savka looked down the road and spotted Mama and Lilia coming from the opposite direction, their shoulders slumped from a full day of foraging. As she waited for them, attempting to quiet her thudding heart, she thought Mama's bad back seemed more hunched than usual as she leaned heavily on her walking stick.

"What did the *banderivka* want?" Lilia said as they drew near, apology in her tone for her earlier behavior.

"A wounded insurgent was—" Savka had just noticed a motorcycle escort on the road to the south, coming toward the village, forcing refugees and their carts into the ditch and making way for a sleek black German staff car with swastika flags fluttering on its fenders—an officer of some importance, judging by the newer make of Mercedes. Lilia smiled foolishly, and edged along the side of the road, joining the women and children around the drum fire.

"SS . . . or Wehrmacht?" Mama asked as the motorcade bore down on them, a triangular beam of driven snow illuminated in the car's headlamps.

"An SS officer and his staff," Savka said as it passed, sidestepping mud splatter from another pair of motorcycles following the car.

In the backseat of the Mercedes, the officer turned his head as they passed, and Savka—an *untermensch* female, lower than the low—dared to meet his eyes. He stared back at her, heavy jowled, his round spectacles reflecting the light and an Iron Cross pinned at the collar of his immaculate uniform.

She looked away. The leader of the Fifth SS Panzer Division had commandeered the empty houses of those who'd been sent on forced labor transports. Villagers who were exempt because they performed essential work or were too old, or those whose husbands were in German battalions, had been coerced to either allow Nazi officers in their homes or move to barns or other outbuildings. And that had brought Gerhard. Was it any wonder her face did not light up at the sight of an SS officer passing through?

A thought broke through the adrenaline still coursing through her blood: was it possible that Marko's division was in the woods? She dismissed the idea. If her husband was still alive, he would have written to tell her if his unit had been assigned to this part of Ukraine.

6

JEANIE

Salt Spring Island
DECEMBER 5, 1972

THE MORNING AFTER PAT'S mysterious late-night phone call, I'm standing in the hall outside my room. Pat's behind on laundry, so I'm wearing my work uniform—coveralls shellacked with multiple colors of paint, and a faded blue sweatshirt—despite this being the very first day of Jeanie's "month-long rest." Yesterday, I completed a pointless landscape, one that took me hundreds of hours and what felt like too many pints of blood to finish. Bone tired, I'm entitled to a break, and Christmas is the perfect excuse to unwind, read, and stay the hell away from my studio.

The floor creaks under my bare feet as I listen to the steady mouse patter of rain on the roof and the sound of Pat down in the kitchen, wrestling an innocent pot in the sink with a Brillo pad. She'd hovered *right here* after last night's phone call and paused long enough to zombie-whisper a terrible thing at me.

I don't think you'd want anyone poking around, would you? Not after what you did.

Insurmountable guilt floods my body, guilt for the mistakes I've made, some I'm not even aware I committed except for Pat's insistence that I did. I glance down the hallway. Her bedroom door is closed, as always—Pat's a stickler for privacy. That charred wax smell permeates the air again, drifting up my nostrils. Angry, I tiptoe toward her door, which seems to quiver with mystery. I'm not sure what I'm planning to do—maybe yank the wick out of the offending candle so I can strangle her with it. I smile to myself. *Imagine.*

I place my hand on her doorknob and turn it ever so carefully. Locked. Just like mine had been last night. How long has she been locking our doors? How long has she been keeping me in my room at night and out of hers during the day?

"What are you doing up there?"

I jump and bolt to the top of the stairs. Pat stands at the bottom, glaring up at me. Something else accompanies her usual contempt for my very being. Suspicion.

When I don't answer, she rolls her eyes. "You need to take your meds." She gallops back to the kitchen, and I descend like a reluctant debutante to a ball, following the enticing aroma of percolating coffee. As I pass the hall table, I notice the drawer is ajar. "What were you looking for last night?" I mutter. "You little nightmare." I stop and peer into the open drawer. Among her scribbled grocery lists, a creamy-white embossed envelope floats like a glamorous castaway, marred by Pat's clumsy attempts to tear it open. No fancy letter opener for her. Nudging the drawer open further, I see the envelope is addressed to *me* and squint at the stamp and return address: it was sent over a month ago from an Octavius Karbuz Gallery in Brussels. Why would a European art gallery be contacting me? I reach for it, my fingers itching to peek at the elegant words written in calligraphy that I glimpse within. But Pat might appear in the doorway any minute, wondering where I am, so I leave it where it is. For now.

"WHAT'S THIS ORANGE PILL?" I ask Pat, trying to sound upbeat, despite her daring to open my mail. "It's positively lurid." A giant fern hangs in the interior of the skylight above the kitchen table and I examine the round glow-in-the-dark pill in the flat morning haze that sifts through its fronds. An ominous looking *SKF T76* is stamped in black lettering on one side of the medication. I don't think I've noticed it before.

"Just take it," Pat huffs, without turning from the sink.

I'm sitting at the table in front of a rapidly cooling bowl of porridge, listening to Tuna whiffle in his sleep in the dog bed near the back door. Dear, sweet chocolate lab, he's curled up in the same position I left him in last night. The kitchen that Aunt Suze built never fails to lift my spirits, even if Pat is standing in it. My aunt designed it years ago to cheer herself up, unaware she'd be dead not long after. She'd chosen the bright yellow Formica counters out of an eccentric's aesthetic rather than any real knowledge of design. Floor to ceiling oak cabinets frame a still serviceable—though dated—fridge and stove. When the kitchen window is open in the summer, one can hear the pleasant trickle of the waterfall. It's one of my favorite things about this house.

I study Pat's uniform. She used to wear what the locals do on this island: flannel shirts and baggy blue jeans. But lately she's shown up in classy threads she must have procured in Vancouver—*trés chic* flared slacks and blouses worn several sizes too small. Does she have a boyfriend in the city? Her dark hair is still in curlers. Thank God she's grown out her pixie cut to a shoulder-length style she'll later wrestle into a side sweep, spraying the flirty bits within an inch of their lives into a helmet she considers the height of glamour.

"But what's the pill for?" I ask, knowing the question will send her over the edge. She doesn't care to have her actions challenged by her lowly prisoner. Pat doles out my medications three times a day from a weekly pill minder. The cocktail is loaded with opiates to block my pain from peripheral nerve injuries, pills that put me to sleep, and pills to get me going in the morning. The bottles are kept in her room, and I wish I'd had the wisdom to seek them out, just to figure out which one does what before she decided to lock her door.

When she doesn't answer, I take a deep breath. Enough is enough. The envelope addressed to me and opened by Pat was the last straw. "You can't lock me in at night," I say to her back. "I need my independence."

She freezes at the sink, pot in hand. "I *thought* you were awake last night. Surely you know why I lock your door."

"You're afraid I'll sneak into your room? Really Pat? If I wanted to kill you, I'd have done it already." She stands so still I know I've succeeded in annoying her. But she refuses to look at me, so I take the opportunity to palm the orange pill and slip it into my pocket, my one small act of rebellion. I get to work swallowing the rest of the tablets with a swig of juice, then gaze at my breakfast. Existential sigh into my oatmeal. Gruel is what happens when you're too afraid of people to go into town for groceries and let a bridge troll do it for you. "An egg would be lovely," I venture. "Could I get some coffee?"

She finally spins around to look at me. "Get it yourself."

The coffee pot is on the stove. I've grown used to being in the same room with a live flame that licks at the percolator, as if at the feet of a witch's pyre, but going anywhere near it? I swallow and try to slow my racing heart. "You know very well I can't."

Pat has a gorilla scratch between her curlers, then surreptitiously smells her fingers before responding. "But you need your *independence. Independent* girls get their own coffee."

"I can't," I repeat, my voice louder than I want it to be. It's difficult to admit just how right she is. And how much I need her. Surely there are kind and helpful caregivers out there. I fantasize what it would be like to advertise for such a person.

Caregiver wanted by thirty-one-year-old woman living on small Gulf island in the Pacific, accessible only by dodgy ferry service. Free food, Irish whiskey, and dog hugs.

I imagine interviewing potential candidates without Pat's knowledge. Maybe when she's hunting and gathering in town, or in Vancouver buying my art supplies.

"I'd be happy to pour your coffee," the potential caregiver might say, "but . . . erm, why?"

"I can't go anywhere near the range—or heat of any kind," I'd say sheepishly.

My imaginary caregiver would be puzzled. "But heat comes out of the furnace ducts," she reminds me. "In the winter?"

"There's no furnace. It's a temperate rainforest—I just bundle up in sweaters and toques. It's fun." I'd laugh to make my point.

"But surely it must get cold. How do you heat the place?"

I'd tell her about the wood stove, which she'd light on those few days in winter when the temperature dips below freezing. My imaginary caregiver would frown. "Only when I'm in the studio, so I can't see it or smell it," I'd continue. "And you must put out the fire before I come back into the house. Oh—did I mention absolutely no candles? Don't even think about them. Which reminds me—you're not a smoker, are you?" Well, of course she'd be—everyone smokes. "None of that in the house," I'd say. "Or anywhere near the house. Or near my studio."

"Where would I smoke then?" She'd be confused, and I'd even feel a little sorry for her.

"Out the back door," I'd say firmly. "The compost heap provides a surprisingly effective windbreak."

Then, before I could tell her I take tepid showers and can't fathom a bath, my imaginary potential caregiver would go up in a puff of smoke. I snap from my daydream, sighing with frustration. I'm hopelessly stuck with Pat.

The truth is, only she knows what really happened that awful night, and my role in it. I can't remember—maybe I don't want to—and sometimes it feels as though only Pat can protect me from the truth, which is a shameful scar of its own, a wound that's very different from the ones I wear on the surface of who I am. My biggest fear is that I'm guilty of some unspeakable crime. That this lonely life, painting pictures hardly anyone wants to buy, is all I deserve.

"I'll be seeing Dr. Reisman," Pat says turning back to the sink, "when I'm in Vancouver next week."

Right, I'd forgotten she was seeing my old doctor, now in private practice as a general practitioner. I'll be left alone, which has its pros and cons. I can roam freely with no one to lock me in at night, yet Pat's absence will simply make me think of Kay, whom I miss more than life itself.

I wouldn't have met these two nurses if Gynecology hadn't been the only ward where a private, sterile room could be outfitted with my massive Stryker frame. When I was discharged from the hospital, I'd been a nineteen-year-old girl all alone in the world, heir to my Aunt Suze's beautiful house on Salt Spring and a generous monthly disability cheque. I needed live-in care. But Kay, my favorite nurse, joined the World Health Organization, so it was Pat who jumped at the chance to be my caregiver. I would never have chosen Pat as a friend, much less a roommate, but I had no choice. We've struggled to make things work, and after thirteen years, the massive differences in our personalities are reduced to small battles we fight daily. Who better to understand your fateful past than the person who nursed you through it? Even if that person liked to remind you of her sacrifice every goddamn day.

Kay and I have stayed in touch over the years she's been nursing in the Congo. In her last letter, she said she was returning to Canada for a break, so I wrote back and urged her to come to Salt Spring and take on my care. It's a big ask, I know that, but I trust Kay. We forged a bond that went beyond friendship. She gets me, and I need a loving presence in my life. Bad. But months have passed with no reply from my beloved nurse.

"I set up a new canvas," Pat announces, drying her hands on a tea towel.

"Thanks," I say, sure she'll miss the sarcasm. "I'll get to it in January."

"You have to finish it by Christmas."

I drop my spoon. "Christmas? I'm taking December *off*." I need to read and be left alone, to feel so quiet and inward it might almost seem like I've ceased to exist. But I feel panicked that Pat dares threaten this dream of mine.

"You have to keep painting." Pat slams the offending pot into the other sink.

"Why?" I'm trying to keep my voice measured even though I feel like screaming.

"Maybe we'll get lucky with this next one." Pat grabs the broom and begins her daily attack on the blue-glazed Mexican tile floor.

I'm tired of painting canvases that so often don't sell. Yet what can I do but doggedly paint as if my life depends on it? Because it does. We only get so much per month from disability cheques and Aunt Suze's estate, and as Pat's employer, I'm responsible to supplement that somehow. But I don't care. "I refuse to paint out of guilt and vague, misplaced hope that this *next* one might sell," I say stubbornly.

Pat turns to face me. "Do you think you're some famous artist? You're mid-level," she says, her eyes narrow, "your work derivative of other painters who've gone on to the highest pinnacles of success. You'll try again, and you'll *like* it. We're in the poorhouse as it is."

A surge of desperation lights my rage and I push away from the table, almost upsetting my chair, and make a dramatic exit, Pat's threat echoing after me.

7

SAVKA

Deremnytsia, Reichskommissariat Ukraine
FEBRUARY 25, 1944

DARK WAS FALLING WHEN Savka followed her mother into the house. She froze in the doorway. An SS officer was seated at the table, face obscured by the bill of his service cap and the lengthening shadows in the room. Her son Taras stood at his side, in the act of drawing the officer's gun out of its leather holster.

Savka braced herself, waiting for the man to tell her that Marko Ivanets had been killed in battle. Thankfully, Lilia had stayed to gossip around the fire in the village square. Savka didn't think she could bear her sister's gloating presence in the face of such news.

The officer struck a match and lighted a candle on the table. He stood, lifting his head. "Have I changed that much, Savka?"

With a startled cry, she flew across the room, burying her face in her husband's broad chest. His wool greatcoat scratched at her cheek, and he smelled of woodsmoke and sweat. "Let me look." She moved her hands along his arms and shoulders, feeling for wounds. Was he really here after a year of war, without a scratch on him? She laughed with relief, brushing away tears. "Tell me that gun is not loaded," she said with a glance at Taras, who trembled with excitement to have the sinister-looking pistol in his hands.

"The safety is on," Marko replied with a smile. "And I removed the magazine."

"Tato's been wounded," their son said, his hair burnished bright from last year's sun, and ears still too big for his head.

Savka tilted her husband's chin to examine an angry red gash on his cheek. "It's infected." She reached for the hook where she usually hung her kit, then remembered that Natalka had just stolen it for the bunker.

Marko's fingers closed around her wrist. "It's nothing," he said with a grin.

Taras could not take his eyes off his father. "Was it a Soviet knife, Tato?"

Marko nodded. "On a reconnaissance mission in Ternopil."

"You're on leave?" Savka asked. Although she was elated to see him—Marko, alive!—she was furious that he'd endangered them all by coming to the house. She forced a smile and reached to take off his cap. A wink of candlelight shone on the SS death's-head insignia, and she dropped the cap as if it had burned her.

Marko laughed and stooped to pick it up. "My battalion is camped in the forest." His sandy hair was cropped short in the manner the German officers wore it—shaved close above his ears and the shorn top standing straight up, like a cockscomb.

"Did anyone see you?" Mama asked nervously. She had quickly shut the door behind them.

He snorted. "Of course not."

Savka kicked off her sodden boots and unwrapped the shawl from around her ears. "You took a great risk coming here," she said, trying to keep her voice neutral.

Her husband's face darkened and there was a quiver of something in his eyes that made her look away. "What are you afraid of?" he asked. "Five hundred soldiers of the Reich are camped in the forest."

"Which the Red Army will soon take back." Savka didn't want to argue, not when they hadn't seen each other in so long, but he had no

idea what the last year had been like in the village, starving and forced
to be polite to Nazi tank officers.

"Tato?"

Marko turned to answer an earnest question from Taras, and Savka
studied her husband as if it were the first time. He'd shaved off the moustache and beard he'd grown while in the underground, and his bare
upper lip looked somehow cruel and unfamiliar to her. He'd surely killed
Soviet partisans—she could smell it on him, like rotting fruit—to avoid
being killed himself. Could she get used to this new version of Marko?

As if reading her thoughts, he looked at her. "You have become
distrustful."

She opened her mouth and closed it again. There was good reason
for distrust. Savka perched on one of the long wooden benches lining
the room and peeled off her thawing flannel leggings, glancing at Marko
shyly as he spoke to their son.

Wind gusted against the house, and she could feel a draft at her
back, storming cracks in the old wooden walls, despite their best efforts
to pack them tight with clay and horse manure. She undid her braid
and finger-combed her hair, then wrung river water and mud from
the flannel strips into a pail near the door, telling herself to enjoy this
moment—her family together again, if only for a moment. Crossing
herself, she murmured a prayer of thanks to the St. Nicholas and Mariia,
Mother of God icons that hung on the far wall directly opposite a wood
stove covered in tiles that had been hand painted by her grandfather.
"We suspect our neighbor is an informer," she said, feeling her heart
jump. "She might tell an NKVD unit she's seen SS officer Marko Ivanets
visit his wife and family."

Marko smiled. "NKVD are miles away yet." Turning to empty the
contents of his rucksack on the table, he glanced back at her, unable to
hide a lopsided smile. "I've brought you something." Forcing a smile of
her own, Savka padded to the table in damp stocking feet, and stood
on tiptoe to peer over his shoulder, her mouth watering at the sight of

two loaves of gray bread, a can of leberwurst, a bag of sugar, and other impossible riches.

Savka's mother regarded a twist of butter with a gleam in her eyes. She snatched up a tin. "Milk! Where did you get it?"

"SS rations."

Hearing the commotion, Sofiy, Lilia's six-year-old daughter, opened the door of the back room, dazed at the sight of her uncle in an SS uniform.

Mama threw more wood into the stove and set to frying some back fat Gerhard had left from his own SS rations—back fat that Lilia had been saving for his return. After Savka's and Lilia's husbands had joined Nazi divisions, and their houses had been designated for the use of Fifth SS Panzer Division officers, the women had moved in with Mama to avoid being forced to live along with their children in a barn. Due to her age and infirmity, Mama was allowed to remain in her own little house. When Gerhard was here, he took the back room, which had once belonged to their grandparents. The rest of the family slept on the wooden benches lining the walls, Mama's bed closest to the stove.

Marko had taken off his greatcoat, and Savka noticed two braids on the shoulder boards of his tunic, and a different rank insignia—four diamond pips instead of two on his left collar. "You've been promoted?"

"I'm the only Waffen-Sturmbannführer among the Ukrainian officers." Marko glanced at her and she felt herself blush like a young girl. She'd forgotten the seductive pull of those clear blue eyes. "We're our own army," he declared, "avenging those we lost."

Revenge for the great Ukrainian famine, Savka thought.

She looked away, abandoned to her dark and bottomless memories, but Taras still clutched his father's gun with a look of fascination. "Is it a Luger, Tato?" He'd been only a babe in 1932, when Stalin began to starve Ukraine. A savage smell still filled her nose, the stench of bodies rotting in the fields, in the street. Would her heart always ache for her younger sister, Halina, and her grandparents, who'd starved and died in their beds? By the end of 1933, millions of Ukrainians had perished—murdered by the Russians. In retaliation, Marko had followed Stepan Bandera, leader of the Organization of Ukrainian Nationalists, and he had risen through their ranks.

"Yes, it's a Luger," Marko said, as Taras ran his finger over two letters etched into the wooden stock. "It came with another SS officer's initials, so I carved my own over his."

"Put it down, Tarasyku," Savka said, chilled that Marko was carrying the gun of a German who'd been killed in action. She was reaching for it when the front door flew open. Lilia, smelling like woodsmoke from the village drum fire, stood motionless for a moment, obviously confused to see Marko, but her expression soon morphed into one of defiance. "You're here while Gerhard fights Soviets on the front lines?"

Marko lighted a cigarette. "Who's Gerhard?"

Savka shared a glance with her sister, the two of them in silent agreement to hide Lilia's forbidden romance from Marko. Lilia strode forward to drop a kiss on her brother-in-law's cheek, wisely deciding to ignore his question and put aside her anger. She beckoned to Sofiy, who ran to her mother's side and hid her face in the folds of her skirt.

Taras had unbuckled the dagger hanging from a short chain on his father's ammunition belt, and Marko drew out the evil weapon.

"You see that?" The wooden hilt was emblazoned with the Nazi eagle.

She smiled, watching her husband and son—with the same golden hair and blue eyes—leaning over the candle flame to examine the knife hilt. Taras had one hand on Marko's arm, his face lit up to be with his Tato again. The memory of Bohdan's festering wound, Natalka's insolence, and Savka's fear over losing Taras retreated to the back of her mind. The smell of frying back fat filled the air, and for a moment, it was as if the war did not exist.

Taras read the etching on the blade. "*Meine Ehre heisst Treue.* My honor is loyalty." He was good with languages, speaking Ukrainian, Russian, and Polish fluently.

Marko cut his eyes at Taras. "Where are you learning German?"

Savka said, "We were forced to billet an officer." She threw another glance at Lilia. "He's teaching Taras German and English," she added, anxious to head off any more questions about Gerhard.

Marko accepted this with a shrug and grinned, the red gash on his cheek somehow making him even more handsome. "That blade is issued only to SS officers," he said to Taras.

Mama arranged the fried back fat, along with a slice of the bread Marko had brought, on a plate, then handed it to him. Lilia had taken off her wet wool stockings and was hanging them on a hook to dry. When she turned back to the table, she noticed what was on Marko's plate. "We were saving that for Gerhard," she blurted, and Savka felt her throat constrict with worry.

Her husband ground out his cigarette in a dish on the table and took up a fork, sending Lilia a dark look. "Gerhard is the mysterious German you are billeting, who dares teach my son his terrible language and provides you back fat?" He speared a piece of bacon. Lilia kept her eyes down and crossed to the stove. She snatched up an old dish towel next to a ceramic bowl they used to wash up.

"Gerhard's a tank commander, Tato." Their son beamed. "He let me climb into his Tiger One and take the battle con."

Marko looked at him sharply. "What unit?"

"The Fifth SS Panzer Division." Taras stroked the dagger handle with one hand and fiddled with the ties on his vyshyvanka with the other, a tunic Savka had embroidered herself to protect him from evil.

"That division was surrounded by Vatutin's army near Lysianka," Marko said between eager bites of his dinner.

Lilia clutched a cup she'd been drying, her eyes wide. "When?"

"A week ago. Heavy casualties. If your Gerhard survived, his tank didn't." The cup dropped from Lilia's hand, and they watched it roll across the floor. When it came to a stop near Marko's boot he looked up at her and said quietly, fiercely, "Lilia, never forget, to the Germans you are *ein untermensch*, a subhuman they've been sent to starve and enslave."

"Marko," Savka began, noticing her sister's eyes had filled with tears, although she quickly composed herself.

"The SS swear an oath to Hitler," Taras interrupted, unleashing one of his glorious smiles and breaking tension in the room. "Say it for us, Tato."

But Marko ignored the question, and Savka watched, breath caught in her chest, as he drew a hand over his son's brush cut, then, out of a pocket in his rucksack, took several items, which he passed around. A small but deadly looking knife for Taras. Hairpins for Lilia, Mama, and Sofiy. Savka waited patiently as he lifted out a silky women's undergarment and handed it to her.

She blushed as the silk slip flowed like water through her fingers. It was beautiful, a soft rose color, and light as a feather. Had she ever owned anything so lovely? Even her wedding dress had been sewn together using old dresses Mama had saved for the purpose. At any other time, Savka would love to wear this for him in the privacy of their own home, but she felt her anger rise again. Did Marko think this expensive gift made up for his long absence? And where did he get such a thing? She'd just spent hours on her knees in the mud and snow, her stomach growling as she foraged for stinking roots, then rushed off with a submachine gun-wielding *banderivka* to treat a wounded insurgent in a war zone. Finally, she'd cowered outside Marko's SS camp because Natalka had shamed her into stealing German medical supplies. And she'd returned with no hope of a decent meal at the end of the day, besides a cup of sour goat milk and some gristled chestnut tubers boiled in water. Before she could stop herself, she burst out, "Fine for you, taking off the last year, too busy to write."

Marko closed his eyes, as if she exhausted him. "You think I had time—"

"And eating SS rations." Breath heaving, she paused, willing herself to stop before she said something she would regret. *Cherish this moment*, she thought. *Do not ruin it.*

"We eat soup made of roots," Taras said, screwing up his face. "And acorn flour bread."

"You will eat better when the Germans win." Marko pushed away his plate and smiled up at Savka. "Come here."

Mama, ever sensitive to the needs of others, beckoned for Lilia to herd Sofiy and Taras toward a bench near the stove, where she started in on one of her stories. "The olden times were not like the days we live in," she said, her gnarled hands resting on her grandchildren's heads. Even Taras, too old to be coddled, seemed captivated as she continued dramatically. "In the old days, all manner of evil powers walked among us . . ."

Slipping a shy arm around her husband's neck, Savka let herself be drawn into his lap, and into the secret universe that was Marko. The first time she'd set eyes on him, his charismatic smile had knocked her senseless. Now, a pleasant, familiar glow bloomed across her chest, as she felt the beating of his heart—that so familiar heart—beneath her hand, and the smell of him as she grazed her cheek against his stubble. There was his old, impish grin, but also something else . . . Marko— familiar, yet different. Was it his long absence or had he changed irrevocably fighting with the Nazis, wearing this uniform that she still couldn't see without a lump of terror forming in her throat? Did every wife look at her husband's hands when he returned from war—which she did now, as they stroked the inside of her wrist—and wonder what they'd done? Kill Soviet partisans in self-defense. That was as far as she would go in her imagination.

From the far side of the room, Lilia sent envious glances their way, as though angry at seeing Savka and Marko together—the SS officer who had brought news that Gerhard was very likely dead. In that moment, it didn't matter what Lilia felt, for Savka needed her husband's strong hands in other places besides her wrist. She leaned close, still holding the silk slip, and whispered in his ear. "May I *speak* to you?"

8

MARKO

Deremnytsia, Reichskommissariat Ukraine
FEBRUARY 25, 1944

THE MOMENT THE DOOR to the back bedroom closed, Marko lit the candle on the nightstand and it shivered in a draft, the flame casting a shadow across his wife's beautifully obstinate chin, her wide and delicate mouth, her cheeks, now gaunt and hollow. He sank his fingers into Savka's glorious long hair. Then they were together, devouring each other, hands seeking familiar yet new ground, mouth pressed hard against mouth as they struggled with buttons and ties, laughing as his mother-in-law began loudly singing a folk song in the other room.

Marko kicked off his boots. One hit the floor with a thud, and he glanced up as the singing paused a beat, holding his breath, then smiling as Mama started in on a more rousing tune. Taking the silk slip out of his wife's hands, he floated it over her head, flinching when she caught at his arm.

"*AB negative?*" she said, squinting at his tattoo in the light of the candle. "What's this?"

"Every SS man has a tattoo of his blood type," he said, his fingers brushing her nipples through the slip draped over her body. She was much slimmer than he remembered. "How else will doctors know what kind of blood to give me if I'm wounded in battle?"

Falling back on the bed, she gazed up at him with a seductive smile. "You will not be wounded, Marko Ivanets."

Lifting her foot, he inhaled the skin of Savka's ankle, her agonizingly lovely calf. He wanted to start at his wife's feet and move his way up, kissing and adoring every inch of her, but he yearned to be inside her. Hovering over her on the bed, he growled. "You think I'm protected by your prayers?"

"My Ukrainian prayers are stronger than your German helmet," she said, pressing her lips to his cheek.

He kissed her neck, the straw-filled mattress whispering beneath them. "I forgot how beautiful you are," he said as Savka pulled his suspenders down over his shoulders, giggling when he fumbled with his breeches. "You laugh at a Waffen-Sturmbannführer?" he teased her.

"You *forgot* I was beautiful?" Savka grasped his shoulders, drawing him into her, inviting him home. The war disappeared as he lowered himself between her thighs, the awful memories retreating when he slipped a hand to the small of her back, quieting her hips as he dug deeper, his blood ebbing and flowing like a great red tide that rose, engulfing him, until he collapsed upon her in blessed relief.

Later, as they lay facing each other, their skin damp with sweat, their fingers intertwined, Savka cleared her throat and said, "Isn't it time Mykola Lebed ordered you to take over the division? The underground needs a Ukrainian army to help them fight partisans."

He suppressed a spark of irritation. "Of course it isn't time, Savka. Do you think me, and the other Ukrainian officers, would get away with killing Freitag and his men and stealing a ten-thousand-strong division with weapons and artillery—a division the Germans poured great effort into training? Lebed must wait on his order until the krauts are in chaos, running back to Berlin. Besides, Freitag has recently begun to trust me. The old Prussian invites me to battle meetings in his tent, asking what I think of the next day's orders from Berlin."

He fell silent, his face burning at the memory of Freitag's recent insult toward him, when he hadn't realized Marko had arrived early for an officer's briefing. He had been standing outside the Brigadeführer's tent, his hand on the flap, when he heard Freitag sneer, "Man from the forest," to his German officers within. That's what his commanding officer really thought of the Ukrainians—simple peasants and nothing more.

"How nice for Hitler to have ten thousand *filthy Slavs* to do his dirty work," Savka said, her normally gentle voice grown harsh with exasperation.

Marko's temper flared. "Do you think I wish to fight with the Germans? Lebed ordered me to join the division. There's a purpose to all of this."

Savka raised herself on one elbow and stared at him. "Lebed sits on his high throne, issuing orders. He's not the one risking his life fighting ruthless Soviet partisans." He could not see her expression clearly in the light of the candle, but Marko chided himself for doubting her. This obstinate refusal to take him at his word was simply a wife's worry for her husband.

And it was true. Mykola Lebed was not on the ground, made to suffer the Germans day after day. Lebed had taken over command of the OUN when Stepan Bandera was arrested and sent to a German concentration camp in 1941 for daring to use the Nazi invasion to declare an independent Ukrainian state. Lebed had allied himself with the Germans, helping to form the Fourteenth Waffen-SS Division—only tall, Aryan-looking Slavs allowed—and he'd secretly inserted a few officers like Marko Ivanets, one of the underground's top commanders.

He shifted in the bed, every nerve and muscle of his body now primed and on high alert. When the entire division was on the march—motorcycles roaring, trucks carrying light field howitzers spinning their tires in the mud—each tree and hillock posed a potential threat. Partisans harassed their camps at night. Sentries would disappear and be found later, their throats cut. Each soldier slept with a hand on his gun.

"Your hand is shaking," Savka said, placing it on her bare breast.

She smiled, like she had the moment their eyes first met in a cafe in Lviv. How he'd been struck by her, a petite, dimpled beauty, with those eyes. But her smile did not soothe him. Perhaps he no longer deserved the comfort of a woman. To avoid her scrutiny, he burrowed under the blanket, his hand snaking up her thigh. "God willing, let us make another child."

Despite their frequent attempts at conception since Taras's birth, Savka had miscarried repeatedly, and Marko had long ago resigned himself to the reality that she'd never have another baby. "Six children!" they'd cried to each other, hands clasped after their wedding ceremony, giddy with delight at the thought of a large family.

Savka's hand was on his arm. "Hitler will soon send you to the front, where too many of you will be killed and Lebed's plan to take the division will be lost. Desert and go back to the bunker in the mountains," she urged him.

Marko blinked in astonishment. "It's Kuzak's now." Until last year, he'd relished commanding a military district for the Ukrainian Insurgent Army, but now the thought of living in a hole in the ground made him shudder. "Do you not appreciate that your husband is a very important man?" he said, forcing jocularity.

With an impish grin, his wife pinned him to the bed, delighting him, surprising him. The slip was bunched around her waist and her gorgeous long hair spread like a curtain around them, shutting out the war and each silver spark of loss they would yet endure. She closed her eyes and ground her hips against his, and he drew her down, holding her close to his chest, stunned at her show of passion, as she finished in a sweat and bit her lip with a relieved laugh. Then she rolled away and curled up in his arms, a blissful smile on her face.

They lay together in contented silence for a few moments, Marko drifting strands of her hair between his fingers, considering how to tell her what she needed to know. "My unit has not been ordered to the front," he said finally. "We're going after Medvedev and his band of Soviet partisans."

The moment shattered between them and Savka lay still, like a rabbit in the grass, hunted by an owl that circled overhead. "I saw your unit camped in the forest."

Marko was surprised that his normally timid wife had wandered into a danger zone. "What were you doing?" he laughed. "Spying on us?"

Savka raised her head to peer through the near dark at him. "A *banderivka* found me at the river earlier. She took me to treat a wounded insurgent."

Marko frowned. "A *banderivka*? There are no women in the bunkers—"

"There are now. This one was fierce," she said, sounding exasperated and weary. "Her name was Natalka."

He remembered seeing Natalka once, a pretty brunette courier who now had somehow found herself a place in Kuzak's bunker. Marko threw back the blanket and sat on the edge of the bed. "Fucking Kuzak," he said. "Always reckless and unpredictable." The small room was suddenly unbearable to him. His heart raced and he exhaled slowly to calm himself. Taking out a paper from one of his tunic pockets, he found a pencil stub and began to compose a *shtafeta* upon his knee, a message in the code of the underground.

Savka knelt behind him on the bed, her arm around his shoulder, hand on his chest. "What are you writing?"

Her hand seemed to sear his flesh, and his first instinct was to push it away, but he forced himself to fold her fingers into his, talking himself down. A sweat broke out on his forehead. Why was he on edge? He was back with his wife; he'd *wanted* this moment. His pencil flew across the paper, and he glared down at it, focusing his anger on the bunker commander. "I'm writing orders for Kuzak to leave killing partisans to us."

"Natalka and Bohdan were obviously starving," Savka was babbling in his ear. "Natalka even took the roots I'd foraged. She said she had a trapline—"

"No traplines!" Marko shook his head and kept writing, his mouth a grim, obstinate line. "Kuzak's insurgents should only leave the bunker in winter to check if a courier left information in the dead drop. It's too dangerous to come down the mountain, even when they cover their tracks in the snow." He finished writing and, after rolling the paper into a tight scroll, handed it to her.

But his wife held the *shtafeta* as if it had just come out of the fire. "There's more than just a warning to Kuzak," she said. "What else does it say?"

"Coded details of the German offensive on the Red Army at the front," he admitted. "Leave this note in the dead drop on the east face of the mountain—Taras knows it—and wait in the forest for one of Kuzak's men to come. He will lead you to the bunker."

"Why would we go to the bunker? And why bring Taras?" Her voice seemed small, choked. "What if we run into Soviet partisans? It's winter . . ."

He lifted a hand to smooth the wildness from her hair, the whites of her eyes stark against her shadowed face. Marko thought of leaving her his Luger, but Freitag would ask where his sidearm had gone and would fly into a rage if Marko made an excuse of losing it somewhere in the forest. What kind of Waffen-Sturmbannführer misplaced his pistol? "We've driven the partisans off the mountain," he insisted. Reaching for his breeches, he drew them on, then the tall boots.

Savka dropped the *shtafeta* and scrambled to the edge of the bed. "You're leaving? Already?"

Marko stared through the window, where snow was quietly falling in the darkness. He could hear her disappointment, but his wife's reluctance to deliver the *shtafeta* made him wish he were out in the snowstorm rather than in here. Marko had thought long and hard of their reunion. He'd envisioned lying in her arms all night. In a real bed. But now he was anxious to get back to his men. "Freitag expects me at an officer's meeting." He riffled through the pockets of his SS field tunic and withdrew an envelope. "After we kill Medvedev, we'll finally be ordered to the front."

Savka fell back on the bed, clutching the sheet to her breasts. "The front? What if you're trapped and can't get away?" She turned her head. "Damn Hitler and this war he started, sacrificing Ukrainian men to a fight the Germans will lose."

Exasperated, Marko leaned forward, elbows on his knees, looking down at the envelope in his hands. "Soon Ukraine will have a great army, Savka. Think of what we can do against the Soviets. But you and I will never come back to Deremnytsia." He handed her the envelope. His wife opened it and pulled out the forged exit visas and false identification papers he'd arranged for her and Taras. She stared blankly, as if struggling to comprehend, then glanced up at him. He said, "The Red Army will be here within the month," shrugging into his field tunic. "NKVD close behind. They're deporting families they suspect allied with the underground, sending them to Siberia. You and Taras will deliver the *shtafeta* to Kuzak and tell him Roman demands that he take you in."

"Taras is too young to live in a bunker," Savka stammered.

"And you're too afraid," he scoffed, jabbing his finger toward the window. "You know what's happening out there? This Gerhard . . . the Red Army soldiers will rape and murder Lilia for sleeping with him, and you, for being married to a Waffen-SS officer."

"We will leave before they arrive—"

"The Russians will catch up and take Taras as cannon fodder. Going to Kuzak is your only hope."

Marko buttoned his tunic and stared at her through the near dark, saw her struggle with the ugly truth and then come to the same conclusion: this was the only solution to save their son. "For how long?" she asked finally.

"When the snows melt, Kuzak's men will take you and Taras to the Polish border. Other insurgents will meet you and put you on a train that will take you to Munich. I'll find you there after the war."

"What of Mama and Lilia . . . and Sofiy?"

He stood up. "I'm working on documents for them."

"Don't send me and Taras up there," she begged, reaching for him. "Hours of climbing through snow and cold, only to be met by . . ."

"Natalka?" he reminded her. "Watch her, listen to her. You will learn to be a fierce *banderivka*."

She reached for his hand, but he was already buckling his holster and dagger. "Promise me you'll get papers for Mama and Lilia, the children," she pleaded, "that you'll get them out."

"I promise, *kokhana*." He left her then, closing the door behind him without looking back.

9

———

JEANIE

———

Salt Spring Island
DECEMBER 5, 1972

AFTER MAKING A DRAMATIC exit from the kitchen—and leaving Pat—I stand in the front hallway a moment, still shaking and furious. There are precious few options for escape when you're a recluse on a Gulf island in the Pacific Ocean.

Stalking toward the front door, I wait for Tuna to scrabble down the hall, tongue hanging and legs bowed underneath him. With a furtive glance over my shoulder, I open the hall table drawer and slip the envelope addressed to *me* into the pocket of my overalls. I shove my feet into Aunt Suze's old garden clogs, pull a wool hat over my long dark hair, shrug on a raincoat, then open the front door.

My clogs beat a tattoo over the wooden pathway that leads to the guesthouse and my studio above. There's a thick smell of rainforest, wet bark, and the competing aromas of growth and decay. I flip up the hood of my slicker against the perpetual rain that has turned the world around me an impossibly vibrant green. The island has been shrouded in storm clouds and fog. You would think I was used to the West Coast winter, but I always dread the rain and heavy stillness, the feel of a damp cellar and air thick with moisture that makes my scars ache.

Beyond the house, in Southey Bay, two low silhouettes of the Secretary Islands rise from a shimmering sea. The tide is out, revealing clumps of glistening, purple sea stars clinging to the wet rocks of a small island out in Houston Passage. To the west, Penelakut Island looms through the fog, a low shadow of Wallace Island to the east, and Galiano Island behind it. Rain and more rain falls, beading on the hood of my coat and soaking the trees that encircle the house, wind moving their lofty branches in a hushed roar. The garden is water-logged, the earth rich with cedar needles fallen everywhere like slivers of light.

"Keep painting, she says. We're in the poorhouse, she says," I grumble. "As Kay used to say, *bollocks.*"

I make my way through the wild, overgrown garden, which Pat is paid a monthly stipend to maintain but claims she doesn't have time. As a result, the surrounding rainforest has strangled Aunt Suze's flower beds and her once-cherished vegetable garden. It's like a jungle, and I love all of it—even the mist rising from the pond—with the affection of a girl who's been *this* close to death.

I stop and wait for Tuna to catch up, his grayed muzzle open in a goofy smile. Years ago, Aunt Suze planted seven palm trees here and now they're gorgeous specimens, over ten feet tall, the fronds rustling and whispering in the slightest wind. I fish out the offending pill, my palm stained orange from the dye coating. I think about flinging it into the forest or the ocean, but I stop myself. The pill has a purpose, and I need to know what it is.

I drop it back in my pocket and glance at my house framed by a stand of cedar and arbutus trees that glow in the pale morning light. Aunt Suze, inveterate traveler and mystic, christened this beautiful place Gladsheim, after Odin's bright and radiant hall of the gods. Massive beams support the sprawling two-story edifice of gray weathered cedar directly upon rocks, which breech like gleaming humpback whales, sloping away from the headland and vanishing beneath the surface of the darkly luminous sea. At night, you can hear the soft lap of waves and imagine you're on an ocean liner that's arrived at an exotically humid port of call. *Gladsheim.*

Aunt Suze died thirteen years ago, while I was still in the hospital, and I can no longer feel her presence in this beloved waterfront estate that lifts from the fog like a ghost ship. The locals—beatniks who came for the wild parties she threw back in the fifties—used to call it *a righteous pad*, but the only souls who've been out here since she passed from this world are her lawyer, the landscaping guy, a few thrill-seeking journalists eager for a story, and the odd, mad squirrel.

I'm overcome by a wave of melancholy, and suspicion that I'm no more than a prisoner working off her sentence in a beautiful purgatory. The lonely trees whisper a brutal reminder: *You are nothing to no one.* Tears come to my eyes. When did Gladsheim stop being home? And where do I belong, if not here?

With Tuna at my heels, I open the door at the side of the guesthouse and slowly climb the stairs to my studio, resentment in every step. When I enter the studio, my dog pads faithfully to his bed beside my easel. Pat calls this place *the den of iniquity,* a reference, I think, to the huge windows and central skylight that, on an actual *sunny* day, shed rays upon a delightfully ratty pink velvet settee in the center of the room that I often recline upon à la Coco Chanel. Glory quivers and thrums around me in a cacophony: sketches and pages ripped from magazines clutter the walls, paint-flecked sawhorses and easels, ladders, and paint tubes, and empty turpentine jugs left where they've been thrown by me, either in artistic abandon or uncontrolled angst.

I fling my raincoat on a sawhorse and wrap myself in a Cowichan sweater, approaching the radio with trepidation. Pat insists the few paintings she's sold in the past were done while I listened to her *lucky radio station of country music favorites,* and as such has direfully fixed the tuner dial to the required station with black electrical tape. It's a warning—*don't you dare change it.* I reluctantly switch it on to Ray Price in the midst of crooning "I Won't Mention It Again."

"Satan tortures her subjects in hell," I gripe to Tuna, who's already curled into a crescent roll in his bed, paws over his ears. I notice that

Pat has sharpened my graphite pencils with the zeal of an executioner honing her axe. Two new canvases, stretched and gessoed within an inch of their lives, lean on separate easels. And she's taken it upon herself to underpaint both in a misguided effort to *save me time.* It's merely a wash of burnt sienna and turpentine meant to banish the stark white of a canvas and give me a starting point, yet this is the artist's job, not her meddling caregiver's. "Insufferable," I say to Tuna. He lifts his head and regards me with those woeful brown eyes I love so much. "Tell me I shouldn't break these bloody things over my knee." His eyebrows have turned white with age, giving him a perpetually startled look. "Right," I say with a smile. "She'd eviscerate me."

Desperate for an idea for this painting—how can it possibly be finished by Christmas?—I sweep my hair over one shoulder and absent-mindedly begin to braid, muttering a little prayer to the goddess of art. There's a heavy, expectant feeling in my chest, like the storm clouds looming over Southey Bay. I dig my sketch pad out from under a pile of old magazines and paw through some of the thumbnail drawings I've done during one of Pat's "inspiration trips" in the double kayak. How can I convey the mystery of a scene and the glorious light that falls upon it, the powerful waiting nature of an extreme and unpredictable landscape on this mere canvas?

"Paint from your dark, unknowable heart," a teacher at art school had once whispered in my ear. I grit my teeth. On the night of my accident a leviathan rose from the abyss to devour my dark, unknowable heart. *It's his possession alone,* I think, throwing down the sketches in frustration. Does every landscape I paint come from my dark, unknowable angst? I go to the window before I succumb to a fresh desire to trash the new work before I've even started it. Rain has stopped drumming on the skylight, and I stare out the window at the profoundly still and watchful ocean beyond the house. I think of the seventeenth-century portrait artist Elisabetta Sirani, who somehow managed to paint and succeed despite male persecution and a raging peptic ulcer.

But I'm not Elisabetta Sirani . . . nowhere close. And besides, she died at age twenty-seven—I've missed the moment.

My hand absently slips into my pocket and touches the envelope. I'd forgotten about it. I draw it out, picking at the fancy stamp affixed to the top right corner, and glance at the return address. "Who the hell is Octavius Karbuz?" I ask aloud.

I'm about to withdraw the thick card stock from the envelope when I see the villain herself exit the house and stump along the driveway, flipping a cigarette into her mouth before cramming her bulk into the Jeep. Pat doesn't turn her head, but I know her eyes have gone to the rearview mirror, expecting a glimpse of me hunched over my easel. I dive behind the curtain, denying her the satisfaction. She backs out and I reemerge, glaring as the Jeep swings down the drive and is swallowed up in the trees.

How I despise her.

"You'll pay for locking me in," I whisper. "You will pay." I slip what looks like an invitation from the envelope, my eyes flitting nervously over the black, stylized writing.

The Great Return
A Pacific Northwest Perspective
PAINTINGS BY JEANIE ESTERHAZY
Saturday, January 21st, 1973
Karbuz Gallery, Brussels

Rumors that Ms. Esterhazy had succumbed to injuries she
suffered in 1958 have circulated through the art world for over
a decade. But those rumors have thankfully been disproven.
Although Ms. Esterhazy's health is precarious, she has begun
painting again. Bravely working through debilitating pain,
scarcely able to hold her paintbrushes with hands twisted and
contracted with scar tissue, her new work raises the bar on

> transcendence and places the viewer squarely
> within her atmospheric world.
>
> The artist will not be in attendance, but please join
> Jeanie Esterhazy's dealer, Octavius Karbuz,
> for a special viewing of her new works.

I stagger toward the settee and sit down hard enough to jangle my teeth. My head spins, and my brain struggles to take in the words I've just read. Never mind the news that apparently my life is hanging by a thread, I'm gobsmacked at the rest. Earlier, in the kitchen, Pat reminded me that I'm a mid-level painter, copying the work of others more talented. But this invitation claims that I'm a renowned landscape artist. "Transcendence" and "atmospheric" be damned, I can't ignore *succumbed to injuries.*

I hold up my hands for Tuna to examine. "Sure, they're scarred, but twisted and contracted so she's scarcely able to hold her paintbrushes?" And *renowned?* That's kind of like *famous.* Why didn't Pat tell me I have an art dealer named Octavius Karbuz? I quiver with a rage that snakes across my skin like live electrical wires. Not only has she lied, but she's also purposefully prevented me from learning the truth. I leap up from the settee, startling Tuna. "I'm not some mid-level artist just getting by, but a celebrated one who raises the bar on *transcendence!*"

I can't quite believe this. Perhaps my art dealer Octavius Karbuz and the gallery he owns are trying to capitalize on my work? Or some nefarious forger has been copying my paintings, which would sort of be a compliment at this stage of my career, I think with a reluctant smile. No. The invite was addressed to me. And Pat hid the damn thing. What has she been up to? Pat always told me she took my paintings to a climate-controlled storage locker in Vancouver to protect them from moisture, but now I know that she's shipped every one of them straight to Brussels. "Sacrificial pay cuts, my arse. She's been pocketing the proceeds." Tuna has settled back into his bed and thumps his tail in solidarity. I have some money hidden in my sock drawer, don't I? It's enough to get on the ferry to Vancouver, but not enough to buy a plane ticket to Toronto, much less Brussels. But why should I be the one to leave? Pat has likely been lying to my face for years. In the past, I was happy for her to take over the shopping and the social necessities of my existence, but now I need to claw it back. My mind is a stutter of confusion and I force myself to slow down and think. I'd ask Kay to send a money order, enough money to buy Pat a special Christmas present for being so fucking nice. Enough money for a plane ticket to my own show, The Great Return. I imagine the surprise and delight on this Octavius Karbuz's face when his reclusive artist actually turns up and tells him she had no idea he existed. But Kay has been incommunicado for months.

My anger swings back to *me*. I've become so damn complacent, letting Pat take over to the point that she's kept me from life itself. She doesn't let me answer the phone, she won't even allow me a stroll up to Arbutus Road for the mail. Now I know why. I might see correspondence from my art dealer and start asking uncomfortable questions. My mind suddenly shifts to the orange tablet at breakfast. There's something very odd about that, and her insistence that I take it without question.

"Who am I kidding?" I confess to Tuna, who sits up in his bed, finally showing interest. "Even if I *can* screw up the courage to attend this show in Brussels, Pat won't let me go." After my first gallery appearance six years ago, she claimed I should never be allowed in public again. I misbehaved, according to her. "I thought I knew Pat," I say to Tuna. "But she's proving to be more than a simple blunt instrument. What else has she been lying about? Maybe I didn't do a damn thing wrong at my wedding reception. Maybe I'm *not* a monster. Maybe the monster is sleeping right down the hall." I stand in the middle of the studio, whispering now. "My god, she might actually be *insane*." Fear grips me by the throat. Is Pat dangerous? I take a deep breath, determined to proceed with caution and watch my back.

I look down at the invitation again. But, if I'm famous, I should be able to paint what I bloody well want. Jaw determinedly clenched, I glance at the blank canvas on my easel, thinking of the one and only abstract I gleefully painted years ago, before giving up when Pat told me it would never sell. I need to see it again, for inspiration.

It's stored in the studio closet where Pat keeps my art supplies. She's piled several boxes in the narrow passage, blocking my way, but I squeeze past them and peer into the murk. The abstract should be stacked near the back wall, but it's gone.

"Miserable bloated swine," I fume. I was proud of that piece. Did she destroy it or sell it to my art dealer without me knowing? A burning, hateful rage overcomes me. Pat has finally stomped over the line, and it's time for things to change. It's either her or me. This is my house, my land, my life.

I find the oil paints on a shelf and fight my way out of the closet. Crossing the studio, I pause to twist the tuner free of its electrical tape on the radio. Dialing in a verboten rock and roll station, I yelp with rebellious glee and crank the volume as the first, epic guitar riffs of Led Zeppelin's "Whole Lotta Love" blast from the speakers. Breath held in glorious anticipation, I squeeze paint onto my palette.

Alizarin crimson, cadmium red. These are the colors I want.

With each slash of oil pigment, I banish Pat by painting her in the style of Edvard Munch—a scream on her face as flames threaten to swallow her, sending her deeper into a hellscape of my own making.

10

SAVKA

Carpathian forest, Reichskommissariat Ukraine
MARCH I, 1944

FOUR DAYS AFTER MARKO'S visit, Taras turned to his mother, one hand on the trunk of a beech tree, the other pulling the knife his father had given him from an inner pocket of his coat. "If a Soviet partisan dares stop us," he promised, "I'll protect you."

"The partisans won't be coming back after SS soldiers so recently camped in this forest." Savka forced confidence into her voice. "And I have our papers. We're an innocent mother and son going to see our relations in the next village." She drew his head to her shoulder and smiled. "You're safe."

A light snow began to fall as she and Taras climbed through the dark forest, and Savka drew the shawl she was wearing over her head. They quickly found a snow-packed trail on the east face of the mountain, with a plan to make the dead drop site by midday, then wait for one of Kuzak's men to venture out and check for a *shtafeta* that a passing courier might have left for them. Beech trees, their distinctive gray trunks and leafless, ice-frosted branches reaching skyward, towered over their heads, massive and ancient. As they walked, an unearthly quiet floated over Savka and her son. The trees and snow seemed unspeakably removed, as if she were in a dream. She looked up, willing birdsong, or a grouse to fly out of the junipers, startled at their passing—anything to show *life* in these lonely woods—but the sky only threatened more snow. Despite a cold wind that flowed down off the upper slopes, blasting through her wool coat, the day was perfect to make an escape. The silently falling snow would cover their tracks.

Only an hour ago, she and Taras had said tortuous farewells to Lilia, Mama, and Sofiy. When Mama held Savka back, a hand on her arm, she wanted to lead her son back into the house and forget Marko's mad plan. "You can't go to the bunker," Mama said. "It's not safe."

Savka's chest ached at her mother's words and at the sight of her heartsick expression. "Mama, it isn't safe for Tarasyku in Deremnytsia," she said, using her son's name in its most affectionate form. "If we leave, a new life awaits us with Marko after the war."

Lilia, holding tight to Sofiy's hand, scowled at her sister. "Where are *our* papers?" Savka could hear panic in her voice. Lilia was a Nazi officer's lover in the path of the Red Army. She had every reason to worry.

"Marko will send them within a fortnight," she promised recklessly. "And we'll all be reunited after the war."

The imprint of Mama's hand on her arm had burned Savka as she and Taras had walked away. A good, brave insurgent would parcel off that memory, focus on the path in front of her. But Savka was not one of those, and it was all she could do to not turn around and run back to her mother and sister.

Now, she struggled to keep up with Taras on the increasingly elevated terrain. They'd not brought much with them, only the layered clothes on their backs and a rucksack filled with a flask of hot tea, dried roots and acorns for Kuzak, her baba's beaded *korali* necklace—which she and her mother had worn at their weddings—and the new, forged exit visas and identification papers Marko had given her a few days ago that announced this mother and son were Irina and Oleh Bzovsky.

Taras was in a celebratory mood, glowing with the news that underground insurgents had ambushed one of Stalin's favorite military commanders yesterday, during a pitched battle deep behind the front lines. "They've mortally wounded Vatutin himself, Mama," he said. "A commander of the Red Army!"

Savka's mouth went dry with fear, and she stumbled, her hand shooting out to steady herself against a tree. Might NKVD patrols have penetrated the front lines and come into the mountains, seeking revenge against the underground? She glanced at Taras. If they were caught by Soviet partisans or NKVD, they were expected to kill themselves to avoid capture, but her son didn't know this. Savka tried to cast the thought from her mind. Marko had been certain that she and Taras wouldn't run into partisans—so certain that he'd not bothered to give her a gun. She was grateful, unable to imagine murdering her own son, then turning it on herself.

Yet the encrypted *shtafeta* that Marko had given her earlier in the week burned a hole in the lining of her coat. Before she'd sewn it in last night, she unrolled the paper to find columns of numbers, a secret code that she'd never learned to decipher. Now she remembered that Marko said it contained details of the German offensive on the Red Army at the front, and her heart skipped a beat at the thought of carrying it through a war zone.

The beech forest ended, and the trail opened to a large, open glade. In the spring, this meadow would be blanketed with yellow and purple crocuses, and in summer, with edelweiss. But now it lay beneath a frigid mantle of white. Savka paused to gaze out at the view—fog over the valley and the river snaking past their village far below.

Taras crossed the meadow ahead of her, mumbling the anthem of the Ukrainian Insurgent Army. To still her mind, Savka tried to focus on the words.

It is sweeter for us to die in battle
Than to live in bondage as mute slaves.

On the other side of the glade, they entered the coniferous forest that grew at higher elevation on the mountain. In the suddenly dim light, the upended and tangled roots of an ancient spruce loomed ahead of them on the trail, torn from the ground by storm or advanced age. When they reached it, Savka brushed snow off the trunk and climbed up, yanking the hem of her trousers—borrowed from Lilia—down over her frigid bare ankles and uncorking the flask of hot tea. She hummed a little tune, determined to not let Taras glimpse even one small fragment of her terror at the thought of them alone in these woods.

Her son patted the trunk. "We may meet the Tsar of the forest, Mama," he said, referring to the story his Baba had told him the other night.

"Maybe," she said with a smile, sipping at her tea. "But I will not let him take you, Tarasyku."

He bounded around the tree as if he were dancing the *hopak*. Savka watched him with affection, a mother's love. After his thirteenth birthday a few months ago, he seemed to have sprouted, growing so suddenly tall and lanky; he was like a puppy who had yet to match its paws. She imagined Marko and her swinging along a street in Munich, Taras between them, laughing and telling them about the most recent book he'd read. *Soon we'll be safe*, Savka thought with a smile. *Soon we'll all be together.*

The back of her neck prickled with foreboding, and she turned her head to look back, the smile dying on her lips. Shapes of brown and black flashed across the snowy meadow they'd just crossed, heading in their direction. Was it possible that Kuzak's men had come out to meet them? Or was it someone else?

"Get down," Savka hissed at Taras, not taking chances. They fell to their knees in the snow behind the fallen tree, the only sound their labored breathing.

Taras's face was pale. "Is it Kuzak?"

Savka raised her head a fraction. Three men had just entered the forest, heads down. Two were clutching their rifles. They disappeared from her view behind dense trees for a moment before emerging in a small clearing one hundred meters away. She felt like a hunted creature, with nowhere to hide. There was no mistaking the distinctive uniforms of the Soviet security police; their bright blue-and-red caps gave them away. This wasn't a full NKVD unit—only an officer and two border patrol soldiers in khaki wool tunics, black pants, and leather boots—but Savka still felt sick as she watched them turn their gaze in the direction of her and Taras's hiding place. She looked at her son, preparing herself to tell him that they must show themselves, but it was too late. Before she could stop him, Taras was up and crashing through the underbrush beside the trail. Panic clawed at her throat. If she didn't run too, Taras would be shot. Prepared to launch herself after him, she was jerked back—her shawl had caught on a tree branch—and she gasped, terrified as she struggled to free herself. Finally breaking away, her shawl yanked from her head and left fluttering on the branch, she followed Taras, tripping on roots hidden beneath the snow.

Guttural shouts in Russian floated behind them, demanding they stop. Savka hazarded a glance over her shoulder. The two soldiers were giving chase. Their officer, a small man wearing a long black leather coat, had paused to train a pair of binoculars on her and Taras. Her son stumbled and she grabbed his arm. "Stop."

Taras went to his knees. "Hide. They might pass us by."

"They've seen us," she said, fear thundering through her.

They crouched awkwardly behind a juniper thicket, holding their breaths. One of the soldiers passed only meters away on the trail, his boots crunching on the snow as he moved away from their hiding place. Savka prayed the other would follow him. Natalka's warning rose from her memory like a specter. *Coward! Destroy the shtafeta!* The end of Savka's long braid lashed her face as she ripped at the hem of her coat and fumbled out the rolled paper with trembling fingers. Tearing it down the middle, she handed half to her son. As they began to stuff the message into their mouths, Natalka again whispered in her ear: *A real insurgent would kill herself.*

When the *shtafeta* had dissolved to a pulpy mess she swallowed it down. Taras scrambled up a knoll before she could stop him, and Savka ran again to catch up with him. As she climbed close behind her son, shots rang out and with a scream she fell forward, her face in the snow, winded and confused. What had happened? As if from very far away, she heard someone approach.

"Mama . . ."

Savka wanted to tell Taras to keep running, but she couldn't get air. It felt as if someone had pulled a poker from a fire and stabbed her in the right side of her chest, and she couldn't move. The snow felt so cold against her cheek. Her entire body was tingling, and yet numb, as though the muscles were going to sleep. She lifted her head a fraction to see Taras standing a few feet away, his face ashen with stunned bewilderment. She stared desperately into his eyes, as if they were a life raft that would float her back to the world.

The grind of boots on snow drifted down to her as the NKVD officer and his two soldiers appeared in her outer vision. One of the soldiers prodded her with his foot, turning her over onto her back, and a sudden throbbing heat blazed down the length of her arm. She could not feel her right hand and tried to lift it, crying out at the agonizing pain in her chest and shoulder.

The officer in the black leather coat regarded her with cold, dead eyes set too close together. He was unnaturally short for a man, and his pock-marked face was flushed with exertion. Snow had fallen on his cap, dusting his cheeks and nose. He brushed at his face with a few irritated swipes of his gloved hand. Savka's vision swam, but she glimpsed two gold stars on his shoulder straps. Her eyes drifted to the treetops far above in stark relief against the chalk gray sky. They seemed to lean toward her, the way a mother would to an ill child.

"How clumsy of you, Comrade Ilyin," the officer said in accented Russian. He collapsed into a coughing fit and straightened, wiping his mouth. "You have broken the wing of this pretty bird."

Ilyin smirked. "Apologies, Comrade Lieutenant Belyakov."

The force of the shot had pushed some flecks of the *shtafeta* up into her mouth, and she could feel them on her lip. Lieutenant Belyakov

seized her coat collar and wrenched her to sitting, his fingers pushed
back into her throat, trying to snag the chewed remnants of the message.
Instinctively, she bit down hard, and he shouted, raising his booted foot
to kick her backward.

Taras launched himself at the officer, the pocketknife in his hand.
She tried to speak, to call to him, and she braced herself, waiting to hear
another shot, but none came. Instead, one of the soldiers easily disarmed
her son and sent him sprawling in the snow.

The initial shock of her injury was wearing off but now the pain
was unbearable. If the bullet had caught her in the left chest instead of
the right, she would be dead now. She began to shiver uncontrollably,
and she thought of her Red Cross training: treat the shock, keep the
patient warm, anesthetize the entry point, remove the bullet, stitch and
prevent infection . . .

"Too many bandits crawling out of their holes," one of the soldiers
said.

"We are not with the bandits," Taras insisted, speaking Russian.

There was a brief silence, marked by the rising fragrance of spruce
and a high sound of wind in the trees. One of the soldiers had lighted
a cigarette and the smell made Savka gag. She could not stop staring at
Lieutenant Belyakov's nose, the bridge crooked, as if it had been broken
at some point in the past. Her eyes reluctantly traveled over the rest of
his face. His mouth was small—to match his compact, almost elfin
body—the lower lip oddly full and sensual but set now in a determined
manner that made her think of interrogation rooms and torture. He'd
wrapped his injured fingers in a handkerchief; she noticed blood seep-
ing through—a small victory. The Lieutenant removed his cap and ran
his other hand repeatedly over his dark hair. Savka fixated on a thick
strand that had escaped from the carefully combed pompadour, slicked
into Stalin's own style—a ridiculous bouffant that had suffered under
the weight of the lieutenant's field cap. One of his men roughly searched
her rucksack and coat pockets. He took their forged papers to his

commander, who studied them for a moment, then looked from her to Taras.

"Who do we have here? Ah, Irina Bzovsky and her dear son Oleh out for an afternoon stroll in the forest." Belyakov lowered his eyes again to the document. "This is an inspiring piece of subterfuge, my dear Savka." At the sound of her name, her pulse spiked, but she fought to keep her expression impassive. When the officer opened his mouth to speak again, she caught the burnished gleam of a single gold tooth. "Did you think your husband's visit to you a few days ago went unnoticed?"

Her neighbor had informed on them. Savka told herself to listen closely to what Belyakov was saying—her and Taras's lives depended on it—but his voice seemed to come from all directions, the sky and trees, the very earth.

A nudge from his booted foot roused her. "What is the lovely wife of a rebel commander and SS officer doing out here with her son?" he asked with a scornful look on his face. "Does Marko Ivanets think we do not have agents in your village?" He cocked his head, waiting for her to speak, but when she said nothing, he continued in a loud, officious voice, as if he were on the stage addressing an audience. "How pleased we were to hear that Ivanets had come to see his wife and son. Marko Ivanets, the fabled underground leader, always slipping through our fingers. An SS officer now! Much more valuable to us than a lowly bandit."

Belyakov glanced around at his men, one of whom restrained a now-subdued Taras, then looked back at Savka. "What high regard your husband has for you, sending his wife and son with a coded message to his bandit friends." He stared down at her. "There is a bunker in the area. You will tell us where."

Taras struggled against his captor's grip. "The *banderivtsi* will murder you," he shouted, "just as they did Vatutin."

The officer smiled ruefully. "Why do you think we are here?" He squatted beside her. "To shoot and interrogate bandits who dared kill our esteemed comrade general." She tried to tell him that she and Taras had nothing to do with Vatutin's assassination, but was overcome with nausea. He placed the toe of his boot over the open wound in her chest, and she screamed. "Admit you're Savka Ivanets. A nod will do."

She squeezed her eyes shut to keep herself from hyperventilating or passing out. For Taras's sake, she would remain conscious; for Taras she would sacrifice anything.

"What must we do to encourage you?" the lieutenant mused. "Bring him here," he ordered. Savka's eyes snapped open, and she watched the two men drag Taras forward. One of the soldiers was brutally handsome: Ilyin she thought his name was, his jet-black hair curled beneath the NKVD cap, dark eyes regarding her with scorn. Would they torture an innocent child? She was in no condition to resist them if they did.

"Yeleshev?" Lieutenant Belyakov nodded to the other soldier—taller, plain faced—who lunged at her across the snow, holding a pair of pliers he'd taken from his coat pocket. He grasped Savka's right hand and held it still as she struggled weakly, struck by raw terror. When Yeleshev angled the pliers over her fingernails, she fixed her eyes on the sky, refusing to scream or cry in front of Taras. She choked as fear bristled and tightened like rope across her throat. They were going to torture *her* to get Taras to talk.

"Don't touch her," Taras sobbed. "It's true—we're Savka and Taras Ivanets."

"No," Savka cried. Yeleshev released her and stepped back, but not before closing one nostril with his thumb and blowing what was in his other nostril into the snow next to her. She let out the breath she'd been holding and tried not to think of her son's shock at seeing her lying crumpled like a wounded deer, helpless in front of these brutes. "Now that you know who we are, let us go," she pleaded.

The officer jerked his head, and his men took Taras a short distance away, out of earshot. Surely NKVD thugs would not shoot a child, yet they harbored ruthless hatred for Ukrainians, no matter how young. "If you hurt my son . . ."

The lieutenant laughed. "You will *kill* me?" He waved a gloved hand. "Look around you, Savka. Absolutely no one for miles."

He knelt on one knee beside her and drew out his Korovin pistol. "Do you know who I am?" He waited for her answer, and when she shook her head weakly, he continued. "I'm high up in the NKVD. Very high. Once I had everything—a fine apartment in Moscow, the best vodka, Western luxuries." He stared out and away from her, his eyes a dark, liquid brown, the irises almost as black as the pupils.

A cruel man, Savka thought, *nothing better than a murderer.*

He looked down at her again. "For years I have been made to slog through forests behind the front lines, into the dens of rats, with only two soldiers at my disposal. When I once had hundreds under my command," he said, smiling. "Hundreds. Now I am kneeling on the snow in a Carpathian forest, wiping my ass with a whore and her mewling son."

She glared at the lieutenant. She would resist him to her dying breath to save that son.

"And yet your husband?" Belyakov continued. "We know he's one of Bandera and Lebed's top men. What plans do they have for the Fourteenth Division? Hmm, Savka? You and I know Ivanets and the other Ukrainian men are not with the SS because they love speaking German."

Savka watched those dark eyes cloud over with displeasure at her silence. "Your husband writes to you? Listen to me. You will encourage Marko's responses and perceive what his unit is planning when they're sent to the front." She opened her mouth to protest, to say that writing letters was like pulling teeth for Marko, but before she could, the Russian lifted the edge of her coat and briefly examined her chest wound. "Listen, peasant—you're bleeding out," he said casually. "And we're leaving you. Surely the underground heard our gunshot from their bunker. If you die before they find you—that is one less bandit for us to kill in the end. If they find you alive, tell them you panicked and ran."

"What?" she choked in disbelief. "They'll never believe such a lie."

"They will. Tell them you were shot and lost consciousness. We captured your son and left, believing you mortally injured." He shrugged. "If the underground can save you, they'll interrogate you, but who knows if they'll trust your story? If they let you go, Savka, you will be mine," he said with a smile. "I will keep your son safe while you write letters to your husband and send me his responses."

She struggled to understand. They wanted her to spy on her husband. And they were taking Taras? The thought of her precious son, her only child, in danger, and the idea of betraying Marko, made her sick. "My husband will not write secret information"—her voice a frantic whisper—"in a letter to me."

"Encourage his honesty," he said simply. "Use your whore ways." He took a pewter flask from inside his coat and deftly unscrewed the top, drinking deeply.

Savka forced herself to look directly into this man's lifeless eyes. "You would use the information to kill him."

The lieutenant returned the flask to his pocket and smoothed his hair back with his good hand. "We will use that intelligence to *protect* him," he said, with a disquieting smile. "The front commanders will be advised of Ivanets's unit. When the Germans are surrounded, we'll capture him alive. He will be returned safely to your village and become our star informant."

"You lie. You'll shoot him . . . or send him to Siberia."

"What's in your future?" The lieutenant asked her with another venomous smile. "Rape and murder for collaborating with the Huns? Or be deported to Siberia? I'll save you from that. If you do what I say, Savka, you'll see your son again. Do what I order, and I will give him back." Lieutenant Belyakov stood and turned, his black coat flapping like the wings of a crow as he strode to catch up to his two soldiers, who'd taken Taras farther up the trail. Savka's son looked back once before Ilyin cuffed him across the ear, and she wailed as they melted into the trees. "Tarasyku," she sobbed weakly, fighting to commit her son to memory. What would happen to him? Would she ever see him again? And what would she tell Marko?

Savka howled into the profound silence, but no one came. Taras was gone. She stared up at the heavy, colorless sky. It was as though she were alone in another universe, detached from everything she'd ever known. Without her shawl, the cold bit into the exposed skin of her neck and ears. Her arm and shoulder were numb, and she didn't know if it was shock or her body shutting down. At some point it had begun snowing and now an icy sleet stabbed at her face like tiny knives. She imagined the snow drifting around her until she became part of the forest, but it didn't matter. Taras was gone and there was no reason for her to live.

A wisp of childhood memory hovered behind her eyelids. A day at the beach in Odessa, a merciless wind coming off the Black Sea, and Lilia scooping sand over her inert form; how she'd laughed, until she felt the relentless crush of it.

With a cry more animal than human, she eased onto her left side and drew her knees to her chest for warmth like a frightened child in a dark room. She felt herself floating in a haze, slipping away, and she sent a silent message to Natalka, to Kuzak. *Come out. Find me.* She struggled to stay awake; she had to live—who else would fight for Taras?

In the quiet of the trees, Savka heard her mother's voice, telling her old stories.

The Tsar of the forest took the son away and they passed into the other world, the world beneath the earth . . .

11

JEANIE

Salt Spring Island
DECEMBER 5, 1972

I'VE JUST FINISHED PAINTING a gleam on the claws of the demon dragging Pat down to hell when Jimmy Page's guitar solo jerks to a halt. I turn to find that my subject has yanked out the power cord on the radio. The studio is so quiet, I can hear her wheezing. "I thought you went to town," I say, voice shaking.

"I knew you were up to no good, so I turned around before I got to Southey Point Road. Someone has to watch you." Pat clocks the canvas, recognizing herself. Her face turns purple with rage, and she bellows, "Who do you think you are?"

Tuna cowers in his bed. And I yearn to curl up next to him and hide. I must contain my rage. Little Jeanie suffers when she dares to face big Pat. "Perhaps I'm a renowned landscape artist who raises the bar on transcendence," I say, feeling too much like a newborn lamb being stalked by a wolf. She storms past me to snatch the new canvas off its easel and breaks it over her knee.

"That might have been worth something," I say, brandishing the invitation over my head. I wanted to play it cool, but with Pat steaming in front of me . . . *hell no.* She doesn't get to be angry in this situation. If I don't confront her now, I'll never be able to live with myself.

Recognizing the fancy invite, her face crumples—in either shame or regret. "You . . . you . . ."

"You better fucking *believe* I know." Choking on the words, but ah, it feels good now, almost weeping with rage. "Octavius Karbuz is my art dealer? And there's going to be a bloody *show* at his gallery in Europe?" I stare at her, breath heaving. "Tell me, evil fiend, how many shows have there been? And how much do my paintings *actually* sell for?"

Pat's eyes dart blindly around the room, clearly struggling to come up with another lie. She gives up and says, "You should be focusing on your work—"

"Really? *That's* where you want to go right now?" My braid has come loose, and I tear hair out of my eyes, still waving the invitation. "This says *a collection of new works*—just how many are we talking about?" I flick the envelope at her like it's a frisbee. "Tell me, Pat."

She raises her chin in poorly misplaced defiance. "Fourteen."

I'm stunned and, for a moment, speechless. "I want to see the books. Right now," I finally manage.

"There are no books."

"There are always books, always a paper trail." I say this with conviction, trying to hide the doubt in my words. What do I know about accounting and paper trails? This is why I'm a patsy. "You've turned my studio into a workhouse, then you complain we never have money. You're a *liar*." Pat is silent, her mouth so tight, her lips have disappeared. With sudden, intense clarity, I realize the truth: She's taken advantage of me since the beginning, telling me I'm useless, but all the while using me to line her pockets. "You told me I'm a lousy artist who sells the odd painting."

I want nothing more than to throw Pat out of Gladsheim, then have her arrested for fraud, but as a tear slides down my face, the reality of my situation hits me square in the gut. I can't really punish Pat, because, for better or worse I need her. She's all I've got.

Pat blinks, solid as a rock in a Japanese garden. "Did you really think this place runs itself?" She gestures to my studio. "That I work for free?"

My anger flares again and I grab some large brushes—that she so helpfully cleaned last night—and throw them across the room. Then I pick up a palette knife, still loaded with paint, and wing it at Pat's head. She ducks, cursing, and I hold up my hands. "Do these look twisted and contracted? I'm going to turn up at this show and tell *my* agent, this . . . this art dealer Octavius Karbuz, that you've been forcing me to work, while feeding me lies that my paintings rarely sell. And pocketing the proceeds." I rub my face in disbelief. Now I understand her stylish new threads. She fancies herself a sophisticated member of the international art world. *Jesus, Pat!*

She smirks at me. "You want to go to Brussels? For your opening?" My heart leaps into my throat, but I know the too-familiar glint in her eye. "You think you'll be able to travel to Europe?"

"I don't have the money for that. But you do."

"You can't even behave in a room full of morons," she snorts. "Remember what happened at your show in Vancouver? You got drunk and made a fool of yourself."

"You can't stop me from going to Brussels." I snatch the invitation off the floor and tap it against my hand. "Octavius Karbuz has called my new show The Great Return. How prophetic. I might perform a few miracles—turn water into wine, or—"

Pat finally snaps, closing the distance between us. I can smell coffee on her breath. "What would you do if your plane crashed and was engulfed by *flames*?" she says. I start so violently my heart seems to stop. Swallowing tears and dread, I wait for my heart to resume its slow, ponderous thud. Why does she always win? Like a dog rolling over in submission to its master, I bend my head, almost feeling the heat of the fire she threatens. "I'm adjusting your medications again. You're acting crazy." She yanks up her sleeve and thrusts her arm out, which is still melodramatically bandaged, as if she suffered a major injury.

My anger simmers on low—much like her morals—for daring to bring this up. I force myself to ask after it politely. "Does it still hurt?"

And I mean that, I'm sorry. It was horrible of me, truly ruthless. Three weeks ago, Pat had been cooking us dinner and rattling on about how Tuna needed to be put down, concluding her diatribe with a woefully cheerful threat to borrow a shotgun from the neighbor and do it herself. Some hopeless part of me broke. Had I sensed this scam she's got going? One moment I was at the kitchen table working on one of the mixed media collages I do for fun, and the next I was on Pat like a banshee, forgetting I still had my blunt-nosed craft scissors in hand. The three-inch-long wound bled for so long, Pat feared an artery had been cut. She'd howled needlessly as she ran around the kitchen, a towel held to the injury, before finally stitching and dressing it herself.

Now my rage ebbs, replaced by a wave of instantaneous, crashing grief. "Is this why you're locking me in at night—afraid I'll scissor you to death?"

"I could have bled out in minutes. You'll stay locked in your room until you can prove to me you haven't gone insane."

"You can't lock me in my room," I say quietly. "This is *my* house."

"Poor wittle Jeanie get mad?" She widens her eyes and sticks out her lower lip, like a maniac.

Despite my thick sweater, I'm suddenly chilled to the core. "Let me come with you to Vancouver next week. I'll prove to you that I can leave this island and fly to Europe for my show."

Pat sucks at her teeth for a moment, considering. "You think you're famous because you're a brilliant artist?" she says. "You've only sold paintings because your accident makes you collectible. If you go to this showing, *any* showing, people will stare at you and whisper. They're not interested in what you paint—they want to see what you look like. They want to know exactly what happened that night."

For a split second I feel crushed, believing her, and my hand flies to my throat, yanking at the collar of my sweatshirt in case any scars might be on display. I force myself to speak. "I may not remember what happened that night . . . I may look like *this* now, but I know Michael loved me—"

"Love?" she laughs in my face. "Michael was simply dragged back to what he'd dismissed as a romp behind the bushes the moment his parents found out Sleeping Beauty was in the *family way*."

Her words land on me like a cannonball. I think of that warm night in the woods. How I'd loved every minute—the sweaty, heated communion of our hormonally charged teenage bodies, the tender moments afterward when Michael held me in his arms. "So beautiful," he'd whispered, stroking my hair. When I told him I was pregnant, he was shocked, but it hadn't taken him all that long to come back with a marriage proposal.

I'd felt so lovely wearing the wedding dress Aunt Suze sewed for me, a confected bodice of French lace and a ballet-style tulle skirt modelled after Audrey Hepburn's frock in the film, *Funny Face*—the fetching bateau neckline, the elbow-length gloves. I'd swept down that church aisle to Charpentier's *Te Deum*, a knocked-up seventeen year old, positive that the boy twitching at the altar was a Disney prince. I never saw him again after that night. Our relationship had been built upon the shaky foundations of teenage lust and supremely unfortunate timing.

"What if I was in a car accident," Pat says. "What then? Who takes care of you? Who goes to Vancouver three times a year to buy your paints and canvas? Who prepares these canvases, cleans your bloody brushes, and makes you grilled cheese sandwiches?" She pauses, glowering at me from beneath her over-plucked eyebrows. "I have to do it all because you're *afraid* of *fire*."

I recoil as if she'd just pointed a gun at me and threatened to pull the trigger. "Kay will do it," I say meekly. "I asked if she'd be my caregiver. She's probably on the next ferry." But I know that Kay likely missed my last letter and is on her way to another, far more exotic place than Salt Spring Island.

I expect Pat to be knocked back on her heels at the mention of Kay replacing her, but her eyes flicker ominously. I'm overcome with a desire to run straight to the window and jump. Anything to escape.

"Kay has better things to do," she says, with an edge to her voice I haven't heard before. "She's probably halfway to South America, or some other third world country."

"South America is a *continent*."

Pat swipes her hand, dismissing me. "I'm going to town now, and you'll behave and paint like a good girl. It's a commission, you know, so make it a cool scene." Then she picks up the broken abstract canvas. Before slithering out the door, she glances back and chucks her final spear.

"It ain't art unless it sells."

12

SAVKA

Carpathian Mountains, Reichskommissariat Ukraine
MARCH 3, 1944

"WHAT DID THE NKVD OFFICER say to you in the forest, Mama?"

Savka's eyes shot open, expecting to find herself buried in snow, but instead she felt a narrow plank bed beneath her, and a smelly blanket wrapped around her against the dampness of a stifling dungeon. She lifted her head quickly, setting her brain on a spin. *Taras*, she thought in confusion. *Where are you?*

When she attempted to rise, pain shot through her arm and a sharp wave of nausea rose in her throat. Her initial astonishment that she'd survived a gunshot wound was quickly replaced by excruciating pain in her chest and the chill of winter creeping through OUN propaganda posters that had been tacked up on the earthen walls.

A single candle burned on an overturned wooden box in the shadowy corner. Someone was there. "I will ask you again. Why were you in the forest, Savka?" She'd met Kuzak several times in the village last summer, when insurgents came down for supplies, but she startled when he stepped out of the shadows into a dim arc of light, absently stroking his horseshoe-shaped moustache. His usually pleasant features were arranged in a scowl.

Someone had rolled her coat for a pillow, and she eased her head down upon it, her chest and shoulder throbbing. It all came back to her like a nightmare. She and Taras had been hunted down in the forest. Not only had she lost her son, she'd been shot and ordered to spy on her own husband by the NKVD officer who'd taken Taras away. Lieutenant Belyakov. His name was burned into her memory. As he'd predicted, Kuzak's insurgents had found her unconscious and bleeding. They'd saved her life. And she was in their bunker. Her skin crawling, Savka's fingers clutched at the blanket. Drawing it down, she tried to move her right arm, but it was pinned firmly to her side by a triangle sling. Carefully she touched the dressing over the bullet wound in her chest, thankfully close enough to her shoulder that it had missed her right lung. As her eyes adjusted to the dim light, she noticed her rucksack on another low bench in the corner. It was open, and all the things she and Taras had packed were strewn on the ground. *Tarasyku, Tarasyku!* When she opened her mouth, a sob escaped her lips. "*Slava Ukraini,*" she said, staring up at the low earthen ceiling above her head. Her voice was so feeble, the greeting came out a hoarse whisper. She waited for the customary response, but Kuzak said nothing. His silence lashed her like a whip. Glory to Ukraine and the reply, *Heroiam Slava,* Glory to the Heroes, was the standard underground salute. It was not a good sign that he refused to give it.

She felt hot, delirious, and she struggled to keep herself from retching. Her wound was most likely infected, but she turned away from Kuzak, turned her head to the wall, picturing her son on a troop train bound for the Soviet Union, starving and afraid. Lieutenant Belyakov said he would keep Taras safe. Surely, her son had been taken to a Moscow safe house or a *dacha* in the Russian countryside, yet she knew he was terrified, too young to be without the protection of his mother.

Whatever medication the underground had given her—possibly one of the opium tablets Natalka had stolen—left her head cloudy and unable to focus, yet the last words of Lieutenant Belyakov rang in her ears:

If you do what we say, you will see your son again. Do what we order, and we will give him back.

"Where's Taras?" she said, forcing herself to look at Kuzak. If he didn't believe her story, he'd order her shot and left to rot in the woods.

The underground leader regarded her with a calculating expression. "You were alone."

She let her eyes widen. Somehow, the insurgents had brought her here, hopefully removed the bullet, and cleaned and dressed her wound, yet she had to keep the facts straight. She must live, *must* obey Belyakov, or she would never see Taras again. These underground insurgents weren't stupid. Savka had placed them firmly in peril—how careless to let herself be shot, to allow her son to be taken by the NKVD. "Is Taras dead?" A low noise of anguish. "Tell me."

"We found you two days ago." Kuzak frowned, arms crossed over his chest. "You would have bled to death if we hadn't heard the gunshot. You've had a fever." Someone ducked their head and came through the doorway. Savka tensed in anticipation of the dreaded Natalka, but it was a male insurgent, his face in shadow. Kuzak gestured to him. "Bohdan saved your life."

Bohdan. Only four days after she'd bandaged his wound in the forest, he'd found the strength to dig out a bullet from her chest. Experimentally, she lifted the fingers of her right hand. They were numb, and she feared nerve damage. "A . . . partisan shot me," she insisted.

Bohdan and Kuzak exchanged a look. "Couldn't have been partisans," Kuzak said, his face etched with concern. "Those cowards slunk out of the forest before the SS unit arrived. You were shot by the NKVD."

"If they shot you, they questioned you," Bohdan added, defiantly, obviously suspicious that she was misleading them.

For a dizzying moment, she feared she might faint if she continued lying to these men. "I blacked out, I can't remember . . ." Tears rolled down her cheeks at the memory of Taras being led away, his frightened face as he twisted to look back at her. "They took my son!"

Kuzak watched her cry for a few moments. "Why didn't they take *you*—interrogate and torture *you*?"

The word *torture* lingered in the musty air. Savka closed her eyes to shut out the image of Taras in a Russian jail cell, beaten and starved. She opened them, alarmed to see Bohdan limping toward her cot. Candlelight glowed through a pair of large ears that stuck out from his head.

"What information were they after?" He had a heavy beard and moustache—why hadn't she noticed when she treated him in the forest?—and his mouth curved in a mocking smile. "Did you give it to them?"

"I was unconscious, I tell you."

"Did they know you were Roman's wife?"

"No," she said, wiping away tears. At one time, she prided herself on honesty. The underground demanded it. She'd failed to aid the struggle, to help Ukraine. Now she was forced to lie to save herself. "Roman said he will soon desert with men and weapons—"

Bohdan's smile had disappeared. "You're now *seksoty*, admit it."

"I'm a courier, not a collaborator," she declared. "Roman had a *shtafeta* for you, telling you to stay in the bunker. Taras and I destroyed it—before I was shot."

"*Stay in the bunker?*" Kuzak snorted. "Roman's belly is full of SS rations, while we starve."

Bohdan scowled at her. "Get up," he demanded.

The thought of standing sent her into a panic. "I need more opium."

"We gave you the last one yesterday." Bohdan peeled back the blanket.

Her trousers had ridden up around her knees and frigid air hit her bare lower legs and feet. When she tried to move, pain shot through her. How would she get Taras back from the NKVD?

Kuzak had gone through the door and Bohdan yanked her out of bed, turning to throw her things into her rucksack. She swayed, the ground cold beneath her feet. Bohdan jerked his head, still holding her arm, and she awkwardly pulled on her wool socks, boots, and coat with one hand, gathered her bag to follow him. She passed through the doorway in time to see Kuzak climb out of the hole—not two feet across—that led outside. The main room of the bunker was small—she could have walked its length in seven steps—and it was filled with box upon box of what must have been encrypted files.

"Hello, you little coward."

A silent figure crouched like a spider near the dugout hole. Natalka, her dark hair now in two long plaits and tied with ratty pieces of leather. Savka could not read her blank expression. Had the *banderivka* argued for her earlier? She got her answer when Natalka leapt up and grabbed her, tied a blindfold tightly over her eyes, and gave her a shove up and out into the forest.

SAVKA'S BLINDFOLD WAS CLUMSILY untied to bright sun that filtered through the branches of towering beech trees in the forest clearing, turning drops of moisture in the air into diamond-like shards that dazzled her eyes. For the last hour, Kuzak and Natalka had dragged her down the same trail she and Taras had climbed only days ago, Savka stumbling blindly, unable to see anything below her blindfold except the tips of her boots.

She blinked rapidly and Kuzak came into focus, standing directly in front of her, levelling a small pistol he'd just taken out of his belt. He remained so still beside Natalka, he might have been a marble statue.

Startled, she glanced at the *banderivka*, who nudged Savka with her *Papasha* submachine gun, positioning her for Kuzak to take aim and fire a single shot at her head. Panic flashed through her. Did Natalka not remember how she'd put her life in danger to save Bohdan? "*Sestra*," Savka begged her, "you can't let this happen."

"Coward," Natalka said, stepping back. "You've been turned, admit it."

Savka retched violently, bent double, then straightened and wiped the sick from her mouth. There would be no gratitude from Natalka, no sisterhood intervention. The wind brought a strong smell of wet tree trunks and sap, and a waft of body odor from one of the insurgents.

Shivering and stifling sobs, her chaotic thoughts tried to land on alternative outcomes to her situation. But there were none. She was in the worst possible predicament: Kuzak believed she'd been turned by the NKVD.

"Why did Roman not give you a gun to kill yourself and your son," he demanded, tightening his grip on the pistol, "in the event you were caught?"

"He didn't think partisans would be in the forest," she said immediately, because it was the truth. The trip down the mountain had sapped her remaining strength, but she found the courage to take a few steps toward Kuzak. "I would never agree to be a Soviet spy." The sun shone bright through the trees, but not enough to warm her, and she concentrated on her breath—in and out, struggling to keep her composure. Some part of her longed to give up, close her eyes, bend her head to let Kuzak take his shot, or allow Natalka to press the trigger on her *Papasha* and unleash a punishing round of Soviet bullets. Perhaps she deserved death. A fitting end for a useless woman who let her child be stolen. Kuzak closed the distance between them, his eyes not leaving hers, holding the gun at waist level. She could smell the wet wool from either his scarf, or her own coat. "You're mistaken," she insisted. "They left me for dead."

Kuzak made a dismissive gesture. "This is what women like you are doing to destroy the underground. A patrol will soon ambush us coming back to our bunker."

"You made sure I didn't know the location of your bunker," she cried, glancing down the barrel of his gun. It was the same kind of Liliput pocket pistol she'd seen on other insurgents before they began snatching Russian-made weapons off the bodies of Soviet partisans.

Kuzak surprised her by turning the handle of the pistol toward her. "In respect to Roman, we're releasing you. You'll go back to your mother's house and wait for this NKVD officer to contact you. Tell him we believed your story."

Natalka grabbed at Kuzak's arm. "She can't be trusted."

Savka shuddered with relief. They weren't killing her?

Kuzak threw off Natalka's hand. "Here's the gun Roman should have given you before venturing out here. There are two bullets in the chamber." Savka reluctantly took the weapon, small but deadly. "Your handler will soon come to visit," he said. "And you will shoot him. When we see his body, we will trust you again."

With the cold steel of the pistol in her hand, she focused on the stippled bark of a nearby tree to conceal a wave of raw terror. *Kill Lieutenant Belyakov?* Agreeing to this plan would confirm that she'd been turned. But did she have a choice? If she failed to shoot the Soviet officer, she didn't want to know what the underground might do to punish her and her family. Savka's only recourse was to gratefully accept the gun and hope a better scheme presented itself.

Natalka lunged at her and thrust the length of her submachine gun against Savka's chest. "If you don't kill your handler," she said, "I'll come for you. I'll hunt you to the ends of the earth."

Savka's knees buckled, and she staggered to keep herself upright in the snow. She could still feel the impression of that submachine gun across her breasts after it was yanked away, and she stood motionless, watching Natalka and Kuzak turn and hike up the same way they'd come down. Only when they were out of sight, did she scream her anguish into the trees.

The underground had provided a way out of her predicament with the NKVD. But they didn't know the deal she'd made with the devil—*spy on your husband or lose your son.* This was a contract impossible to break, yet she feverishly schemed a solution. Lieutenant Belyakov had been right—the underground had saved her. Now he owned Savka Ivanets as surely as he did his own boots. Had he also known they would order her to kill him? If so, he wouldn't be alone when he came to find her in Deremnytsia.

She stared at the gun, imagining Belyakov and his soldiers coming to her home, as threatened. She'd enlist Mama and Lilia's help to over-power them, then Savka would hold a butcher's knife to the officer's throat and take him hostage until the Soviets agreed to trade his life for her son's. If the officer refused, she'd eviscerate him and scatter his guts in the forest to be devoured by wolves. But if she killed the only man who could free Taras, she'd lose him forever.

Savka stumbled, falling hard on her wounded shoulder in the packed snow. Moaning, she rolled onto her back and stared up into the trees, struck by a raw and gutting truth: she couldn't kill the officer, she must betray the underground and her own husband in order to save her son. She'd have to be smart and muster her courage. Somehow, she'd find Marko and he would rescue Taras.

With grim determination sharpened by grief, she pocketed the gun and began to descend through the silent forest.

13

JEANIE

Salt Spring Island
DECEMBER 5, 1972

I STAND UNDER A MASSIVE Garry oak tree on the headland near the house. The wind whips Aunt Suze's ceremonial Japanese kimono around my bare legs and the scars that traverse my back and stomach in whorls and channels. Across the palm of my hand lies a length of rope, one end fashioned into a noose. My nostrils fill with the brine smell of kelp drying on the beach at low tide. My eyes fill with angry tears.

Rain has ebbed, the sky now rinsed clear of cloud. Across the Strait of Georgia, snow dusts the summits of the Coast Mountain range only thirty miles to the east. A short ferry ride to the west, the mountains of Vancouver Island jut skyward. A hundred yards to my left, a long wooden staircase descends from the deck that wraps the house and leads to the beach path. Over thousands of years, ocean waves pounded this coast, creating Southey Bay, and the headland—made of harder rock that resisted erosion—plunges away on all three sides in a sheer cliff drop to the sea. Ghost forms of monolithic rocks shimmer below the surface of the bay, and out in Houston Passage the restless ocean churns.

I scrape away my tears and tighten the knot on the noose, using my thumb to test the strength of the rope, still damp from the shed where I found it among the boxes of screws and light bulbs. Careless Pat had forgotten how dangerous a length of rope can be in the hands of a heartsick woman.

A sudden gust bothers a few shreds of rabbit fur strewn in a dismal still life upon the moss at my feet. Bunnies are shy, yet extremely talented at evading predators—just the shadows of those wings send them scurrying for cover—but sometimes an eagle catches a rabbit out in the open, on land such as this, and then it's a fight to the finish. Fur and sometimes feathers or thatches of down are often the only sign such an epic war has taken place. I stare down at the battle scene, wondering if this bunny fought to the bitter end, or ceased to struggle as it lay helpless in the raptor's talons, admitting defeat to the stronger opponent. Perhaps it got away—slipped from the vise, because that's what rabbits sometimes did.

After Pat had destroyed my abstract canvas, thoroughly berated me, and finally left for town, I headed back to the house and stood in the hallway, glaring at the telephone. There was no one to call even if I wanted to, and it rarely rang these days. I yearned to speak with Octavius Karbuz, but what would I tell him? That I had no idea I'd been selling paintings all this time? That I had zero clue as to where the money had gone? I'm an artist so dumb I didn't even know I had an art dealer, or a "new collection."

I climbed the stairs in a fury, like a wounded animal caught in a trap, willing to bite off my own leg to survive. In my bedroom, I stripped off my clothes and put on Aunt Suze's Japanese kimono. It seems the right thing to wear to stage a death scene. What a spectacle I'll make when Pat comes down the drive: my long hair lifting in the wind, the white kimono fluttering around me, like a butterfly that's landed on a flower, its wings outstretched.

I'm not really going to hang myself. Horrors. I don't have the nerve, or the real desire. This is an act of desperation, a petulant kind of performance art, a chance to enjoy the expression on Pat's face when she thinks the disability cheques and cash from art sales that keep her in Cheerios and Irish whiskey are coming to an end.

"Your cash cow is no longer giving milk for free," I mutter as I squint up at my Garry oak and toss the rope. It falls uncooperatively across my garden clogs, and I bend to throw it again until it finally hooks over a gnarled branch. "Oh man, it's going to cost you going forward." If there *is* a forward with her.

At one time, I considered the world out there hostile and depraved, a world to escape from. The fear of other people's judgment and their curious stares sent me into hiding, and, in turn, that fear became my prison. Yet when I close my eyes and feel the wind burn my cheeks, hearing waves crash below and spray salt into the air, I'm free. I stretch out my arms and pretend I'm a bird, hovering over the bay and striking out for lands unknown. I'm smiling into the wind like an idiot, when, from behind my eyelids, an image rushes at me like a freight train—a man in a dark coat and fedora hat standing in a doorway, his looming form silhouetted against the light behind him. I sink to my knees, terrified, the image haunting my every nerve synapse and cellular function.

By the time I raise my head, the memory train has thundered around a corner and disappeared from sight. Who was that man? I might not remember the night of my accident, but I have many childhood memories. Not all of them pleasant. My father was a traveling salesman, often away for weeks at a time on the road. When he returned to our little bungalow in Vancouver, he'd go out at night to get himself *stinking drunk*, as my mother used to say. This intrusive memory can't be of him. He wasn't the kind of father who opened his daughter's room to gaze at her with affection. And not the kind of dad who stuck around to see her grow up, either.

I haul myself up by the rope and onto a moss-covered rock, experimentally slipping the noose around my neck. But I still feel uneasy. If the man in the doorway was a memory, and he's not my father, then who the hell is he? My clog slips and the rock wobbles. I claw at air, panicking for a moment as my upper body swings away, then laugh darkly at the irony of possibly managing to hang myself while attempting to foil Pat.

She won't be long now, I think, cocking my ear to the driveway. I picture her spotting me, rope around my neck, and freaking out, terrified her meal ticket is about to swing.

Years ago, when the two of us first moved to the island and into Gladsheim, Pat told me there were rumors we were a couple of lesbians who'd bought Aunt Suze's isolated property to avoid the judgement and live in domestic contentment. "Nothing could possibly be further from the truth," I shout to the wind. Pat is nothing more than a freeloader and a glorified jailer.

A stiff breeze buffets me, and my kimono flaps open, to the dismay of a fat gull that's drifting along the shoreline, hunting for sea stars. It screeches, lifting away on a current of air and Tuna sets up a furious bark from somewhere near the compost bin out back, startling me. The rock seesaws beneath my feet. Pat must be home. I frown. How has she managed to sneak down the drive without me hearing? I turn, prepared to savor the look of shock on her face, but it isn't her at all. A man stands near the garden walkway. He stares up at me, astonished, then takes a few tentative steps before breaking into a run. I watch, unnerved, as he scrambles up the path to the headland, his face contorted with effort and distress at the spectacle of me trying to off myself.

He barrels right at me, grabbing me around the waist without hesitation and lifting me, his hand slipping the noose off my neck in one quick movement. I push off his lean chest and struggle away, falling onto the thick moss. The kimono flies up to my knees, and I pull the hem tightly around my ankles to hide my scars.

But he's already seen them, this man who has somehow showed up just in time to *save* me. I expect him to flinch where he's standing, but he's got a strange light in his haunted, cerulean eyes, almost as if he anticipated finding me like this, trying to hang myself. I study his face. He's marvelous, the kind of man you see in old films, striking in the Humphrey Bogart manner—expressive nose, his eyes aloof and brooding. I notice his light hair, trimmed close to his head in a no-nonsense army buzz cut, and the scars on his blighted cheeks. The skin's surface has been irreparably damaged. He looks away, and I wonder what other injury lies hidden beneath his brown leather coat and worn gray corduroy pants, his scuffed boots.

"What were you thinking?" he says, still out of breath.

Tuna chooses this moment to emerge, stiff-legged and sleepy, from behind the house. The man and I watch my old dog meander up the path. This stranger seems otherworldly, someone who went into the forest a long time ago to remove himself from humanity and, after many years in the haunted wood, has emerged a kind of mythical figure, fraught with secrets and slightly stunned at what he's found in the world.

But what he *doesn't* do—to his credit—is fidget and stare at me, like others who've come across my kind of awkward. He stands perfectly still, mountainously still. It's unsettling. I catch him glancing with concern at my cadmium red paint-splattered hands. Does he think it's blood? He leans forward, his hand out, and I catch his scent—a heady blend of rain, cigarette smoke, and leather. I feel myself blush. His gaze is disarming; its cool, distant quality makes me feel vulnerable and seen. I turn my head, struck mute and aware of how ridiculous I must appear, cowering on the ground, legs tucked under my kimono.

Tuna has arrived and sniffs at the stranger's hand companionably. He absently scratches behind my dog's ears. His jacket and pants seem to float on his frame, as if they're an afterthought, or were chosen only for the warmth they might provide. "I would speak with Pat O'Dwyer," he says formally, clearing his throat. He has a slight accent that I can't place.

I scramble to my feet with as much dignity as I can muster. "Has she done something wrong?" I ask, curiosity trumping my fear of strangers. "Is she going to be arrested?" I try not to sound too hopeful.

He takes a step back, almost tripping over an exposed tree root. "I'm investigating a man's disappearance from your hospital ward in 1959." He removes a small plastic bag from his coat pocket and opens it to reveal a battered collection of hand-rolled cigarettes. When he selects one, every muscle in my body primes to bolt. Cigarettes mean matches and matches mean *fire*. Pat usually smokes huddled by the compost bin and even that's not far enough from the house for me. I squeeze my eyes shut, bracing myself for the distinctive sound of a match strike. But it doesn't come, and I open one eye to find him simply holding the cigarette, as if it's somehow dear to him. Does he *know*? It's then I notice that the tips of his fingers are missing. "Your fingertips," I gasp.

"Frostbite," he says, as if this covers it.

Frostbite. How in God's name? "Were you lost in the Arctic or stranded on a Himalayan peak in a snowstorm?"

"An assignment in Antarctica," he says cryptically. He seems to suddenly notice the view from the headland and turns his head, in awe at the ocean, and a long serrated cloud that's flung itself across the sky.

"I was still in the hospital in 1959," I venture. "But I didn't hear of a man disappearing."

"His name is Marko Kovacs—he changed his last name from Ivanets when he came to Canada."

"I don't recognize the name, but maybe Pat will. She'll be back soon." I try to pay attention when he tells me the police made a mess of Marko Kovacs's missing person's investigation. As he speaks, something odd happens in my chest, a gloriously painful efflorescence, of which I'm unable to pinpoint an exact cause.

"I am Danek Rys," he says. "Researching cold cases for the *Vancouver Sun.*"

"Did you come from Europe?" I ask, shyly.

"Czechoslovakia," he says, and I get the impression he was there during the war and doesn't wish to dwell on that time in his life. He holds the unlit cigarette between two ravaged fingers and pulls out a well-thumbed notebook from his jacket pocket, flipping a few pages. When he looks back at me, his expression is maddeningly ambiguous. "The police report says Pat O'Dwyer was the last person to see

Mr. Kovacs. But she tells me on the phone she never heard of him. I've come to face her in this lie—"

"You'll find she does a lot of that."

"—and interview *you*."

"Me? You were the one who called last night. Pat never told me that a man disappeared off the face of the earth from my hospital ward." The very idea of it weirds me out. You'd think she would have mentioned it at some point in the past thirteen years. The wind sweeps hair across my face and as I lift my hand to brush it away, the sleeve of my kimono falls to my elbow, revealing the shiny twisted scars on my arm.

"Why do you do this?" the newspaperman asks, indicating the rope, still swinging from the tree.

Why exactly *did* I come up here with a rope? To upset Pat? I can do that with a word. No, it's something more. Much more. I stare at Mr. Rys for a moment. There must be some way to articulate how very isolated and desperate I am out here with a caregiver who's forcing me to paint and stealing the proceeds of my art sales. I clear my throat and try on a tentative smile. "Don't you think you should have to fight?"

14

SAVKA

Kraków, German General Government, Poland
APRIL 23, 1944

"WE TOOK BETS ON what color your eyes were," a woman said to Savka. "I was right—they're brown!" A thermometer was stuck rudely into her mouth. "I'm Ewa."

Savka opened her eyes in the strange room. Warily, she turned her head on the pillow and eyed the Red Cross nurse. Ewa wore a crisp blue dress and sat on a chair beside her bed, gazing at Savka expectantly, arms folded over the bright red cross sewn over her heart. She was beautiful. Short blonde hair framed fine features arranged in an expression of veiled curiosity. Her flaxen eyebrows and lashes only made her pale blue eyes more arresting. Savka knew some Polish, but her first instinct was to not trust this nurse. The conflict between their neighboring countries was epic—fighting over what constituted the borders of Western Ukraine and Eastern Poland. Although Nazis were still in control of that disputed territory, the Red Army would soon push them out.

The moment that Ewa took the thermometer out of her mouth, Savka said, "Where am I?"

Ewa frowned as she held the thermometer to the light. "Finally, your fever has broken." She smiled at her. "You're in a Red Cross clinic in Podgórze Kraków, and we've dosed you up to here with penicillin."

The nurse eyed the bandage on her patient's chest. "You were brought in by a Ukrainian doctor."

A Ukrainian doctor? Savka lifted a tentative hand to her scalp, thunderstruck to feel rough stubble beneath her fingertips.

"You got lice on the road," Ewa said, noticing her distress. "It had to be shaved."

Savka glanced around the ward, eyes wild. Without her long hair, she felt like a chick newly emerged from its egg. A wave of nausea overwhelmed her, and she tried to settle her stomach by studying the ceiling high above, intricately carved with cherubs and angels.

Ewa glanced up. "It was once a grand salon in a Jewish house, converted to a clinic after fucking Nazis sent the family to a concentration camp."

The smell of antiseptic and chloroform drifted in sunlight that poured through high windows, illuminating rows of narrow, white metal beds and a large wooden cross that had been hung above the door. Some of the other patients were propped up on pillows; others lay motionless beneath their blankets. Fragments of memory coalesced in Savka's mind—the panicked, resolute expression of her son as he was dragged away by the NKVD, lost to her. And the impossible task laid out by two entirely different parties, both demanding her obedience:

Spy on your husband to get your son back.

Kill your Russian handler to prove you are not a spy.

She remembered collapsing near Mama's barn in Deremnytsia after Kuzak and Natalka had released her. "Mama, Lilia . . ." She turned her throbbing head, recalling their worried faces as they carried her inside. "How long have I been here?"

"Two weeks."

"But, how . . ."

"You have Dr. Humeniuk to thank," Ewa said, scraping her chair closer. "He told us your mother stood on the road that runs through your village, calling for a medic among the refugees, and he put up his hand. He agreed to see you and told them you were dying—obviously whoever dug out the bullet and stitched your wound didn't sterilize their instrument, and infection set in. Your family surrendered you to save your life." She laughed. "Do you know the doctor's wife reluctantly parted with an antique washstand to make room for you in their cart?"

"A *cart*?" Ewa's words triggered a kaleidoscope of memories—waking in sudden lucid moments to starlight, and feeling rain on her face, the mutter of distant voices and cart wheels turning, the smell of woodsmoke in her nostrils and broth being spooned into her as she lay in a fever of confusion. Ewa told her how Dr. Humeniuk had hoped to bargain for sulfa and opium from Polish partisans as they journeyed west for six weeks, retreating from the Soviets advancing to Berlin. But he hadn't been successful, and her infection had worsened.

Savka's hopes soared. "The war is over?" Soon she would see Marko, and they would find Taras.

"Over?" Ewa said. "Far from it. Red Army shits are marching on Stanislav in west Ukraine. They'll be here before spring."

Savka turned her head away, crushed. Deremnytsia had been taken. And here she was, no better than one of those Red Army shits, safe and sound in a stolen Jewish house while her son was in the hands of monsters. "Mama," she whispered. "Lilia, Sofiy . . ." Had Marko sent papers in time, as he promised he would? If he hadn't, it was possible they'd been raped and beaten to death by Soviet soldiers in Ukraine. She had to go back and find them. Savka threw back the covers and got her bare feet on the floor, but the room spun, and she wavered.

"What are you doing?" the nurse cried, leaping up.

"I must find Taras . . . Mama, Lilia . . ."

"You're too weak," Ewa soothed, easing her back. "And anyway, you'd have to be crazy to enter a war zone when you're pregnant. Think of the baby."

Savka blinked with incomprehension. "What did you say?"

Ewa smiled as she tucked her back into bed. "We're not sure of course, but Dr. Humeniuk said you didn't have a monthly on the road."

Stunned, Savka placed a hand on her stomach. She remembered Marko's words the last time she saw him: *God willing, let us make another child.* Had one of their prayers finally been answered?

Ewa glanced down at her own stomach. "I'm pregnant too."

"I can't possibly . . . ," Savka insisted, not really listening as Ewa chattered of how they'd receive extra rations, but her happiness at the prospect of another life growing inside her was swallowed by thoughts of Taras. Almost two months she'd been close to death, two months that her son had suffered elsewhere. Captive and alone. *He is safe, in a dacha,* she convinced herself, to avoid thinking of the alternative. That Lieutenant Belyakov might have sent Taras to a prison in Moscow or . . . a thirteen-year-old boy in the Gulag? Anything but that.

Savka remembered Kuzak's pistol and tried to raise her head. "Where are my things?"

The nurse bent to pull her rucksack out from under the bed. "It's all here—what you arrived with."

Savka dragged it to her across the blanket and pawed through the contents, her fingers grazing the silk slip Marko had given her, and Baba's *korali* wedding necklace. "Where is it?"

"What?"

Savka licked her dry lips. "Where is my . . ." she searched for the Polish word ". . . gun?"

Ewa looked surprised. "Why would you have a gun?"

Savka frowned. "It was mine and it's gone." She felt grateful to this Dr. Humeniuk for saving her life and her baby's, yet there were too many questions left unanswered. Did Mama and Lilia know what had happened to Taras? She wondered if she'd told them about her encounter in the bunker before passing out. And where was her gun? The secrets in Savka's head floated in jumbled chaos.

Ewa sat back, arms crossed, regarding her with interest. "Perhaps you can tell me how you were shot."

"I would tell you," Savka said, staring down at her hands resting on the blanket. "But I can't remember a thing." Another lie. She could remember well enough what had happened, but to relate the story of how she'd been captured and betrayed twice made it all too real. And she was not ready to face the truth—the NKVD officer would never find her here. Nor would the underground. She refused to let herself feel relieved and safe when her son was not. How could Taras be gone when she could still feel his head against her shoulder and the warmth of his smile?

Ewa leaned forward. "I can see you've not had an easy war. Where's your husband? Mine was in the Polish Home Army. He was shot like a dog in the street in '41, by German spies." She ran a reluctant hand over her belly. "I used to go out with my little girl, Maja, late at night, looking for food, but a German patrol finally cornered us two months ago. They stole my Maja, and a Nazi prick is the father of this child," she said through gritted teeth. "Hitler despises the Poles, but he's not above stealing our blonde, blue-eyed children to bring up as good Germans. Or impregnating Polish women. This is why I want to kill some Huns."

"You kill Huns, I'll kill Soviets."

Ewa sat back and crowed, "I knew I would like you." She prattled on about how Savka was welcome to stay in her flat as long as she liked. "The Krauts hunt women at night," she was saying. "It won't matter if we're pregnant . . ."

Savka stared in disbelief. How did Ewa speak so casually when she'd recently been raped by Nazis and lost her daughter to their *Lebensborn* program? She wasn't sure if she could trust this tough Polish nurse who had extended a generous welcome to her, a stateless, homeless, possibly pregnant Ukrainian woman, but she knew she had no choice. She was alone in this world, and she and Ewa were united in grief and in war, a Pole and a Ukrainian meeting across the divide to fight their common enemy.

15

JEANIE

Salt Spring Island
DECEMBER 5, 1972

"YOU DIDN'T TELL ME you were one of the last people to see Marko Kovacs," I say, as Pat glances from Danek Rys to myself. *You're outnumbered, dear girl.* "Mr. Kovacs disappeared off our ward," I peer inquiringly at the newspaperman, "when was it? Thirteen years ago?"

Pat arrived fifteen minutes ago and she's still out of breath from climbing the path to the headland. Scrambling out of her Jeep and gathering four paper grocery bags in her considerable arms, she had stopped suddenly on her way to the house, the way you might if you suddenly spotted a cougar or a bear. Head down, she continued, pretending she really hadn't seen us, and took her time unpacking the groceries before curiosity got the better of her and she ventured out.

Danek stands a few feet above Pat on the headland, one boot up on a rock, looking down at her with mild distaste, as if he's finally met the object of his quest and is disappointed by what he's found. I think of the photograph of a sculpture I once saw in one of Aunt Suze's art books, of the demigod Perseus, holding aloft the severed head of Medusa. If only.

When Pat sees me pull the kimono close around my body, she breaks into a smile, pointedly ignoring Mr. Rys. "Dear, what are you doing out here wearing that old thing? You should go back to the house. You'll catch your death of cold."

"You do know journalists can read police reports," I say, leveling a stare at her. "Yet you told Mr. Rys when he called last night that you'd never heard of this Marko Kovacs." Pat glances from the journalist to myself, and I feel a frisson of pleasure at her obvious discomfort.

"Please call me Dan," he says, as Pat takes a step toward me, but I'm saved by a gust of wind that destroys her carefully hairspray-lacquered bangs. Futzing them back into place, she sends me a poisonous glare. I know she'll find some way to punish me after Dan leaves. I glance at the journalist, firm in my resolve to keep him here as long as possible. Tuna is licking his fingers. My old dog doesn't like strangers. He's even surly to the landscaper, who Pat hires each year to trim the arbutus trees. I smile then notice Dan's uncertain expression. He doesn't look all that comfortable with my dog. Or life itself, for that matter. He has the features of a boxer, his nose broken long ago and healed slightly crooked. A face marked by trauma. As someone who bears her own disfigurement, I don't let my eyes linger there or on the large, work-toughened hands, strange tattoos like hieroglyphs dancing across three of his fingers.

Danek Rys is a sign, an obvious, tragic wreck. God has turned his back on us both.

Pat erupts, "This is criminal! How did you get our address?"

He grips his pen, seemingly scratching her every word in his notebook. "Someone on the ferry gave it to me."

"The *ferry*," she says through clenched teeth.

"What joy it is, living on a small island," I say cheerfully. "Everyone knows where you live."

"Give me the name of your paper," she demands. "I'm going to call your editor right now, tell him you're harassing us."

Instead of answering her, Dan turns to look at me. "Maybe Jeanie will tell the truth to your lies. Did you see a man, the night Marko Kovacs disappears? Maybe you hear something in the hallway?"

"The only men who came into my room were doctors," I say, gazing back into his eyes, his razed features. I want to draw him. I want to *paint* him!

The rope, my carefully crafted hangman's noose, still hangs from the tree branch above us, and a gust of wind blows it toward Pat. She swats it away without looking up, too busy taking in the columnist. Tapping a finger to her temple, she says, "Anything Jeanie says can't be trusted. It's the painkillers—screwed with her head."

"Why did you say you had never heard of Marko Kovacs on the phone?" Dan asks her.

I rack my brain, trying to remember Pat's half of the conversation last night, my memory working the jigsaw puzzle, pieces sometimes landing in their rightful places, other times flying off into the void.

What makes you think you can call this late?

No interviews. Out of the question.

Never heard of him.

"I'd forgotten his name," Pat says simply. Then grabs my arm, adopting her stern nurse look. "This is too upsetting for you." She digs in her fingernails. "Go back to the house."

I try to object, but the look on her face is murderous. She's left me little choice but to turn, the kimono swirling about my legs. Pat shoves me ahead on the path, while she hangs back, presumably to keep her conversation with the newspaperman private, but I close my eyes, ears out on stalks to hear every word.

16

SAVKA

Kraków, German General Government, Poland

JUNE 28, 1944

EWA'S APARTMENT WAS LONG and narrow, with a bricked-in fireplace and large windows at one end, overlooking Mikołajska Street, which, Savka had been told, had once been an ancient trade route that led straight to Kyiv. The flat was only a stone's throw from Market Square, the very heart of Kraków, where Savka had just spent an hour lined up for her and Ewa's meager weekly food allotment. She let herself into the flat, a cloth bag of rations slung over her arm. Kicking off her shoes at the door, she headed for the kitchen, luxuriating in the feel of the rich parquet floors—laid in a herringbone pattern—beneath her bare feet.

Now that Savka was no longer in Ukraine, her days of serving the underground were over. Ewa had given up nursing at the Red Cross clinic to work as a forger for the Freedom and Independence movement, an organization that supported the Polish government in exile, supplying resistance insurgents with false identity papers when it got too hot for them in Kraków. The job didn't seem dangerous, but Ewa often disappeared for days at a time, leaving Savka alone with her ghosts.

She had just unpacked the last of their rations, wondering when Ewa might return from her latest assignment, when a voice called from the bedroom.

"What are *you* doing home?"

Although this was not Ewa's usual welcome, Savka smiled and went to the bedroom door. "The lines weren't as long as usual. I thought you were out . . ." She trailed off at the sight of Ewa, with one leg on the bed, in the act of rolling a stocking up the length of her calf. Bright spots of pink colored her friend's pale cheeks. Ewa—who usually charged about in trousers and blouse and old boots—had slipped on a blue, crepe print dress and styled her flaxen hair into marcelled waves that made her look like an American film star.

Savka's hand went to her own hair, which had begun to grow back surprisingly thick and wavy, like an unrepentant nun's hair that had been freed from its wimple. She raised an eyebrow. "Where are you going?" Ewa looked stylish, as though she had a reason to dress. "Don't tell me you have a secret lover."

Ewa refused to meet Savka's gaze. "I'm going to deliver papers," she said, drawing the stocking up her thigh and fastening it to a garter belt.

"In *that?*" Savka asked, amused.

Ewa turned to examine herself in the wardrobe mirror. "I don't even look five months pregnant."

"I'm bloated as a cow already." Savka's laugh strangled in her throat. She'd sworn never to feel joy or happiness again, never to forget that each moment was a torment, each moment was a raw wound. But four months after leaving Deremnytsia and losing Taras to the Soviets, she still caught herself at odd moments, profaning his memory.

Her eyes filled with tears at the memory of her son's smile. She treasured a moment from a summer's night last year, going out in the dusk to find Taras in the garden among the flowers and carrots and staked green beans. "Come in, Tarasyku," she'd called.

"Just one more page," he begged.

She'd gazed back at him, his dear face illuminated by a single candle, immersed in a book. "Your eyes will cross with all this reading, and then what will I do with you?"

"Love me?" he said with a mischievous smile.

How I wish to be carried back to one such night as this, she thought, turning away before Ewa noticed her tears. "It's too close to curfew. You'll be arrested." Savka had learned to talk to her friend as if she were a child, for even a child would not be so impulsive.

"Nonsense, *piękna*," Ewa said, using her pet name for Savka. *Beautiful*. She began to apply pancake foundation to her face. "I'll be home before then."

"Where did you get powder?" Savka asked. Along with soap and shampoo, cosmetics were a luxury only to be found at a price on the black market. Ewa laughed and struck a match to light a cigarette, waiting for the match to burn down and cool before using the charcoal to line her eyes.

Shortly after moving in, Savka had finally shared a version of her story, one peppered with a careful lie—that Taras had been stolen by the Red Army. As much as she wanted to tell her friend the truth—that she'd been shot by the NKVD and made deals with the Soviet officer and Kuzak to save her son—she knew she couldn't. Ewa reminded her too much of Natalka, the fierce *banderivka*—a mystifying mix of courage, gumption, and annoying hubris—and Savka knew she could not fully trust her. Not yet.

She went to the window, her hands roaming gratefully over her pregnant belly. Everything had been taken from her, except for this miracle, this baby that grew within her.

Late afternoon sun glanced off the red tile rooftops. Across the Vistula River, a spiral of smoke from Soviet army cooking fires curled ominously to the sky, more battalions joining them each day. There'd been news that the Fourteenth Division had suffered heavy losses in a battle at the front, but they'd pulled back and marched south into Slovenia. If Savka's husband had died, she'd never know. And if he was alive, how would he find her after the war?

"Why are you so on edge?" Ewa asked.

Because the Red Army is camped on the other side of this river, Savka wanted to say. *And I fear a certain NKVD officer is coming for me.* It was unreasonable, of course. Lieutenant Belyakov had no idea where she'd gone. She imagined him showing up in Deremnytsia months ago and learning that she'd been taken by a refugee doctor. Kraków was facing a Soviet invasion, and once again, so was she, who'd so recently escaped the front with her life.

"With our luck," she said, looking over her shoulder at Ewa, "we'll go into labor in the middle of the Russian advance."

"A new baby will make you forget Taras," Ewa said thoughtlessly, exhaling a plume of smoke.

Savka's throat went dry. "No new baby could make me forget my son." There were too many mornings where she awoke shuddering in horror, Taras's shouts in her ears. The Soviet officer had demanded she perform an impossible task—*spy on your husband, or your son dies*—but she took no relief in the fact she no longer must follow his orders. Taras was innocent, taken as a bargaining chip and now faced a lifetime in purgatory because Marko was gone, and with him, the reason for their son's kidnapping. She'd lost Taras forever.

In weaker moments, she let herself hope that the NKVD officer had handled her teenaged son with care and left him under the supervision of a kind Russian couple. Taras would surely charm whoever held him captive.

"Taras will survive somehow and come back to you," Ewa said, although she believed he was in the Red Army, perhaps even camped with his unit across the river. "He's a strong boy."

"And Maja will be returned to you after the war." Always they traded these same platitudes in a bid to keep their missing children alive, if only in memory. Dreams perhaps, but comforting nevertheless.

"Maja will be seven years old now," Ewa said distractedly.

Savka smiled. Whenever Ewa mentioned her daughter, it was always in the past tense. "How wonderful to hear you speak of her like this."

Ewa awkwardly fussed with a tube of lipstick and Savka allowed her a private moment of grief, this generous woman who'd taken her in and become a best friend.

"They say Hitler hates red lipstick on a woman," Ewa said with a secretive smile as she painted her lips crimson.

"You aren't going anywhere near Nazis," Savka said sharply. "It's too dangerous."

"Safer than what *you've* been up to," Ewa shot back.

Savka colored. Since the Germans had invaded in '39, the majority of Kraków's sixty thousand Jews had been deported by the Nazis for extermination, leaving only a few thousand who were held outside the city in the notorious Płaszów work camp. Savka thought of Taras when she saw the pale, gaunt Jews with their Star of David armbands, being herded through the streets to slave twelve-hour days in armament factories or stone quarries. She, along with many Poles in the city, often left them food in hidden drop spots organized by a doctor she knew from the Podgórze clinic.

"Anyone might report you—even a neighbor." Ewa carefully extinguished her half-smoked cigarette in a glass ashtray, so that she could relight it later. "You would be executed, and I'd lose this flat."

Savka knew the risks, but if she couldn't save Taras or her family, she would do one small thing to ease another's suffering. The Nazis were panicking, desperate to hold the city, as the Soviet army waited like vultures only miles away, anticipating the arrival of Allied forces battling their way north on the Western front. "The SS is forcing the Płaszów Jews to dig up mass graves of their people—those murdered earlier in the war," she said with a violent shudder. "The Nazis are burning all proof of their unthinkable crimes."

"Let's talk of more pleasant things, *piękna*," Ewa said, taking Savka's chin in hand. With a conciliatory smile, she glided the silky blunt end of the lipstick across Savka's upper lip with slow, hypnotic strokes.

"It's too late to go out." Savka said, glancing at the alarm clock on a table beside their small bed. "Curfew is two hours away."

But Ewa was already packing away the cosmetics. "I'll be back by then."

Savka could no longer ignore the elephant in the room. "Where are you going looking like a prostitute?"

Ewa studied her own face in a small handheld mirror. The pancake makeup was too dark for her complexion, yet she looked like a beautiful doll. "A woman paints her face, and you immediately think prostitute." Savka slipped an arm around her friend's shoulders and Ewa sagged against her for a moment. "You are thinking of your mother and sister," she said, breathing against her neck before pulling away, taking with her that cigarette and perfume smell, so familiar. *Family.*

Four months after Mama had procured a doctor to take her eldest daughter to safety in the West, Savka's nerves still pulsed with a profound unease. Had Marko managed to get Mama, Lilia, and Sofiy exit visas before the Reds invaded? Or had they been deported by the Soviets to a labor camp in Siberia? Baba's *korali* necklace could not be the only thing she had left to remember her family.

Ewa had a strange, morose expression on her face, yet when she turned for a final glimpse in front of the mirrored wardrobe, that sad look was gone.

Savka tried again. "Where are you going, *really?*" But Ewa kept her head down, silently searching for her small handbag and keys. "You aren't leaving for days, are you?" Savka hated herself for pleading, but the thought of being alone in that bed—especially at night—with her own private grief, terrified her.

Ewa sighed. "I promise I'm not *leaving for days*, but it's best you don't know, Savka." She sashayed out of the bedroom, then through the apartment door as though she were heading to a dance. When she'd gone, so had all the light in the room.

IT WASN'T DIFFICULT FOR Savka to remain hidden from view on a shop stoop, staring across Szpitalna Street at the unlikely sight of Ewa loitering in an alleyway. A few off-duty SS officers were going in and out of restaurants and cafes, feasting on Polish delicacies while Krakówians starved on mealy rations. Unlike Warsaw, Kraków hadn't been destroyed by Allied bombing raids. The Renaissance and Baroque style buildings and churches remained virtually untouched.

When Ewa left the apartment ten minutes ago, Savka had grabbed her keys and quietly opened the door, listening as her friend's shoes tapped down the stairs. She'd hurried after her, ignoring the voice inside, telling her to trust her friend, to stop being so obsessed with her and whatever secret life she was living. Why did Ewa leave for days? It couldn't be to pass forged papers to a member of the Polish resistance. Savka had to see what she was up to for herself. Only then would she trust her.

Savka watched as her friend nervously glanced up and down the street. It seemed too dangerous to hand over false identification papers in such a public place, but Savka carefully examined each person who passed Ewa, waiting for one of them to veer into the alley.

A Nazi staff car turned into the street and passersby ducked their heads and scuttled away, as if a predator had slunk onto the stage. Everyone except Ewa, who, at that moment, ventured out of the alleyway with quick glances around her. The car came to a stop and the back door opened. Savka watched in disbelief as Ewa slipped willingly into the car.

Savka shrank back and watched it pull away. Had she really seen her best friend and confidante, a forger for the Polish resistance, get into a Nazi Mercedes? She thought of Ewa getting dressed up earlier, her stubborn secrecy over where she was going. There was only one reason a woman would willingly climb into a Nazi staff car painted like a prostitute.

Ewa was a collaborator.

Stunned, Savka turned in the direction of home. By the time she reached the flat, her shock had twisted itself into raw anger. In a craze, she tore through Ewa's wardrobe, ripping dresses from their hangers and leaving them scattered on the floor. Then she ran to the kitchen and yanked out every box and container in the cupboards, running her fingers through buckwheat groats and split peas, not sure what she was looking for exactly, but *knowing* that Ewa had more secrets she was hiding in that flat. *Moody,* Ewa would say when Savka questioned her long, brooding silences. *I am moody.* But now Savka knew it was something more. Something much more.

She stormed back into the bedroom and turned to the dresser she shared with Ewa, pulling out drawers, and going through their meagre clothes. Frustrated, she lifted each drawer back into place and noticed the lowest one wouldn't slide in as easily. Getting down on her knees, she saw that a thin board had been clumsily nailed to the underside of the drawer. A false bottom. Quickly she pried it off and a small pistol clattered to the floor. She sat back on her heels and stared down at the gun Kuzak had given her in the forest months ago, right before he demanded she kill her Russian handler. When Savka had asked about it after waking in the clinic, Ewa had pretended not to know what she was talking about.

Gun? Why would you have a gun?

When she'd hidden it away. Seething, Savka tucked the pistol into her skirt pocket, threw herself on the bed that she and Ewa shared and stared at the ceiling. *I'll wait all night,* she thought darkly. *I'll wait to face you with this gun.*

True to her word, Ewa showed up just before the curfew horn sounded in the streets. Savka sat up on the bed and listened as her friend put on the kettle in the kitchen. When Ewa eventually came into the bedroom with the kettle, Savka, unable to keep the scorn from her voice, said, "Did you open your legs for him?"

Ewa didn't look at her as she poured boiling water into the basin on the dresser. "Of course I did."

Savka flew off the bed. "You have no shame!"

"You think I fucked him for silk stockings?" Ewa's voice was deadly cold. "I was getting information." She poured cold water from a pitcher on the dresser into the steaming basin and dipped in a finger to test the temperature.

"What do you take me for?" Savka said, her throat burning with unshed tears. "You're a Nazi collaborator."

Ewa looked up at her. "Trust me, I'm not."

Savka blinked back confusion. *Could* she trust this woman, who'd taken her gun and hidden it in a dresser drawer? "You lied to me—"

"We need submachine guns," Ewa said, her face closed, secretive. "And grenades for the uprising."

Savka took her by the shoulders. "What uprising?" She felt an icy chill of fear, as if Lieutenant Belyakov was already breathing on the back of her neck.

"To attack the Germans," Ewa said in an eerily calm voice, before shaking Savka's hands off and turning. "Why should only the Allies and Red Army get to kill Nazis, when Poles have suffered the bastards for so long?"

Savka felt like a heel for doubting her. Ewa wasn't a collaborator or traitor to Poland. She was a hero of the Polish Home Army, the most powerful resistance in eastern Europe. Admirable work, dangerous work. And yet . . . Savka drew the pistol from the pocket of her skirt and held it out. "Why not use this?"

Ewa glanced back, her eyes on the gun. She stood rigid, gripping the washcloth she'd dipped in the steaming water. "You don't understand . . ." she began, her eyes filling with tears. "I took it to protect you, Savka."

"From *whom*?" Savka cried, her anger mounting.

"In the hospital," Ewa shouted. "After, you were suicidal, heartbroken over losing Taras! You don't remember—"

The pressure in Savka's chest was unbearable, a silent scream, waiting to snake its way out. "I'm not suicidal now," she said, suddenly hating Ewa for daring to remind her of those dark moments of despair when she had struggled with the finality of losing her son. "Why didn't you give it back?"

Ewa dropped the washcloth and snatched up her cherished Hummel figurine on the dresser. "Because you're still a grieving fucking *mess*," she screeched, flinging it against the wall and smashing the delicate porcelain.

Savka jumped back, terrified, then collapsed on the bed, violent sobs racking her thin body. Ewa was right—she was a shattered woman, a pregnant, stateless Ukrainian in the middle of a war. She had no home, no husband or family, and she'd lost her son.

Ewa calmly picked up the washcloth, dipped and squeezed it again. She drew it up her arms and under them, then soaped and scrubbed her hands, as if she hadn't just destroyed one of her treasured possessions, as if she hadn't just cut Savka with her harsh words. "You're jealous," Ewa remarked, taking up a small towel to dry herself.

"I'm simply concerned." Savka got off the bed with as much dignity as she could muster, wiping tears from her face.

"Concerned." Ewa was suddenly behind her, trailing her hand over Savka's shoulder, across her old wound. *The same hand*, Savka thought, *you used only an hour ago to pleasure the SS officer.* She imagined them in a sumptuous apartment sequestered by the Nazis for their top men, the officer rutting on top of her dear Ewa, gasping and finishing in the messy way men did. Had she gripped him with her legs, cried out?

"You still stink of him," Savka said.

Her hand still on Savka's shoulder, Ewa circled to stand in front of her, smiling. "I would rather smell of you, *piękna*." She leaned in and Savka closed her eyes as she felt Ewa's tongue flick over her upper lip, leisurely, maddeningly slow. Without an agenda.

Savka gasped and held her breath as her friend lifted her skirt and snaked a hand up her thigh. She trembled at Ewa's touch and with a soft moan, grabbed the edge of the dresser to keep herself upright. *Never again will I do this sinful thing*, she'd promised herself what felt like a hundred times, but she couldn't refuse Ewa, she craved her touch.

Ewa's fingers had worked their way into her undergarments, into the slick wetness that Ewa knew, with confidence, she would find, smiling when Savka's own fingers turned white gripping the dresser.

They fell onto the narrow bed, clawing their clothes off, breaths ignited, almost sobbing. Ewa's kisses were urgent. Savka's grief and despair disappeared in an instant and she felt herself suspended higher and higher until she tilted on the very edge. A sudden, shattering orgasm ran the course of her body, and she floated in blessed relief, but Ewa would not let her rest. She slid downward, lips trailing over her breasts, her stomach, before opening her, and tasting her with that glorious tongue. Savka clutched Ewa's head, her friend's hand slipping between her own legs, bringing herself to quick climax in a shout that she muffled against Savka's thigh.

Afterwards, they turned away from each other in shame and bitter longing. Outside, dusk was falling and the shadows in the room lengthened.

"This has to stop," Savka breathed against the pillow.

Ewa remained silent, her back radiating waves of frosty remoteness. Her inherent wariness disappeared only when they fell into each other at night beneath the blankets to satisfy not a need, but an agonized want. And Savka already wanted more, yearning for Ewa's velvet tongue, those beautiful, terrible fingers gripping her, even the red marks and bruises on her buttocks and thighs that lingered for days after.

It had begun late in the night a few months ago when Savka woke from one of her nightmares beside a sleeping Ewa and sought her own comforting form of release. But Ewa had reached for Savka, her fingers not rough and inexperienced, as a man's would be, but soft, almost aimless, skillfully bringing Savka to a shockingly intense orgasm.

"I'm sorry," she whispered now, a slave to Ewa's mood, desperate to bring her out of her brittle silence. She inched closer on the bed, placing a tentative hand on her back. "I only wish I had your courage," she whispered into her friend's hair.

But she was met by silence. Resigned, Savka drowsily closed her eyes, and she was back on the mountain, where Kuzak and Natalka had given her the pistol. She wondered what it must look like now with all the snow gone, wildflowers in the meadows. "I can almost see Natalka," Savka muttered, drifting into sleep, "out checking her trap-line for rabbits."

Ewa had roused herself. "Who?"

Savka's eyes snapped open. She hadn't meant to speak aloud. Ewa turned to face her. "Natalka," Savka said reluctantly. "A ruthless *bander-ivka* I once knew."

Ewa's eyes glittered in the murky shadows of the room. "You were lovers?"

Savka snorted. "Anything but."

"How did you meet her?"

"I was in the Organization of Ukrainian Nationalists," she said, relief flooding her heart that she'd finally told Ewa one of her secrets.

Ewa stroked her cheek. "I would never have believed you were a warrior."

Savka's face burned hot with confusion. Was the pressure in her chest anger or hurt? She hadn't been much of a warrior with the underground, but Ewa made it sound like it was all but impossible. "That's how I lost Taras, on an assignment for my husband." She wanted to tell Ewa more, but the truth was poison on her tongue. "An NKVD patrol found us—" A sob hitched in her throat and the dam finally broke. Ewa gathered her into her arms, and it poured out of Savka, the events of that day in the Carpathians that had been burned into her heart—how she'd been shot, the promises she'd made to Belyakov and the underground.

How Taras had been stolen. When she finished, she was surprised to feel her heart had lifted in relief. Losing Taras was a burden too heavy to bear alone.

Ewa tenderly wiped Savka's tears away and studied her face. "I understand. One of those soldiers is the father of your child."

"Never." Savka froze in Ewa's arms, a chill running down her spine like ice water. She cupped her small pregnant belly protectively, as if to ward off her friend's words. "This is Marko's child."

Ewa inched close and whispered in her ear. "When will you learn this simple truth, Savka? That's what men do—to claim your soul. A woman gives life. Men take it."

Savka pushed Ewa away. "I was not violated," she insisted.

"They turned you by using your son," Ewa said, rolling onto her back. "Despicable."

"The Soviet officer tried, but I escaped him. I'm free of him."

Ewa glared up at the ceiling. "I'm desperate for a cigarette, but I'm too lazy to get up. Keep my mind occupied by telling me more of these brave insurgents living in their bunker in the mountains."

"I say bunker," Savka began, grateful to change the subject, "but it was more of a hole in the earth. Two small rooms. Natalka told me there are seven of them living in there. How brave they are. Now that the front has moved past them, there will be many opportunities to fight Red Army and NKVD patrols."

"The bunker was high on the mountain?" Ewa asked, her voice oddly calm. "Near Deremnytsia?"

Savka hesitated. A good insurgent would die before revealing even a vague description of a bunker's location. But this was Ewa, another revolutionary, and now Savka trusted her implicitly. "Very cleverly hidden on the east face of the mountain, in the spruce tree forest. There was a creek nearby, I remember hearing it—"

She broke off as Natalka's parting threat rang in her ears:

*If you don't kill your handler, I'll come for you. I'll hunt you to the
ends of the earth.*

Ewa's voice pulled her back into the room. "I hope the NKVD
hasn't got to them."

Savka smiled to herself. "Kuzak and his insurgents will hold out
forever."

17

DANEK

Salt Spring Island
DECEMBER 5, 1972

UP ON THE HEADLAND, Danek Rys watches as Nurse Pat O'Dwyer takes a few moments to compose herself. He has seen this kind of person many times before. A liar and a thief.

But he's been lying, too. He's come to Salt Spring Island on a mission. He is no better than the nurse.

Pat steps closer. "Jeanie suffered a traumatic accident at the age of seventeen. She was in the hospital for two years, and on heavy drugs. There are no memories in that daft, vacant head. Do you know what the papers called her? Wait, of course you do."

Dan notices that Jeanie has come to an abrupt stop on the path to the house, thin shoulders bowed, as if she's heard these hateful remarks.

His gaze returns to Pat. "You told police you saw Marko Kovacs last, heading for the back stairs of your hospital ward. Another man arrived soon after this, says he is Mr. Kovacs's brother and runs down the hall after him." Dan waits while Pat stares at him, obviously angry that he's dared bring up the police report. It has been difficult tracking her down, but now that's she's standing in front of him, he waits for her to admit the truth.

"He didn't *run*, but you could say he was in a hurry." Pat folds her arms across her chest.

Dan hides a smile. Now he's got her. "What does the man look like?"

"How should I know? A hat hid his features." She frowns. "And it was many years ago."

"Did he have an accent?"

"Like yours, you mean?" Pat narrows her eyes. "You know, Mr. Rys, maybe you're in on it." She takes a step toward him. "Maybe I should call the police."

"Mr. Kovacs vanishes into thin air after this," he presses her, watching those dark eyes for a hint of reaction. "His car is left in the parking lot. You have seen or heard *something*."

Pat snorts with derision. "Kay and I saw nothing."

Jeanie is inching back toward them, dejected and shivering, and he suffers a fractal image of dark figures hunched in a long line before him, snow blowing so hard they cannot see. He shakes his head to rid himself of the memory and focuses on the young woman. Before his visit to the island, he read several articles about Jeanie Esterhazy on the microfiche in the Vancouver library, about her dreadful accident and how she disappeared after an art show in 1966. Beyond that, there was only speculation as to her whereabouts.

". . . and the baby," Pat is saying. "Poor thing never stood a chance. Even a house cat possesses better sense and proper instinct than Jeanie did that night."

He scratches this into his notebook: *Baby?* There was no mention of it in the articles. He feels a tentative hand on the sleeve of his coat, and he jolts, unaccustomed to touch. It's the artist. Jeanie is obviously terrified of Pat, yet she's managed to creep past her caregiver to stand next to him. Her long hair, the color of a raven's wing, blows across her lower face. She smells of the wind and salt, she smells of the sea. He stares into her luminous green eyes. Intoxicated, he forces himself to look away, dropping his gaze to Jeanie's hands. Her fingers, runnelled with scars, are strangely beautiful.

"Could you leave your card, Dan?" she says, her voice a whisper. "I'll call you if I remember anything else."

"That won't be necessary," Pat says loudly before Dan can respond.

He stands dumbly for a moment. He's prepared for any eventuality but didn't think of having a business card made. How bad he is at this. Dan quickly scribbles his telephone number on a blank page of his notebook then rips it free. Pat leaps forward to take it, but he deliberately hands it to Jeanie, who folds it in half and in half again.

Pat looks more furious than ever, and Dan is confused. Why would a caregiver be so *uncaring*? She's turned to lead Jeanie down the path toward the driveway. He follows, intent on pressing Pat further.

When they near the house, she tells Jeanie, "Take a hot bath and get into your pajamas."

Jeanie stubbornly shakes her head. "I won't let you talk to him alone."

With a tight smile, Pat slips an arm around her charge and steers her to the door. Jeanie resists. After a brief struggle she gives up and shuffles inside with a final glance back at Dan. He opens his mouth to say something, but unsure of what those words should be, he stops himself.

Pat turns and looks at Dan, her smile gone. "As you can see, she's fragile," she tells him. "You coming here, bringing up that traumatic time in her life—it's devastating to her."

He watches the nurse intently. "She would be dead now if I did not come." He turns and gestures to the rope hanging from the tree.

"You think Jeanie would try to kill *herself*? That's all performance! She's gone mad. I have to hide anything sharp for my own safety." Pat lifts her sleeve and shows him her bandaged arm for emphasis. "Even her craft scissors."

He files this away, though he only feels sympathy for the artist. Any attack was undoubtedly the act of a broken-hearted woman with no other choice. "And yet you left enough rope for her to die."

Pat's eyes flare with indignation, and he knows he's struck a chord. "Jeanie is a sick individual. Strong drugs have affected her mind."

He's silent for a moment. "She survived a terrible accident," he says finally. "She is no coward."

Pat laughs, as though she suddenly finds him amusing. "You're foreign, aren't you? What's your name? What miserable country gave you those scars?"

"You don't remember me?" he says, for she deserves to be put in her place. "I come from your nightmares."

Pat rears back and glares at Dan, her eyes and tone sharp. "You'll never show up here again to upset Jeanie."

He glances up at the house and spots Jeanie's lovely, pale face hovering in a window. She lights up when their eyes meet, but he tries to keep his expression neutral. He hasn't had much experience with women, yet there's something about this one that compels him. His eyes shift back to Pat. What is she hiding? "You are lucky to live here, in paradise."

"Lucky?" Pat's face contorts in anger, a hand to her hip. "This is not paradise. Far from it. You try taking care of Jeanie! Do you know Kay and I were her two vigil nurses? We held her close when her mother and aunt died in a car accident Jeanie's second year in the hospital. Her father's been out of the picture since she was a child." She pauses, clearly agitated. "When Jeanie got out of the hospital, she was nineteen. She needed someone familiar with her care, the medication. She got *me*. And I've sacrificed more than she—" Pat clamps her mouth shut over these last words.

He gives her an appraising look, eyebrows raised. What else did she mean to say?

There is only a foot between them, but he steps closer to Nurse O'Dwyer and slips one hand into his pocket to caress the leather sheath that holds a knife he made long ago with a surgeon's scalpel, the handle wrapped in a compress bandage and wound tight with an old shoelace. He's kept this blade for one purpose—to sing across the neck of the one he's been hunting with singular focus. Pat looks too smug, too sure of her place here. "What will happen to you if Jeanie is successful in . . . what do you call it? *Performance?*"

Pat stumbles back and he sees he's scored a hit. "You seem a little too invested in this cold case," she says. "Who was Marko Kovacs to you?"

Dan remains silent. Pat doesn't need to know that he's been obsessed with Marko for many years. He's tracked his actions in Europe with the Fourteenth Division and with British Intelligence in England. When he finally traced Ivanets to Canada, he was surprised to learn that the man had changed his name to Kovacs, and he'd disappeared without a trace in 1959. Dan doesn't believe it. He suspects there is something else behind Marko Kovacs's disappearance. And he's here to find out just what that is.

Pat is staring at him. "Show up here again and I'll call the police."

He turns and walks up the drive, Jeanie's declaration, "Don't you think you should have to fight?" ringing in his ears. What a question. He has never heard anyone put his own experience into words quite like this. During the war, he fought with everything in him to survive. Yet, parts of him are dead. His heart or his spirit? He still doesn't know. Glancing over his shoulder, he can still see her woeful face in the window, like an animal in a cage, watching its only chance for escape leave forever.

It's clear he'll get nothing further out of Pat O'Dwyer. The nurse had claimed on the phone that she'd never heard of Marko Kovacs. She can't be trusted. The police had questioned both nurses, the only ones who worked on the ward at the time Kovacs disappeared. They'd not questioned the patients. Jeanie is the true lead, the only one he's got. He'll use her to get to Pat, find out what she's hiding.

But Jeanie has already been used.

He puts this away from him, surprised to feel a moment of pity, of attachment. Some part of him desperately wants to run back, grab Jeanie and take her away from this place.

Jeanie is the key—she has all the answers in her head. And he must get them out. Surely she will remember hearing something the night Marko Kovacs disappeared. And when she does, she'll call and tell him why her old nurse lied. Or he'll return and show Pat just how far he's willing to go to find Marko Kovacs.

18

SAVKA

Kraków, Polish People's Republic

JANUARY 19, 1947

"IS THERE A PARADE, *Matka?*"

"Yes, Paweł." Savka smiled at the little boy. "A parade just for us."

Ewa's son held Savka's hand with a grip stronger than any three-year-old she'd known. The image of Taras at that age, his own precious hand in hers, invaded Savka's memory and her heart ached. *My son, where are you?*

She pushed away the grief and steered Paweł and her own small daughter, Zoya, into the doorway of a cafe just as a Red Army battalion marched through the entrance of St. Florian's Gate at the center of Kraków, where, since the twelfth century, Polish armies led by kings and princes had passed through in processions of victory to Wawel Castle.

As she watched the Soviet soldiers file into Market Square to the ugly shouts of their captain, Savka's scarred wound throbbed, a perpetual reminder of the day she lost Taras. She tried to stay calm as she took in the distinctive puce-colored Red Army uniforms and this alarming display of force on the day of country-wide elections. One of the soldiers was tall, gangly, and her heart briefly soared with hope. She'd not stopped frantically looking for her son in the face of every young man on the street, nor had she stopped asking herself questions that hung like vapor in the frigid air:

Has he been tortured? Does he get enough to eat? And in her lightless moments: *Is he still alive?*

Her son was fine, she convinced herself. Healthy, safe. *Taras has his own room in a beautiful* dacha—*riding horses, and with access to a library filled with books.* She took a deep breath, the glacial smell of melting ice from the Vistula River in her nose and an eerie foreboding in the air, as if a ghost cello played in the streets of Kraków on Polish election day.

This morning, Ewa had been eager to arrive early at the polling station to vote. "Stalin is finally permitting the democratic election he promised the Allies at Yalta," she'd said excitedly, getting ready to leave after breakfast.

"And you trust he will deliver this promise?" Savka had been wiping buckwheat porridge off Zoya's face. Her own dark experience living in Soviet Ukraine made her skeptical, yet Ewa was optimistic that democracy would rule.

But that had been hours ago, and as Ewa's absence stretched into late in the afternoon, Savka had come out with the children. Now she could see the polling station in the corner of the square, Polish voters in neat lines, doing their best to ignore Soviet soldiers and their bristling *Papasha* submachine guns. Savka worried that Ewa had run into trouble.

The Russian soldiers goose-stepped in front of Savka and the children, and past a massive banner of Stalin that fluttered in the chill breeze. She searched the crowd for the old gray hat that Ewa wore all the time, even indoors in winter, blissfully indifferent to its shabby condition. Where was she? Surely her friend had not anticipated so many Soviet soldiers here to intimidate voters.

Little Zoya flinched at a sudden shouted order from the captain of the Soviet battalion, and Savka picked her up, burying her face in her daughter's dark, curly hair. The miracle of carrying a child to full term had almost made the loss of Taras and Marko bearable.

Almost.

Savka glanced around the square, expecting to see Ewa's grim and stormy face. Surely her friend had now accepted that this election was a façade. Stalin cared not a whit for decency and democracy. The strong military presence was not here to protect Poles' right to vote, but to demonstrate that only *one* person was in charge—an evil warlord who hunched like an ogre in the dark stronghold of the Kremlin.

The clock in the watchtower of St. Mary's Basilica struck five, and the *hejnał* hourly trumpet call sounded. Savka listened as the plaintive melody lofted over the Gothic spires that rose into a cloudless sky. It was a haunting Polish anthem that ended abruptly—symbolic of a time when a trumpeter in the thirteenth century had spotted an invading Mongol horde and sounded the alarm, only to be interrupted mid tune when he was shot in the throat by an arrow.

She felt a sudden pain in her own throat and the eerie sense that she was being watched. She spun on her heel to look behind her. *Stop it*, she told herself. Who could be watching? Lieutenant Belyakov, the brutal NKVD officer who'd shot her? Ever since that day three years ago, she couldn't stop looking over her shoulder, wondering if he stood right behind her. But it was impossible that he'd been assigned to Kraków alongside an army sent by Stalin to enforce communist rule in his new vassal state. Still, she couldn't shake the feeling that he loomed closer than ever.

It's grief that haunts you, not a random Soviet agent.

Savka was lucky. If there was such a thing as luck anymore. Millions of Ukrainians had not survived the war. Families were torn apart. Survivors had limped away and struggled to recover. When the Allies had liberated many Ukrainians from German forced labor camps, they became displaced persons. And what of those who'd been beaten, raped, or murdered by the Russians? Savka brushed away a sudden tear at the thought of Mama and Lilia. She'd written many times to the house in Deremnytsia, but each letter was returned. Submitting a tracing request to the Red Cross had been her only hope. After the war, she had also made inquiries into the fate of Marko's Fourteenth Division, but her husband was missing in action and presumed dead. It had been impossible to find information on how he'd died.

A biting wind came off the river, and Paweł shivered in his threadbare coat. "I'm cold, *Matka*."

She smiled down at him. Paweł and Zoya called her and Ewa *Matka*. Mother. The children shared a cot on the floor of Ewa's bedroom, and the two women still slept in the same bed, no longer turning to each other at night. They'd put aside their brief affair and were simply companions now, responsible mothers. There was little time for misguided passion among two best friends trying to keep their children safe.

Savka glanced at her wristwatch. Too close to curfew. She couldn't endanger the children further, hoping to find Ewa in this crowd. They had to head home. Reluctantly, she led the children through one of the Renaissance arches in Cloth Hall. Shopkeepers piled rationed items like bread and tea in the same stalls where traders had sold exotic spices and silk hundreds of years ago. A hand on her arm set her heart pounding. *He's found me.* Bracing herself, and still gripping the children's hands, she turned, prepared to face Belyakov. Savka gasped with relief when she saw that it was Ewa, her bright blonde waves peeking from beneath the old woolen hat.

"Let's get out of here," Ewa said, her face flushed with anger. "I don't know what's going to happen."

"What do you mean?" Savka's heart was still hammering in her chest.

"I tried to vote, but my name has been struck from the electoral roll. A filthy Russian told me I was an *anti-government bandit*." Ewa glared at her. "The propaganda they spew—in my own country!"

Savka grabbed her coat sleeve and pulled her friend close, waiting until Ewa's breath slowed. Ewa couldn't lose her temper, not in the presence of the *filthy Russians* all around them. Criticizing the regime was dangerous. Still, she whispered in solidarity, "Yalta and its empty promises. The West can't control Stalin. He's a criminal, a beast."

"These thugs," Ewa said, twisting away to look over her shoulder at the Red Army battalion. "Poles have been arrested. At a democratic election."

Savka composed herself for the children's sake. "The dark wizard in the Kremlin has added Poland to its slave states, another spoke in the wheel of the USSR," she said softly. "Poland will be eaten, just as Ukraine was."

"I will not let it be eaten," Ewa said, her teeth clenched.

"You have no choice. Do you want to end up in the Gulag?" Savka tried to keep the frustration out of her voice but was unsuccessful. "You would never see your son again."

Ewa nodded and took Paweł's hand. Together they all headed toward Planty Park. After her son was born, Ewa had fallen in love with being a mother again and vowed to protect Paweł the way she'd been unable to protect her daughter. She'd decided to lay low and do less perilous work for the Polish resistance, which had gone even further underground.

Pigeons flew up before them and light was already failing, the streetlamps starting to wink on along the wide, snowy pathways. In summer, the plane and beech trees formed a glorious canopy high above, but now they stood silent, leafless, frozen in winter slumber.

Paweł raced ahead along the path, Zoya squealing with delight as she attempted to catch him. Savka stopped to remove a pack of cigarettes from her coat pocket. She lighted two, and handed one to Ewa, who took it, glowering at several people who were hurrying past, coming from the polls in numb defeat. The strangers glanced back at her, for everyone noticed beautiful Ewa. "Stalin got his wish today." She exhaled a stream of smoke. "The West has abandoned us."

"Keep it down," Savka warned. "Stalin has agents in every organization—he penetrated the Ukrainian underground. He can penetrate yours." Her fingers trembled as she lifted the cigarette to her lips and inhaled. In her mind flashed a vision of the NKVD breaking down their apartment door and dragging Ewa away. The image was quickly replaced by a whisper of memory from Lieutenant Belyakov on that dreadful day on the mountain when Taras was taken from her.

We have been piecing together information on all of you.

Ewa dropped her voice. "They're arresting any Pole they like, without provocation." She watched Paweł and Zoya, jostling each other playfully, then turned to look at Savka. "Thousands are disappearing quietly—voters and opposition candidates, either murdered by the NKVD or sent to Siberia."

Savka's breath rose in clouds of vapor in the cold air, Belyakov's voice ringing in her head again. *Did you think your husband's visit to you of late went unnoticed?*

Ewa stared at her. "Look at you, shaking like a rabbit." She paused. "Why did you come out with the children?"

"I worried about you. Where have you been?"

"Getting something," Ewa said mysteriously. She took off after the children, who shrieked as they scooped up snow and threw clumsily rolled snowballs at each other.

Savka took a final drag on her cigarette and followed, her heart settling on an even, careful beat. Ewa's vague pronouncements were troubling, but it at least took her mind off the NKVD officer. Savka caught up to Zoya and bent to pull her daughter's hat down over her dark curls. When she straightened, she started at the sight of a man in a long coat leaning on a light standard near them, reading a newspaper. From this distance, he seemed tall enough to be Lieutenant Belyakov's soldier, Yeleshev, and perhaps handsome enough to be the other one, Ilyin. But her fears were allayed when a woman came up the path toward him. The man slipped his arm around her waist and the couple made off toward Market Square, unaware that Savka stood rooted to the spot, hardly breathing and her spine still tingling with dread.

"Don't worry," Ewa said lightly over her shoulder, "your Russian handler has forgotten you."

Savka ground the cigarette butt under the heel of her boot. "Quiet." Her voice held a warning: *Say no more.* She would often tell Ewa, in the privacy of their flat, how vividly the NKVD officer still haunted her— why was her friend speaking so freely about it now? Paweł and Zoya were roughhousing in the snow, and Savka pulled her daughter away. They didn't need attention drawn to them. She straightened and looked at Ewa. "Why are you being so cruel?"

Ewa passed a hand over her eyes. "I'm sorry, Savka. I just can't believe my country is going to these red dogs," she said in a savage whisper. "The Kraków I love is dead."

Savka forgave Ewa, as she always did. "You mustn't do anything rash."

Ewa scowled, flicking away ash from her cigarette. "I *will* do something rash—leave Poland forever." She took out a handful of folded documents from her coat pocket and showed them to Savka. "Forged USSR exit visas—for us and our children, *piękna*," Ewa said with a secretive smile.

Savka let out a relieved sigh. As much as she trusted Ewa, sometimes she worried that one day her friend would tire of her and demand Savka and Zoya leave the flat. These papers quieted those fears. The four of them would always be a family.

"We'll flee to Germany—even to America," Ewa said excitedly. Then she slipped two sets of papers into the pocket of Savka's coat and scanned the park, making sure that no one was watching them. "We'll take the train to Allied-occupied Berlin," she continued, satisfied they were safe. "A friend has an apartment there."

Savka blinked in surprise. "Is there room for all of us?" It was dangerous to brandish forged papers and talk of escape from a Soviet state. They could be stopped at any time and searched.

"We will make room," Ewa said, her eyes burning with enthusiasm. "And somehow . . . somehow I will find Maja, and you will find Taras."

They walked in the direction of home, snow crunching under their boots, and Savka squeezed Zoya's mittened hand, looping her other arm through Ewa's, who excitedly laid plans for their new life. Her friend was a true warrior and had the means and connections to get her and Zoya out. Savka was confident that, one day, she would find Mama and Lilia, and Taras.

Savka looked back. No one was following them. After three years of worry, she finally allowed herself to breathe a sigh of relief. Soon she would leave the Polish People's Republic, and the NKVD officer would never find her.

AN HOUR LATER, Savka and Ewa stood in the hallway of their apartment building, the children loudly chattering after their mad dash up three flights of stairs. Ewa turned the key in the lock and opened the door, stepping aside, allowing Savka to usher Zoya in ahead of her. Savka staggered back into the corridor at the sight of a shadowed figure sitting at the kitchen table.

"Hello Savka."

She stifled a scream as the shadow smiled and she registered his face. Lieutenant Belyakov.

Fear hummed down Savka's legs, as Ewa crowded in behind her with Paweł. They exchanged a terrified glance. "How did you find me?" she whispered, the Russian words like ashes in her mouth.

Belyakov grinned. "No one escapes me, Savka."

She had not seen the officer since he stole Taras, and yet here he was on the same day Ewa had given her newly forged exit visas.

Ewa pushed past her and the children, who stared, instinctively fearful of this strange man. "How did you get in here, you troll," she shouted in surprisingly good Russian. "She's suffered enough, can't you see?" The lieutenant studied her, his lip curled in distaste. "Savka still cannot raise her arm without sharp pain in her shoulder," Ewa cried. "You know nothing of her nightmares!"

Savka sent her a look of gratitude. Thank God for Ewa. How long had it been since someone had defended her?

For a moment, Belyakov's full lower lip and cleft chin made him appear kind, even genial. But this illusion was dispelled the moment he opened his mouth. "Do not speak to me of suffering." He buckled under a wet cough that ended with a disturbing gabble in his throat. Belyakov got to his feet and moved about the room, picking up their few possessions, and turning them over. She'd forgotten how small he was—she and Ewa towered over him—yet he gave the impression he might strike at any moment. Finally, he turned his gaze to her.

"You are looking well, my pretty bird. The food is good in Kraków."

Emboldened by Ewa's presence, Savka demanded, "Where is my son?"

Belyakov regarded her for a few moments before responding. "Safe."

Thankful tears filled her eyes. She doubted anything else Belyakov might tell her, but she'd gratefully accept news that Taras was safe.

Ewa stepped toward him. "Her husband is dead. You have no more need of her—give back her son."

Belyakov sprang at her like a cat and Ewa shrank back with a gasp. He stood in the center of the room, his eyes now on Savka, who'd inched toward the kitchen, hoping to slip a knife out of the drawer. She might never have this chance again. "Your husband is alive," the lieutenant said. "I found him in a British prisoner of war camp in Italy."

Savka's vision blurred and she let out an involuntary cry. Marko was alive? She had mourned him so thoroughly over the past three years, it seemed impossible. Zoya echoed her cry with one of her own, looking up at her mother with wide eyes. Ewa quickly gathered the frightened children and ushered them into the bedroom. When they were alone, Belyakov walked slowly toward her until he stood only a few feet away. "You have nothing to say, Savka? I thought you would be pleased to hear Marko is alive."

"I am," she whispered. But she wouldn't let herself believe this Soviet. "He's in Italy?" All this time, Savka had thought she'd escaped Belyakov, the spider, when, all along, she'd been suspended in his web, until he decided to crawl down and eat her. But now she must remain calm, she had to outwit and placate him, until she and Ewa and the children could escape. She thought of Kuzak's pistol that she and Ewa agreed should be kept in the false bottom of the dresser drawer, taking it out only if Soviets came bursting through the door. Savka tried to send Ewa a silent message: *Get the gun—shoot this Russian in the head,* but she could hear her friend reading a book to the children in the bedroom, her voice too loud and tremulous.

Belyakov regarded her with a quizzical twitch of his lips, as if he were conducting an experiment and taking note of its effect on his subject. "A survivor, your Marko," he remarked. "The Fourteenth Waffen-SS Division slipped away from the front to the uprising in Slovenia and then to Austria. They surrendered in May '45 and were sent to a POW camp in Italy." Belyakov removed his blue-and-red cap and ran a hand through his dark hair. "Your Roman god of a husband has been there all this time."

Roman god? It seemed an odd phrase for him to use. Unless—like everyone who met Marko—Belyakov had become obsessed with her husband's height and good looks. "You've seen him, haven't you—in the prison camp?"

Surprise flitted across Belyakov's features. "I interrogated him, *da,* but the British imperialists blocked our every effort to repatriate him." He stood as close to her as he had that day in the forest three years ago. Savka noticed Belyakov had gray hair at his temples and hoped she might have put a few of them there herself. Several fingers of his right hand were twisted and crooked at the second joints, she observed with satisfaction, remembering the sour taste in her mouth and his crazed shout as she bit down hard on them after she'd been shot. He turned away in frustration and strolled to the kitchen window, hands folded behind his back. "At Yalta, the Allies promised Stalin they would help us pursue these men to the ends of the earth, but instead they protect him."

"Repatriate?" Savka forced a laugh. "You would ship Marko to Siberia or shoot him." Belyakov turned to look at her and she resisted the urge to touch her pocket. He couldn't find out about the two exit visas, not before she discovered what had happened to Taras.

The Russian's voice cut through her thoughts. "There are consequences to actions, wouldn't you agree?"

"Yes." She leaned against the counter, bracing herself for the worst. *Where was Ewa with the gun?*

"Your husband has committed a crime against the Soviet state and must be punished for treason."

"He's in a prisoner of war camp—that's punishment enough."

"The British have let them form choirs and orchestras," Belyakov said before collapsing into a spasm of coughing, a bleak sputter of phlegm in his lungs. Hands trembling, he pulled a pewter flask from his pocket and unscrewed the lid before taking a long pull. Recovered, yet clearly agitated, he slipped it back into his pocket. "The men are staging theatrical performances," he said, now fiddling with his field cap. "Your husband flourishes, eats better food than you and I do, and breathes the healing air of the Adriatic Sea. He is not suffering."

The floorboards in the hallway creaked and Savka turned to see Ewa in the bedroom doorway, staring at the NKVD officer. "What more do you want of her?" she asked, her voice dripping acid. Savka glanced down at her friend's hand. Empty. Why hadn't she taken out the gun?

Belyakov did not take his eyes from Savka. "The imperialists will soon move Marko and his division to England, to work in their fields. The British wish to keep these traitors out of Soviet hands and MI-6 plans to recruit the Ukrainian officers. You will write to your husband, tell him you escaped Ukraine with the clothes on your back."

"Marko sent me and Taras to a bunker in the mountains to wait out the war. You think he did not hear from Kuzak—even in this prisoner of war camp—that he suspects me of being turned into a Soviet spy?"

"Do not concern yourself with Kuzak."

Savka's heart plummeted at the sight of Belyakov's sly smile. "Why?"

"A unit of NKVD agents was sent to exterminate the vermin. Kuzak died with your name on his lips."

"Not the entire bunker."

"Every rat in the hole."

She thought of the lion-hearted Natalka lying dead in the snow. "How could you kill a woman in cold blood?"

Belyakov's eyes narrowed. "There was no woman in that bunker." He coughed. "We had to ensure your husband would never know Kuzak took you in or learned of the deal he made with you," he said, regarding her with a cold detachment that destroyed every last vestige of confidence she'd built for herself in Kraków. "Did you not think I knew those bandits ordered you to kill me?"

Suddenly Zoya appeared behind Ewa, clutching her doll, and Savka glared at Belyakov. "When Marko learns that Taras was stolen by the NKVD and I somehow turned up safe and pregnant in Kraków, he'll know the Soviets turned me on the mountain."

"You were at it like rabbits when Marko came to the house, yes?" Belyakov's tongue flicked over his lips. There was something in his eyes she didn't like, as if he'd imagined, in great detail, how she and her husband had come together that night in Deremnytsia. The Lieutenant gestured toward Zoya. "And here is the residue of that union. Marko sent his dear pregnant wife and his son on a fool's errand into enemy territory. You were shot by NKVD, left for dead, your son spirited away. A doctor took you to Kraków to save your life. There is nothing to doubt."

"Marko's not stupid. He'll suspect the NKVD hold Taras as a bargaining chip," she said, desperate to squirm her way out of the corner he'd backed her into. "He will suspect *me*." She paused. "But if you release our son, I'll consider your request."

Belyakov scratched briefly at the top of his head. He had long nails, remarkably clean, and she pictured him carefully scraping under them to remove the dirt and blood of his interrogations at the end of each day. He finally spoke. "I cannot release your son. That is beyond my control."

"Where is he?" Savka's voice rose in a howl.

"Safe." Belyakov smiled and glanced again at Zoya. Savka crossed the room and stepped in front of her daughter, as if she could somehow protect her from the Russian's gaze. But Belyakov reached around her and stroked the child's soft cheek with his thumb. "She is beautiful, like her mother. Will she be as obedient?" Savka nodded, afraid if she said anything, she would scream.

In an instant, Ewa was there with a hard push to Belyakov's shoulder. Savka held her breath as Belyakov lurched, then, just as quick as Ewa had been, he struck her—one quick slap that sent her sprawling. He dusted off his tunic, straightening the buttons, and looked up at Savka with a glint in his eye. "You are one of the lucky ones—you are *alive*." Belyakov opened the door and glanced back at her clutching Zoya, ignoring Ewa, her cheek still red from his slap. "I will be in touch when I receive intelligence that Marko and his division are being moved to England. Do your job well, Savka, and you will see your son again."

The moment he was gone, Zoya began to cry softly into her doll's dress. Savka held her, feeling the frantic beat of her daughter's heart. Yet another of her children had borne witness to the cruelty of Lieutenant Belyakov. Ewa reached to embrace Savka, but she shrugged her off. "Why didn't you take out the gun and shoot him?" she demanded.

Ewa let her arms drop. "Think, Savka. You almost have Taras back. If I had killed this Soviet, you would have lost your son forever."

Savka closed her eyes briefly, anger overcome by gratitude for her friend. Ewa was right—they must do nothing to threaten her reunion with Taras. She turned to stare at the closed front door. Belyakov was in Kraków as an undertaker, raising her from the dead, conjuring her from a deep and pitiless grave. How naive of her to think she could escape his bondage.

19

JEANIE

Salt Spring Island
DECEMBER 9, 1972

A WINTRY SUN BEAMS through the skylight in my studio where I stand before the canvas on my easel—a canvas that Pat has despoiled yet again with her ham-handed attempt at underpainting. She left for Vancouver this morning in her usual dramatic leave-taking, reminding me ad nauseam how to conduct myself in her absence, but also making sure I had my marching orders: *Get that landscape commission done.* Her brake lights had hardly disappeared through the trees when I dragged myself out to my studio, Tuna at my heels, too depressed at the thought of completing this picture by Christmas.

You'd think I would enjoy seeing the back of her, but not quite. In our early days on Salt Spring, when I rebelled and made Pat angry, she would take off for days, leaving me alone, unable to care for myself— just to show me how much I needed her. Deep in my mind are shameful memories of me ransacking the medicine cabinet in her bathroom— only to find she'd taken every last one of my medications. How could a nurse do that, leaving her patient to a nightmare of chronic pain? I'd taken to bed in a haze of agony, curled up in the fetal position. Only when I was hungry or thirsty did I try to get to the kitchen, falling down the stairs in a pathetic display worthy of a heroin addict. She knows I'll behave. I'll do anything to avoid that terrible pain and withdrawal. Not only is Pat my caregiver, she's my drug dealer.

I stand in front of my easel and take a breath. I've learned this commission is for a financier in Paris, and I have no idea what to give him. When I begin framing a new composition, it's always with an art teacher's voice in my head: *This is how you find your focal point, this is how you position islands to ocean to sky* . . . I flip through some sketches and find a drawing I once did of a sweet little cove on Wallace Island when Pat took me out in the kayak. This will do. Taking up a 4H graphite pencil, I reluctantly begin sketching. Somehow, my pencil leaps out of my hands and hits the floor, its lead fracturing to bits.

Now this is a sign, I think. *Paint what you really want, Jeanie.* I head to my drying racks. Skimming through, I find a canvas that I underpainted a long while ago, when I still worked with oils. After setting it on my easel, I let my hands move of their own volition, squeezing oil paint onto my palette, and dancing a brush across the canvas. Danek Rys has become my muse. He whispers in my ear, and I lose all track of time as I layer these paints, these colors—how can I have used them so mindlessly on landscapes I didn't really want to paint!—alizarin crimson is my life's blood. Lapis lazuli becomes the transcendent shade of Dan's fine eyes. He's here with me, in this room, closer than my own soul.

Each painting I've begun in my life was for someone else, in hopes it might pass the grade—and with Pat's long shadow haunting me, in hopes it might sell. *Paint like this work will soon hang in the bloody Guggenheim*, she'd often say, adding, *even though it never will*, just to keep me in line. Before this moment, I've cobbled together images, painting in the dark. There's nothing of me in those landscapes.

The sun-drenched morning passes, and an androgynous form takes shape on my canvas as shadows slant sideways through the studio windows. It's the journalist, his eyes staring into mine. He has awakened something in me, a holy and sacred thing I thought long consumed. As my brushes move across the canvas, the leviathan, the monster that has long held my dark, unknowable heart, finally releases it, and a strange sensation rises to meet me.

"Everything I've painted before this moment was a lie," I whisper, tears swimming down my face.

All I can think of is Dan Rys: I see him running toward me on the headland, and later, walking slowly up the driveway after Pat told him to leave, one long glance over his shoulder at me in the window. When all three of us came down the path from the headland, I knew she would rip the note with his phone number out of my hands as she wrestled me through the front door and harangued him in private. But Pat had no idea that I rushed to the kitchen and tore a piece of paper from a notepad on the counter near the phone. I scribbled his number on it, hoping I had remembered it right. Then I stood at the window and listened to her feed him lies. If he believed any of those slanderous falsehoods—about me and my relationship with Pat—I'd never see Dan again.

I paint well past noon, composing a figure pieced together in cubes, the face indistinct, the eyes at different levels—almost Picasso-like in its construction. Awash with reverence, I step back and observe Danek Rys. "Please let this not be a fleeting moment," I breathe, "but a gift that no one, not even Pat, can take away."

Famished, I plunk my brushes in a jar of turpentine and head to the house for lunch, Tuna dawdling behind me. The weather has held; there's not a cloud to be seen. It's crisp, even cold, but the sun is a welcome gift. The house feels damp, and I bundle into a sweater and knit hat, picking up one of the white medication cups Pat has so thoughtfully lined up like soldiers on the kitchen counter. I immediately trash the orange pill, then down the rest with a gulp of water and remove a scrap of paper from the pocket of my overalls—Dan's telephone number. For the past four days, I've kept it with me during the day and under my mattress at night.

His haunted face floats before my eyes. I want to charge to the phone and dial his number. But what would I say? *I miss you?* I don't miss my mother, the person I once wanted more than anything in the world to love me, yet she somehow didn't. I dearly miss Aunt Suze and Kay. And another cherished soul—my baby, who would have been fourteen years old this January. I hardly know Mr. Rys, yet I miss him as much as I do my daughter—for I knew she was a girl right from the start.

My heart hurts at the thought of who she might have been today. Would she like swimming in the ocean? Would she love to paint, like me? I blink back tears and take a breath. *Time to occupy my mind with something else*, I think and slip Kay's last letter out of my sweater pocket to reread, savoring details of camp life in the jungles of Africa. I wonder where she is now and if she ever thinks about me—but I know that I probably never cross her mind; that she's already settled in a new clinic or hospital in Bangladesh or Ethiopia, settled into a new life.

Brushing away tears, I clasp the letter to my heart. "I need you, Kay."

I stare down at the orange pills marked *SKF T76* in the other medication cups, glowing like radioactive waste material. What are they for?

I must see those pill bottles.

20

SAVKA

Kraków, Polish People's Republic
AUGUST 1947

THROUGH THE WINDOW of the flat, Savka stared down at the man on the sidewalk directly across the street from their building. Spotting her, he lifted his hand in an insolent wave, his black hair curling from beneath a wide-brimmed fedora. Comrade Ilyin. Over the past seven months, he'd taken turns with Yeleshev, Belyakov's other man—who'd also been with him that fateful day in the Carpathians—to linger in doorways or pace at the corner, smoking and watching to ensure she didn't escape Poland. After Belyakov had turned up at their apartment in January, he'd ordered her to wait until Marko and his division had been shipped to England, and as the months passed without further word from her handler, Savka often watched his men watching *her* like hawks.

Sweat was gathering under her arms, and she fanned herself with a newspaper, lifting damp hair off her neck. A heat wave had descended on Kraków, and even this early in the morning, the city was wreathed in a scorched haze, the sun blazing down and wilting those who dared wander the streets. If Ewa were home, she would come up behind Savka and whisper, "These beasts can't stand out there forever." Savka had resisted Ewa's plan to flee Kraków for Berlin. Belyakov held Taras, and if he found out she'd escaped, Savka was certain she'd lose her son.

Until she'd received Marko's first letter from Rimini.

After Belyakov's visit, Savka had written to tell her husband how she'd escaped Ukraine and was hiding in Poland with their daughter. His reply had come within weeks, followed by others, and his letters and Ewa's forged exit visas were in her purse on the kitchen table, along with the small gun Kuzak had given her.

She stuck her head into the bedroom to check on Zoya and Paweł, who were playing quietly with wooden blocks, then she glanced toward the door of the flat where two small suitcases stood, packed and ready for them to leave at any moment. Irritable and impatient in the growing humidity, she took out Marko's most recent letter, unfolding it to read his hurried scrawl, and seeking reassurance that escape was her best option.

Savka—

I remain devastated that you lost Taras. Unforgivable. How could you survive while our son was taken by the NKVD?

Every moment I grieve his loss.

The British are committed to protecting our division from the Soviets. We are getting out of here soon. When I arrive in England, they will help me send a message to Kuzak. He will discover where Taras is being held and launch a rescue.

We will bring back our son.

Your husband,
Marko

A tear dropped on the page, blurring his words. "Soon you will know Kuzak is dead," she whispered. "And that *I* killed him—"

The door to the flat flew open, and Ewa burst in, breathless from racing up the stairs. "That gorgeous beast isn't there," she shouted. "He's not *there*." Savka rushed to the window. The sidewalk was indeed empty, save for a few people walking along Mikołajska Street toward the market. She and Ewa mobilized, moving around the flat in a frenzy, stuffing slices of rye they'd toasted this morning, and a few more clothes into their suitcases. Once their bags were packed, they bolted with the children to the station, leaving behind their life in Kraków with nothing but a few furtive glances over their shoulders.

But on the train to Berlin, Savka could not let her guard down, nor shake a sense of foreboding, even as Ewa sucked at cigarette after cigarette and winked at her through a cloud of smoke that rose in ribbons to the ceiling of their third-class compartment. Paweł was occupied, playing a game of jacks on the floor of the carriage, but Zoya was tugging at her mother's coat, wanting something to eat. "In a moment, darling," Savka said, her eyes on Ewa and the new jaunty red felt beret that she wore angled down over one eye. Savka thought it looked expensive but would not begrudge her friend a luxury.

Savka had just handed Zoya a slice of toasted rye when the door slid open, and she jumped in her seat. "Papers!" A Soviet conductor glared down at the women, his hand out. She tried to smile, to act naturally, as she fished the exit visas out of her handbag. The conductor glanced at her photograph. "Savka Ivanets." He looked up to study her and Zoya, who had slid to the floor to join Paweł in his game, the toast still clutched in her hand. "Your daughter?" Savka nodded without a word, holding her breath.

After the conductor reviewed Zoya's visa, he turned to Ewa and examined hers and Paweł's with a frown. Finally satisfied, he handed them back and left the carriage. Savka gratefully exhaled.

Ewa clasped her hand, stroking each of her fingers. "We did it, Savka," she said, her eyes gleaming with excitement.

Savka looked out the window and allowed herself a sigh of relief. When Belyakov had shown up seven months ago, his order for her to spy on Marko in England sent her into a deep depression, but now her heart soared with quiet elation. With Ewa's help, she and Zoya had escaped the clutches of her Russian controller. Every blast of the locomotive's whistle brought her closer to freedom, closer to her husband. And perhaps to Taras.

But something still niggled. How had they escaped so easily?

"Bye-bye Belyakov." Ewa zipped her hand in the air. "*Bzzzt!* You will see, soon he will be erased from your memory, Savka. Zoya will lead a normal life—and finally meet her father." Ewa glanced at her. "Why the long face?"

"One of Belyakov's men has been out there every day," Savka fretted. "Why would Ilyin suddenly leave without Yeleshev taking his place?"

"Maybe he's got a girlfriend," Ewa said with a shrug. "Oh, *Ilyin, Ilyin*," she cooed, her eyes closed, and a dreamy expression on her face.

Savka frowned. "What are you doing?" Sometimes Ewa's joking irritated her.

"Kissing that magnificent creature," she said with a naughty, schoolgirl's grin. "Don't tell me you wouldn't kiss him, given the chance."

"Stop it." Savka's gut cramped. It was Ilyin who, on Belyakov's orders, had shot her that day in the Carpathian Forest. She could *never* imagine kissing that monster.

Their train had just crossed the frontier between Poland and Germany. Savka had never been this far west. Leaving the Polish People's Republic was exhilarating and distressing, for it meant leaving Ukraine behind forever. A Soviet exit visa was a one-way ticket. She watched German village after German village pass with a feeling of dread growing in her chest, and thought of her father and brother, working in this strange country during the war. What had become of them? She'd likely never know.

Ewa took her hand again, eyeing her impassively, and for a moment Savka felt dizzy under her friend's gaze.

"You must breathe, Savka," Ewa said, giddy amusement stealing around the corners of her mouth.

"I will breathe when we're safe in Berlin." Savka smiled reluctantly. The sun was high overhead, the heat oppressive even with the window down. She gazed at the miles of farmer's fields flying by. Two years after the war had ended, eastern Europe was still struggling to recover, but the wheat would soon be ready for harvest.

The train approached a station and slowed, whistling to a stop, black smoke drifting past their window. Some passengers disembarked, others boarded. She and Ewa had been lucky to have the compartment to themselves, but with the train now at capacity an older woman opened the door, searching for a seat. Savka and Ewa lifted the children to their laps.

Zoya had been quieter than usual on the long trip, as if she knew that she and her mother were running for their lives, but as the train gained speed again, she turned and gazed up at her with those beautiful dark eyes. "Where are we going, Mama?"

Savka hugged her dear, small body close. "Somewhere safe, my love," she said, "where you and Paweł can make friends and play."

"What a lovely child," the new passenger remarked, as Zoya shyly ducked her head. "She must look like her father."

Her daughter resembled neither her nor Marko. Savka was certain that when her husband met Zoya for the first time, he'd sweep her into his arms and tell them stories of an aunt or great grandmother who had such dark, wavy hair.

Several hours later, the train rolled through the outskirts of Berlin. Inside the compartment, the air seemed to heat another few degrees. Savka held a now sleeping Zoya, even as a chill of anticipation ran over her skin like a rat. *Berlin*. How many times had she heard the name of this city drop from the mouths of Nazi soldiers in her village? Berlin, home to the Reichstag, to Hitler and his minions, who'd raged across Europe, leaving it in ashes.

Ewa lit another cigarette and smoked pensively, staring out the window. Savka noticed her friend's hands were shaking. Approaching the birthplace of her rapists, how could they not? "Over three hundred Allied bombing runs," Ewa smirked, "and not one of them managed to kill that bastard Hitler." The new passenger, obviously a German, quickly looked away. As Ewa blundered on, relating how Germany had been carved up by the Allies—the Americans and British holding West Berlin, the Soviets occupying the eastern part of the city—Savka watched the destruction pass by their train window. Buildings were bombed to shadows of their former selves; they resembled drawings she'd seen of Roman ruins, ceilings blown out, insides reduced to rubble. Two years after the end of the war, only the outer brick structures remained standing.

The train slowed as it came into the station, and Savka closed her eyes with the conviction that here was one of the supreme moments of her life. *Freedom at last.* When she opened them, the German passenger had already left and Ewa was standing to take down her bag from the overhead compartment.

"We did it," Savka whispered. "How can I ever thank you?"

Ewa leaned to kiss her cheek, then rubbed off the lipstick mark she'd left there, smiling. "Give me your little gun, *piękna*. Police will stop you at checkpoints. If they find it . . ." she trailed off.

Savka fumbled in her handbag for Kuzak's pistol and handed it over to her friend. "What if *you're* stopped . . ." But Ewa had already gathered up Paweł and turned, leaving the carriage so quickly, Savka had to scramble with Zoya to catch up.

IT WAS EARLY EVENING when they got off the train. Years later, Savka would often think of how she and Zoya descended the narrow steps to the platform, Savka—her dress sticking to her legs from the humidity—trying to keep her daughter from being crushed by the crowd on the platform as she searched for Ewa and young Paweł. She spotted the top of Ewa's red hat bobbing toward the street and recalled Ewa saying that her friend would be waiting in a car to take them to the apartment. Savka followed, diving headlong into the tidal current of disembarking passengers, dragging Zoya behind her, the travel bag under her arm.

But other passengers streamed forward in a crush to board the train, and it seemed impossible to reach the street. Savka was consumed by a sudden, aching exhaustion after almost seven hours on the train. Years later, she would remember her pulse quickening, the smell of engine grease and coal steam, and the sweat of passengers being greeted by friends or family. She would remember the feeling of being watched, and the sudden crystal-clear directive from somewhere inside her:

Run.

Someone grasped her by the elbow and she turned to find a man dressed in an overcoat, his face shadowed by the wide brim of his hat. Terror gripped her and she tried to pull away, but another man had already snatched up Zoya and their suitcase, moving toward the street.

"No," she screamed as they dragged her through the station. "Zoya!" Savka would rather die than lose her daughter the way she'd lost Taras. She scratched and fought like an animal, shouting into the crowd for help, but people silently passed her, tight-lipped and eyes down. *What's happening? Where the hell is Ewa?*

Out on the street, a black car was waiting at the curb. Savka was thrown roughly into the back while a crying and frightened Zoya was deposited in the front passenger seat. One man climbed in next to Savka and the other got behind the wheel, steering the car onto the busy street.

"My papers are in order," Savka said in stilted German, her voice shaking so much she could barely form the words. "You can't detain me." The man next to her finally turned to look at her, and her blood chilled. It was Yeleshev, the second of Belyakov's deputies. Savka's old wound burned hot with memory. She flicked her eyes to the driver next to her sobbing daughter. As he wove expertly through traffic, he turned his head to steer the car down a wide boulevard, and Savka took in his profile. Ilyin. *They found me.* Devastated, she looked out the window and stared with dumb incomprehension at the passing tableau. Most of the trees had been destroyed, leaving only a few leaning precariously, scorched black by fire or the heat of bomb blasts. Battered light standards hung over the bomb-damaged street like ghouls. Under a large banner of Stalin that flew from the top of a broken statue in the center of the boulevard, a work crew of women in a long assembly line moved a rubble pile, piece by piece, from the street.

Within a few minutes, their car crossed a short bridge. Now they seemed to be on an island in the middle of the city. The car slowed in front of a grand bombed-out relic, the towering limestone walls and columns pitted with shrapnel fragments from artillery fire. Savka imagined it might have once been an impressive museum. "Where is my friend and her son?" she cried.

Her captor opened the back door, and she was yanked out onto the sidewalk. She pounded her fists on the Russian's chest and looked back at Zoya, her small palm flat against the car window, her face wet with tears. "Let her out!"

"She stays here," Yeleshev said, his voice a surprisingly rich baritone.

Savka struggled as he led her up a series of wide steps into the building and down a warren of abandoned corridors. The air was thick with dust and the musty scent of ancient history. She tripped over rubble from the collapsed ceiling as they passed through an arched entrance to a massive gallery. Would she be reunited with Ewa and Paweł in a bombed and deserted museum?

Savka's heart almost stopped at the sight of a figure in the middle of the gallery, his back to her. Belyakov waited next to a huge stone structure of time-worn bricks glazed a vivid lapis blue. Exotic animals stood out from the wall in bas relief—enameled tiles depicting lions, dragons, bulls. Boards lay on the ground, presumably pried away from the installation, the rest of which was covered by other boards and extensive scaffolding. Several NKVD border soldiers stood in the archway, smoking. The Germans had done what they could to protect this antiquity from Allied air raid damage, but there was no protection from the invading Soviets.

"Nebuchadnezzar, king of Babylon!" he thundered, without turning to look at her. "Isn't it magnificent, Savka? The Ishtar Gate brought here stone by stone. What I would have given to be on that dig—fifteen years to unearth this beauty."

She ignored his comment. At another time, she would have studied the gate with fascination, but this was the man she'd hoped never to see again, the same dark eyes under his cap, his immaculate khaki uniform, and burnished black boots, Lilliputian as ever. When he removed his cap, she saw that he'd pomaded his hair, slicking each hair so close, she could make out the disquieting shape of his skull.

He opened his arms and turned to the gallery. "We have all this glory to ourselves, Savka. See where it was walled in during the Allied air raids? If not for the meddling of American troops, we would have disassembled it and taken it to Moscow, like the Pergamon Altar." A sour look. "Now it must be guarded day and night." He gestured to the NKVD border soldiers. "They have taken off the cladding so we can see it. What a gift to stand before one of the Seven Wonders of the World—entrance to the ancient city of Babylon."

Savka glanced up at the spectacle, hardly seeing it for worry over Zoya and barely listening as Belyakov prattled on about how German archaeologists had painstakingly reconstructed the gate in Berlin, any missing tiles replaced to show what the edifice must have looked like in its day, one hundred years before the birth of Christ. It was obvious that he expected her to show some kind of awe, but she refused to give him the satisfaction.

"If you hurt my daughter, I'll kill you," she said quietly, fixing Belyakov with a cold, dead stare.

"Did you hear that, Yeleshev?" Belyakov tilted his head back to look at the roof of the gallery, parts of which were open to the sky. "Do you see the destruction Hitler wreaked on Germany's treasures?"

"They shouldn't have stolen it in the first place," she said.

"Savka, I had no idea you shared my love of archaeology." Belyakov smiled broadly. He took out his pewter flask, slipped a small white pill into his mouth, and gulped it down without taking his eyes off her. "Did you know this gate was built to venerate Ishtar, the goddess of love and war?" He chuckled to himself. "One must appreciate a woman who forced gods and men to their knees." Belyakov stole another drink from his flask before returning it to his pocket. Then, hands folded behind his back, he stepped closer to examine a golden dragon set within the bright blue tiles, its long tongue lashing as it prowled the netherworld.

Savka was sick of his games. "Where is Ewa?" she demanded.

"Safe."

"What have you done with my friend?"

"If you wish to be a successful operative, you would do well to follow Ewa's example." Belyakov turned to face her, laughing at her obvious confusion. "You ignored the signs, my dear Savka. Did you not question why your *friend* took you in so readily?"

She blinked rapidly. He was trying to make her doubt Ewa, and she wasn't going to let it happen. "Why would I question a woman so welcoming and giving of herself? Ewa is a true loving soul, who would give me the shirt off her back."

Belyakov smiled. "And . . . *did* she?" he asked with a wink.

Stunned, Savka backed away from him but Yeleshev, who'd been leaning against the wall behind her, stepped out and pushed her forward. Her thoughts stuttered over Belyakov's sly suggestion. As she tried to convince herself that he knew nothing of the relationship between her and Ewa, moments with her friend replayed in her mind like one of the war-time romance films they often went to see at the playhouse in Kraków: In bed with Ewa, her lovely fingers tracing a pattern on her naked back, taking her, sobbing, into her arms while Savka wailed Taras's name into her shoulder. Ewa angry at the treatment of Jews on the day Savka had caught her getting dressed for her SS officer informant, yet warning her for trying to help them. Ewa handing Savka the exit visas, willing to leave her lovely flat and Poland forever. The film ended like so many of them did, with a close-up of the Hollywood starlet wearing a stylish new red hat, fingers trembling as she lighted a cigarette on the train. Savka's heart turned over and a hot, hard lump formed in her throat. "Ewa . . . just took my gun to keep Berlin police from arresting me at checkpoints."

"Dear Ewa," Belyakov said, his eyes dancing with amusement. "Protecting innocent women from harm."

Yes, Savka thought, with a low moan, *she protected me . . . didn't she?* "Ewa loves me," she murmured aloud, shivering as if she had a fever.

"Love?" he scoffed. "Ewa does not love."

"She does," Savka insisted. "She loves *me*. Ask her."

"I would if she wasn't leaving tomorrow for New York with her son Paweł and daughter Maja," he said with a sick smile.

The shock of betrayal rose slowly, forcing Savka to examine the truth in utter devastation. *Maja was alive?* With shame and humiliation, she thought of every secret she'd told her friend. How had she been so stupid, so trusting? And how could Ewa have lied so easily? Paweł had become another son to Savka, and Ewa loved Zoya to distraction. *It can't be true.* But she knew that it was.

"Ewa is one of your agents," she said, her voice wretchedly toneless.

"Not mine," Belyakov said conversationally. "A comrade turned her and two other Home Army operatives a few months before I turned you. You'd flown the coop and I'd written you off but imagine my delight to hear from my comrade that you had shown up at his agent's clinic in Kraków." He looked at her with hooded eyes, ignoring her tears. "It wasn't personal, Savka. Ewa kept you safe until I needed you. She did what she had to do to get her daughter back."

So Ewa had delivered her to Belyakov to save Maja. Savka knew she'd do the same to Ewa if it meant being reunited with Taras. Still, her hands formed into fists, tight against her sides. "You're a monster," she spat at the Soviet. "You used Maja the way you use my son."

Belyakov merely shrugged. "Let Ewa inspire you, Savka. Do a good job and it's possible to get your son back."

The scene in their flat seven months prior came hurtling back at Savka: Ewa shouting at the Soviet agent, shoving him to protect Zoya; his hand darting out to slap her. It had all been a charade, a show they'd staged to convince her to trust Ewa completely. She trembled, thinking back to how cooly her friend had seduced her. The sex had been casual, meaningless—simply what she did to ensnare her victims, male or female. And that damned new red hat—undoubtedly purchased with money Ewa had earned double-crossing Savka and Zoya and delivering them to the NKVD.

Belyakov was watching her with a sober expression. "You will never escape me. Show me Marko's letters from Rimini."

She opened her handbag and blindly handed them over. As the Russian scanned each one, she glanced up at a figure of a striding lion on the Ishtar Gate, its savage eyes wide and fangs bared in the pursuit of ancient prey. How she yearned to become that lion, leap upon the Soviet agent, bite into his bony neck and bleed him to the ground.

Belyakov swore and threw the letters. They fluttered around her like lost doves. "He has said nothing of MI-6. You must ask him direct questions."

It was Savka's turn to scoff at him. "He would suspect me."

The Russian practically pulsed with rage, his dark eyes resolute. "Do not waste my time," he shouted. "Ewa's forged exit visas got you here. Now you will go to Marko." He suddenly stepped back and clapped with mock joy. "What a reunion it will be!"

"Why did you bother with this deception?" she asked, startled at how easily his moods shifted. "You could have given me the visas instead of making Ewa forge them."

"Marko knows the Soviets would never issue you an exit visa. But if you tell him your good friend who'd once been in the Polish resistance helped you get papers, he will suspect nothing."

Savka still didn't understand. The Soviets had hunted Marko's Waffen-SS division since its inception in 1943 and had been one step behind them as the division marched across eastern Europe, fighting partisans. But that didn't explain the trouble Belyakov was taking with this case. "Why do you still want him so badly?"

His mouth twitched, as if he were suppressing a smile. "There was a camp muster list—a roll call. The British commander would not let me have it. But it was stolen by your husband before he left the POW camp. He somehow took the Rimini List from under Brigadier Block's nose," he added with reluctant admiration.

She stared numbly at him. "Why would Marko steal this list?"

Belyakov's eyes danced. "To safeguard his men. Think of what that list means. The names and places of birth of every man in the Fourteenth Waffen-SS Division. Over eight thousand Soviet citizens—traitors who must answer for their collaboration with Germany."

She allowed herself a merciless smile. It gave her joy that Marko had unwittingly made her Russian handler's job difficult. "And he's escaped your clutches yet again." But there was an aura of smug satisfaction about Belyakov—as though he'd expected Marko to steal this list— that unsettled her.

Belyakov's face was now an expressionless mask. "You will go to your husband in England. You will find the list."

"Marko has surely burned it by now," she said, staring him down.

"Your husband is an arrogant man. I wager he has kept it."

"He'll never just give me this list," she said, but the thought of spying on her husband, of living a lie of that magnitude made her break into a cold sweat.

"Did you suspect Ewa of being a spy?" Belyakov smiled when she shook her head. "You will do it seamlessly, as effortlessly as she did with you. You're Marko's wife. You have your methods of persuasion—pillow talk can be illuminating."

"I want news of my son."

Belyakov reached into the breast pocket of his coat and held out a photograph, which Savka took, breathless with fear, and expecting to see Taras standing in a Russian field, perhaps embracing a horse that loved him. A scream died in her throat at the sight of a now sixteen-year-old Taras emaciated and drawn, his head shaved and wearing rough, felted clothes, the barren, snow-covered Siberian taiga behind him. Her son was not looking at the camera. He seemed lost, staring out somewhere she could not see, the whites of his eyes stark against the smudges on his face.

Savka wanted to lunge at Belyakov. "He's in the Gulag?" she choked. "You said you would protect him. I thought—"

"I snapped this photograph myself," he said proudly, reaching for it. She held it tight against her heart and he grinned, his gold tooth gleaming, dropping his hand as though he realized it was better for her to keep the photo, if only to remind her what was at stake. "The gold mines are infamously torturous." He raised an eyebrow in affected concern. "Taras looks near to death, wouldn't you say?"

"You agreed to keep him safe . . . ," she trailed off, her voice hoarse with emotion.

"Your memory, Savka! I agreed that you'd see him again if you did what we ordered. Your son was charged with counterrevolutionary activities, which carries a twenty-five-year term. Once in Siberia, it's either the mining or the logging crews for political prisoners. Your husband writes of mobilizing bandits to find Taras. Impossible when he's in a gulag. But now you're in a position to help him."

Her Taras, a political prisoner? She'd heard stories of the many camps within the Gulag, of the mines—long workdays in minus fifty-degree weather. Savka was suddenly furious at Marko, who'd escaped to safety while his son was being worked to death in Siberia. And now she must keep that terrible fact from her husband. Her chest was weighted with so many secrets, she feared she could no longer carry them. "You cannot punish the son for his father's crimes," she said finally.

"You will go to your husband and bring us the list."

"No."

"Do you want Zoya to grow up in your dark shadow? Do you want her to grow up knowing her mother was a traitor?"

Savka ground her teeth to stop herself from shouting. "You will move Taras to safe work, out of the cold."

Belyakov blinked and nodded at Yeleshev, who strong-armed Savka back down the long hallways of the ruined museum. When they got to the car, she came to an abrupt stop. "My daughter," she said, throwing off his hand, "will be in the back with me."

The Russian reluctantly obliged her and opened the front passenger door.

Zoya leapt into Savka's arms. "Mama?" the little girl whispered in her ear. "I thought you were gone forever."

Savka clung to her daughter, devastated that she'd made her fear such a thing. "I'm here, my love," she said before steering Zoya into the backseat.

As Ilyin silently navigated the car through the ruined streets of Berlin, Savka contemplated her situation. She held tight to Zoya, who buried her face in her mother's dress collar. Only hours ago, she'd exulted in the certainty that she'd finally escaped Belyakov; now she felt his hands around her throat. Worse, she had learned that Taras was suffering in a gulag.

She thought of Ewa with Paweł and Maja, soon on their way to America, a place she'd always dreamed of going—to a clean, bright apartment supplied by Belyakov for a job well done. *Does she feel guilty for her betrayal?* What did Savka know for certain, except that she could trust no one? She hugged her daughter close, stifling a sob. Her beloved friend had delivered her like a hog to the butcher, and Savka would never forgive her.

But she was now bound for England, and soon she and Zoya would be reunited with Marko. For now, she was a bird set free from her cage—even if the master kept the door open in anticipation of her return—and she would spread her wings and fly. She would turn the tables on this ruthless Soviet and tell Marko everything.

21

JEANIE

Salt Spring Island
DECEMBER 9, 1972

WHAT'S SHE HIDING IN HERE? Vibrating with excitement and dread, I kneel in front of Pat's bedroom door, frantically jiggling a hairpin in her lock. I've seen this technique in a detective movie, but it's harder than it looks.

Ten minutes later, I'm sweating, ready to give up when there's a click and the lock gives, almost like magic. I open the door and stare wide-eyed at Pat's inner sanctum. It's immaculate, of course—the sheets snugged tight with hospital corners, the quilt on top smoothed of wrinkles. The trinkets on her dresser are neatly lined up, the books on her nightstand perfectly stacked. Every surface clear of dust.

Tiptoeing across the wood floor, I hover in the doorway of Pat's bathroom; the distinct funk of her Irish Spring soap makes me want to retch. Aunt Suze had the house built in the early 1950s and the entire bathroom is stuck in that decade—pink tile up the walls edged in black, with matching soap dishes above the sink. When I step onto the cold pink-and-black tiled floor and approach the mirrored medicine cabinet, I can't help but pause. It's one thing jimmying her lock, another to be snooping through her things.

There are no mirrors in my own room—to avoid unexpected glimpses of my naked, marred flesh. I glance up at Pat's before remembering not to. And gasp. Dark hair hangs listlessly around my face, not having been cut in at least a decade. It's almost to my waist. I'm only thirty-one and yet I look thin and drawn and *old*. My scars mark the places where my wedding dress ended and began. Nothing on my face or neck, my upper arms, my lower legs, but lurking just beneath the neckline of my sweat-shirt, there lies puckered and webbed skin worthy of a character out of Grimm's fairytales.

Drawing a deep, mutinous breath, I focus on the task ahead of me. Taking care not to leave smudges on the pristine mirror, I open the left cabinet first. Each shelf is crammed with Q-tips, Nivea, and Noxzema, along with some prescription cream with Pat's name on the bottle and the directions, "Apply as needed." *Ewww.* I open the right cabinet and allow myself a cry of triumph. I've found the mother lode. Standard pill bottles fill one shelf, another with hypodermic needles, the third with first aid supplies—gauze and butterfly bandages.

Getting down to business, I work my way through the medication bottles, carefully reading each label prescribed to me. Pain killers have a starring role, in pill and liquid form, followed by my sleep drug. I remember the names of these from when I was discharged from the hospital. There's a bottle on the top shelf with a strange name that I can't recall from that prescription list. I open it to find the mysterious orange pills and squint at the label.

Chlorpromazine.

Also on that shelf are several chlorpromazine ampules.

I remember that Pat owns an old pharmacology textbook from her nursing days, and I steal back into her bedroom. I have to find it. Pushing down my rising sense of dread, I riffle through her closet with deep disdain at the many new outfits I find, some still sporting price tags, then paw reluctantly through her unmentionables in a low chest of drawers, finally going to my knees and locating the textbook under her bed. It's well-thumbed, as if it might be Pat's bedtime reading. I flip to the index, dragging a shaking finger down to find the name of the medication. When I turn to the right page, I find the corner has been turned down to mark her place.

Chlorpromazine® brand of chlorpromazine antipsychotic • tranquilizer • antiemetic

Tranquilizer? I read the word again and again until it blurs in front of my eyes. An electric charge zings along my damaged nerve endings, forcing my hands into claws, and I drop the book. "You're a *nurse*," I repeat to the room, for it's my only reliable witness. "You aren't helping me; you're trying to *kill* me."

But why is she giving me a tranquilizer? What did she tell Dr. Reisman to make him prescribe this to me? I snatch up the book and frantically page back through the *Cs* to find my place.

. . . Schizophrenia

For the treatment of severe behavioral problems in children marked by combativeness or explosive hyper excitable behavior and poor frustration tolerance.

"Severe behavioral problems." I blink hard to bring the words into focus, scanning the side effects: *Sudden death from cardiac arrest, convulsive seizures.*

I sit on the floor and rub my face in disbelief. Can this be real? Can the woman I've trusted to dispense medications to ease my pain and suffering be drugging me senseless? Or, rather, drugging me into just enough of a stupor so I won't give her trouble yet can still finish my *commissions*. I haven't taken these pills for three days now, and I'm admittedly much less nauseous and dizzy. Why did Dr. Reisman prescribe it if I don't have *severe behavioral problems*? Because Pat has obviously shown him her dramatically bandaged arm, and told him about my outbursts, the small rebellious acts that make it possible to survive the stress of living under her thumb. Are those indications of mental illness?

I jump at an ominous rustling noise, quickly realizing that Pat has left her window open a crack. It's only her hideously striped curtains drifting back and forth, like some kind of otherworldly creature.

I close the book and slide it back under the bed, careful to leave it exactly as I found it. I'm about to get up off my knees when my eyes fall on Pat's night table. Thinking of the numerous times she's invaded my privacy, I crawl over and ease the drawer open. Inside are a few trashy novels—*really Pat?*—and some migraine medication. I rummage beneath the bodice rippers and touch something rubbery and nobbled. My fingers close around a handle. I slowly draw it out.

Nothing prepares me for the sight of an old revolver with a long, sinister-looking barrel. I jump to my feet and drop it on the bed, staring in revulsion and horror at the words *Webley Mark IV* embossed just above the trigger. And the intials *M.I.* scratched beside it. A gun. In *my* house. In a trance, I back away until I feel the wall behind me. *What do I do now?* Spin the round thingamajig to check if it's loaded? I stare down at the menacing weapon. I can't bear to touch it. Why does Pat own a gun?

I creep back into her bathroom, hating the dumb, obedient puppy I've become, emptying the contents of every white medication cup she cobbles together into my mouth without question. Before I can stop myself, I open the chlorpromazine bottle with a flick of my thumb and hold it over the toilet, prepared to dump every one of the offending orange tablets. But then I think better of it and snap the lid shut with a frustrated shout. If I flush the pills, Pat will know I've seen them. She'll know I've been in her room, a place I'm *not* supposed to ever be. And who knows what she'd do then to subdue me. I glance back at the gun on the bed. Would she dare use it to wound herself, then blame it on my supposed psychoses?

Reluctantly, I replace the pill bottle and turn to leave. Outside, the sun has slipped behind a bank of clouds and by a trick of the fading light, a shadow appears in the doorway. Like a shard of glass, the nightmare image I suffered four days ago on the headland slices through me again. The phantasm shimmers and looms closer, as if stepping into the room. I'm immobilized by dread. Now I can see his face, eyes hidden under the brim of a fedora hat. It's a memory, I'm sure of it; something locked deep in my mind, of a man who once stood in the doorway of my hospital room. *But who is he?* Then I remember Danek Rys's handsome scarred face, and the question he asked me:

Did you see a man, the night Marko Kovacs disappeared? Maybe you hear something in the hallway?

I need to tell Dan that I *did* see someone—and perhaps it was Marko Kovacs. But why would a strange man visit me at night?

I notice a folded piece of paper on the floor. It must've slipped out of the drawer when I was pawing through Pat's stuff. I pick it up, unfolding the page carefully. It's a letter, with so many crossed out words, it more closely resembles a redacted government document. Reading other people's mail is wrong on so many levels, but Pat is exempt from civil niceties. Taking the letter to the window, and the light of the fading sun, I raise it to my nose and begin reading.

I'm writing this into a void, Kay. Where the heck are you, anyway? The last letter I wrote was returned by the camp hospital marked, No longer at this address. *Don't tell me . . . no, I can't imagine any other reason why you might leave that damn place you like so much.*

Remember I wrote you about the last will and testament Jeanie secretly got Aunt Suze's lawyer to draw up? The will I found out about quite by chance when I called him about increasing my monthly salary. During one of my trips to Vancouver, he came out here as a favor to Jeanie, because she's such a damn recluse. How kind of him. Don't worry, he has no idea. Still, you don't know what I've had to do to keep myself from jumping off the headland and into the sea. The only thing stopping me is the thought of her celebrating that, maybe even dancing over my bloated, drowned corpse.

"You're feeding me antipsychotics," I say, a corrosive anger eating at my heart. "And locking me in at night for having the nerve to draw up a last will and testament?" I blink a few times and make a mental note to find a new lawyer, one who won't whisper in Pat's ear, then I try to focus on her next words:

Things have become dire. She's trying to kill me, you know. I have to hide everything sharp. Anywho, back to the blasted will. The nerve of her thinking she could leave Gladsheim to the Salt Spring Historical Society! Now do you see why I can't trust her?

How I wish there was a way we could talk on the telephone. Where did you go? You can't hide, you know.

If only there hadn't been that nasty business at the hospital. Imagine how different things would be if you had moved here to help me take care of an increasingly volatile and dangerous patient instead of escaping to the Congo? And it was an escape, you can't deny it any longer. I know very well what happened that night . . .

I'm about to turn the page and read what's on the back when I hear a car roll into the driveway. A door opens then slams shut, and my heart skips a beat. Pat can't be home; she just left this morning. From the window, I watch a taxicab leave the same way it arrived. There's a knock on the front door and I almost climb the curtains. Since the beginning of the Vietnam war, draft evaders have been crossing the Canadian border and coming to the island to disappear. Perhaps it's one of them, or yet another journalist, arriving—as they sometimes do—on the last ferry, shamelessly canvassing people in Fulford Harbour for my address. These visitors have tapered off of late, but they still occasionally turn up. Pat always sends them on their way with a few choice words while I hide in my studio.

The front door handle rattles and I hear it whine on its hinges. The nerve! Of course I didn't lock it. *Dammit Jeanie, someone's in the house.* I know for certain it's not Pat because she always slams the door and clomps down the hallway like an ogre. My heart racing, I look at the gun, innocently lying on the bed. If only I had the courage to pick it up. The intruder moves to the kitchen, and Tuna growls from his bed near the back door. Fearing this interloper might hurt my precious dog I step toward the bedroom door, and the wooden floorboards creak loudly.

Whoever is downstairs stops and I imagine a thief, thinking no one is home, suddenly realizing that someone *is*. I stand frozen in Pat's doorway, tension clawing at my chest, as the intruder leaves the kitchen and walks slowly to the foot of the stairs. Then they begin to climb.

22

MARKO

Moorby, Lincolnshire, England
SEPTEMBER 1947

OUTSIDE THE CAMP MESS hall in Moorby Village, Marko Ivanets eyed the long, distant plume of dust from the British Army Jeep that was carrying his wife and daughter toward him at last. Tyrsa Dorochkin, a nurse who'd been with the Fourteenth Division since its inception, was loitering nearby, her eyes sparking with indignation and understanding that her nights sharing a bunk with the division's Waffen-Sturmbannführer were over.

Marko turned away and twisted his hat in his hands. He was nervous, but what man wouldn't be after not seeing his wife for four and a half years and meeting their daughter—born in his absence—for the first time? Especially a wife who had lost their only son. After arriving at the Rimini prisoner of war camp, he'd written letter after letter to Deremnytsia, desperate for some word from his family. When the letters were all returned, he'd assumed that Savka had disobeyed his order to leave with their son and she had died when the Red Army swung through the village, Taras taken as cannon fodder, perishing somewhere on the front.

The Jeep turned down the road between the village and the resettlement camp, passing hectares of potato fields the Ukrainians worked for the English. Besides the one thousand Ukrainians from the Fourteenth

Division in the camp—and the other seven thousand who'd been sent to different villages in England and Scotland—most of the inhabitants of Moorby were spread across farms that still struggled to recover from reduced manpower during the war.

How surprised he'd been to get Savka's first letter at Rimini in February of '47, handed to him by a British guard while his unit was on the beach, taking their daily exercise. He'd stared blankly at the unfamiliar return address in Kraków, astonished to find Savka's distinctive handwriting, and ecstatic that his wife had somehow survived the war, although she'd managed to get herself shot by the NKVD in the forest and lose Taras. His son haunted his every thought when he wasn't seething with rage and devastation. How could Savka have let this happen? Could he ever forgive her? When MI-6 had recruited Marko to contact insurgents in Ukraine, he'd sent a coded message to Kuzak, only to discover that his bunker had been wiped out by the NKVD. Now Taras was lost to him, perhaps forever.

Marko hadn't wanted to think of the NKVD. But the visit last summer at Rimini from the short, disturbing Soviet agent still haunted him. Marko remembered all too well the oily presence of the man, uttering his empty threats.

Your British commandant will not let me have the camp roster list of your men. But it will soon come into my possession. Each one of you will be hunted down and assassinated.

Not on Marko's watch. The NKVD agent had thrown down the gauntlet and Marko could not resist taking it up. Unable to trust the British to protect a list with the names and birthplaces of eight thousand Ukrainian men who'd fought with the SS, he'd stolen the Rimini List, fully intending to burn it immediately. Yet each time he'd held it over the flames, he saw the NKVD agent's shrewd, dark eyes. Marko still had the list in a safe place, but he thought of it constantly, perhaps a little obsessed with it himself, for it remained a distinct *fuck you* to the little man who wanted it so badly.

The approaching roar of the Jeep roused him from these dark thoughts. It finally pulled up in a cloud of dust—they'd not had rain for weeks—in front of the canteen, and Marko broke out in a cold sweat. *Do not berate your wife,* he reminded himself. *She has suffered.* He took a step forward and hesitated, waiting for the back door to open. Suddenly, there was Savka, somehow more beautiful than he remembered. He thought her eyes looked sad, clearly burdened with guilt at losing Taras, but they lit up the moment she saw him.

When she ran to him, he held her close, his cheek against the top of her head and her surprisingly short hair. "Where is Zoya?" he asked, looking behind her at the Jeep still parked outside Moorby Hall.

Savka laughed. "The driver offered to make her a matchstick doll—she left hers on the train. But she's excited to finally meet her father."

Another Jeep had arrived and parked beside the one that had brought Savka and Zoya—one driver shouting to the other. Marko flinched and closed his eyes. The memory of the big 150 mm howitzer thundering over his head, leveling huts, partisans scattering . . .

Säubert das Dorf!

Clean the village. The German words shouted by Nazi officers would haunt him to the end of his life, images flying at him, unbidden; a repetitive frame, or photograph, forever imprinted on his brain.

Savka was telling him of the journey from Poland, how she and Zoya endured the long, dusty line of trains across western Europe, and a boat over the channel to Dover, then London, and another train for Lincolnshire, where the army Jeep had been waiting for them. "How stunned I was to see these lush green fields," she gushed, "and quaint cottages. We're blessed to leave the USSR."

Savka's voice seemed too shrill, her smile forced, and he thought back to her letters, her admission that she'd run afoul of the NKVD, and had come to in Kuzak's bunker, screaming for Taras. He studied her face, still captivated by the seductive allure that he'd fallen for in Lviv so long ago. Had she lied? Impossible. She'd never lied to him in sixteen years of marriage. His wife was timid and could not possibly have been turned by the Soviets. And yet . . . "I wonder how you so easily came to England," he said, carefully observing her reaction. "Many of my men have tried to get their families out of Ukraine, but are blocked by the Soviets, refusing to issue exit visas."

"You forget I was in Kraków," she replied, her eyes flashing. "A friend who worked in the Polish resistance forged an exit visa for me."

He wavered, eager to press her further, but instead, he forced a grin. "Let us not argue at our reunion," he said, rubbing his hands together in anticipation. "Where is my daughter?"

The Jeep's driver had come around to open the back door, and a pair of small black boots dangled briefly before the driver lifted her out. His daughter inched forward shyly, clutching a crude matchstick doll.

"Zoya . . ." Marko trailed off, staring at the child with incomprehension. He'd expected a little girl with blonde hair and blue eyes, who looked like Taras—who looked like *him*—but the child Savka was passing off as his own stared up at him, her hair dark and curly, eyes almost black. "This is not my daughter," he choked, backing away.

Savka blanched, her lower lip quivering. "Surely she takes after one of your ancestors—"

"Get her away from me," he shouted and stormed off toward the canteen, leaving his wife and whoever's bastard had come along with her.

Re: File #924073—Family Tytovsky

Dear Mrs. Ivanets:

We apologize for the delay in contacting you. You might appreciate that we have been backlogged with requests.

In your letter, you mentioned that your family could have been forced out of Ukraine by the Red Army as it pushed the Germans west in retreat. We have compiled lists of displaced refugees who were relocated in forced labor camps, persecuted or imprisoned in different locations during and after the war.

There was no mention of your mother, Mrs. Tytovsky, or your sister (or her daughter) in any of these camps. Your father and brother were listed in a German forced labor camp, but there was no record of them among the Allied Expeditionary Forces Displaced Person Registration cards. Not one labor passport, exit visa, declaration on a transport list, or record of death.

Sincerely,
Desmond Abrams
The Red Cross

23

SAVKA

Moorby, Lincolnshire, England
SEPTEMBER 1948

FROM A CORNER OF THE Moorby village hall, her eyes brimming with tears, Savka watched Zoya skip and hop across the makeshift stage with a group of other four-year-olds. One hand in the pocket of her coat, Savka stroked her thumb across the letter from the Red Cross as if it were a genie in a lamp that might grant her three wishes. The first wish? To be reunited with her son, who she knew would never appear in this room, this country, this life she now led so far from home. The second, to find her family, who'd seemingly vanished without a trace. Her third wish? That Marko might love Zoya. A formidable task, even for a magical genie. At least she had her husband and daughter, but without Taras and her family, it felt as if an essential part of her had died.

The children's teacher was leading them in a song for the *Kolomyika,* an ancient Ukrainian folk dance, and Savka smiled through her tears. She'd never seen Zoya so excited and happy. How could Marko continue to ignore her, when she was learning the language and dances of her people? Moorby's annual Harvest Supper was approaching, and the Ukrainians had planned a pageant, keen to convince their hosts that they still celebrated their culture and traditions, despite what the war had done to them.

The children sang as they joined hands, rollicking one way and then the other with a great deal of giggling and mishaps. The teacher coaxed a young boy into the center of the circle to attempt some squats and high kicks, which made the other three mothers who were watching laugh. Savka beamed at Zoya, who looked decidedly English in her hand-me-down skirt and blue cardigan, white socks, and a pair of worn brown Mary Jane shoes.

Shivering, Savka pulled her coat close around her to keep out the cold. She and Zoya had been here for almost a year, but she was still not used to the rain and damp. At least Belyakov and his men could not follow her to England. Three months ago, the USSR had blocked Allied access to Berlin, and tensions were high between Russia and the West. She picked up her market basket and moved closer to the stage where the Ukrainian mothers were standing. She'd just waited in line with them for their weekly rations. Everything from clothing to tea, meats, sweets, and soap were doled out with precision and care, the coupons in their ration books stamped to cancel their allotments.

Surely Marko didn't wish to remain in this godforsaken country. The food was awful, and although Savka had learned a decent amount of English, she still couldn't understand a word the locals said. Yet away from the dark eye of Belyakov, she'd let her guard down. It was all too easy to lapse into her native language rather than speak English, with so many men here from Marko's battalion and a few of their families who'd managed to escape eastern Europe during the war, along with several nurses and a priest, who'd also been with the division.

The mothers were twittering, sending coy glances at the door to the hall. Savka turned her head to see what they were so excited about. A handsome man was leaning against the wall near the entrance, smoking, a tweed cap set like a tea cozy over his dark, unruly hair.

Savka felt a scream in her mouth, her muscles twitching in a desperate need to run, and an unbidden image of Ewa swooning on the train to Berlin.

Don't tell me you wouldn't kiss him, given the chance.

It was Ilyin. Somehow, Belyakov had managed to get one of his spies into England to watch her watch Marko.

Savka held her breath and closed her eyes, striving to remain calm. She had to relax, pretend that she didn't recognize him. Yet, she could feel Ilyin's eyes on her. The scar on her chest burned with memory and other images of that day she was shot—Russian leers, guns, threats, and Taras's pale, frightened face as they stole him away. When she opened her eyes, Ilyin was still there, inclining his head ever so slightly as he turned to leave.

Intent on confronting the man who had shot her, Savka followed Ilyin outside. It was dusk, the rain had stopped, and the sky was rinsed free of cloud. On the air was a smell of meat cooking in broth from the canteen, and the unnerving sight of the Russian waiting for her, the end of his cigarette glowing like an otherworldly creature.

Savka glanced around to make sure no one had seen her slip between the community hall and a series of tents and prefab huts the British had erected to house the Ukrainian men from the Waffen-SS division. In a flash, she crossed the space between them and planted two hands on Ilyin's chest, giving him a shove that made him stumble backward. "Where did *you* come from?" She glared at him, but he simply brushed off his oilskin coat with a wry smile. "If Marko, or any other Ukrainian man sees you here—"

Ilyin frowned and gestured at his get up. "I look Russian with this?" She had to admit that he did look remarkably like a British farmer, completing his disguise with corduroy trousers and muddied rubber boots. "Besides," he added, speaking English with a surprisingly genuine accent, "your men are all *down the pub.*"

Savka exhaled with annoyance. "Why are you bothering me? I've looked everywhere for the Rimini list. Marko doesn't have it."

He turned his head at a sound from behind one of the huts, and she grudgingly admired his profile—his lips full and sensual as a woman's—

in the dying light. It wasn't easy to admit with a hot course of anger vibrating every cell in her body, but Ilyin was a good-looking man.

Confident they'd not been heard, he turned back to her. "You have a new assignment," he said, continuing in English. "We've received confirmation that Marko has been recruited by MI-6. He leaves tomorrow, yes?"

"He . . . he told me he's going to London," Savka sputtered, confused. "To petition authorities for English language lessons for everyone in camp—"

"Lies. MI-6 is sending him to Ukraine."

Savka struggled to understand. "But why would he go back into enemy territory, where the NKVD want to kill him?"

"That is what you will find out," Ilyin said, creeping closer to her. "I want to know how many of his old and trusted soldiers are going with him. And what kind of arms MI-6 is supplying to the underground."

She could smell cheap British ale and the bangers and mash Ilyin had eaten for lunch. "How would they get back to Ukraine?" she asked, bewildered.

"A transport plane will parachute them into Czechoslovakia— they'll cross the border into Ukraine at night. We need confirmation of a landing site."

"My husband will not tell these things to me," Savka said, but couldn't help picturing Belyakov when Marko's parachute landed, waiting to arrest him. She choked back panic. "And I will *not* send him into a Soviet trap."

Ilyin's hand shot out, lightning quick, clutching her forearm. "Whose life do you value more? Your husband's or your son's?"

Savka stood perfectly still. It was an impossible choice. *I can't make it,* she thought, then paused. *Or can I?* It was Marko who'd sent her and Taras into that forest. Since they'd been reunited, she'd wrestled daily with the feeling that all of this was her husband's fault. Although he'd promised to get exit visas for Mama, Lilia, and Sofiy, those had never materialized. Did she still love her husband enough to save him from the Soviets? Or could she send him to his death in the hopes of getting Taras back?

She swallowed a sob. It seemed incredible that she hadn't told Marko the truth by now, that she'd been turned into a Soviet spy, with their son Taras dangled as bait. But her husband was a different man after receiving a wound near the end of the war, when a bomb went off as his unit crossed a bridge in Slovenia, the shrapnel missing his right eye by inches. He suffered now with debilitating headaches and his temper was terrifyingly short, usually directed at Zoya, who'd done nothing to deserve such treatment. This Marko would not tolerate a wife who'd agreed to spy on him. He would send her and Zoya away immediately—and then how would she survive, a woman with a daughter, stranded in England?

Now, Ilyin's fingers on her arm reminded her too much of her impossible predicament. "I will do nothing until I know Taras is safe." Savka stared him down in the fading light. "Marko already doubts me. If I ask him these questions, he'll know I'm a spy."

"Find a way to get it out of him in the bedroom—when his defenses are down." Ilyin raised an eyebrow and flashed her a vulgar grin. She flinched when he lifted his hand to touch her shoulder-length hair. "I like this style on you." His insolent gaze traveled over her body, that disturbing half smile still playing on his lips. Then, hands in his pockets, he slouched away and disappeared like the shadow he was.

A WEEK LATER, SAVKA found herself striking a provocative pose in the living room of their house in Moorby, wearing the rose-colored silk slip Marko had gifted her the night he came to visit in Dermenytsia. Shortly after she and Zoya had shown up, their family had been allocated a two-room prefab home near the edge of town—a special privilege, she speculated, that he was afforded by MI-6.

That afternoon, while she'd been kneeling in a field with the other Ukrainian women, harvesting potatoes, she spotted Ilyin beckoning to her from behind a shed. She made her way down the rows toward him, and he passed her a note from Belyakov.

Your son has been taken off the mining crew, the note read. *He works in the camp infirmary and receives extra food.*

When Savka cried out and clutched it to her chest, Ilyin glanced around to ensure none of the women in the field could overhear and told her that Marko would return that night.

Although she was relieved that Taras now worked in a safe, warm place instead of the mines, and was getting extra rations, she couldn't hide her frustration. "I told you Marko wouldn't admit he was going anywhere but London."

Ilyin made a gesture of dismissal. "You must search his pockets for valuable intelligence he might have brought back from Ukraine."

Terror and anger roared in her ears. "You expect me to rummage through his coat?" she almost shouted.

To subdue her, Ilyin pushed her against the shed wall. "He'll be tired from a long flight back to London and then a train to Moorby."

"I can't do it."

Ilyin, standing too close, looked into her eyes. "You're expected to do it. Or . . ."

Savka turned her head at the implied threat. *Do it—or Taras will be sent back to the mines.*

Now, hours later, she stood like a common whore in the cramped English house, waiting for her husband to come through that door. She'd arranged for Zoya to spend the night with one of her friends, so that she and Marko could be alone. But it was too quiet. She hoped that seduction might work on her husband when vague questions had not. The thought of what she must do—draw Marko into the bedroom, and afterwards, while he lay in post-coital oblivion, steal into their cramped living room to search his coat—left her mouth dry with fear. She was no better than Ewa with her SS officer in Kraków, using sex to get information. Savka pushed the thought away. She would never be like Ewa.

She didn't have long to wait, for the door opened abruptly and Marko came in, looking tired, his face bloated with drink.

"What is this?" He demanded, taking in the silk slip.

Savka closed the door and threw her arms around his neck. Snaking a bare thigh up the side of his leg, she felt the bulk of something in his left coat pocket. "I missed you."

"I have just come back . . ."

"Yes?" she breathed, waiting for him to admit he'd just returned from Ukraine. But Marko was more interested in what she was wearing, leaning in to sloppily kiss her neck.

"Come," she murmured in his ear. "Make me pregnant again." The word *pregnant* gave her the chills. She'd been with child a few months ago and was allowed extra rations of milk and cod liver oil, but she and Marko had suffered another heartbreak when she'd lost the baby. He desperately wanted another child to make up for his groundless suspicion, she knew, that another man had fathered his daughter. Marko hadn't accused her outright, but his disregard for Zoya was shameful. Savka wanted to scream at him, remind him that she'd never been with another man—Zoya was his. But he refused to accept their daughter.

She kissed him and Marko responded swiftly, violently, all but devouring her naked breasts, hardly pausing when she stripped off his coat and threw it on a chair. Soon he led her into their bedroom, and she lay on her back in the small bed, staring, eyes wide at the ceiling, dreading what she must do next.

Ten minutes later, with Marko asleep, Savka drew back the covers and tiptoed naked into the living room, heading straight for his coat. She knelt on the nubbly rag rug, searching his left coat pocket. Instead of a document, her shaking fingers closed around the unmistakable handle of a revolver. Slowly she drew it out. Not the German Luger she'd seen in Deremnytsia, but what looked like an English gun, a Webley Mark IV, its manual safety lever in the off position. Marko had carved *M.I.* into the stock and Savka thought of the Luger he'd had in Ukraine, how he'd scratched over a dead man's initials. Did her husband covet his firearms so much, he had to personalize every gun he owned? Ilyin was right. It was obvious that Marko had been recruited by MI-6 and been given this gun on assignment for them in Ukraine. Another memory intruded, of Ewa taking the pistol Kuzak had given her to shoot her Russian handler. *No,* she thought, *banish it.*

She still had the gun in her hand as she fumbled his coat open to search the inside breast pockets. Something was there, sewn into the lining . . .

"What are you doing?"

She yelped in surprise as Marko appeared in the doorway of the bedroom in his underwear, rubbing his eyes.

Her pulse jumping, she lifted the gun. "You think I didn't feel this in your pocket?" she said, finding her voice. "Why have you brought a loaded weapon into the house where there's a young child? It's too dangerous."

Marko snatched up the revolver and opened it, removing three remaining bullets from the cylinder. "Now it is unloaded." He regarded her for a moment, hopefully ignorant of the many secrets she was keeping from him, then carefully hung his coat on a hook and lowered the kitchen table from the wall—the room was too small to have it down at any time other than at meals—and pulled up one of the chairs.

The knife wound Marko had received in Ternopil was now a jagged scar across his cheek, which somehow made him look more handsome—not to mention deadlier. The scar would turn a frightening white when he was angry, which it did now. Savka watched as he field stripped the gun with well-rehearsed movements. Her eyes went to his coat hanging on its hook. She'd felt the outline of a document in his pocket. If Marko hadn't caught her, she'd have found what the NKVD wanted, some kind of intelligence or information—maybe even the Rimini List—and secured Taras's release. But she'd missed her chance.

She glanced at her husband and tried to remind herself of his sacrifice. The fight for Ukraine's independence had taken him from the underground to the SS, then to a prisoner of war camp, where he'd stolen the only list in existence of those Ukrainian men now being protected by the British. He had never turned from the ongoing struggle. *Savka* was the one expected to betray Ukraine.

You must ask him direct questions, Belyakov had said in the ruins of the Pergamon museum.

"There's talk . . ." she began, her voice calm, even as her heart pounded in her ears. "That some men have been parachuted back to Ukraine."

Marko's head snapped up. "Who told you that?"

His expression was shrouded, and she was unable to read it. "I heard women talking, in the fields."

"Back to Ukraine?" he scoffed. "That would be madness." He massaged his temples, a tell-tale gesture she'd become familiar with over the past year. Another headache.

"You would be proud of your daughter," she said, changing the subject. "She's learning the *Kolomyika*."

Something moved like a shadow deep within Marko's blue eyes, and his brows knit together with a look of disdain. "Get your things together. We're leaving tomorrow."

"Where?" Savka whispered. Ukraine was out of the question of course, but she hoped for somewhere in eastern Europe. "Yugoslavia?" she asked. "Or Hungary?" It would mean struggling with another language, but at least she would be closer to finding Lilia and Mama.

"Have you learned nothing?" he said, lighting a cigarette. "All of eastern Europe is behind the Iron Curtain. We're going to Canada."

Savka hardly listened as Marko outlined plans to move them to a country even further from Ukraine, and from Taras. She allowed herself one bright spot of hope: her son was safe, working in a Gulag infirmary. Canada was not a dictatorship; it was not war-torn Europe. Marko would no longer take orders from MI-6 and with the USSR's growing dominance in eastern Europe, cold war animosities between the Soviets and the West were escalating. Surely Canada, a dedicated ally to Britain and the United States, had strict emigration policies and would be alert to Soviet spies trying to cross its borders. Belyakov and his men could not follow her there. Someone in Canada would help her find Taras, get him out of the Gulag, and back into his mother's arms.

24

JEANIE

Salt Spring Island
DECEMBER 9, 1972

THE STAIRS SQUEAK AS the intruder prowls upward, so close now, I can hear his breathing. I back away, almost tripping over Pat's bed, trying to keep myself from screaming.

A face comes into view. I brace myself to scream at the sight of a stranger, but it's someone entirely unexpected, someone I know so well. Someone I love.

Kay.

I utter a cry of delight and rush at her, pulling her close, then hold her at arm's length, hardly able to believe she's actually here. When I last saw Kay, back in 1959, she wore her mouse brown hair in the same shoulder length style but now it's long and straight, parted in the middle and combed Madonna flat over her ears, then gathered into a no-nonsense bun at the nape of her neck. An enormous pair of glasses amplify her kind brown eyes.

"Pat's in Vancouver," I say, squeezing her in another hug. "She'll be back in a few days. I'm *so* happy to see you."

Kay pulls away and studies me. "What are you doing in her room?"

I watch, heart in my throat, as she picks up the gun from the bed and cracks it open. I didn't know she knew how to handle weapons. To my horror, there are bullets in the chamber. "It's *loaded?*" I gasp. "Why would Pat keep a loaded gun in the house?"

"To protect you, of course." Kay rubs her thumb contemplatively over the initials cut into the stock. "Nice Webley IV. Where did you find it?"

I point to Pat's bedside table and Kay opens the drawer to sling it back beside the ammunition. When she closes the drawer, it seems to throb with danger.

"Don't you think you should unload it?" I ask, gnawing at my cuticles.

"You never know when you might need a gun," she says, with a smile. "Especially out here—no one around."

I frown, thinking of the newspaper articles I've read about brutal unrest in the Congo, but I never stopped to consider that Kay may have experienced violence. For all I know, she may have had to use a gun there. Then I remember that Pat's letter to Kay is still in my hand. I try to slip it quietly into my pocket, so I can read the rest of it later, but I'm not fast enough.

"What's that?" She takes the letter and scans it briefly, an amused expression on her face. "Pat always did like talking to herself," she says, before folding the paper and throwing it beside the gun in the drawer. She slams it closed then holds a finger to her lips. "We don't want her to know we've been in here, do we?"

I drag her into Pat's bathroom and show her what I found. "Kay, someone who's giving me antipsychotics without my knowledge would *not* keep a loaded gun for my protection." I search her face. "Right?"

"Chlorpromazine," she mutters, reading the label on the bottle. "I'm not familiar with this medication."

I'm damn paranoid by now, my trust so thoroughly eroded, I can't resist adding, "Please don't tell Pat—"

Kay returns the bottle to the cabinet and catches my hands. "I'm the last person to tell Pat anything." She was never fond of my zookeeper, either. "Why do you think I stayed away so long?"

IT'S CLOUDING OVER BY the time we're lounging in the living room drinking red wine that Kay has brought, which is a real treat. Since my disastrous art show in Vancouver six years ago, Pat hasn't let me touch a drop. Kay sits in one of the yellow-patterned wing chairs flanking the couch, where I'm curled up, my scarred legs tucked under me. During the day, ethereal ocean light suffuses this space; at night, a floor lamp with a fringed scarf draped over the shade emits a moody vibe that never fails to delight me. It's a room built for parties, for conversation. In Aunt Suze's day, beatniks sat around playing bongos and smoking grass on the colorful carpets and floor pillows she'd brought back from Istanbul.

While we work our way through the bottle, I get a little tipsy and pester Kay with too many questions. "What was your life like in the Congo? Twelve years. It's such a long time." She answers with hesitation, but I slowly get a picture of her early days in a jungle medical clinic and her relief when a Canadian medical team arrived to build a field hospital. How Kay became the head nurse there.

The lines in Pat's letter float at me in fragments. *I can't imagine any other reason why you might leave that damn place you liked so much . . .* "Why did you leave?" I ask Kay.

A shadow passes over her face. "I was frustrated at the political situation, the warring gangs, and . . . troubles getting medical supplies." She looks away, toying with a loose thread on her sweater.

I laugh nervously. The Kay I knew years ago was forthright and honest; this Kay is cryptic and a little cagey. "You haven't accepted another job?"

The shadow vanishes as quickly as it appeared, and she looks at me brightly, as if banishing unpleasant memories. "I'm afraid I don't know where I'm going next, darling."

I'd explained the Pat situation in my last letter, but Kay obviously wants to hear it in person. "Kay, you know how impossible Pat is. Come live here."

Kay stands and takes her glass to the bank of windows facing the sea. Aunt Suze designed the space so you can come through from the kitchen and feel as if you're on the deck of a ship. Outside, the sun is now a blurred facsimile of itself, shrouded with fog and hanging low in the sky. The days are getting shorter; it's almost four o'clock and within an hour it will be dark. "Living on a small island in the Strait of Georgia," she muses, gazing out at the ocean. "Sounds bloody perfect to me."

"Our lives here must seem small after all the good you've done—saving the world."

To my surprise, Kay seems annoyed. "I went to save the children, but they couldn't be helped . . . not in the end." She turns from the window and smiles at me—the dearly loved closed-mouth smile that hides her crooked teeth. "Let's talk about sunnier things, Jeanie, shall we?"

I really want to know more about what wasn't so sunny about her time in Africa but am reluctant to press her. "Come live with me," I repeat.

Kay wanders the room, pausing to scrutinize the bookcases. "Pat got here first. I won't depose her." She takes one volume from the shelf and cracks it open, and suddenly there's a delicious smell of old books in the air mingling with the dreadful undercurrent of spent ashes in the wood stove, and fumes emanating from a half-finished glass of Irish whiskey that Pat left after one of her benders, on a drink trolley in the corner.

"You don't know what she did." I take a deep breath. "Would you be surprised to learn I'm supposedly a pretty good landscape painter? That my commissions are in demand?" I lean forward, elbows on my knees and look up at Kay. "I really need you—an actual sane person who isn't going to sell my paintings behind my back and pocket the proceeds."

Kay shakes her head and tsks as I tell my little story, but she seems too distracted by a pair of antique Buddha heads on the mantel. "Were these your Aunt Suze's? I liked her—a proper character." She turns to look at me. "I learned years ago to never be surprised at anything Pat does."

"Then be my caregiver," I say, swinging my stocking feet onto the massive black lacquer chinoiserie coffee table. "Save me from the beast."

She finishes off her wine in two practiced gulps. "I despise Pat, too. But I couldn't do that to her."

I groan in frustration. "But *I* could. She hates me. It's a strange thing to be despised so vehemently by someone you're forced to live with."

Kay laughs. "Sounds like most marriages."

"If it is, I want a divorce."

"Poor love," Kay says, picking up the bottle of wine off the coffee table. "Did Pat ever tell you about her childhood?"

"Thankfully, no." I watch her pour herself another glass. "We don't share meaningful moments."

"Her father liked his whiskey. Pat answered to him *and* his drinking, answered to her mother, too . . ." Kay trails off almost reluctantly and gulps at her wine. "Everyone has their secret pasts," she adds in a moment. "Did you know Pat ran away from home when she was only fifteen?"

The idea of Pat on her own at such a young age makes me feel a little more sympathetic toward her, but I usher the feeling aside. I won't let anyone, least of all myself, forget what she's doing to me. I tell Kay about Danek Rys's visit—omitting, of course, the embarrassing bit about my staged death-scene art installation. "Pat told him she'd call the police if he came back—imagine calling the police on a journalist." My eyes fill with tears, and I swipe them away. "She told him about my accident, Kay . . . she mentioned the baby."

Kay frowns. "The bloody cheek. It must have felt like a betrayal."

Three months after I awoke from the coma, doped up with enough morphine to stun an ox, Aunt Suze was tasked with the unenviable job of telling me what had happened the night of the accident; a night built on a series of beautiful disasters—a teen pregnancy, and a boy two years older than me, coerced by his parents to do the right thing. Apparently, the wedding ceremony at the church was perfect, no signs of the tragedy to come only hours later. *How young you were,* Aunt Suze had whispered as I hung upside down in the Stryker frame, my tears puddling on the floor. *And how horribly mismatched you were, too, but willing to make a go of it, for the baby's sake. Michael made a mistake. But you survived, dear heart. If only your new mother-in-law had not been a religious freak with an unnatural love of candles,* she added, trying to make sense of life and its series of *what ifs.*

What ifs worked both ways. What if my wedding dress had been long-sleeved, like many in the late fifties? What if I hadn't removed my veil before we cut the blasted cake? Perhaps some part of me can still smell the singed material of Michael's suit sleeve as it caught fire on one of the candles, can still hear my own screams as I hit at the flames, the tulle of my dress acting as kindling. What I do remember is the unbearable agony as fire burned through French lace, skin, and muscle. Smells fused with sound, fused with images, in a cacophony of tortuous, ruinous, entangled memories.

It was Aunt Suze who told me that Mother had sold the wedding photos to the *Vancouver Tribune.* One photo made the front page—a pretty girl, dark hair pulled tight in an Audrey Hepburn chignon, the full skirt of her dress successfully hiding her four-month pregnancy. Me, as I once was. All directly beneath the headline:

Fire Bride Not Expected to Live.

Kay is studying me, and I let my eyes meet hers. How wonderful it is to gaze upon a sympathetic face. She sits down beside me and takes my hand, the other still holding her wine glass. "You were so brave, Jeanie. Six months on that Stryker frame. I don't know how you did it."

"Brave," I scoff, gazing down at her dear hand, which seems so much more wrinkled than it used to be. "You mean a putz, don't you? Trying to save the unsaveable."

I watch Kay finish her wine and stare into the empty glass, as if it might hold the answer to her life. "There wasn't much alcohol in the Congo," she says softly, releasing my hand. "I thought I'd never want another drink again, but really, I missed it, that feeling you get, your blood burning . . . like you're the best thing that ever happened on this earth."

The look in her eyes as she peers into that wine glass sends a chill up my spine.

"Remember," Kay says, "how inconsolable you were, over the baby . . . ?"

The baby. *My* baby. This memory is literally burned into me—I can still hear my screams in those first few months, waking from a drugged stupor and calling for my daughter, only to be given more drugs that sent me straight back to a murky underworld. Several months passed before I truly understood I'd lost her. Pat's voice intrudes, even louder, from a few nights ago, standing outside my locked bedroom door. *I don't think you'd want anyone poking around, would you? Not after what you did.* I'm hit with a devastating realization. "I literally set my unborn child on fire," I whisper, my lips quivering. "I destroyed a *life*." This was the terrible, awful thing Pat has alluded to over the years. I look up into Kay's kind brown eyes. "Do *you* think I'm a monster?"

"Of course not—" Kay's cut off by a sudden coughing fit, hacking until sweat breaks out on her forehead.

"Are you okay?" I ask, worry for her immediately consuming my grief.

"Just a bit of malaria," she chokes. "Comes and goes."

"Malaria?" I practically shout. Her face, usually so composed, has taken on an odd expression. "What did Africa *do* to you, Kay?"

She glances up, a contemplative finger running along the rim of her glass. "Africa did not appreciate the lengths to which my duty drove me . . ."

I always thought she had a face worthy of a Brontë heroine—pale skin and downcast eyes, a doe-like expression—but now that face looks *haunted*. Besides the worrisome malaria issue, there's something different about her, something I can't quite put my finger on. "You were always such a good nurse."

She's fixes me with a curious stare. "They didn't understand my genius is what I'm saying. Whereas *you do*. You always did."

25

SAVKA

Vancouver
OCTOBER 16, 1950

ON THE SECOND FLOOR of the Museum of Vancouver, Savka trailed down a long hall to the Antiquities gallery, her wet umbrella leaving a drip trail across the floor behind her. The climate in Vancouver had been a surprise—a damp cold so cyclically pervasive it made her bones ache. Two years after leaving England, Savka still felt like a displaced refugee, but Canada was a reprieve, an escape from Belyakov and the USSR's growing power in Eastern Europe. Stalin had tested his first atomic warhead only last year, and the Western allies had closed their borders. Neither her Russian handler nor his toughs could reach her here, where she was safe, where she'd begun to live again.

A tall young man came out of the gallery, and she felt the breath go out of her lungs. There was something about the flop of blonde hair over his forehead as he lingered at a statue in the hallway, stepping close to read its description, and, unthinking, she sprang forward. Taras! She was sure of it. As she hurried down the hall toward him, her heels clicking, he looked up in surprise, eyes dark as ink, and she came to a dead stop. Taras had blue eyes. Like his father. This was not her son. It could never be him, for Taras would toil in a Gulag infirmary until she could find someone to help her get him out.

Blinking back tears, Savka smiled politely at the young man. "I am sorry," she said to him in pained English. "I thought you are someone else." *I thought you were my son.* She turned away, thinking of the many applications she'd made to Ottawa, after her local member of parliament claimed he had no jurisdiction in the USSR. Marko knew nothing of her efforts. They had a large two-bedroom apartment in West Vancouver, and Marko was considered a leader in the Ukrainian Immigrant Association, a group of émigrés that had formed an underground government, operating in different cities across North America. For a reason unknown to her, he'd changed their last name to Kovacs and instead of working in potato fields, she was now a stay-at-home mother and wife. It should have been a luxury to lounge all day, but not when Marko continued to refuse Zoya and make their lives a living hell.

Most of the people she'd met at the Ukrainian Cultural Centre had either been sent to Germany as slave laborers during the war or had slipped away as refugees to western Europe when the Red Army advanced. After the women heard she'd recently come from Ukraine via Poland and England, they begged for news. Savka suffered their desperate hands on her arm, claiming she knew nothing of her own family, how would she know of theirs? Her father and brother had surely been killed by the Red Army in Germany, but she still held out hope that Mama, Lilia, and Sofiy had survived the Soviet onslaught and would somehow find her.

Savka entered the Antiquities gallery. The museum had become a surrogate home of sorts. Rather than wait among the women while Zoya was at rehearsals for the children's dance troupe, Savka came to visit relics of history. Here, she could hold the past close, even as she struggled to accept that some things were fated to disappear forever.

She crossed the room to her favorite exhibit: a mummified boy who had been discovered near the Valley of Kings in 1915.

Penechates, son of Hatres, the card read.

"Beloved son," she whispered. The boy looked so sad and alone lying there, bound in his linen wrappings. Savka placed her hand reverently upon the display case. She'd adopted the Egyptian child as her own, and when she visited, showered him with affection, and a mother's love. Filled with a renewed sense of peace, she moved on to the display of animal mummies. This museum did not compare to those she'd visited in Kyiv, but somehow a damp, rain-soaked city at the end of the earth had managed to acquire the gruesome remains of cats and crocodiles. She bent to study a mummified cat. An ancient Egyptian artist had drawn a stylized version of the creature contained within, its whiskers and huge, soulful eyes. The cat had sustained a skull fracture and broken neck, evidence—the note card informed her—that it had been beaten to death as an offering to Bastet, warrior goddess of the sun. Savka straightened, remembering the cats that starving Ukrainians were forced to eat during the great famine, when from behind her, a man said, "*Slava Ukraini.*"

She gasped at a sudden, blinding pain in her old shoulder wound. Was it someone from the Ukrainian Cultural Centre? No. *That voice.* It buzzed up the center of her spine like a saw. She would know it anywhere.

Slowly she turned to find Belyakov feigning interest in a nearby display case, hat in hand.

If she opened her mouth to speak, the pain in her heart would flow out like water from a broken dam and drown her. But she composed herself and forced a scornful laugh past the stone in her throat. "*You.*"

He smiled, gazing off into the middle distance. "Savka," he said. "Have you missed me?"

It was a declaration of ownership, nothing more. Tears smarted in her eyes. "*Heroiam Slava,*" she said ruthlessly. "Glory to the Heroes!" It seemed impossible, but somehow, this man had found her in Vancouver, thousands of miles away from the USSR.

Belyakov laughed and turned to admire the gallery. "How fitting we should meet again in a museum. A far cry from the Pergamon."

Two figures sauntered into the room and Savka's skin crawled at the sight of them. Belaykov's men skulked toward the far corner where they could keep an eye on the door. They wore matching dark coats and failed miserably at affecting a Western nonchalance. Ilyin wore a fedora slanted over one eye, obscuring his handsome face. He sent her a brazen glance and looked away.

A security guard had followed them into the gallery and stood with his arms crossed just inside the entrance, eyes magnified by a pair of thick, black-framed glasses. He studied Belyakov, this small man in the long, tan-colored trench coat speaking Russian on his watch. The Cold War between America and Britain on one side, and the USSR on the other, had made everyone—even this museum security guard—fearful of an impending nuclear attack from the Soviet Union.

Savka raked her eyes over Belyakov, assured that at least the guard was on her side. "How did you find me?"

Belyakov regarded her with solemn gravity. He'd always taken great care with his grooming, and now wore his hair in a severe side part, combed over and slightly puffed at the front, not a strand out of place. She saw that his eyes were bloodshot. Was he drunk? His cheekbones were like razors. He'd lost weight and seemed to disappear in the trench coat that was too big for his frame. Yet there was something still whip-fierce about him, the suggestion of a coiled serpent waiting to strike.

"You came here just for the Rimini list?" she ventured, wishing she had the courage to add, *Or are you still infatuated with my husband?*

"How kind the West has been," Belyakov said, with a quick glance at the security guard. "Taking in war criminals like your husband and making nuclear weapons to hurt Mother Russia."

Not just the list, then. She wondered how many other NKVD agents like him were in North America, hiding in plain sight, running intelligence networks, recruiting those who might trade military secrets and atom bomb technology with the Russians. *Deception.* Savka hadn't known it would define her life. It had been three long years since she'd seen Belyakov. And yet, in a matter of minutes, her dreams of a safe, quiet existence had vanished like the sun slipping behind a bank of cloud.

"You're the war criminal—here illegally," she finally said. "You think three Russians can walk freely among westerners?" The guard entered her field of vision as he circumnavigated the room, his hand on a bully stick attached to his belt, marking his territory. It was obvious he had an ear cocked to their conversation and was suspicious of Belyakov's men, who watched him with dispassionate expressions. She was sure the guard didn't understand Russian, but perhaps he suspected the lot of them were Cold War spies.

"I haven't found the list," she said to Belyakov. "And you will not treat me like one of your throwaway spies."

His bleary eyes sharpened. "Our former allies are now our enemies. We are fighting a new kind of war, Savka. One in which you will prove invaluable."

Savka felt faint. A mist of perspiration began to form on her upper lip. Did he expect her to spy on others besides Marko? *Report him to the police*, she thought, but immediately dismissed the idea. If Belyakov went down, he would take her with him. A hot tear and then another rolled down her cheek, and she fumbled in her purse for a handkerchief, summoning her courage. "I refuse to work for you."

Belyakov inched closer, then smiled broadly at the security guard. "A lover's quarrel," he said with a surprisingly authentic Canadian accent, complete with the flat vowels and rhythms of speech she had yet to master. With a hand to the small of her back, he guided her toward another display case. The Russian might have had a gun to her head, so easily she went, like a marionette leaping to life at the touch of a puppeteer.

Through eyes blurred with frantic tears, she realized she stood before Penechates's case again, the Egyptian boy mummy—*her boy*. She did not notice Belyakov reach his arm across her shoulders—as a husband would, comforting his wife—until his thumb found her puckered scar, clawing at the place she was most vulnerable. Savka went limp in his hand, a frightened rabbit whose neck he might twist at any moment. His coat was damp with rain; he smelled of unwashed hair and some other sour odor she couldn't place. Her arm went numb to the tips of her fingers, and she was transported back to cold snow against her cheek and the unbearable pain coursing through her after she'd been shot, the last terrified look from her son before he disappeared over the rise.

Belyakov leaned to her ear. "Resume spying on your husband, and I will allow you letters to Taras."

Her heart, long frozen over with grief, roused with a flutter of joy and she almost cried out. The thought of writing even one simple letter to her son! "I'll do what you say—I will find the list," she whimpered, and he let her go. She glanced at him warily. Now was the time to negotiate, when he'd already made concessions. "I want you to find out what happened to my family."

"Your *family*?" Belyakov's eyes flickered ominously, and suddenly she *knew*.

"Mama, Lilia . . . tell me you didn't hurt them." When he wouldn't reply, she pictured, with sudden devastation, his interrogation of her mother and sister, in the brutal manner known only to the NKVD. An interrogation so ruthless, all mail going to their house had been returned. Savka felt her world tip and spin, her entire existence crashing in on itself. "You slaughtered them," she whispered, an exhale of grief.

He fiddled with the belt on his trench coat, as if he meant to take it off and strangle her with it. "They refused to tell me where you had gone, and our army was advancing on the village—your family already marked for death as collaborators."

Belyakov handed her a business card, and she looked down at it, her eyes blurred with tears.

Jaska Hanninen
Furniture and Restaurant Supply

And a phone number where he could be reached. She was aware that Belyakov regarded her with a smug smile. "You see, I am a respectable Finnish businessman eager to start a new life in Canada."

Out of her shock and grief, she blinked with sudden, lightless understanding. Belyakov and his men had taken on Finnish identities, most likely stolen when Russia occupied Finland during the war.

Belyakov sent an almost imperceptible nod to his two men and stepped back. "Don't forget, Savka, I know where you live." He let the threat hang between them, then strolled past the security guard with a smile, as though he were out for a walk and had not just reestablished control over Savka Kovacs, his most valuable asset.

The Russian's men followed obediently. Ilyin took off his hat and ran a hand through his dark hair. When he turned his handsome face to glance back, the breath went out of her. There was something about the set of his shoulders that took her back to that Carpathian forest. Ilyin loping toward her as she lay alone on the snow. Where was Taras in this memory? Already taken over the rise, by Belyakov and Yeleshev.

Her blood turned to ice. Why had Ilyin returned?

She could still see the wavering image of him kneeling before her as she lay bleeding on the snow, could still feel his hands on her, rummaging in her pockets and leaning so close, she could smell his musk scent. Had Belyakov ordered him back to check that they hadn't missed another *shtafeta*? Or to ensure that she was still alive?

26

JEANIE

Salt Spring Island
DECEMBER 10, 1972

"YOU DON'T SEEM VERY HAPPY," Kay says, skipping a stone across the flat water of Southey Bay.

"I can't stop thinking about that letter Pat wrote to you."

"Don't waste your time." Kay's hair is still wet and gleaming in the morning light. She's become one of those hardy souls who, even in December, enjoy getting up with the birds for an early swim in frigid water.

We've just followed Tuna's dear, wagging bottom down the path to my crushed-clamshell beach. Rafts of seaweed, a few crab carapaces, and waterlogged driftwood form an ever-changing still life artfully designed by the tide. A mid-winter sun climbs the sky, casting shadows across the shores of the Secretary Islands, less than a kilometer north of us in Houston Passage; the air is liquid and golden, like it might have looked at the beginning of time.

"I remember you and Pat coming into my hospital room right before I was discharged, trading insults. Didn't she call you a *Cornish Sow?* That's why I wonder why she wrote you that letter." I regard Kay thoughtfully. "You two hated each other."

She runs her fingers over a large boulder, its dark gray surface etched with divots and circles and channels carved by the waves of many storms.

"Pat has always been deluded. And that letter proves it—writing to the ghost of a nurse she once worked with?" Kay snorts. "Terribly sad when you think about it."

"She does enjoy the sound of her own voice," I agree, looking back up at the house. But there was something *off* about the tone of Pat's letter. "Had she written you before?"

Kay turns with a smile. "Pat wrote me letters over the years, but I always threw them in the bin. I moved halfway around the world to get away from her." She shields her eyes and watches Tuna with a grin. "Crikey, if she really did succeed at jumping off this headland, I'd join you in dancing over her *bloated drowned corpse.*"

We cackle joyfully at the image, horrible I know, but it feels so good to finally be part of a team—me and Kay against evil Pat. No one else in the world seems to know or understand how awful she really is. I still think of braving my way back into her room again, but Kay insists that Pat's obsessive letter writing is an exercise in futility, so I let it go. I wind up and throw an old tennis ball into the ocean. Tuna splashes in, furiously paddling out, droplets beading on his dark head. If you live by the water, you must own a Labrador. It's almost a rule. The dear old soul is thirteen years old and crippled with arthritis, but I can't bear the thought of life without him. Despite his age, it's impossible to keep him out of the sea. I still get a thrill seeing him retrieve the ball and turn on the swim, with that profoundly resolute look on his face. Besides Kay, he's my only friend.

Kay squints out at the water. "You never swim?" she says, in the same tone someone might ask why you didn't breathe or eat. "I would think the ocean would be your friend. Are you afraid of drowning?"

Now I'm positive that she's here to recover from something terrible. What had Pat said in the letter? *I can't imagine any other reason why you might leave that damn place you liked so much.* I slip an arm around Kay's waist. "You can trust me with whatever happened in that jungle."

Her eyes take on a hooded quality. "What?"

"I don't know, but it was *something*. I mean, those rebel soldiers—I've heard they harbor little mercy for Western peacekeepers in the Congo. You weren't a victim of . . . a victim of violence—"

"You always had a wild imagination," she says dismissively.

Tuna emerges from the ocean, more sea lion than dog at this point. Kay breaks away from me and reaches to take the ball out of his mouth, but he shakes himself vigorously and walks right past her. She laughs, yet her eyes harden in a flash of emotion.

"Rudeness doesn't suit you, Tuna," I say, throwing the ball farther this time.

A double kayak that Pat uses to take me out on sketching trips lies at the far end of the beach, near the tree line and an impressive thicket of blackberry bushes. An old aluminum rowboat reclines beside it, a relic of Aunt Suze's time. Kay glances up at the headland to our right, which rises in a sheer, moss-covered cliff face, stunted arbutus and fir trees growing from any foothold of earth they can find. A great blue heron stands like a sentinel in the shallow water below. I think of him as *my* heron, for he's been there every morning for years, the bay his exclusive fishing territory. "It's so beautiful here," Kay sighs. "You're lucky."

"My French penal colony?" I say, glumly. "I'll never escape."

"Why would you want to? If I owned this place, I'd never leave." Kay shades her eyes and stares up at the house, surveying the surrounding garden and trees with the proprietary eyes of a real estate agent. "It *would* fetch a good price in today's market."

I hesitate before speaking again. Kay read Pat's letter; she deserves to know why I drew up a last will and testament. "You understand why I'm leaving Gladsheim to the Salt Spring Historical Society, don't you, Kay?"

"Of course."

"I thought of leaving it to you, but Pat would be furious. It's best left to the island that embraced Aunt Suze with such love." When Kay nods sympathetically, I decide to finally tell her more about Dan Rys. "He asked Pat about a missing person he's investigating. She freaked out."

Tuna returns, shaking his coat and thoroughly soaking us, and Kay laughs, saying, "What missing person?"

"A man named Marko Kovacs." I clasp my hands under my chin like a smitten teenager, seized by a wonderful idea. "I've got Dan's number, I can call and invite him out, Kay. Maybe you'll remember the man who disappeared off our ward."

Kay's eyes go cloudy. "Tell me more about this journalist."

I smile, remembering his stern, immovable face. "He's . . . inhabited by a great stillness, as though he's purposefully withdrawn from life."

"Sounds rather like an enigma."

"Pat said he was a foreign hulk of a man who loped out of the woods like a stray dog." I roll my eyes. "Just because he's got tattoos."

There was a droll little smile at the corner of Kay's mouth. "And you happen to like stray dogs . . ."

I blush furiously. "I only saw him once."

"He could be a murderer for all you know!" she says, almost gaily. Her last few words are drowned out by the distinctive shuddering cry of a bald eagle. I look up into the treetops, the word *murderer* dropping like a lead weight on my heart. How disappointing that Kay doesn't get how very special Dan has become to me.

Her head is down as she bends to examine the beach, searching for the odd skipping stone among the crushed shells. "Can I see his business card?"

"He didn't have one, but he wrote down his telephone number," I say, watching a sailboat that's appeared farther out in Houston Passage, tacking south toward the long, low profile of nearby Wallace Island, the sun glancing off the limestone cliffs along its shore, shading them a dusky orange.

She licks her lips and smiles. "What journalist doesn't have a card?"

I decide to ignore Kay's contentious tone. It's so not like her. "I've had a memory since then—I think this missing man appeared in the doorway of my hospital room."

"You were drugged up to here," she says, shaking her head. "And wheeled into surgery for skin grafts almost every week." Kay stoops lower to study the tide line, as if she's searching for buried treasure. "You can't have remembered anything."

I'm silent for a moment. The sun's rays on the beach have released a distinct ocean smell of seaweed left behind at high tide, and it's like ambrosia to me. "I do remember seeing . . . this man, in my doorway. Why was he there?"

Finally, Kay palms a suitable rock and straightens. Maybe it's the blood flow to her face, but she looks decidedly *bothered*. I chide myself for pushing. This conversation about men lurking in doorways has obviously brought back awful memories for her.

"You're remembering a visitor," Kay says, distractedly, then winks. "And you had *so* many of those."

I'm hurt by her insensitive joke—I had no visitors besides Aunt Suze and, on occasion, mother—but decide to dismiss it as a little gentle sarcasm between friends and watch as she leans to skip the rock she's found. It dances only briefly across the surface before plummeting straight to the bottom. She glares after it with a stormy expression, as though the rock has somehow failed her. "If this so-called journalist was disrespectful to Pat," she says at last, "never speak to him again. You can't live out here without her."

I'm dumbstruck. "Didn't we just agree how awful Pat can be?"

Kay looks around at me, eyes bright, like she's trying to prove she isn't sad or gloomy, that maybe her years in Africa didn't break her. "I'd never defend that woman. What does she do in Vancouver, anyway?"

"I always thought it was just to buy my art supplies and deliver paintings that sold occasionally to a gallery. But now I know she couriers them to my dealer in Brussels and goes to see Dr. Reisman."

Kay raises an eyebrow. "Reisman? Did he leave New Westminster General?"

"He's now a GP," I tell her, "in private practice." He trusts Pat's knowledge of my medications, which means I don't have to face real people. She never fails to remind me that, over time, full thickness burn pain becomes increasingly complex to control. Dr. Reisman started me on hydrocodone last year, but it gave me insomnia, which meant I needed stronger sleep medication. "I imagine she's telling him that I lunged at her, my craft scissors becoming a Bowie knife. She'll probably show him the stitches she gave herself."

"Pat was always one to exaggerate." Kay's face is a mask, like someone who's recently come out of a war zone. The bright light dims, wind off the water suddenly colder, and the two of us look up at the same time. A small cloud—the only one in the sky—has obliterated the sun.

"She's hidden everything from fondue skewers to garden shears. I had to steal a screwdriver from the shed in case I need to protect myself." Kay might be different than the beloved nurse I once knew, but it's such a relief to share all of my *Pat secrets*. "She's started locking me in my room at night."

Kay looks shocked. "Why on earth would she do that?"

"The other day she told me I'd stay locked in until I could prove to her I hadn't gone insane."

"That's rather dodgy. I'll have a little chat."

"Would you?" I look gratefully into Kay's eyes and without warning, a vision descends—her leaning over my hospital bed. As the image comes into focus, I see Pat standing next to her. They're whispering in hushed tones, complaining bitterly about a stint they'd been forced to do while in nurses training at the only mental hospital in Vancouver. Riverview. Disturbing words drop out of my memory: *padded rooms . . . lashed out in rage . . . lay in their own filth.*

The image fades, and I shudder, uncertain if my brain can be trusted.

Wind ruffles the water, and I can taste salt at the back of my throat. "She drives me too hard," I say, determined that Kay hear the truth.

"Jeanie, you took her in when she had nowhere to go."

I nod. "Yep, saved her from the poorhouse."

"If you hadn't it would have meant she'd never work as a nurse again—" she breaks off.

My heart stops for a moment, attempting to process this declaration. "*Why* exactly wouldn't she work as a nurse again?"

Kay looks around at me, wide-eyed. "I'm jetlagged and spouting rubbish."

I step toward her. "You're not getting off that easy."

She snatches up another stone and pitches it into the waves, taking out her unnamed frustration on the natural world. "You deserve to know the truth, Jeanie," she admits, watching as the rock dribbles weakly across the surface. She sighs, then turns to me. "There was a little episode on the ward near the end of your stay. Pat made a mistake—"

"A mistake?" I lean closer. "She gave too much of something to someone, didn't she?" Kay doesn't answer immediately, and my nerves are suddenly on high alert.

"Perhaps you should ask what you would have done if she hadn't been available at the right time, the right place." Kay finally says with a brave smile. "You would have had to hire a stranger as caregiver. Imagine that."

"I *have* imagined such a scenario, and my life with a stranger comes out on top." My heart now thuds alarmingly against my ribs. "What kind of mistake are we talking about?"

"Pat was caught siphoning off some of your morphine—" When I let out a startled squeak, Kay hurries on. "Just *incremental* amounts, for her bad back. I forgave her—"

I can barely breathe for the dagger in my chest and the swirl of conflicting emotions there—despair, rage, hopelessness, and something else

I can't identify. "My *morphine*?" I finally manage, staring blankly down at the crushed clam shells beneath my feet. How can the waves go on lapping at them, as though a quake has not just riven the earth? I can't look at Kay, who abandoned me to a criminal without telling me, because she forgave her transgressions.

But she's telling you now, a voice intercedes on her behalf, *and that means something, doesn't it?*

Kay looks out at the sea, hands on her hips. "I'm going to take another swim—clear my head."

A steely resolve washes over me. "I'll need your help," I say, my reckless plans finally crystallizing. "When Pat returns from Vancouver, I'm going to fire her."

I turn to go back up to the house, but Kay loops her arm around my neck and hauls me in for a hug. I can smell alcohol on her breath. Not wine but something stronger. Gin or whiskey, it doesn't matter. *This is Kay*, that voice again, *her strong shoulders beneath your hands, shoulders that have squared off against Pat in the past and will do so again.*

"You don't realize how very much we love you," she whispers into my hair. "We nursed you back from the dead. Do you know that? Watching you suffer—you have no idea what it did to us."

Tears spring from my eyes as I return her embrace. Kay is here to save me from Pat.

I DRAG MYSELF UP to the house, fatigued, my scars aching, but I'm too devastated at Kay's news to think straight. I peer out the living room windows. She's stripped off her slacks and sweater and is standing on the beach in her navy one-piece bathing suit. Donning a pair of swim goggles, she wades in a few feet, performing a lovely, shallow dive and surfaces, water dripping from her hair. As she eases into an overhand crawl, my heart swells with so much love for her. Kay knows that Pat's the *real* monster. I might not have enjoyed her blunt delivery, but my old nurse had some good points to make.

What journalist doesn't have a card?

Maybe Dan ran out? I'm not sure, just that I really need to speak to him. *Now.* Without this obviously traumatized version of Kay listening in. My fatigue forgotten, I head for the hallway, digging out the piece of paper with his number on it and pick up the telephone, fumbling with the rotary dial. I hold my breath when a man answers on the third ring.

"Hello?"

"Danek Rys?" I exhale in relief. But his voice is gruffer than I remember.

"You have the wrong number." He hangs up and I stare at the wall, stunned. I dial the number again. The same man answers and slams down his handset the moment he hears my voice.

I dart into the living room and glance anxiously out of the windows. Kay is still doing laps across the bay like an Olympian. Pat isn't here to stop me, but I have the sense that Kay, if she knew what I was doing, would disapprove.

Looking at the paper again, the numbers jump off the page, raffish and impertinent: 735-2390. When I scribbled them down from memory, chlorpromazine—a drug meant for the mentally ill—was still smoking its way out of my system. Tears prick my eyelids. In the few moments between looking at the number Dan wrote out so carefully, having Pat take it from me, and getting to the kitchen to write it down, my brain messed things up. I might as well accept it. Now I'll never talk to him again. Why am I so eager to speak to him anyway? What do I really know about Danek Rys?

He stood up to Pat for you.

Then it occurs to me. Perhaps I transposed the numbers. Surely I can figure out the true combination. Dashing back to the hallway, I yank open the side table drawer and find a small pad of paper. I sit cross-legged on the floor and jot down different variations of the number, the musty smell of carpet that hasn't been vacuumed regularly wrinkling my nose. Dragging the phone down onto my lap, I dial now with purpose, crossing out each combination as I get a wrong number. One woman mistakes me for her husband's mistress and calls me a hussy. Another man tries to keep me on the phone, claiming he's lonely and needs someone to talk to after his wife died.

When I check on Kay again, she's heading to shore with dedicated strokes. There's time for one more try, I think, and fly back to the phone. I quickly dial another combination of numbers and a man answers.

"Hi," I say, waiting for whomever is on the other side to tell me I can take a long walk on a short dock.

"Hello." A slightly foreign accent.

"It's Jeanie!" I can hardly keep the excitement out of my voice.

"The artist," he replies. Is it my imagination, or does he sound happy to hear from me?

I close my eyes in relief. An awkward silence ensues, and I rush to fill it. "It was lovely meeting you last week. I hope you don't think I'm crazy?" The line hisses. "Because I'm not."

"Pat—she is suspicious, guilty," Dan says finally. "But of what?"

"Maybe from years of telling me I'm an average artist?" I say, gripping the handset. "My other nurse just told me Pat was stealing my morphine—she's probably still siphoning it off. If that's not a burden of guilt, I don't know what is. Pat should never have worked as a nurse again, not taken a job as my caregiver." I hear him take a deep, careful breath.

"What does she sacrifice for you?"

Good question. "Pat thinks me an idiot to throw myself on my husband's *funeral pyre*. She said if it had happened to her, she would have watched him burn, maybe run for the fire extinguisher, but not attempt to put out the flames." I pause, thinking Dan might ask for details, but he remains silent after my little rant. "That's the story of my life. I don't think things through."

"But you remember something?"

"You asked me if I saw anyone the night Marko Kovacs disappeared, if I saw anyone in the hospital. I thought I was hallucinating, but I think

I *did* see him standing in the doorway of my room. He was tall—he wore a dark coat and a hat."

I can almost hear his disappointment. A tall stranger in a dark coat and hat is hardly enough to go on. Then another memory imprints itself on my retinas and I speak without thinking. "I can see his face, Dan. There was a scar—a jagged line that went from his mouth to just below his eye."

There's a pause on the line, static and another deep breath. I brace myself for a sudden click and the dreaded dial tone, or an admonition—*don't waste my time*—but he sounds excited.

"Jeanie."

"Yes?"

"I need to see you."

27

SAVKA

Vancouver
OCTOBER 10, 1959

"THERE HE IS," SAVKA said to Lev Podolyan, ducked low in his front seat. She looked out the windshield and squinted to bring her husband into focus.

Marko had parked his '52 Pontiac in an abandoned lot not half a mile in the distance, and Savka watched him as he jogged toward an old blue car—what looked like a Dodge Coronet that had been waiting nearby, its engine still running.

Lev turned to look at her, a puzzled expression on his face. "You really think," he said, "that Marko might be fooling around on you?"

Of course not, but Savka had asked Lev to follow her husband today on just that pretext. In England, there had been a nurse attached to the Fourteenth Division, a woman named Tyrsa Dorochkin, who had often gazed at Marko adoringly, much to Savka's annoyance—but she knew he would never cheat on her. Yet when she craned her neck over the dashboard, she noticed, even at this distance, that her husband's head was held high, a playful grin on his face. As he slipped into the front passenger seat of the car, she thought, *I have not seen him smile in years.*

The day was gray and overcast, the sun swallowed up by an impenetrable fog. The side street Lev had parked on in Yaletown's warehouse district was quiet this morning, but she urged him to drive closer.

"Too dangerous," he said, peering through the windshield. "Do you want Marko to see you?" A few moments later, the Dodge pulled out onto Smithe Street and began making its way east. Lev put the car into drive and followed at a distance.

Savka glanced back at her husband's prized Pontiac. "He's reluctant to leave his car in the apartment parking lot, much less in this run-down area," she said as they drove past abandoned warehouses lined up like haunted houses behind the sea wall.

Haunted. She sobered at the irony of the word. It was how she'd describe the woman she'd become over the last fifteen years—robbed of her son, dying in a loveless marriage, and forced into servitude by a cruel master. Grief and desperation tore at her heart, where it remained caged in a frozen wasteland, the deep caverns of her chest. Savka had done everything she could to find the list—checking Marko's drawers each time he returned from a trip, even going through their apartment's basement storage unit. She'd hidden behind doors to listen in on his hushed phone calls; she'd watched and waited for some kind of hint that would direct her to the location of this damned list that Belyakov demanded. And found nothing.

Lev frowned as they slowly followed the Dodge along Smithe Street. "If your husband has another woman, what a good time he is showing her—a tour of deserted warehouses," he said. "Marko Ivanets, the romantic."

A smile tugged at the corner of Savka's mouth, tempered by a twinge of guilt. She did not enjoy lying to Lev, but it had been necessary. She gazed at her friend's thin, aristocratic face and eyes that were kind even though the NKVD—or the KGB, as it was now called—had not been kind to him.

After Ewa's betrayal over a decade ago, Savka had sworn she would never trust anyone again. Then last year, when she had arrived to pick up Zoya from dance practice at the Ukrainian Cultural Centre, Lev Podolyan had been there, waiting for his own daughter. Another mother had whispered to her that the new arrival had attended the National Economic University in Kyiv and was arrested by the NKVD in '44. Savka had sidled over to him, and they'd struck up a conversation. After learning that he'd been sent to a gulag, she peppered him with questions, hoping he had run across Taras. By the time they'd established that Lev was released in '53 and had neither seen nor heard of a teenage boy of her son's description in his camp, Savka found herself charmed by Lev's gentle demeanour and shy, sincere smile.

When Belyakov and his two thugs had appeared in Vancouver in 1950, she'd thought she could simply watch Marko at home, waiting for him to grow careless and leave the list somewhere she might find it. But of course, years had passed and that still hadn't happened. Then, yesterday, she had received a call from Belyakov.

"Your husband has spotted our car," he'd said, slurring his words. "And is performing some . . . evasive maneuvers. *You* will follow him tomorrow. We are out of town." Belyakov paused, and she heard him take several lusty swallows from his flask.

She mulled this over, wondering what three Soviet spies did in Vancouver under the cover of a furniture and restaurant supply business. "You forget I don't have a car, or a license," she said, anxious to put him off. "Do you want me to follow my husband on the bus?"

"Ask your friend Lev Podolyan to drive you," her Russian handler had said breezily, as if he was prepared for her protests. "Tell him you suspect your husband is having an affair."

Savka was stunned. *How did he know about Lev?* She tried to find the right words to respond. "Where are you going?" she finally sputtered.

Between swigs from his flask, Belyakov ranted several phrases she struggled to understand—*fucking imperialists . . . Princeton University chemist*, and . . . *radioactive heavy water*. He took another swig from his flask, before shouting, "The vodka here is shit," and hanging up the phone. Savka stared at the receiver in her hand. Was Belyakov finally falling apart after years of being kept like a dog on a long leash by Moscow?

As Lev steered the car slowly down the street, Savka tried to calm the worry growing in her chest. She knew that the Soviet and his men tracked every move she and Marko made, but it troubled her that her only trusted friend was being watched by them too.

She twisted in the seat to ask Lev, "What's *radioactive heavy water?*"

He gave her a confused smile, as though wondering how she knew the term. "A material they use for making nuclear bombs. I've heard that Canada is building nuclear arms processing plants for the Americans."

The pieces finally fit together. If Canada was hosting a U.S. chemist and radioactive heavy water had been on Belyakov's mind, he was obviously sending intelligence back to Moscow.

The Dodge had just made a right turn onto another street, and Lev followed. "If only they would bomb Russia into oblivion."

He looked almost hopeful. When Savka had asked for his help, he'd jumped at the chance. Lev was a loyal friend, but he knew Marko was not often around. Savka wondered if Lev had feelings for her that were greater than fond friendship.

Would that be so terrible? Lev was the kindest man she'd ever met, a stark difference from her tortured husband.

Over the past few years, Marko had become increasingly volatile, perhaps because of his work with the CIA. Belyakov had long ago confirmed that her husband had been recruited by the intelligence agency when Ilyin and Yeleshev followed Marko to the airport, where he got on the first of many flights to New York City. And Mykola Lebed. Belyakov grudgingly shared that a power struggle had erupted between the two former leaders of the Organization of Ukrainian Nationalists: Stepan Bandera in Munich and Mykola Lebed in New York, over who had the most influence among their émigrés in the West. "The émigrés have not given up the fight," Belyakov said. "Bandera and Lebed are thorns in Khrushchev's side. He wants Lebed eliminated. But that *svoloch* is slippery—hides behind the skirts of CIA and won't let anyone near him but trusted advisors and friends."

The danger of assassination was very real for top Ukrainian émigrés working against the Soviets from the West, and that looming threat made Marko unstable. At times, he lashed out at Savka and Zoya for the smallest mistakes or perceived infractions. He still rejected Zoya and could care less that she was now an integral part of the Ukrainian dance troupe. But then there was Lev, who praised Zoya and his own daughter, Olena, who was also fifteen and often came for pajama parties, the two girls staying up all night gossiping and giggling. Lev would appear at Savka's door the next morning to pick up his daughter, and she would invite him in for tea, the two of them sharing old, pleasant memories of Ukraine. Each time she was with Lev it felt as if the sun came out from behind the clouds. Unlike Marko, Lev was funny, sweet, caring.

And she needed those things like she needed air.

Savka bent her head to hide her face, which now burned with an emotion impossible to name. Her heart was racing. She'd grown to care for Lev, but she hadn't realized how much. Yet she was *married.* What would Marko do if he found out? And what would Lev say if he learned the truth—that she was a spy forced by her KGB handler to watch her own husband? He'd want nothing to do with her. The ever-present rage toward Belyakov boiled inside her. That monster had forever ruined her for love.

The Dodge Coronet finally pulled up in front of an old brick warehouse on Cooperage Way. Judging by a faded sign above the door, the place had once been a processing plant. Lev parked behind a neighboring warehouse—not so close that Marko would notice them.

"Why aren't they getting out?" Savka watched the back window of the Dodge and saw the silhouette of her husband's head and shoulder leaning toward the driver. Were they whispering secrets?

Marko had so many of those.

"Maybe it's not a woman," Lev offered. "Maybe it's just an old friend of Marko's and they're catching up." Savka glanced at him with gratitude. Thank God Lev was here. *Of course it's not a woman*, she thought. Her husband had little time for those of the female persuasion.

Marko suddenly emerged from the car and Savka and Lev slouched low, their eyes on the driver, who was finally climbing out, a hat shadowing his face. The driver was shorter than Marko, slighter too—strangely petite and narrow. Savka's heart lurched. "It's a *woman*," she whispered, aghast. "Marko is meeting a woman."

Lev squinted through the windshield. "Who is she?"

Savka watched Marko and the woman—now clutching his arm as if it were a life preserver—stroll companionably about the parking lot for a few minutes, talking and laughing. Savka could only see the woman's mouth beneath the brim of her hat, and she wished she had binoculars. "I know her from somewhere," she said, her ears humming with irrational panic, and a nagging memory. She'd seen that defiant smirk before.

Savka sat back in her seat, stewing in anger and frustration. So it was true, Marko was having an affair. She felt diminished somehow, but jealous? She paused to consider. *No.* The truth was, her husband had become a stranger to her, and she felt more like his cook and laundress than his loving wife. Still, even though he'd been returning home late the past few weeks, she never would have suspected him of cheating.

Lev turned to her. "What will you do now?"

Savka studied him. Was it her imagination, or did he appear almost pleased? When Lev had been released from the Gulag and come back to his daughter and wife in Kyiv, he found she'd left him for another man, nine years too long for her to wait. Perhaps there really *was* something more to Lev's feelings for Savka. The thought made her feel surprisingly giddy and guilty at the same time.

"I don't know what I'll do," she admitted, her pulse jumping. Savka looked away and gazed unseeing at the old rail tracks and run down warehouses. False Creek lay flat and gray in the near distance. More fog had rolled in, and it started to rain. *Perfect weather for a dying marriage.*

Her early years with Marko had been exhilarating—the strong and handsome commander of the underground fighting for Ukraine's independence, and the studious but passionate village girl falling in love at first sight. Perhaps she should have run the other way. She might have chosen a less manly man, one who would not let his head be turned by other women. She glimpsed her own image in the side mirror of Lev's car. A new hairdo could not mask her harried look and the weight of fifteen years of servitude. Savka usually didn't care about her chestnut hair, leaving it in an untidy shoulder length style, if only to win one small battle with Marko, who still begged her to grow it long. But she'd visited the salon last week, and now she wondered if it was vanity, shamelessly preening under Lev's admiring gaze. Why would he find her attractive, a married woman who'd been beaten down by fate and bad luck?

A pain in her lower abdomen made her wince. "It's nothing," she said, when Lev looked at her with concern. She'd been having increasingly difficult monthlies and was only comfortable in bed cradling a hot water bottle to her stomach.

"What's this?" Lev said, and Savka jerked her head up to see where he was pointing. Marko and the woman were getting back into their car. "They came here to walk around an abandoned parking lot?"

Savka held her breath, and her hand inched toward Lev's passenger door. Her fingers curled around the handle but then she paused. What did she intend to do if Marko crawled into the back seat with his lover? Stalk over and scream at him? She slipped her hand off the door handle and folded it in her lap. Not when she was also harboring conflicted feelings for another man, blood stirring in her veins again.

The strange woman started her engine, and the car quickly swung out of the parking lot. Lev gave them a head start before he pulled out into Cooperage Way, then onto Smithe Street. A truck had somehow come between them, but Savka kept her eyes glued on the Dodge. When it turned right, they did too.

The three vehicles stopped at a traffic light. When it changed, they waited. Savka jumped when the truck just ahead of them honked. "What is it?"

Lev's face had taken on an odd, tense expression. "The Dodge isn't moving."

Savka craned her neck, trying to see the dusty blue car, but the truck now blocked her view. It honked again and when the Coronet refused to budge, the truck pulled out into the next lane, passing the Dodge with an angry rev of engines. Was this one of the "evasive maneuvers" Belyakov had complained to her about on the phone? If so, Marko and his friend had noticed Lev's car. He didn't advance to fill the empty spot between them. Savka glanced at her friend. He was sweating, and it looked as though he were holding his breath. "What should I do?" he asked Savka. "Pass Marko and we lose him—or, worse, he'll see *you*. If we stay here and wait—he'll confirm we're following him."

The Coronet's brake lights were red as a Soviet star, the eyes of a beast. "Can we back up and—" Savka stopped on a gasp. Lev had pulled out to pass the car, and took her by the shoulder, drawing her down on the passenger seat. Would Marko look to see who'd been following him and recognize Lev Podolyan? Her husband went to the Ukrainian Cultural Centre as much as any other émigré.

Lying flat across the seat, her head was close to Lev's leg, and she felt the heat of him, so near. She held her breath and closed her eyes when his trembling hand moved from her shoulder to her head, stroking hair back from her face. *No one has touched me like this in so long*, she thought, with an unbearable ache in her chest. Perhaps she could remain forever curled up beside him. Perhaps she could tell Lev to keep driving, out of the city, and away from the sinking wreck that was her marriage.

28

MARKO

Vancouver, British Columbia
OCTOBER 11, 1959

THE RAIN HAD TAPERED off to a mist and the chill lay close around Marko, the kind that bled through whatever warm coat you might put on against it. He crouched behind a dense row of yew bushes near the monkey pen at the Stanley Park Zoo, watching Savka at the polar bear enclosure, 150 meters away.

He flicked ash from his cigarette and looked over at his companion. "She looks sad and alone," he said.

No one else was about in this area of Stanley Park. It was ten in the morning and cold for October, but the grass and towering old-growth cedars were alive, green. Marko yearned for the mountains of Ukraine, where, at this time of year, snow would lie several inches deep on the ground. But he would never return to his beloved homeland.

He parted the branches of a yew and glanced at Savka again, who was leaning over a chain link fence to watch the menacingly large white bears. Three of them paced the jagged cement walkways, while the fourth bear swam about in the pathetically small pool. His wife wore an old, threadbare coat, wool tweed skirt, sensible brown walking shoes worn down at the heel, and a plastic rain cap over her new hairstyle. The first time he'd seen her in a cafe in Lviv, she'd been the most beautiful girl in the room. When had she become a drudge?

Natalka stood close beside him, also staring down at his wife. "There was no sadness on Savka's face when I finally tracked her down in the summer of '44." Natalka cursed under her breath. "That Polish bitch and your wife, setting up house and *sleeping* together. It's a wonder she walks around freely, never fearing I'll turn up, when I told her that day in the forest, I'd hunt her down if she didn't kill her Soviet handler."

Marko kept Natalka on a short leash, worried that she might slip away and make good on her threat. He still couldn't believe the story she'd shared after turning up at the Ukrainian Cultural Centre a month ago, newly arrived from Eastern Europe. She'd been surprised to see him, believing him dead in battle with the Fourteenth Division, and he hadn't recognized her at first, for she'd suffered privations during the war. She fidgeted beside him, her thrift store coat and high-waisted slacks miles too big for her frame. When he'd met the *banderivka* in the Carpathian Mountains in the early days of the war, her dark hair had been long and unbound beneath her fur cap. But it had been shaved in a German prisoner of war camp, and instead of coming back thicker, like Savka's hair did in Kraków, Natalka's had grown in sparse and lackluster, hanging in cheerless waves around her beautiful face.

She felt his gaze and smiled, leaning close to whisper a dirty something in his ear, then pulling away with a throaty laugh. He felt the heat of those dark eyes, remembering them on him last night . . . and berated himself for falling for a woman other than his wife.

Natalka turned to check on Savka, who'd removed the plastic rain cap and swung it in her hand. "Your wife the traitor," Natalka said, with a wicked smile. "She's meeting her handler here. I'll prove it to you."

"I don't believe it," he said, as they watched Savka stroll aimlessly toward the penguin pen, which was attached to the polar bear enclosure, a set of long, iron spikes the only barrier separating predator from prey. Savka shrank back when a penguin waddled down its cement pathway and a polar bear lunged at it, almost impaling itself on the spikes, before falling back into its pool with a tremendous splash.

"Then why did your wife and her lover follow us?" Natalka sulked.

"Savka does not have a lover," he said with certainty, although yesterday, after Savka had shown up with Lev Podolyan, whom Marko recognized from the Ukrainian Cultural Centre he couldn't be quite so sure. He and Natalka led them on a wild goose chase, but Marko knew his wife was on to him. "She doesn't drive, so she dragged Podolyan out to seek confirmation I'm having an affair before kicking me out." He thought of Podolyan's face when his car passed them. Amateur. He didn't know what he'd gotten himself into. And Savka, suddenly disappearing behind the dashboard, believing she could hide by cowering like a thief beside him.

"She doesn't care if you love another woman," Natalka mused, not taking her eyes off his wife. "The black town car that tailed us last week—I'd wager it was Savka's KGB handler. He knew we clocked him, so he tasked *her* to follow us."

Marko laughed. "Savka isn't a spy. You've met her. She's incapable of lying." He turned his head and coughed into his sleeve. His cigarette had burned down, and he ground it out beneath the heel of his shoe, the base of the bushes they hid behind already littered with several butts. He wanted to light another, but his cough was getting worse.

It was unthinkable that Savka had been with a woman in Kraków when, on the rare occasion they still had sex, she lay rigid beneath him, no longer capable of the passion they once knew. In England, he'd harboured doubts about his wife, but believed her story that a Polish friend helped her escape Soviet Poland—unaware that that friend had been her lover. When Savka assumed her wifely role and worked diligently alongside other Ukrainians in the fields, he'd scolded himself for suspecting her of subterfuge. Then after coming back from a mission to Ukraine for MI-6 he'd caught her going through his pockets. But he'd been too distracted with guilt over something terrible he'd had to do in Czechoslovakia to think much of it.

If Natalka was right, and an NKVD officer had turned Savka the day she was shot, he'd surely ordered her to question her Waffen-Sturmbannführer husband about Freitag's battle plans, hunting Soviet partisans. He thought back to Savka's letters to him in Rimini, how he'd dismissed the awkward questions about what the British might be planning for the Fourteenth Division as concern for their future together. *But that was fourteen years ago.*

As though she knew what he was thinking, Natalka said, "Savka has been spying on you all along, hoping you'll lead her to the Rimini list."

Marko shook his head. "The KGB couldn't possibly know I stole the list. Moscow presumes it's locked away in London, classified by MI-6."

"Really?" She gave a short, mirthless laugh. "You don't know the KGB."

If anyone knew the KGB, it was him, he thought with annoyance. Over the past year, Moscow had escalated its fight against the Ukrainian émigrés in the West, sending operatives to assassinate Bandera in Munich and Lebed in New York, but the attempts had failed. Those men were heavily protected, and no Soviet agent had managed to penetrate their inner circles. Last week, Marko had received an urgent call from Lebed, with intelligence from the CIA. The émigrés who Lebed's people were training in New York had been parachuted into Romania and were killed when they tried to cross the border into Ukraine, confirmation that the KGB had infiltrated the CIA's training program. Lebed had wired CIA funds for Marko to start a similar program for émigrés in Vancouver, but the black town car had made that impossible, following him and Natalka out every day.

Natalka was staring down at Savka with daggers for eyes. "I will soon let her know who has stolen her husband," she glowered.

He almost felt sorry for his grief-stricken wife. Savka would never find the Rimini list. It was the one thing that kept him alive—the KGB knew better than to capture and torture him. For Marko would go to his grave rather than give up eight thousand Ukrainian soldiers.

Unless . . .

Paranoia crawled like a spider up his back as he recalled an evening last week when he was followed home. He'd parked in the apartment lot, noticing the same black town car that Natalka and he had shaken earlier in the day. Somehow it had picked him up again and he'd been careless, not checking his rearview mirror, and now they—whoever *they* were—knew where he lived.

He'd hurried up the stairs to the apartment he shared with Savka and Zoya, pausing to listen for steps behind him. But there was only silence. Lebed had told him stories of Simon Wiesenthal, and operatives belonging to Israel's spy agency hunting ex-Nazis complacent in their new lives in the West. And in the eyes of Mossad, former Waffen-Sturmbannführer Marko Ivanets of the Fourteenth Waffen-SS Division, was an ex-Nazi. For years now, he'd managed to operate in secrecy in Vancouver, helping Lebed in New York, employed by the CIA to resurrect the underground and protect the Rimini list. But now he felt hunted. He'd entered the apartment with a splitting headache, only to find Savka in bed clutching a hot water bottle. She'd scrambled to her feet, claiming she hadn't expected him so early, and ran into the kitchen, taking up a cleaver to split cabbage for soup.

"What happened to your hair?" Marko had asked, incensed.

She raised a tentative hand to the nape of her neck. "I had it . . . *done.*"

Her hair had been a bone of contention between them in England. In Canada, he'd pleaded for Savka to grow it long again. Now, in willful rebellion, she'd gone to a hair salon, where it had been cut short and curled close to her head in a style he found reminded him too much of Doris fucking Day.

But there'd been more important things to worry about. Marko had paced, agitated, then sat down heavily at the kitchen table. "Someone's following me."

"You're too distrustful," his wife said absently, chopping the cabbage into pieces.

He shook his head. "It's one of Wiesenthal's Mossad."

"Do they think you committed crimes for the SS?" she asked absent-mindedly, throwing chopped cabbage into a pot of water. The words were hardly out of her mouth before Marko leapt from his chair and grabbed her by the arm.

"I did not commit *crimes*," he shouted. "Do you not understand we were fighting the Soviets—"

The apartment door suddenly opened, and he cut himself off mid-sentence. He and Savka listened to Zoya kick off her shoes in the living room and throw her school bag into a corner. She appeared at the kitchen door, her pretty face flushed, and long black curls flying out of her braid.

"Guess what happened at school—" she said in Polish but saw Marko and stopped short.

His rage was like grit in his mouth. He could never forgive her for speaking Polish. And now he had proof the girl was not his, believing Natalka's story, that she'd found Savka in the forest, in '44, trousers down around her knees, neck abraded, and the smell of Russians on her. Sure signs of rape. "What did I say about that language in this house?"

Zoya studied her hands, eyes slanted downward, like a cat's. Already she'd learned to avoid his wrath by acting the ingénue. "That you'd punish me if you caught me speaking it."

Marko pointed his finger. "To your room."

"But I'm hungry," Zoya said, staring at him angrily.

"As long as you're under my roof, you listen to me!"

When Zoya had slunk off to her bedroom, Marko was already on his way to the door. At least he'd be welcome in Natalka's arms. But Savka flew into the hallway and blocked his path, shouting, "Do you believe I was screwing another man as the Soviets advanced?"

Marko opened his mouth to finally tell Savka he had proof that her daughter was a dirty Soviet's bastard, when Zoya yelled to him from her bedroom, something that, days later, still made Marko sick with fury.

"I hate you so much, I wish you would *die*."

He'd stepped into her doorway to find she'd crawled under the covers, still wearing her school clothes—and he thought of pulling her off the bed and beating her, but decided it wasn't worth the energy and he stalked to the front door, slamming it behind him.

Breaking into his memory, Natalka slipped into Marko's arms; her heady fragrance and the feel of her breasts against his chest stirred his desire. "Do you have it?" she asked.

In England, he'd kept the list sewn into his coat lining, and in Vancouver, in a safe deposit box, but he'd obsessed over its security, even in a bank, and moved it to a locker at the airport. Now it was with him again. With a surge of anxiety, he ran a hand over his coat, reassured when he felt the distinct edge of the ten-page document that he'd kept hidden since he stole it from Brigadier Block's office in Rimini. He would soon stash it somewhere else. If Nazi hunters were here, it was too dangerous a thing to keep with him.

Natalka pulled away to stare down at Savka, who kept looking at her watch and glancing up at the opposite pathway that led to the aquarium. "She and her handler have no idea the list they've searched for is within smelling distance," she chuckled, taking out her pack of cigarettes.

Marko fumbled for a book of matches and lighted one for her. He didn't like the eager expression on Natalka's face. Could he trust her? Of course he could. She'd been Kuzak's insurgent. "You're enjoying this too much," he said, shaking out the match before it burned his fingers.

She spun to face him. "Don't forget," she hissed. "While your wife cavorted with her Polish whore, I waited to catch her alone. It's Savka's fault I was arrested by a Nazi patrol. You had it good in Rimini, playing on the beach, getting a suntan, but *my* prisoner of war camp was not so cushy."

Natalka had told him how she'd suffered in the German prison brickyard, then the stables, kept alive by stealing oats from the horses and by the thought of slicing his wife's throat. When her camp was liberated by the Allies, Natalka had struggled to regain her health in displaced persons camps, unable to get back to Kraków until '47, only to find that Savka had disappeared. Savka Ivanets, who she believed had shared secrets with her Polish lover—also a Soviet spy—and was responsible for sending an NKVD patrol to the location of Kuzak's bunker. Natalka had been checking her trapline in the summer of '44 when she heard shouts and then gunfire. She'd rushed back to find a small army of Soviets surrounding the bunker. They'd thrown in tear gas and waited for Kuzak and Bohdan and the others to run out, then machine-gunned them like dogs.

Kuzak and five insurgents had been shot dead, and the encrypted files were taken. Natalka would have fired on them if she'd thought she had a chance, but she wished to remain alive and find the woman she knew had betrayed the location of the bunker so carefully hidden in the mountains.

Natalka fidgeted, taking a deep drag on her cigarette. "Look at her," she said, "enjoying a visit to caged animals, when she has the blood of hundreds of insurgents on her hands."

Marko scowled. Surely it had been someone else who betrayed Kuzak. Not Savka. It took time for the Soviets to decipher the encrypted files they'd found in that bunker, and when they did, it was like dominoes. Over the past twelve years, they'd dismantled the entire underground network. But the NKVD hadn't bargained on the Ukrainian émigrés in the West, who were intent on rebuilding the resistance with help from the CIA and MI-6. It was time to bring it back in full force and fight Russia from the mountains again.

From its enclosure, one of the polar bears set up a pitiful howl and Natalka smiled to herself. "Savka still thinks her handler will kill Taras in the Gulag if she doesn't find the Rimini list. When Taras has been dead for years."

Marko flinched. "You will not speak of my son this way," though even he believed that Taras had perished.

A son for a son.

God continued to punish Marko for what he'd done in Czecho-slovakia in '48, on assignment for MI-6. He and his men had been para-chuted near the country's border with Ukraine and were surprised by Czech police. One of the officers had been particularly vicious, engaging him in hand-to-hand combat, Marko finally drawing his Webley and shooting him point blank, in the heart. Although Marko had killed many partisans during the war, the look on the officer's face still haunted him—the brutal way he'd had to take him out, and the man's last words, calling out for his son.

Natalka pulled hard on her cigarette. "If you won't let me kill Savka," she said, exhaling, "I'll expose her as a Soviet spy to the Canadian government."

Marko shook his head. "I will not see her in a prison cell. Savka would never betray me."

"She's betrayed Ukraine, she's betrayed *you* for years. Why don't you believe me?" Natalka pouted, her small, bow mouth turned down. Irresistible.

Marko remained silent. Not for the first time had Natalka made him doubt his wife. She'd recounted in great detail how Kuzak suspected Savka had been turned and insisted that she kill her handler. But Savka had avoided that directive by escaping to Poland.

"You believe the story she told you?" Natalka had cried when Marko initially expressed misgivings. "Her mother surrendering her to a Ukrainian doctor who just happened by? Savka was sent to Kraków by her handler while he hunted you down." Marko admitted it was strange that his wife had made it to Poland, when her family had disappeared.

"I want to be there when the police arrest her," Natalka said, blowing smoke out of her nose. "They'll force her to expose her Soviet handler and we're free to train our insurgents without worry a Russian will shoot us in the back of the head."

Marko looked away. Natalka had edges—some that managed to wound him, and others . . . well, he could only smile quietly to himself and think of her riding him like a she-wolf in bed. Savka had no edges to speak of, yet he would not punish the mother of his son.

Natalka grabbed him by the elbow. "Someone's coming. I told you she was meeting her handler."

Marko ducked lower, parting the bush in front of him with one hand. A man had come down the pathway from the aquarium, his pace quickening when he saw Savka. Marko laughed with relief. "It's only Lev Podolyan."

At the sight of Podolyan, Savka stuffed her plastic rain cap in her purse and touched her hair. Marko watched as the two of them awkwardly circled each other. What were they doing? His wife said something, and Marko's breath caught in his throat when Podolyan took her playfully by the shoulders, Savka smiling up at him in a way Marko did not like. They exchanged a few words, a laugh, then Podolyan leaned in and kissed Savka on the mouth. With a stomach-lurching swoop, Marko took a step forward, his fist clenched, but Natalka threw down her cigarette, dragging him back.

"You're jealous?" she said in disbelief. "You love *me*."

Marko shook her off. He wanted to kill Podolyan for daring to kiss his wife against her will, but now he could see that Savka did not pull away. She leaned in, returning the kiss with ardor.

Marko hardened his heart. Every last doubt, every last vestige of affection or loyalty to Savka evaporated. Natalka was right. Not only was his wife a traitor, she'd been spying on *him* all these years. She was still getting her Soviet handler's instructions from Moscow.

"Now do you believe me?" Outraged and vindicated, Natalka kicked grass over their spent cigarette butts—an old habit from her days in the underground. A family came down the path behind them, and Marko took her arm, leading her back to the parking lot, the *banderivka* gesturing wildly, making threats to kill Savka. Marko felt panicked, exposed. How was Moscow getting orders to his wife in Vancouver?

Then he remembered the short NKVD agent who'd interviewed him at Rimini, threatening him with violence, and hinting at something else.

What of your wife? Your son? That secretive smile. Before he'd come to Italy, the *Moskal'* had already turned Savka and taken Taras. And had never stopped searching for the Rimini list, a list that was so important to the Soviets they'd sent the same agent halfway around the world in order to find it. How long had that fucking Russian been in Vancouver?

When Marko and Natalka were back in his car, he turned to her, his heart pounding.

"I think it's time I put Savka out of her misery."

29

JEANIE

Salt Spring Island
DECEMBER 10, 1972

"WHAT IN GOD'S NAME do you hope to accomplish with *this?*" Kay touches my braided leather headband as if it's a snake.

"I don't know—christen a Viking ship?" I joke, wilting under her fearsome stare. Kay has all but dragged me into the kitchen, out of hearing distance of Danek Rys—who stands in my living room, legs akimbo, fresh from the early afternoon ferry.

It isn't often I dress up, and I thought I looked kind of groovy. This morning, I'd torn through Aunt Suze's trunk and all her mod outfits, finally settling on a swingy maxi dress in shocking orange and pink that she might have worn dancing around a fire on the beach. "I wanted to look nice for our guest." I say, hiding a shiver. Wool socks and clogs do *not* go with a maxi dress, so I'm wearing my favorite summer Jesus sandals. My feet are freezing.

"Who happens to be a *man*." Kay says the word as if it were poison in her mouth. She watches me closely. "And you invited him here?" Her eyes have narrowed. "I don't trust him."

Who I invite to my house is my business, but I invited Kay here too, didn't I? To be my new caregiver, which lends her some authority. "Pat lied to his face," I tell her. "I can set the record straight without her here to shoot me down."

"And you think *you* know the truth."

I suddenly understand how Kay rose through the ranks to become head nurse in that Congo hospital. She's more overbearing than I remember. I say, "Dan thinks I was the last person to see Marko Kovacs."

She makes an exasperated noise and sails to the fridge, removing a freshly chilled bottle of wine. With the focus of a brain surgeon, she sinks a corkscrew and begins turning. Just how much alcohol has she brought with her?

I bolt back to the living room, where I find Dan standing at the window, hands deep in his pockets, gazing out at the Secretary Islands. I circle the room, circle *him*, with a dorky smile on my face. Under his leather jacket, he's wearing an old-fashioned white shirt with a long, pointed collar, and a patterned sweater vest, the kind I expect my grandfather would own, if I still had one. He's so quiet and still, which is delightful, but a strong urge overtakes me—*make him smile, Jeanie, make him laugh.*

Rain clouds have cleared and it's sunny again; the ocean lies flat and wide before us, the horizon dotted with small islands that rise out of the water like a pod of killer whales. Dan seems hypnotized by a lone bald eagle, who—despite buffeting winds—flaps lower and lower over the water. "Hide dear, darling fishes," I say, sidling closer to him. "*Hide.*"

"Eat or be eaten," Dan says. Instead of making him laugh, or even smile, he appears more melancholic than ever.

You're traumatizing him, Jeanie. Shut up.

He turns and looks at me properly for the first moment since he's arrived. The old scars that mark his cheeks make him seem more fiercely handsome than when I first saw him five days ago. His frank, blue-eyed gaze unsettles me in all the good ways.

"How can you be sure," I stammer, "that the man I remember seeing in my hospital room doorway was Marko Kovacs?"

"I read in the police report that Kovacs was wounded by a Red Army soldier in battle during the war and had a scar on his face—like this scar you described to me on the phone."

Ah, his voice—the way he holds himself! Dan regards me with expectation, as if I'm about to tell him a whole lot more. But Kay ruins the moment by meandering in and sitting in the big wicker chair. She's dispensed with the restriction of a dainty, stemmed glass and has poured her wine into a beer stein.

Dan glances at her, seemingly anxious to ask her a few questions of his own. "Pat O'Dwyer said in the police report you both saw a visitor when he came to the nurses' station."

"That's right," she says, taking a manly swig of her wine.

"What did this visitor look like?"

"I was busy charting and didn't notice. Pat handled it, told him to leave." Kay meets my eye and raises her brow, as if to say, *I see what you mean—he's rather compelling.*

Dan has taken a few steps closer to her. "And the visitor doesn't listen to Pat telling him to leave?"

Kay looks up at him, blinking. "Pat saw him press the elevator button, but she told him Marko Kovacs didn't leave that way. The man bolted for the hallway. He must have followed Kovacs down the back stairs." Kay huffs an indignant sigh. "What newspaper do you work for, anyway?"

"The *Vancouver Sun.*"

"That bloody rag?" She narrows her eyes at him. "Listen, Pat and I were at the nursing station, charting, then we had a patient call. What do you hope to write about this case? It's stone cold for a reason. One bad actor chased another. Both bad actors disappeared. Who knows why."

Dan regards Kay for a moment, as if he wants to say something else, but instead, turns to me. "If you close your eyes, can you see anything?"

I realize that he wants to know if I saw this man follow Mr. Kovacs into my room, and I do as he asks. Suddenly I'm back in my hospital bed, a form coalescing behind my closed lids, silhouetted in the light from the hall. He steps into my hospital room and the door swings shut behind him. *Shadows, dancing along the wall.* And a worrisome foreboding. I will my memory to be cooperative, eager to share what I couldn't when Dan was here last, but it's no use. I can't coax anything more out of my broken brain than the frozen image of a man dressed in a black coat and hat standing in a dark corner of my room, staring at me. Is he even real?

My eyes fly open of their own accord. "You've read the articles about me. People have a morbid curiosity when it comes to burn survivors."

"It's true," Kay says, crossing her legs. "Newspapers like yours made Jeanie famous. People found her appealing—they still want to *touch* her in some way."

I wonder, vaguely, how Kay knows that the odd thrill seeker still stalks me when she hasn't been here, but I'm transfixed by Dan, who has gravitated to Aunt Suze's bookshelves, his hand floating across the spines. He jiggles one book halfway out, as though he yearns to touch the velvety pages within, but reshelves it immediately, thrusting his hands deep into his pockets.

"You're welcome to borrow anything, anything at all," I blurt. When he turns to examine one of the Buddha heads, I add, "Aunt Suze brought that back from the Orient." The poor man. He can't notice anything without me providing baseball commentary.

Dan glances at Kay, then out the window, his expression suddenly shrouded. "I do not stop thinking of this place."

"My aunt came to visit a friend on Salt Spring in the early fifties," I babble. "Fell in love with the island, and, well—this is weird for some people, but not me of course—she fancied herself a Viking shield maiden in a past life. So, she called this place Gladsheim. Odin's hall of the gods—"

"You know, there was something strange that night Marko Kovacs disappeared," Kay says, cutting across my bow. "A girl not more than fourteen showed up. She just stood there outside Mrs. Kovacs's door."

Dan turns abruptly and stares at Kay. "What did she look like?"

"Pretty, I suppose," Kay says after another gulp of wine. "Long dark hair—curly, I remember. I surprised her in the hallway. I asked if she was family, if she was going in. She admitted that she was Mrs. Kovacs's daughter but ran back down the hall. We didn't see her after that."

Dan frowns. "What time was this?"

"9:30, I believe—past visiting hours." Kay doesn't notice that Dan seems flummoxed by this new piece of information.

"Do you see anyone else in the hall?"

"*Did* I see anyone else in the hall . . ." Kay smiles as she corrects his English, and I cringe. "It's all starting to fall into place," she declares. "Pat and I blundered into quite the fight between Mr. and Mrs. Kovacs. And then he disappears. Can't you see he obviously left her? Bloody selfish of him not to just tell her directly instead of dragging us all into a missing person's investigation."

Dan's expression has hardened, and I really can't blame him. "If Kovacs left his wife, why did he not take his car?" he asks Kay. "It was in the parking lot."

"I think that Russian is the key to this little mystery," she says casually. "The one who visited Savka Kovacs just before her husband arrived." Kay looks at her watch, ignoring Dan's stunned look. "You should keep your eye on the time. The last ferry leaves at 5:15."

30

SAVKA

Vancouver, British Columbia
OCTOBER 11, 1959

HAS A MAN EVER *looked at me like that?* Savka thought. She'd just broken off Lev's kiss and opened her eyes to find him gazing back at her with a devotion she didn't deserve. Perhaps Marko had, in the early years of their marriage. She and Lev were standing so close together, she could see the gold ring circling his pupils. Even his smell was intoxicating, a clean, spicy scent with a hint of tobacco and aftershave. She felt feverish and aroused for the first time in years.

A shout issued from the path to the back parking lot, and she quickly stepped out of his arms, anxiety clutching at her stomach. But it was only a group of visitors, laughing and eating the hot dogs and cotton candy they'd bought from a concession stand. Savka blushed furiously, suddenly dismayed that she'd returned Lev's kiss with equal passion. She was forty-six years old, and Lev closer to fifty—they were a bit long in the tooth to be gawping at each other like teenagers. But her body still pulsed with the beat of her own heart. The kiss had scalded her with its erotically charged heat, like nothing she'd ever felt before. She raised a finger to her mouth, where the memory of his lips still lingered, forbidden and sublime.

All around them, pigeons strutted, waiting to swoop down on a discarded bit of food. A polar bear had raised himself on hind legs to sniff at the new arrivals. Why had she asked Lev to meet her in a place where captive bears paced within their enclosure, waiting for visitors to toss in scraps of bread? The sight of them managed to break the spell of Lev's kiss and Savka's heart. How dare she try to steal a moment of happiness when Taras rotted in Siberia?

She brushed away a tear as Lev took her hand and led her toward the monkey enclosure. There were too many of them in the pen; they fought like criminals over food in a metal bowl. A lone monkey hung from an iron pole by its tail, repeatedly slapping its paws against the cement wall. Savka turned away.

"Taras does not fight to eat," Lev said, reading her thoughts.

One of the polar bears set up a miserable howl, triggering a sharp pain in her womb that made her gasp. Savka shifted from foot to foot, cold wind blowing through her nylons. The back of her neck prickled, and she turned to scan the surrounding trees.

"What is it?" Lev asked.

"Nothing." She was simply feeling guilty. But why when she knew Marko had been committing adultery? Couldn't his infidelity grant her license to have an affair of her own?

Lev stared silently ahead, immersed in his own thoughts. "I know the feeling," he said.

Savka had a sudden, chilling premonition. "Has someone been following you?"

Lev blinked a few times, as though weighing whether he should say anything or not. "Last week, I was heading to Olena's school," he replied, haltingly. "A black town car was idling at the corner. As I passed, the back window went down. A man spoke to me in Russian."

Sick rose into Savka's throat. "What did he say?"

"That if I told anyone you and I were following Marko, I'd never see my daughter again."

She was stunned into silence. How had she managed to bring Lev and Olena into danger? "I can't let you take the risk—"

"I'm not telling anyone," Lev insisted. "There is no risk." He looked confused, and rightly so. Yet he was too much the gentleman to ask her awkward questions and had already dismissed the strange Russian.

Savka was not convinced. Belyakov had proved himself ruthless and unfeeling. She didn't trust him to keep his hands off Lev or not use Olena as another bargaining chip. She felt her legs wobble. *You deserve this,* she told herself. *You destroy everything you touch.*

But she wouldn't destroy Lev Podolayan, whose thoughtful, amiable face was now wreathed in a smile. Her stomach fluttered madly. How could she let him go? In the space of a year, Lev had become so important to her, she couldn't imagine facing life without him.

"We don't need to follow Marko anymore," she said. "I know he's having an affair." Savka raised a hand, warning Lev away, but he took it, lacing his fingers in hers. The warmth in his hazel eyes melted the edges of her heart, melted the woman she'd become after years in Marko's increasingly unbearable company.

Lev leaned closer. "Let's run away tonight," he said, as if he sensed that he was losing her. "You, me, Zoya, and Olena."

Savka looked quickly away from Lev's firm resolve, his bright light. She couldn't tell him that it was impossible to leave; that Belyakov was the only link left to her son.

She'd read in a Vancouver newspaper that Khrushchev had dismantled the Gulag, and political prisoners incarcerated under Stalin's regime were being released. The joy she'd felt at this news was quickly crushed when she'd called Belyakov to ask when Taras was coming home.

"When you bring me the Rimini list," her handler replied. "Taras has been transferred to the Black Eagle correctional colony, where the worst serial killers in Russia are held." The list was still so important to Belyakov, he'd ensured that his bargaining chip remained in captivity, even after Khrushchev had decided all political prisoners should be free. And perhaps Taras was in even more danger at Black Eagle penitentiary. The sinister name alone made her worry for her son.

"I must be here," she said to Lev. "When Taras is let out of prison."

"You've already lost him," Lev said, and when he saw Savka's sudden tears, "I didn't mean to upset you." He frowned, and she knew he was kicking himself. "Do you think Taras is a good man?" he asked her.

Her lip quivered with emotion. "I only knew him as a boy, but yes . . . good."

"Then he will come back to you."

Savka lifted her chin, desperate for courage to bear this aching loss. A shift in the wind brought the sharp, feral smell of captive monkeys who'd been torn from their mothers and sent thousands of miles away to a cold, unfriendly place. When Belyakov had told her nine years ago in the Vancouver Museum that she could communicate with her son, she'd written letter after letter, pouring out her heart to Taras, and her Russian handler had taken them, but she'd received none in return. The silence had been so absolute, Savka feared her son was dead. After the devastating news that he'd not been released, she'd confronted Belyakov at their next meeting. "I have sent many letters to my son," she said, unable to stop herself from shaking. "Why has he not written me back?"

"I said you could *write* letters," her Russian handler intoned. "Not receive them."

If Ilyin and Yeleshev hadn't been standing nearby, she would have lunged at Belyakov and strangled him with her bare hands. Instead, she demanded proof that Taras was alive, and another photograph had been provided—of her son bending over a patient's bed in the Gulag infirmary, some twelve years after the first photo had been taken of him in the mines. Taras had looked up at the very moment the shutter clicked, surprised by the camera, his expression shrouded and his eyes wary. He was then a man of twenty-five, and taller . . . but still painfully thin and haunted.

She was not meant to love in this life.

Taras had been stolen. Marko had drifted away from her when he left to join the Waffen-SS, and now she knew the reason for Tyrsa

Dorochkin's pained glances at her in England: Marko had started an affair with the nurse, perhaps before he'd visited Savka in Deremnytsia that night in 1944. And Ewa had broken what was left of her heart. Now she must let Lev go to protect him from Belyakov.

It had started to rain, and the other visitors began to peel away, opening umbrellas and running for their cars. But Lev still held her hand, gazing at her with stars in his eyes.

It's the last time he will touch you like this, she thought, and suddenly she was back in the Carpathian Forest, after Belyakov and his men had taken Taras away, lying alone, the snow fallen almost an inch thick over her, and the surprise image of Natalka grabbing her by the shoulders, yanking her to sitting.

Look at you, your trousers down, smelling like a dirty Russian.

Savka's body began to tremble, a sad, vibrating hum, and she bent double at a searing pain in her abdomen, one that managed to eclipse the pain in her heart.

"What is it?" Lev went down on one knee, peering up into her face with concern. "*Tell* me."

Another jarring pain shot through her. She felt her legs give out, then she collapsed to the ground as she had after being shot that day in the woods.

"Savka!" Lev took her hand and tried unsuccessfully to raise her to her feet, then ran up the path toward the aquarium, shouting back that he would find the nearest pay phone and call an ambulance.

Breath coming in gasps, Savka closed her eyes, willing this torment to end. In Kuzak's bunker, delirious with fever, the excruciating pain in her shoulder had been all encompassing. She'd lost consciousness after being shot and remembered only fragments. Now she knew why Belyakov had sent Ilyin back. No longer able to ignore the *other pain*, the secret her body had borne to this moment, Savka curled into a fetal position on the cement path, the sound of a polar bear's tormented growl in her ears.

Zoya wasn't Marko's child; she was the progeny of Ilyin, a man who had returned to her as she lay unconscious in the snow and raped her while she lay bleeding.

31

DANEK

Salt Spring Island
DECEMBER 10, 1972

DAN'S MUSCLES TENSE AS he tries to process what Kay has just told him. "A Russian"—he can barely speak this word without his blood running cold—"came to visit Mrs. Kovacs before her husband did?"

The woman is looking at him from the sofa like a cat who's caught a mouse. "Pat saw a Russian in Mrs. Kovacs's room the night her husband disappeared."

Dan is frozen in place. "How does Pat know this visitor is Soviet?" A black cloud that he left behind over a year ago now seems firmly anchored above his head.

Kay gets up from her chair and strolls to the window. "Pat said she interrupted a heated conversation—foreign. She heard the word *nyet* . . ."

"Is that Russian for *no?*" Jeanie says and Dan turns to where she's standing near the sofa. She's more beautiful than he remembers, in that long, colorful dress with bell sleeves, her straight, dark hair brushed out over her shoulders. Emotions wash across her face, desolate as the Lady of Shalott, open as a flower. *She's like the goddess Devana, from ancient times,* he thinks in a fluster, *daughter of the moon and wild things.*

"Why did Pat not tell the police of this Russian visitor?" he asks Kay, getting out his notebook. His breath is shallow; the air feels like fire in his lungs.

Kay shrugs, gazing out at the view. "She clearly thought it had no bearing on the case. But wouldn't you agree, you're obviously looking in the wrong place—it's Mrs. Kovacs you should grill, not us." She heaves a theatrical sigh. "I see someone has to be Miss Marple. A mysterious Russian appears in Mrs. Kovacs's hospital room after visiting hours. They engage in a heated discussion. About what, you might ask. Mr. Kovacs shows up soon after, fights with his wife, then he's chased down the back stairs by another man with a foreign accent—perhaps also Russian? I'm surprised you missed this." She drains her beer stein. "Or the daughter did something she shouldn't have." Kay sends a pointed look his way, sees that's he's been madly taking notes. "You've got what you came for. You can leave Jeanie and me alone now."

Dan hesitates. He's been dismissed, but his thoughts surge in a Prokofiev symphony of discord and chaos. A Russian visited Savka Kovacs just before her husband disappeared. Why hadn't she mentioned this when he first spoke to her? He must get back to Vancouver and question her and Zoya Kovacs. Nurse Kay lingers at the window, staring out at the sea as if she owns it.

Jeanie is trying to get his attention, mouthing something his way. He frowns, attempting to understand, and her pale cheeks flush with sudden opposition. "Dan is staying," she announces to Kay. "Pat won't be back for another two days."

"Pat wouldn't allow it," Kay says without pause.

Every particle of air has been sucked out of the room. *Perhaps Kay is just as wounded as I am*, Dan thinks, but he doesn't pity her. He's wary of what she might be capable of.

"He'll stay in the guest cabin." Jeanie crosses the room, her long dress swirling around her leather sandals. She takes out the paperback he touched earlier, placing it firmly in his hands. A conspiratorial whisper. "You're gonna love it."

To Kill a Mockingbird. He almost drops the novel, then studies the cover with wild longing. "Tell me—this Harper Lee, why does he—"

"He's a *she*—a famous American writer."

Dan nods appreciatively. "Mockingbirds do not have much meat on them. Why does she wish to kill one?"

Jeanie breaks into a smile that illuminates her face. "It's about . . . oh, it's about good and evil and fighting—yes, fighting—especially when you're not allowed to fight."

"'Not allowed to fight,'" Kay repeats. "You always were melodramatic, Jeanie."

He slips the paperback into his coat pocket, fearing this too might be stolen from him, along with the life he should have had, a life filled with books and art and poetry.

Jeanie takes his arm. "I'll show you the guesthouse."

Kay watches with disapproval as Jeanie bundles him out the front door, the dog rising stiffly from his bed in the kitchen to follow them. For the first time since Dan has arrived, he and Jeanie are alone. On the boardwalk, he slows to rummage in his pocket for the plastic baggie filled with his hand-rolled cigarettes. He needs the nicotine but will not strike a match in her presence. Simply holding the cigarette calms his blood enough to think. Clouds have obliterated the sun and the sky has turned the same steel gray as the ocean. Jeanie's dog catches up to them, heading straight for Dan, nudging his hand and hoping for a scratch. Dan obliges him, if only to stop his hands from shaking.

Kay's shocking pronouncements have set off bombs, the shrapnel flying about in his mind. Marko Kovacs wasn't murdered by a thief in the parking lot; he could have been killed either by his daughter or an assassin, someone sent by the Russian who Pat had seen earlier, in Mrs. Kovacs's hospital room. Marko Ivanets had been a high-ranking officer in the Fourteenth Waffen-SS Division during the war and obviously changed his surname to Kovacs in order to elude the KGB. Was the Russian visitor a KGB agent who had singled him out for assassination? If so, it had taken him long enough to find Kovacs in Canada, a Ukrainian traitor to the motherland.

Pat should have mentioned this KGB officer to the police, but it was Marko's wife's failure to admit that the Soviet had visited her, obviously demanding she hand over her husband, that bothers him the most. Somehow, the agent was no stranger to Savka Kovacs.

Dan has an uneasy feeling. He thinks of a black town car that he recently thought was following him, but when he sped up and quickly turned down an alley to test his theory, the car drove straight ahead, and Dan had shaken off his fear as mere paranoia.

But now he knows: Someone *has* been following him. Had the Russian who visited Mrs. Kovacs at the hospital discovered that a journalist had been poking around, resurrecting the cold case?

He turns to Jeanie. "When I first came here, I asked if you remembered seeing a man in the hall. You couldn't. What has changed since then, to make you remember?"

Jeanie stares back at him for a long moment before answering. "I stopped taking this orange pill Pat's been giving me for a while. And some memories . . . they're starting to come back."

When they pass his gray car parked in the drive, Dan turns to eye the front door of the house. "It is strange that Kay comes the day Pat leaves."

"Kay said she and Pat suffered watching *me* suffer. They just want to protect me from further harm." As if to punctuate this statement, Kay's face appears at the kitchen window.

"Harm from what?"

"You? Kay said she thought you could be a murderer."

He stares out over the ocean. Perhaps he was a murderer, for he'd thought of killing so many times. When they arrive at the guest cabin, he lingers on the porch. "You are sure the man you saw in your hospital room has a scar near his mouth?"

"Positive."

He frowns. If Jeanie saw Marko Kovacs in the doorway of her room, she knows—somewhere in her drug-and trauma-addled brain—what might have happened to him. Dan must coax the memories out of her somehow. They've arrived at a two-story guest house. "This is where you work?"

"Would you like to see?" Lifting the hem of her long dress, she opens a side door and is already heading up the stairs. Dan follows her through an almost tangible wall of paint fumes. Her studio is large, filled with light and he feels intimidated by the tools of her mysterious art. Jeanie—suddenly shy—removes the dust cover from a painting and he walks slowly toward it. "Normally, I only do landscapes," she says, "but with Pat gone, I can fool around a little. This one is . . . personal."

Dan is dimly aware of Jeanie turning on a radio and fiddling with the channels. He doesn't like to admit it, but Kay is right—he's been looking in the wrong place and wasting his time with the police report, when the KGB could have killed Marko Kovacs. He might still wonder why Pat didn't tell the police about Savka Kovacs's Russian visitor, but Jeanie's old nurses are innocent of any wrongdoing.

A guttural wail bursts forth from the radio, and the room fills with the rich twang of guitar and harmonica. Dan turns in astonishment. "What is this music?"

"John Lee Hooker," Jeanie says with a laugh. "I think my aunt might have worshipped him."

He stands completely still, listening. The raw melody reminds him of every day, every moment he was denied music. Swallowing past the burn of grief in his throat, Dan notices the figure on the canvas for the first time. He finds himself drawn closer, as if in a dream, or hypnotized, until he stares straight into the face of a spectral figure.

Its eyes are a void. He peers closer and there's something about the figure that's so familiar to him—perhaps its vague, disjointed reality, that Jeanie has rendered in cubes, which drift away, never to return. He steps back, stunned. The cubes aren't drifting away. They represent long-lost fragments the figure is calling back to itself. Jeanie has painted *him*. Not a monster or a ghost, incapable of love, but a survivor, standing on the earth. How can she know his heart, his grief, his loss? "He leaves nothing, not a shadow on the earth," Dan says, his voice hushed, his shield lowered for only a moment—long enough for his grief to rise like a falcon in the wind.

"I didn't mean to remind you of . . . anything," Jeanie ventures.

He almost doesn't hear her, he's so riveted by the figure. A strange sensation within him—a warming of something long gone cold. But a part of him has been touched by evil. He fears this part of him is essential to life. "What do you wish these eyes to see?"

Jeanie tucks a strand of hair behind her ear and stares up at her work, as if comprehending it for the first time. "Perhaps he sees everything in existence."

Although neither of them has moved, he's left with the impression that Jeanie's come closer, and he feels the heat of her skin, the faint thrum of energy that floats, somehow, between them. This feeling, this attraction frightens him, and he turns from the painting. He's standing so near Jeanie, he feels himself attuned to the rhythm of her breath. Afraid of what else might break open within him if he looks at her again, Dan backs away. When she takes a step after him, he turns and lifts his hand to point at her painting. "How do you do this?"

"Do what?"

"Shine light into the dark corner and see . . . it's more than a corner."

"It's an ode to freedom," she says with a tentative smile, perhaps a little puzzled at his reaction.

Freedom. A dirty word. He glances at the artist, not quite trusting himself with her. There's something here she's ignited, and he's afraid for the first time in years. Dan pretends to examine her paint collection, the colors so rich they make him feel like a blind man whose sight has been restored after a lifetime in darkness, before he finally speaks. "When does Pat return?"

"Not for another two days. I have lots more to tell you." She reaches to touch his arm, as though reluctant to break the magic spell that has drifted over them. "Yesterday, Kay let slip that Pat stole my morphine

when I was in the hospital. How could Kay leave me in the care of someone who was fired for stealing my pain medications?"

Dan stares at her. "Your old nurses are afraid of what you'll say
to me—"

There's a noise on the stairs and Jeanie rushes to the door. Kay's on
the landing, swaying and shivering in her cardigan. Her eyes are bloodshot with drink. A strange sensation creeps up Dan's spine. She could've
been listening to their conversation.

He pushes past Kay and down the stairs. "Dan, wait." Jeanie catches
up to him on the porch. Already, they can hear Kay making her sloppy,
drunken way down the stairs behind them.

Dan turns to look at the Fire Bride. "How can we be alone?"

32

SAVKA

Vancouver
OCTOBER 12, 1959

HER WOMB WAS MELTING from her slowly, *drip, drip*, echoing in a deep, icy mine shaft. Taras's voice came to Savka from tunnels that opened on all sides of the shaft, but when she stumbled blindly from one entrance to another, desperate to find him, she encountered only inky darkness.

She awoke with a start—panting and dry-mouthed. It was night and she was in a hospital bed, her head propped up on pillows. By the low illumination cast by a lighted recess on the wall behind her, she could see a shadow at the end of her bed. A dark remnant from her dream.

If only it were Lev. But she'd broken his heart. A low table had been rolled over her bed, and she reached for a plastic cup of juice on the dinner tray, setting off a terrible pain in the incision area in her lower belly and sending dishes rattling. Vaguely, she remembered someone—a Nurse O'Dwyer—bringing the tray earlier and explaining that Savka had an emergency hysterectomy. She'd been too groggy to eat anything, devastated by memories of her collapse that morning and her frantic shouts to Lev—*I don't love you! Leave me alone*—as he ran behind the stretcher in Stanley Park. Tears tracked down her cheeks. Would Lev visit her, even after her cruel parting words? She would tell the nurses no visitors. And if he called when she returned home, she would hang up the phone. She'd stop going to the Ukrainian Cultural Centre, Zoya would no longer dance with the troupe. Savka had to save someone, if not herself.

She sipped at the juice, raising a hand to wipe away her tears, and the dream figure moved in the shadows; it lifted something to its mouth and drank deeply. She watched, fascinated. What kind of painkillers had the nurse given her to make her hallucinate like this?

The creature drew a vicious hand across its mouth. "You filthy *whore*."

She started violently, the sound of his voice flaming along her nerve endings. Belyakov.

With shaking hands, she set her glass of juice back on the tray, unable to look at him, her usual vulnerability made worse by this hateful waking in a hospital bed after surgery. She summoned her voice. "How dare you call me a filthy whore when you ordered Ilyin to rape me in the forest."

Belyakov seemed unnaturally agitated as he prowled around her bed. "You would deny a soldier his reward?"

"Reward?" she gasped. "You couldn't attack Marko—so you attacked *me*." Her body was nothing but a hilltop in war, the conqueror taking his spoils. She ground her teeth to keep from screaming. "Why are you here?"

He moved closer. "Yeleshev . . ." Belyakov paused, his voice breaking. Savka's eyes widened with astonishment. She'd never seen her Russian handler unmoored, upset. "Yeleshev . . . followed you and Lev Podolyan to the zoo." Belyakov straightened and seemed to get hold of himself. "Imagine his surprise to find Marko spying on you, with that woman. Later, Yeleshev called me from a payphone across the street from her apartment building."

Savka got her hands under her on the mattress. Trying to sit up was impossible, and she collapsed against the pillows when an agonizing pain shot from her lower abdomen and into her heart. What did she care if Belyakov had come to share his distress? She would not suffer the outrage of a man who had invaded not only her country, but her body, her soul, her mind. And left them dying.

"Marko gave this . . . woman, this bitch, something in the car." Belyakov continued, unaware that Savka despised him with every inch of her being. "Yeleshev said he thought it might be the list—he was going to follow her."

An image of the woman hanging on Marko's arm in the parking lot, petite and hiding her face under her hat, obscured Savka's own devastating memories. She felt a sudden crawling feeling between her shoulder blades. And a voice from her long ago past.

If you don't kill your handler, I'll come for you. I'll hunt you to the ends of the earth.

Savka squeezed her eyes shut. She suddenly knew the identity of the woman she and Lev had seen with Marko—the woman with the defiant smirk.

Natalka had made good on her threat, somehow tracking her to Vancouver and seducing her husband. She imagined the *banderivka* after she'd climbed the stairs to her apartment ahead of Yeleshev, her head bent to the task of fitting a key into her locked door and turning to find a KGB agent behind her. Savka shuddered, her voice reduced now to a whisper. "Did he . . . ?"

Belyakov lunged forward, so close now, she could smell his familiar sour odor and dizzying waves of alcohol fumes. He was drunk, or high on his little white pills. "When Yeleshev did not return," he said, "Ilyin and I went to find him." As Belyakov rummaged blindly in the inside pocket of his coat, Savka wanted to cover her ears. Lifting his flask once again, he drank deeply. By the dim glow of the recessed lighting, she could see his Adam's apple move as he gulped vodka like it was water. She thought of Yeleshev, the man she'd first seen in the Carpathian Forest, the tall soldier with mournful eyes and baritone voice who had taken out pliers to pull out her fingernails. "Yeleshev was lying . . ." Belyakov stuttered, ". . . on the floor of her apartment. Blood everywhere—"

He lowered the flask, a defeated gesture. "Before she died, that bitch fought like a cat. She turned on him with a knife—stabbed him again and again." He broke off abruptly, gripping the bed rail, as if Yeleshev had been his own son. The intensity of her Russian handler's reaction set the blood pounding in her ears. "Ilyin and I will avenge him." He made a wild cutting motion with his hand. "We will finally slit Marko Ivanets's throat."

She faltered, momentarily speechless. "He will never tell you where the list is under torture." Had it really become her job to talk this brute, this criminal, off a cliff's edge? "When you kill him without getting the list, Moscow will send someone to take you out."

"Fuck Moscow!"

She looked away from Belyakov's tragic expression, his raging grief. *This is the end*, she thought, *I can't survive another day under his thumb.*

But there was more. There was always more.

A rattling noise startled her. Belyakov's hand crept along her bed-rail. "Do you know when I questioned Marko in Rimini, he refused a luxury apartment in Moscow for you and him, and your son?" His voice had grown louder. She licked her chapped lips. *He's lying.* Yet Belyakov continued his relentlessly destructive report. "When I mentioned his wife and son, your husband laughed and said he would not trade you for eight thousand Ukrainian men." He paused, watching Savka with a sick smile on his face. "Marko placed your safety below that of his compatriots."

The air in the room felt suddenly cold and her skin chilled. "Not Taras," she whispered. "He loved his son."

"You could have been a family again, Savka. But your husband was quite clear—neither of you would make him give up his men."

Her head drooped to the side. She was too tired, too ravaged to hold it up and look Belyakov in the face. Some part of her grieved for the life that she, Taras, and Marko could have had in Moscow—alive, together.

Fifteen years she'd missed, fifteen years of her son's life. What a wonder and a privilege it would have been to watch him grow to be a man, even under the watchful eye of Stalin.

"You have not been in Moscow." Belyakov's voice betrayed a sudden note of melancholy. "It is beautiful."

"You *knew*—in Poland." Her Russian handler didn't answer, and the pain from the old shoulder wound snaked its way down her arm. "Why didn't you tell me?"

"Would you have gone to Marko in England?"

Savka remained silent, too stunned to utter a response. Why had he waited to share these details when she lay helpless in a hospital bed? A crazed and unbearable anguish scaled its way from the depths of her like an old ghost. Slowly, her fingers curled into fists on the bedcovers. On that fateful day in Ukraine, Belyakov had dragged her below the waves of a vast ocean, and she still drifted there, in a kind of trance, deep beneath the surface.

It should be Marko you rage at, she thought, feeling numb, shattered, and achingly aware that the signs had been there all along, if she'd only chosen to see them. Her husband had made cutthroat decisions to save his men over the lives of his wife and son. To hurt her, he took Natalka as his lover. Yet Savka had made her own devastating choice during the war to spy on Marko for the KGB—a choice that, in peacetime, seemed abhorrent. But she'd done it to save Taras. Something Marko had refused to do when faced with the opportunity.

"Why tell me this now?"

Belyakov was silent, back to his usual intractable self, and Savka already knew the answer. He'd come to unload his grief and anger, and he did it in the one way he knew would crush her.

She suffered another image of Natalka's bloodied body on the floor of her apartment. Despite the *banderivka*'s threat and her betrayal with Marko, she'd not deserved to be murdered. She pictured Marko finding her, devastated. He would surely run straight to New York. Shaken, Savka thought of Belyakov ruthlessly ordering the raid on Kuzak's bunker. "How dare you use Kuzak's files to exterminate every bunker in Ukraine!"

Belyakov stared blankly down at her, as though attempting to switch gears. Suddenly, he made the connection. "You think we raided the bunker because we needed Kuzak's files?" he scoffed, insulted. "Everything in code and when you break it—anything of use? *Nyet!* Careful interrogation of captured bandits—that is how we exterminated every bunker in Ukraine."

The door had opened and Nurse O'Dwyer stood silhouetted in the hallway, light playing over her crisp white cap, and a uniform that bound her stocky form like a sausage casing. "What's going on here?" She stiffened at the sight of the black-coated figure standing in the near dark beside Savka's bed. "Visiting hours are over," O'Dwyer said, stepping into the room. "Your wife needs to rest."

Belyakov stormed past the nurse without a word and disappeared, like the sick phantom he was, leaving her standing with hands on her hips, glaring after him.

33

JEANIE

Salt Spring Island
DECEMBER 10, 1972

"YOU CAN GO OUT on the sea with *this*?" Dan looks doubtfully at the rusted aluminum boat pulled up high on the beach, its ancient motor attached by what appears to be a few loose screws.

"Not this one," I reassure him. "It leaks like a sieve. The boat is from Aunt Suze's day—practically prehistoric—but Pat's too lazy to get rid of it." I glance back up toward the house. No sign of Kay. Yet. I wonder if the only reason we've successfully dodged her is that she's getting progressively more inebriated. She's obviously trying to protect me, but I decidedly *do not* welcome her interference.

Dan follows me toward the double kayak. I trip over the hem of Aunt Suze's maxi dress, turning it into a cheeky caper across the clam-shells. "You're gonna love this skookum boat."

"Skookum?" he asks, trying to hide a smile.

"It's West Coast speak for strong . . . good."

Dan picks up one of the double-bladed paddles. "I have not seen the ocean for many years."

That smile was fleeting. Now he seems troubled. Of course he is. Damn Kay for her pronouncements about a girl running down the hospital hallway and Russian visitors. In my studio, Dan said, *He leaves nothing, not a shadow on the earth,* realizing that he was the subject of my painting. What exactly is going on behind those tortured blue eyes? He seems like a man clinging to a life preserver in the middle of the ocean. I remember the expression on his face when Kay told him a Russian had visited Savka Kovacs the same night her husband disappeared—the same look he has now, glancing up at the house, his eyes narrowed. I whirl to find Kay picking her way down the path to the beach, beer stein of wine firmly in hand.

Dan and I exchange a look and make a silent decision. Together we wrestle the double kayak down to the water. I curse my choice to wear Aunt Suze's dress, which is decidedly unsuitable paddling attire, but it doesn't stop me. We set the boat down with a splash and Dan climbs into the bow cockpit as I steady the kayak. His foot braces are adjusted to my shorter legs, yet there's no time for me to change them. As soon as he's in, I bunch the dress around my thighs and wade out, pushing the kayak in front of me. With a practiced leap, I slip into the stern cockpit, grabbing the other paddle and pushing against the rocky bottom to propel us out into the bay. Can I do this? I'm used to sitting up front, where I have freedom to sketch, while Pat takes the stern, keeping up a steady pace and steering the boat.

"Stop," Kay shouts. "I just called the *Vancouver Sun* and there's no Danek Rys working there."

I roll my eyes. To what lengths will she go to prevent me and Dan from being alone? "I'm fine," I cry, refusing to look back at her. When we're deep enough, I tell Dan to drop the rudder and he fumbles with the line on the deck, almost losing his paddle in the water. I finally hear a satisfying thunk as the rudder descends into the ocean beneath us.

"Just paddle straight forward," I say, peeling the wet dress off my legs. "I steer from back here."

Dan soon gets the hang of the paddle—digging left, then right—and before long, we've put some distance between us and shore. I lean back against the low-slung seat, and turn to find Kay standing on the beach, watching us. Suddenly, she chucks her beer stein, and begins tugging the old motorboat toward the water. "What's she trying to do?"

Dan glances back. "She will follow us."

"Not in that old thing—it's practically a colander!"

Dan resumes paddling, his leather jacket stretched taut against his back muscles. He's a lot stronger than Pat, and I desperately work the rudder, my soaking wet sandals squelching on the foot pedals, trying to keep the kayak moving forward in a straight line.

"*Why* is she following us?" I shout with frustration. "She can't honestly think you're going to hurt me." I bite my lip. What if Kay is telling the truth and Dan really doesn't work for the *Vancouver Sun*? Of course he does. Why else would he be here?

Without breaking his stroke, Dan says over his shoulder, "Kay is sent by Pat to watch you. They are afraid of what you might remember."

This declaration, which seems to come out of nowhere, stuns me. Pat and Kay colluding? Ridiculous. "Kay loves me too much, that's all," I protest. "And she hates Pat." I trail off as a distinctive, juddering mechanical sound echoes across the bay. Twisting in my seat, I see Kay standing in the old aluminum boat a few feet offshore, her feet braced against the gunwales and yanking hard on the manual starter. The motor roars to life with a few coughs and a spume of blue exhaust.

"How can she follow us in that tin can?" As if the boat hears me, its motor dies suddenly and we listen to Kay's repeated attempts to get it started again drift on the wind. Along with a few *bloody hells*. "She'll realize it's not safe and row back in," I say, trying to convince myself she really won't persist.

Dan has quickly powered the kayak forward, and I realize with a start that we're almost across Houston Passage, South Secretary Island looming closer. I can see the rock formations on the beach. A lone harbour seal pops his head up, his breath a spray of mist, and Dan looks momentarily awestruck. We watch it dive and resurface farther away, an eerie sense of disquiet descending as we slowly resume paddling.

Dan does not glance uneasily at the ocean's surface; it's me who eyes it with trepidation, the one who lives here, knowing what creatures lurk beneath the surface of this deceptively dead calm sea. Over the years I've witnessed packs of killer whales cruising the bay and Houston Passage, hunting for seals, or whatever other seal-shaped prey they can scare up. But that was always from the safety of Gladsheim.

Rounding the tip of Secretary Island, we lean back in our cockpits, relieved to be out of Kay's sight.

Dan takes off his jacket, folds and tucks it behind him and rolls up his shirtsleeves. He studies the shoreline, entranced at the appearance of a little brown mink running along the water's edge.

Finally, we're alone. "Paddle left and we'll put ashore," I direct, breaking his reverie.

After a few minutes of awkward maneuvering between two sheath folds of rock, three or four red-beaked oystercatchers dart along the shore as we make landfall. Dan yanks on the rudder line and we clamber out—decidedly not an exercise in grace—to stand on a crushed-shell beach.

34

SAVKA

Vancouver Regional Hospital
OCTOBER 12, 1959

"THIS IS NOT A private room," Marko said, standing in the doorway. "I thought you would have a private room."

Savka jolted in her bed, her eyes burning, hardly able to lift her head from the pillow. It had to be late, yet Belyakov's visit still reverberated in her bruised and frail body.

Marko placed your safety below that of his compatriots.

How much time had passed since her Russian handler had been chased out by the nurse, leaving Savka to cry soundlessly at all the ways her husband had betrayed her? And yet Marko had somehow got past the nursing station after visiting hours were long over. He closed the door quietly and stepped toward her bed. Had he just come from Natalka's apartment, discovering her body on the floor? In the dim light from the recess behind her, Savka watched, terrified, as her husband circled the bed, his tormented, hateful eyes gleaming like a hawk tracking a mouse.

"Before I left, I had to see you for myself, see the traitor to Ukraine," he said, in a level voice that she found more disquieting than his usual shout. "You deserve to be as dead as your useless womb for losing Taras." Earlier, an orderly had wheeled in another patient, and Marko turned to look at her sleeping soundlessly in a bed by the window. He yanked the curtain around Savka's bed, but it snagged on a broken track, and he lost his temper, jerking it into place. Her heart jumped in her throat as her husband loomed over her. "When Natalka arrived in Vancouver, she told me how you were turned, how Kuzak gave you the chance to kill the man who made you a Soviet spy."

With trembling fingers, Savka drew the hospital blanket up over her chest, as if it might protect her from Marko's wrath. The pain in her incision was unbearable. "Don't you think my handler knew the underground would demand I kill him?" she cried weakly. "He's responsible for Natalka's death. Not me." Her husband looked stunned. *He doesn't know*, Savka thought, losing her nerve when Marko made a strange, low noise in his throat, as if he were choking off a scream. Had he *loved* the *banderivka*? "My handler's man . . . killed her. I—"

"It was that *Moskal'* who interrogated me in Rimini!" Marko raged. "He sent you to England, and he followed us to Canada." His hand shot out and snatched her wrist, twisting mercilessly until she begged him to stop. "Your handler hoped to finally get his puny hands around my neck and find the list. But I'm standing here because he'll never succeed."

She let out a gasp when he finally released her, feeling the little strength she had left fading rapidly. Marko knew everything; it was time to make demands. "Do the right thing—give the list to me and save Taras."

He looked away, unable to meet her eyes. "You think your Soviet will honor his part of the bargain?"

She drew down a deep, painful breath and marshaled her emotions. "You're here only to punish me before you leave."

"You're surprised I should want to leave a wife who watched my every move for the chance to *betray* me?" His voice was sharp, almost shrill. "You think I should not leave that wife's spawn—a Soviet man's child? No, Savka. You left *me* the moment you agreed to become a Russian spy."

"You think I could say no?" The pain medications were wearing off and she felt herself descend into a cold, white rage. "You sent me and Taras into danger."

"A Ukrainian fights Russia or dies," he exclaimed, then fell silent, watching her. She could not clearly see the look in his eyes, but imagined it narrow and unforgiving, as though he'd planned this moment.

"I took you back out of love," he said, his voice hoarse. "But in England, when I found you searching my coat pockets, I should have known you'd been turned in Ukraine. That boy was my *soul*, and you lost him! The Soviets keep me alive until they find the list, which will never happen. I have been free to do my work for the underground."

"You had an opportunity," Savka said, possessed and insanely wretched with fury, "when you were in the Rimini camp, to take Belyakov's offer and save me and Taras. But you chose to save your men."

Marko practically convulsed with indignation. "Can you blame me?"

"You *sacrificed* me, Marko," she said coldly, tears rolling down her cheeks. "You sacrificed your own *son* to the devil himself."

"You wished me to save one boy for all those men?"

If she was not so feeble and in pain, she would shoot from the bed and take her husband by the throat. "Those men could defend themselves. Taras is an innocent. You sent him to hell."

"Taras is dead!"

"I have photographs—Belyakov moved him out of danger—"

"And you trust your handler's word?" Enraged, Marko swept the dinner tray off her rolling table, sending it clattering across the floor.

The door opened suddenly, revealing the form of a nurse whom Savka had not met, a taller nurse who stood like a statue, a white cap on her head and a pair of glasses glinting in the light from the hall. "How did you get past the nursing station?" she asked Marko in a British accent. "Crept up the back stairs, did you? Visiting hours are over."

He rounded on her. "Why is my wife not in private room?"

The nurse glided in, ignoring the spilled tray, her shoes squeaking on the linoleum floor. She handed Savka a white medication cup and a glass of water, then turned on the bedside light, watching as her charge obediently swallowed the pills. Savka glanced at her nametag. "The ward is crowded; every private patient has to share," Nurse Lewis responded without turning. "Except for Jeanie, of course."

Marko stared defiantly at her. "What is special of this *Jeanie?*"

"You haven't read about the Fire Bride?" The nurse said quietly, almost baiting him. "She's famous, you know—burned forty percent of her body in an awful accident. And she's on this very ward, in a special room with *special* care."

Marko pointed at the other patient, lying so still, she could very well be dead. "This woman can go in special room, too."

"Stop!" Savka cried, dismayed when the admonition came out much like a kitten's mew. But Marko was glowering at the nurse and disregarded his wife.

Nurse Lewis turned slowly to face him "You were told earlier—you can't come in after visiting hours, getting your wife riled up. She needs rest, not argument."

"I was not here earlier." Marko's dark gaze shifted to Savka. His eyes clouded over as though he were possessed. "Get out," he said to the nurse.

Nurse raised her hands. "You're the one who has to leave."

"Get *out*," he repeated.

Her back stiffened, and she became very still, then she took her time rearranging Savka's pillows and did not look Marko in the eye before leaving the room. Savka watched her go reluctantly. In the light cast by the lamp, her husband looked more dangerous than he ever had.

Marko glanced at the other patient, then eyed the pillows beneath Savka's head, as if he contemplated removing one to hold over her face. "Poor Savka Kovacs—who would argue if she died suddenly, so soon after having her barren womb cut out of her?"

Fear thundered through Savka like an earthquake. If this had been a private room, Marko would have smothered her—a brutal farewell to the wife who had lost his son, spied on him, and betrayed his lover to the Soviets.

Marko turned to go, then stopped in his tracks. She followed his savage glare to her bedside table. He snatched up a newspaper Nurse O'Dwyer must have brought in earlier with the dinner tray. "What is a picture of Bandera doing on the front page?" He scanned the English words. "Stepan Bandera has been assassinated in Munich." Marko's face went deathly pale. With plaintive exclamation, he threw down the paper. "KGB murdered him. Next, they will come for Lebed, then for me."

"Run away to New York—*leave* me," she shouted as the door opened again and Nurse O'Dwyer charged into the room.

"What's all this commotion?" She pointed at Marko. "You're disturbing my patient."

"I am going!" As he strode past the nurse, he clipped her with his broad shoulder, and she lost her balance. Marko was already gone, the door swinging closed, when she hit the floor with a sickening thud. Savka watched in horror as Nurse O'Dwyer leapt to her feet like a cat, dusted herself off, and with a cry of outrage, rushed from the room.

35

DANEK

Salt Spring Island
DECEMBER 10, 1972

NO BOAT MOTOR CAN be heard in the distance, and Dan exhales with relief, thankful to be on dry land. Kay can't bother them here. If Jeanie's old nurse was confident she'd solved the mystery of Marko Kovacs's disappearance, why did she climb into a leaky boat to follow them after drinking the better part of a bottle of wine? Something's locked in Jeanie's memory—something so damning that Kay and Pat will do anything to keep him from discovering it.

Jeanie is wringing sea water out of her long dress. She rubs her shoulder and looks up at him for a weighted moment. "A desert island and thou . . ." she says softly, her long hair lifting in the cool breeze.

He gazes into those spectacularly sorrowful eyes and his lips curve in a wry flash of a smile that makes him feel as though he's arisen. But the smile fades quickly when Kay's voice comes back to him.

. . . there was something strange that night Marko Kovacs disappeared. A girl not more than fourteen showed up. She just stood there outside Mrs. Kovacs's door.

Dan sits upon a large piece of driftwood burnished almost white from years in the sun, and turns to study a low bank of limestone to their right, the circular, cave-like formations etched by ocean waves pounding it smooth with the surf of many storms. Zoya Kovacs was surely too young, too small to have killed her own father and disposed of the body. Kovacs was disappeared by the KGB. Still, he cannot dismiss Zoya Kovacs from his list of suspects.

He looks up at Jeanie, wishing he could tell her why he's really here. "You remember Marko Kovacs came to your room. You must have seen an assassin follow him in." He waits breathlessly for her answer. "*You are key, Jeanie. You were there.*"

Jeanie's rapturous expression has vanished. "I obviously blocked it out." Dan explains that Kovacs had fought with the Germans during the war, and the KGB could have finally caught up with the ex-SS officer and assassinated him, yet she doesn't seem to hear him. "I *can't* remember."

"But your *nurses* do. They're trying to make sure you don't remember anything else."

Jeanie is fanning the hem of her dress to dry it and he glimpses her delicate ankles, those fantastic scars snaking up her calf, which pull at him like a map to the constellations. "If he was killed in my room," she says with a frown, "what happened to his body?"

He shakes his head. "The assassin overpowered him, dragged him down the stairs to an accomplice, who helped get him into a car. How do two nurses not see anything?"

"Maybe *I* saw Mr. Kovacs killed?' Jeanie says, glancing at him with wide, startled eyes. "And Kay and Pat are making sure I don't remember, to protect me. I didn't have a chance to tell you, but Pat's been lying about my commissions, she's been giving me anti-psychotics and locking me in my room."

At the sight of a tear rolling down her cheek, his heart lurches in his chest. They're twin volcanoes the two of them. The containment of their grief like a lava flow that threatens to burn everyone around them alive.

"Pat has an agenda," he says, "to make sure you do not remember."

"An agenda?" Jeanie's voice is barely more than a whisper, as though an unreasonable fear has seized her by the throat and won't let go. "Pat's not protecting me. She wants me to seem crazy to Dr. Reisman!" Jeanie paces the beach like a jungle cat. "Pat's seeing him in Vancouver right now. If he believes her, he has the power to commit me. She wants Gladsheim."

He's sure that not just Pat is plotting to commit Jeanie. How far will Pat and Kay go to shut her up? Send her to a sanatorium? The thought of her in one of those places . . . He grits his teeth. "You are *evidence*," he says. "Your nurses plan to be rid of you and hide it forever."

Jeanie stops pacing. Shivering, she rubs her arms, her face pale. "But you said Mr. Kovacs was killed by an assassin." Dan stands to float his leather jacket over her thin shoulders. "When Kay arrived, I was in Pat's bedroom." Jeanie gratefully clutches the coat around her, color rushing back into her face. "There was a gun in her bedside table."

"A gun?" Dan takes her by the arms, surprised at the feel of her, the frail bones beneath his jacket and something else too, a heat he can't ignore. He imagines taking her chin between his fingers, drawing close enough to smell her intimate perfume. She's gazing up at him, tears not dry on her cheeks, her lips open slightly and enticing, inviting his kiss. He finds himself leaning until he feels the softness of her mouth against his, then he lifts his hands from her shoulders, shocked at himself. He cannot lose focus on the investigation, he must keep his mind sharp. "What did Kay do with this gun?" he manages.

Jeanie blinks rapidly. She's just as surprised as he is. "I . . . she checked to see if it was loaded—which it was, but she just slung it back into Pat's side table. You know, it was weird seeing someone's initials engraved on that gun . . ." She trailed off. "What's wrong?"

"What were these initials?" he asks, a muscle in his jaw twitching.

"I can't remember."

"I must see this gun, before Pat comes back," he says, noticing that Jeanie is looking over his shoulder at the channel behind them, the water calm and flat and still.

"It's *too* still," she whispers. "Pat watches the tides when we go out on our sketching paddles but look—the levels are low right now. It's slack tide, I'm sure of it."

He studies the ocean, his senses on high alert. "What does this mean?"

"Why didn't I pay attention to Pat's annoying lectures about the pull of the moon on the waters?" Jeanie says, in a panic. "Those harangues about timing our sketching forays to avoid large tidal exchanges and powerful rapids. All these bays and small islands make such things complicated. The tide is about to change—"

He still doesn't understand. "What is wrong?"

"The term 'flood current' is woefully inadequate to explain the force of the incoming tidal stream." Shading her eyes, she studies the ocean, her lips moving, as though she's praying silently that this flood current hasn't happened yet. But even Dan can see there's a slight disturbance in the water at the center of the channel. He can't tell if it's the wind.

"There," he exclaims, pointing at what looks to him like low rapids.

"It's the current. Rushing in like a tidal bore." She looks up at him helplessly. "And we must cut directly across it to get back." He follows her at a run toward the kayak. "It's only going to get worse," she says. When she hands him back his leather coat, their fingers touch briefly, and a jolt of anguished longing passes through him like an electrical charge. As Jeanie struggles with the paddle, her face colors. Did she feel it too? "When flood tide progresses," she says, "all the water that left the channel at ebb tide flows right back in. Why didn't I bring lifejackets? We'll be hooped if we tip. Can you swim?"

Of course I can't swim, he thinks as they splash their kayak into the water. The old rowboat suddenly appears off the point of the island, Kay plowing the oars with determination. He'd not thought he would feel trapped again, but here he is on a wide ocean, heart pounding, and fearful of what this woman might do.

Kay hefts one oar when she sees them, almost losing the other. "Pat called," she yells. "She's coming back tomorrow morning."

He and Jeanie slip into the kayak. Digging deep, they're soon away from the island and passing Kay's boat. She half stands, as if they will somehow ask her to come aboard.

"Get back to shore," Jeanie shouts to her. "The tide's coming in."

Then they hit the full force of the current. Dan dips his paddle low and applies his weight to the shaft as though the hounds of hell are after them. And maybe they are. He can hear Jeanie frantically work the rudder, but the current violently shoves the front of the kayak sideways and waves splash over the deck, almost swamping them. Coughing sea water, he glances back at Kay, sitting quietly now in the motorboat, oars cocked, and a chill comes over him. The watcher, watching. Jeanie shouts as the boat tilts and pitches. He pictures them flailing in the frigid ocean. Would Kay help them? No, she'd watch them drown and sink below the waves, a smile on her face. Dan throws himself to the right and slices the paddle left. Finally, the bow of the kayak points into the waves instead of across them. Scooping the paddle's blade, he feels the boat right itself and shoot past the current and into calmer water.

His hands tremble at the close call. When they beach the kayak fifteen minutes later, exhausted, Dan can see Kay struggling about five hundred meters offshore. Is it his imagination that the hull of her boat seems lower in the water?

"I may have to call the Coast Guard," Jeanie says, biting her nails.

"She will make it. Her kind always do." The persistence of the truly evil still astounds him. He looks up at the house, then back out to the bay, where Kay is rowing with effort, her back to them, pulling hard, even as the boat fills with water.

Dan draws a deep, shuddering breath. They won't have time to search Pat's room. He turns to Jeanie. "Do you have pills to make you sleep?"

"Pat's still toying with the dosage," Jeanie says, as if wondering why he's suddenly interested in her medications.

"Slip one in Kay's wine. Then we go to find this gun."

"I could never drug Kay!"

They watch her row closer, and Dan catches a glimpse of Kay's expression when she turns her head to gauge her progress between strokes. She looks at him directly, as if she knows that he also has history, and perhaps some unfinished business with Marko Kovacs.

36

—————

MARKO

—————

Vancouver Regional Hospital
OCTOBER 12, 1959

MARKO RUBBED HIS FOREHEAD, where an iron vise had tightened itself—a headache coming on. He squinted at a sign hanging on the door just down the hallway from Savka's room.

Do Not Enter

Sterile Environment

The Fire Bride lay within, he'd stake his life on it.

If he weren't still devastated to hear that Natalka was dead—followed so closely by news that Bandera had been assassinated in Munich—he would open the door and look in, see what all the fuss was about. But he must flee Canada for New York, where Lebed and the CIA would protect him. The nursing desk was hidden from sight around the corner at the end of the hall, and he could hear one nurse complain loudly to the other that she'd been accosted by a visitor. *Accosted.* He snorted. She would know if Marko Kovacs had accosted her.

Hands thrust in the pockets of his coat, he turned to head for the stairs, when he heard the elevator ding. Who would be coming up this late? Glancing back, his pulse jumped as a man in a dark coat and black hat with a wide brim that hid his face, sidled toward the nursing station. Marko backed himself into the Fire Bride's doorway, certain the man had not seen him.

A nurse's grating voice floated down the hall. "Another one? Visiting hours are over—come back tomorrow."

The stairwell suddenly seemed miles in the distance.

He thought of the short, vicious NKVD agent, who had interrogated him in Rimini, vividly recalling his threat.

Do not mistake it. One day, my hands will find your throat.

Marko had always presumed the Rimini list kept him alive. But they'd killed Natalka, and Bandera, too. He could hear his own breath, coming now like a train, and a jolt of raw fear passed through him. After exterminating the underground in Ukraine, had Moscow sent word that *all* Ukrainian émigré leaders in the West must be eliminated, the list be damned?

When in fact he didn't have it. After dropping Natalka off to pack her bags, Marko had returned to his apartment to pack his own things. Seeing Savka kiss Lev Podolyan had filled him with such hatred toward her, he knew he couldn't leave with Natalka until he'd ensured that his wife no longer drew breath. It had been a risk, coming to the hospital so late; a Nazi hunter might follow him. Driven by revenge and panicked that the list might fall into the hands of Wiesenthal—Marko had torn it out of the lining in his coat and hidden it in a familiar place. But Savka had not been alone in her hospital room, and now a Soviet assassin or Mossad agent hunted him, perhaps the very one who had murdered Natalka in cold blood.

Soundlessly, he opened the Fire Bride's door. He would wait for the assassin to leave, then scramble to retrieve the list before escaping to New York. Pausing for a moment to let his eyes adjust to the dark room, he stepped in, letting the door click shut behind him. The Fire Bride's room was bigger than he had expected, but it was windowless, stuffy, and he drew a breath against the scent of bleach, and the lingering old-soup smell of a dinner tray that hadn't been cleared. Light glowed softly from the low recess behind her bed, casting her figure in shadow.

The Fire Bride did not stir.

Something swung ominously over her head, bothered by air displaced at his entrance, and he hesitated by the door, his first, disturbed thought: *rope.* When his eyes adjusted to the dim light, it transformed into a metal trapeze attached by a chain to the ceiling, a contraption for her to pull on, he understood, to sit up or strengthen her arms. What parts of her had been burned so badly, he wondered, that she was still in hospital two years after her accident?

Marko waited, his back against the wall, finally exhaling a hesitant sigh of relief. He was safe, hidden from the assassin who had obviously become impatient waiting in the parking lot and come up to find him. The nurses had surely sent him on his way by now. Marko still itched for revenge, and he thought of Zoya, in their apartment earlier, standing quietly, hatefully, in the living room as he charged toward the door with his suitcase. Yes, he would return for the Rimini list—and strangle Savka's bastard daughter while he was at it.

The Fire Bride moaned in her sleep, and he found himself taking several tentative steps toward her, yet when he approached the bed, he noticed that her eyes were open. He stopped dead, but she gazed blankly, possibly too drugged to acknowledge his presence. Her eyelids fluttered as he stared down at her.

Slowly he lifted the blanket, then the sheet. He just wanted to look. He'd bent low enough to feel her hair against his cheek, when a chain rattled above his head, like a guillotine blade descending. The first blow came by surprise, and he was thrown across the bed, the toes of his shoes grazing the floor. He lay there, stunned in the sudden quiet, feeling her legs jerk beneath him.

Deep in his coat pocket, against his hip, he could feel the cold press of his Webley revolver. He twisted to wrench his arm around when the chain clanked again. A relentless force smashed down over his head and back, and out of the shadows came muffled cries, a bitter, repetitive chant. His shoes scrabbled on the tile, but he'd fallen too far over the bed to get back on his feet. Jumbled words fell like shots from a cannon, reverberating with each strike. Willing his other hand to life, he fumbled blindly for the far bed rail. He seized it and the earth swelled and rose beneath him, along with a memory—the deck rolling as his ship crossed the Channel, the sight of England on the horizon, a distant roll of thunder. How vast the sky was, how alive with light.

Another blow came down. He lifted his head and cried out in Russian, pleading with the assailant to stop. But he was silenced by a strike to his face, blood in his mouth and a spray of it across the white blanket beneath him. The blows raged until he lost his grip on the bed rail and slid to the floor.

"The list," Marko groaned, this time in English, and the assault stopped. He felt quick hands searching through his pockets, patting the lining of his coat, then the door opened and closed; a flicker of light from the hallway sent a lone shadow up the wall—the assassin slipping from the room as soundlessly as he had slipped in.

With a shout of pain, he rolled and thrust himself to standing. Fumbling for his gun, he was overcome by dizziness, and fell like a tree across the bed again. A nurse would come. He had only to wait. As he lay there, half on his side, he felt a light touch on his face, a cautious, tentative contact that made him think of his mother in Ukraine, how she always reached out to him before he would leave for school, as if imprinting his face on her memory.

Ukraine.

A black hole opened before him, the land pulsing beneath his jackboots, and stars wheeling above. Moonlight glinted off the death's-head insignia on the brigadeführer's steel helmet—Freitag with his ghost eyes, fresh from the death squads at Babyn Yar. Below them, a dozen soldiers were at work, widening the trench, a raw wind at their backs.

He blinked away the memory, blinked away a sudden slice of light that appeared on the far wall. Cooler air wafted about his exposed ankles as the door closed, pitching the room into shadow. "Help," he gasped. Was it the short nurse or the tall one with the English accent?

He felt rough hands on his shoulder and knew in an instant: it was the assassin, returning to finish the job. With frightening certitude, something was slipped over his head, the cold rubber pinching his neck. He lifted his good hand and groped frantically behind him, but the arms of his assassin were unrelenting and steady, squeezing with brutal efficiency—with the confidence of a killer.

Blood roared in his ears, and behind the lids of his closed eyes, the sparking brightness of a thousand stars.

37

JEANIE

Salt Spring Island
DECEMBER 10, 1972

"WHY DID YOU LEAVE ME out there?" Kay is standing in the dark hallway when I come in from getting Dan settled in the guest cabin. A sliver of moonlight from the living room windows falls across her lower face, and I can see that her lips are chapped, and she's completely sloshed. It's obvious she's shaken from having to row against a frighteningly robust current as her boat filled with water. Now, after a hot bath, she has a highball firmly in hand, which I suspect is not her first of the evening.

"I could have drowned," she says, her voice slurred and shaky.

"It was really . . . dumb to follow us. Didn't you see the boat was leaking?"

Her eyes look larger than ever behind her glasses. "I imagined him tipping that kayak and both of you in the ocean. Hypothermia—"

"Dan isn't dangerous."

Kay gulps some of her drink. "You have no idea, Jeanie."

"Really? Why don't you tell me?" I think of Dan's idea to slip her a sleeping pill. I just can't do it. This is Kay, my old nurse and confidante.

Suddenly she's in my face. "He doesn't work at the *Vancouver Sun*. So why is he *here*? Her breath smells like grain alcohol, with a low note of cheese. "He thought Pat was gone, that you'd be alone—"

"I invited him," I say, stepping back.

"*Did* you invite him?" She comes closer, until I'm backed against the wall. "Or was he too eager to jump on a ferry and question you without Pat to protect you? When you told me you remembered seeing Kovacs in the doorway of your hospital room, I couldn't help but wonder if you'd asked yourself *why* he was there. Or what had happened to him. I think Danek Rys is a private investigator, who's here because he suspects you of having something to do with Marko Kovacs's disappearance."

I press a hand to my forehead, sudden doubt clouding my thoughts. But I say nothing; the raw scraping pain in my throat makes it difficult to speak. Kay's eyes glint in the moonlight. She's obviously concerned, but I don't need someone afraid for me right now. I need a friend.

She takes my hand, squashing my fingers. "Forgive me," she says in my ear. "I can't seem to stop trying to protect you."

I pry my hand out of hers. "Why does everyone want to protect me? I'm not seventeen anymore."

"Mr. Rys refuses to see that Marko Kovacs's daughter had something to do with her father's disappearance; the girl was positively venomous. I've seen men like Dan before—shattered into a million bits, and there's absolutely nothing you can do about it. They're compelling, yes, but you can end up hurt . . . or dead."

"Shattered into a million bits?" I say, stepping back. "Is that what you think of *me*?"

She sobers briefly and fishes around in her pocket, before drawing out a little white cup. "Time for your medications," she says, the white of her crooked teeth bared in a smile.

I take the cup reluctantly, realizing that it's just the nurse in her coming out.

Kay finishes her drink and spins drunkenly, before careening into the living room. "He's dangerous, I tell you," she calls over her shoulder, before collapsing on the sofa, her head lolling back.

I make a beeline to the kitchen and peer into the medication cup.

A full moon shines through the skylight, illuminating an unpleasant surprise. Hidden among my pain and sleep meds, tucked away at the very bottom, is an orange chlorpromazine tablet. The faint, moldy smell of the drain makes me feel like retching. Plucking out the orange pill, I angrily flush it down the sink, thinking of what Dan said earlier.

Kay is sent by Pat to watch you. They are afraid of what you might remember.

I told Dan I trusted Kay with my life. But why would I, when she's been following us around all day and dared sneak a medication for schizophrenia and severe behavioral problems back into my medication cup? She still thinks of me as a child, a teenager who got herself into the trouble of a lifetime. I'm sick of behaving for everyone. I'm sick of being managed.

The guest cabin is visible from the kitchen window, and I can feel Dan's presence behind the warm glow through the curtains cast by the kerosene lamp he lit when darkness fell. What's he doing in there? Bursting with resolve, I extract my sleeping tablet from the white cup. On the counter, it almost glows in the moonlight. I hesitate. It's a crime to drug someone, to ease them into sleep without them knowing, but I raise a glass and crush the pill, pulverize it into dust. With a shaking hand, I drift the powder into a water glass and stir while my heart flips over like a dying fish.

When I bring the water to Kay, her eyes are open to slits, through which she regards me with something that approaches curiosity. "You've always been considerate." She tosses back the water as if it were whiskey, then slides the empty glass onto the side table. It teeters on the edge, and I lunge forward to catch it before it crashes to the floor. "Now sit down and talk to me," she laughs, her eyes already closing.

Back in the kitchen, I look out at the cabin again. Danek Rys *dangerous*? I trace a finger across my upper lip, remembering the feel of his mouth so very briefly on mine this afternoon before he turned away.

Almost as if I've conjured him, the front door of the cabin opens, and he steps out on the porch. He closes the door, and I watch a match flare, the glow of yellow that seems to jitter and jump as he lights a cigarette.

I quickly pull on a sweater, then head to the linen closet and gather two bath towels. My heart skipping beats, I follow the boardwalk across the garden. Moonlight shimmers over the shrubs, mist rising from the leaves like steam. These things so familiar to me, and yet I gaze upon them with new eyes. Is it possible I'm falling in love with a man who might very well be a private investigator here to prove I'm guilty of a crime I can't remember committing?

$$38$$

SAVKA

Vancouver
MARCH 19, 1972

WHEN MARKO HAD DISAPPEARED thirteen years ago, Savka found a job as a cleaner in a nursing home. The work was hard, but on her one day off that week, she made her slow, painful way through the park across from her apartment building juggling three paper bags of groceries in her arms. She was tired and irritable and her back ached. When she got home, she planned to finish making a few dozen *varenyky*, then go right to bed and recover from six straight days of scrubbing toilets and mopping miles of linoleum floors.

She paused reluctantly in front of a park bench, dark memories swirling in her mind. The place was deserted, not as it was that day in 1959, when she'd stumbled upon Belyakov on her way home from the hospital. The ghost of her Russian handler was still there, flicking away his half-smoked cigarette. Elbows on his knees, he had glanced at Ilyin, who stood nearby at the edge of the small pond, looking adrift without his old sidekick, Yeleshev. Savka had had the sense the two Russians circled her like lions hunting an injured zebra on the plains. Belyakov had looked up at her. "Where is he, Savka?"

She'd waited for her racing heart to slow, remembering his distressing visit to her hospital room only days before. "Where is who?"

"Your husband leaves on another trip and you do not contact me?"

After Marko had threatened her several nights before, she had presumed he'd climbed into his car and driven straight to New York. "He came in after you did," she said. "A nurse thought he was you. Marko flew into a rage, demanded to know who you were."

"You didn't tell him . . ."

"I didn't have to tell him," she said, her womb-less body aching and yearning for her own comfortable bed. She wanted to tell Belyakov that news of Natalka's death had undone her husband, but knew better than to mention the *banderivka's* name and set her Russian handler off. "He remembered you from Rimini. We had words and he left. He's escaped."

Belyakov's eyes narrowed. "I would think the same thing, but why did he leave his car in the parking lot?"

Savka winced as pain snaked its way along her hysterectomy incision. Marko would never leave his prized Pontiac. "A Soviet assassin found him?" she gasped, struggling to take in the fact that Marko's worst fear had come to pass. "An assassin who worked without your knowledge?"

"No operatives are here without my knowledge," Belyakov said. "It was Mossad." He looked up at the gray sky. She flinched when he swore, calling her a "train station whore" in his despicable Russian. If she had the strength—and a gun—she'd shoot him dead. Reaching into his coat pocket, he took out his trusty flask. "I should be in Moscow," he said, after a long swig, "not in this shit country—rain, rain, rain." He seemed still grief-stricken at the loss of Yeleshev, and now of Marko. He'd spent years and a great deal of effort tracking her husband across continents, desperate to bring him back to Moscow, this traitor to the motherland, a rebel who had something he dearly wanted. And another predator had snatched his prey without warning.

But Savka wasn't buying this act. "In the hospital, you threatened to kill Marko. You've done it and now wish to make me think he ran afoul of a Nazi hunter. Is this the lie you're telling the KGB?"

Belyakov seemed so startled by the accusation, Savka had to presume he had nothing to do with Marko's troubling disappearance. But there *was* an upside. With her husband gone, and presumably the Rimini list along with him, Belyakov didn't need her anymore. She was free to turn her Russian handler in to the Canadian police. Without orders from him to the Black Eagle prison, someone would notice that a certain political prisoner had not been granted release when Khrushchev set so many of them free. And Taras would be liberated. Savka felt power thrum in her blood. She was a warrior at last, authority and dominance finally in her hands.

Emboldened by this new burst of confidence, she didn't notice Belyakov studying her. "You think you can turn me in now?" he said. "Who do you think has kept Taras alive in Black Eagle? If a year goes by and the commandant does not hear from me, he has direct orders: shoot your precious son into a ditch."

At the time, Savka had hung her head, chastised, but now she clutched her groceries and shook off that memory, leaving the park, and climbing the front steps of her apartment building. Wedging her bags against the door, she juggled her keys. Belyakov had insisted she file a missing person's report. "The police are useless here," he'd said, "but they might turn up something. A friend of Marko's could have waited for him in the parking lot. Left the car behind to throw us off. Until I see a body, I will assume Marko is still out there."

She'd filed the report and learned from a detective that the nurses had noticed a man come in shortly after Marko had left her—most likely a Nazi hunter, who might have chased her husband down the back stairs and into the night. Belyakov was right: there *had* been a car and accomplice waiting. But not a friendly one. Marko had likely been forced inside, driven somewhere remote and been tortured to give up the list. Refusing, he would have taken a bullet to his head for daring to join the Waffen-SS. The list was lost forever, and Marko's body buried in a shallow grave.

Savka went through the front door of her building, pausing to listen for the distinctive click of the lock behind her before she checked her mailbox, breath held, still looking for a letter from Taras. Of course there was no letter, and she climbed the stairs to the third floor. Grief for Marko did not lie heavily on her heart, but grief for Taras? It was a never-ending spiral. She was afraid that her husband had been right, their son was dead. Perhaps Belyakov—no longer in need of his bargaining chip—had simply let her son perish in prison.

"A smart woman would rent a smaller apartment, on a lower floor," she muttered to herself as she gained the first landing, breath now coming in gasps. To keep her loneliness and grief from overpowering her, she often talked to herself. Sometimes Savka wondered why she still held on to an apartment she could ill afford. Perhaps to give Zoya a place to move back into when she left her boyfriend. Savka approved of her daughter's job—she was an X-ray technician—but not that she lived with a welder in West Vancouver, with no talk of marriage.

After Savka had put away the groceries, she took out the *varenyky* dough she'd made that morning, and the mixture to fill them—potatoes she'd mashed with cheese and onion. Weariness settled in her bones as she rolled out the dough, and a sharp pain in her heart, remembering Mama making hundreds of *varenyky* at a time in the old kitchen in Ukraine, and how Taras would wait beside the stove, eager for a first taste. Tears in her eyes, Savka cut circles in the dough with the rim of a glass and folded the stuffing into the dumpling rounds, pinching the edges to seal them. After her nap, she would boil them for her lunch.

Savka had just filled a hot water bottle when there was a knock on the door. She froze at the sink. On her days off, Belyakov sometimes ordered her to follow certain people—*targets* he called them—on buses around the city, reporting back to him in detail of where they went, what they did. He still considered her an asset and would never give her peace, not until she was dead.

But Belyakov had never turned up at her apartment door. It could be a vagrant, with his hand out—at times, other tenants would unwittingly let one slip in behind them into the lobby. She stood still in the kitchen, waiting for this person to go away, but the knocking had become a delicate, questioning tap.

Could it be Lev Podolyan? No. It had been thirteen years since she refused to answer his calls or gone to the Ukrainian Cultural Centre, and he'd finally given up. She'd imagined his hurt, she imagined it, still.

The knock sounded again, more insistent. Angry and ready to blast whoever had dared disturb her, she stalked to the door, yanking it open.

A man—or what approximated a man—stood in the hallway. He was emaciated, haunted, a walking corpse among the living, and she swayed on her slippered feet, sorry she'd opened the door to this homeless beggar. As he reached out to her, she moved to slam it shut.

Until he said something in Ukrainian.

She hesitated, breathless with fear—had one of Natalka's compatriots hunted her down? But then the strange man suddenly whispered, "Mama."

Savka's heart came to a jolting stop, and she fell to her knees. *Mama.*

The ghost of her son stepped into the apartment and closed the door behind him. These were his hands, weren't they, gently hauling her to standing? These were his eyes, glancing at her shoulder. "I am sorry." His lips moved, that dear mouth she remembered. "Does your wound still hurt?"

"Taras," she cried, falling into him. He smelled of the hard road that had brought him there—rain and cigarette smoke and sorrow. She held onto him, clutching his wasted body to her—so thin!—and finally held him at arm's length, hardly able to believe her eyes that Taras stood before her in Vancouver. How she had dreamed of this moment. "I thought you were . . . *dead!*" Her voice rose from a whimper to a terrible cry that shook her body in convulsive sobs.

Her son awkwardly wiped away his own tears. "For the first years, in the camps, I thought you had died on that mountain—"

Fearing she might faint, Savka took his arm to steady herself. Still shaking, she drew Taras into the warm kitchen and eased him into a chair at the table. "But how . . ."

"I learned you were alive in 1950, when your first letter arrived." Taras looked up at her with wounded eyes. "How happy I was to know you were in Canada, that I had a little sister, and Tato had survived the war. But after 1953, your letters stopped coming. I thought you were all dead. I would not rest until I could prove it for myself."

She faltered, momentarily speechless. Why, after only a few years of her writing letters to Taras, had Belyakov simply stopped sending them on? How she hated him. If he were here, she would kill him with her bare hands. She shook her head, taking in her son's lean form and the gut-wrenching scars on his cheeks. What had happened to him? It no longer mattered, for Taras was here, *safe*. He had not looked away, and she saw there was a kind of desperate madness in his eyes, a disjointed sorrow. The Gulag had stolen his spirit and left him a shell of the son Belyakov and his men had stolen from her.

"Thank God you got my letters," she cried, raising her eyes to the ceiling. "I prayed and prayed, and here you are. Tarasyku, when were you released?"

"Last year," he said haltingly.

Her mouth dropped open in disbelief. "Why did you not send word?"

"At first, the Soviets would not issue an exit visa. When they discovered I was writing for the underground newspapers in Kyiv, they let me go, not wishing political prisoners in Soviet Ukraine stirring up sedition. Now I am an exile."

To hide her tears, Savka put on a pot of water to boil and went to the fridge, taking out the *varenyky*, lined up in rows on a baking sheet. "You should eat," she said, intent on putting meat on her son's bones.

"Where is Tato?" He glanced around the kitchen, as if he expected his father to appear at any moment.

She left the sheet of dumplings on the counter and sat beside him, taking his hand in hers. "He disappeared thirteen years ago."

Taras stared down at the table, blinking. "Where did he go?" he finally asked, his voice quiet.

"The last time I saw your father, he visited me in hospital, after I had an emergency hysterectomy."

"Where did they find his body?" he asked, his eyes brimming with bitter tears he would not shed.

"They didn't. I filed a missing person's report with the police."

"Then there is hope," he said, stubbornly.

"His car was in the parking lot," she whispered. "He wouldn't have left it. The police thought a thief might have surprised your father when he came out of the hospital, a fight ensued, and the thief accidentally killed him, disposing of the body." But that was all she said. Savka would move heaven and earth to prevent her son from learning that his father had surrendered his wife's and son's fates to Belyakov in Rimini. She would never tell Taras what Marko had become after the war, nor that she had spied on him for the Soviets. Never *that*.

The look on her son's dear face broke her heart. Fingers trembling, he took out a baggie that held tobacco and papers and began to roll cigarettes. She returned to the stove and spooned *varenyky* into the pot of boiling water. Taras appeared at her side, handing her a cigarette. She placed it between her lips and let him light it, inhaling a long first drag. "Where is the police station," he asked, "where you filed the missing person's report?"

Savka coughed, so that she would not burst into tears at the sight of his ruined fingers. The tips had been lost to frostbite, most likely early in his incarceration, for there were still nails on the ends of his stunted fingers. "The case has gone cold."

"Cold," Taras said, surprising her with English. "How could this case go cold?"

"Your English is good. You hardly have an accent." She forced a smile, watching the dumplings float to the top of the boiling water while he explained that he'd learned more English from other political prisoners in the camps, and had taken lessons in Kyiv after being released, working hard to lose his accent.

"Why did you wish to lose your accent?"

He took a deep pull on his cigarette. "I will not be mistaken for a Russian," he said quietly, exhaling. Savka regarded him with an anxious eye. If Taras knew how close his mother had been to one particular Russian, how he still kept her on a long leash, he might run from her and never return. She must now guard him with her life. If Belyakov caught wind that Black Eagle authorities had released Taras Ivanets without the KGB's knowledge, he would rage. But incredibly, he could now do nothing. *Finally*, she thought, *I am free of my master.* She had her son back, the bargaining chip was no longer in play. Still, she would protect Taras with her life, and somehow prevent Belyakov from learning he was here in Vancouver.

Scooping half a dozen *varenyky* out of the water, she arranged them on a plate with a little fried onion and set them in front of her son. She watched in disbelief as Taras stubbed out his cigarette in an ashtray. It seemed impossible that her child was now a man. Back in Ukraine, she'd often thought of how handsome Taras would look fully grown, and she was right. Despite the horrors of the Gulag and Black Eagle, he looked so much like a younger Marko, her heart throbbed with memory.

As her son ate, the two of them filled in the blanks of their dual history like two people working a puzzle long abandoned, finding pieces that had suddenly appeared before them. While she'd been delirious with fever in Kuzak's bunker, Belyakov had put a terrified Taras on a train for Moscow, where he spent a month in the massive Lubyanka prison. A shiver went down Savka's spine when her son said he was charged with counterrevolutionary terrorism and sentenced to twenty-five years of hard labor in Siberia. Despite Belyakov telling her that Taras had been sent to the Black Eagle penal colony, she did not feel any less horror when Taras related that he'd spent years there, somehow holding his own against some of the worst serial murderers in the Soviet Union.

Savka shared how she'd crawled down the mountain, pregnant with Zoya, and been saved by a Ukrainian doctor. Then, her voice wavering, how she'd ended up in Kraków. The knife Ewa had plunged into her back in 1947 was still there, twisting in painful reminder of that betrayal. When Taras lifted the fork to his mouth with the last dumpling, Savka noticed a set of still-red scars visible below the cuff of his jacket. "What's this?"

"Tattoos I got in Black Eagle. I am . . . removing them."

"How?"

"A razor."

She tapped ash from her cigarette into the tray, imagining, with anguish, her son using a razor to scrape at his own skin. With every tattoo scoured away, she suspected he was also burying his past.

In halting words, Savka related how she'd stayed three years in Poland, when a sudden ache in her old gunshot wound spoke to her: *Tell Taras the truth.* But she couldn't reveal the secrets she'd held on to for so long. "Kraków," she said finally. "That was where I learned your father was in an Italian prisoner of war camp."

Taras looked up. Was that suspicion in his eyes? "How did you find him?"

"I made inquiries. I contacted your father in Rimini. When the British moved him to England, he sent for us."

"The NKVD officer," Taras said, as if sensing a connection. "Comrade Belyakov—he visited my camp once." Eyes burning with intensity, Taras set down his fork and took a leather sheath from his pocket. In a move he must have perfected over the course of years, he quickly withdrew a crude knife from the sheath and placed it on the table. "When I got out, I meant to kill him with this. But I could not find him."

Savka stared down at the odd and dangerous-looking weapon— a shiv that Taras had somehow fashioned out of what looked like a surgeon's scalpel, the handle wrapped in a bandage and tied fast with a weathered shoelace. Her eyes crept again and again to the knife as he told her of overhearing Lieutenant Belyakov demand that Taras receive extra food, which made him a target of the criminal prison population, who couldn't understand why a lowly Ukrainian political prisoner was kept alive when others perished with the hard work and thin gruel they called rations.

Tears ran down her face. Her sensitive boy had survived twenty-eight years in prison because Belyakov had needed his bargaining chip alive. She said, "You will move into Zoya's old room."

"I need to work," he said.

Savka thought of the work her son had done in the mines and then the camp hospital and felt suddenly ashamed to gripe at having only one day off a week. Already, she worried for Taras. Who would hire a forty-one-year-old man without a work history? "You don't need a job," she said. "Rest and sleep."

"I must buy a car," he said, clearly agitated.

"There are buses—"

"I need a car. I need to find out who killed Tato."

She held her breath, regarding him with dismay. "Your father was different after the war—complicated and unpredictable. He received an injury."

"You were happy together," he said, a new kind of despair haunting his features. "I remember."

"Taras, what do you know of marriage?" She cut herself off, but not before seeing his hurt. She'd wounded him, and he had very little reserve left.

"It's true," he said, his voice flat and emotionless. "I know nothing."

Part of him had closed off to her and she regretted her words. "There is still time—you will find a woman."

Taras glanced sidelong at her. "I have no love in me."

"I remember the boy who loved his family, his country."

"He has died."

Her heart spasmed with grief and she reached her hand across the table, but he would not take it. By the determined look on Taras's face, she realized he would unravel the mystery of his father's disappearance if it were the last thing he did.

And that was *unimaginable*.

Taras had escaped the Soviet system that broke him. He could not enter that world again, for investigating Marko's disappearance would take him down a dark path. Her son was too vulnerable. He wished to see his father as a hero, and she would preserve that memory at all costs.

39

———

DANEK

———

Salt Spring Island
DECEMBER 10, 1972

ON JEANIE'S GUEST HOUSE PORCH, Dan leans against one of the posts, smoking. He's taken off his jacket and rolled up the sleeves of his white shirt, hearing Kay's voice from earlier today: *I surprised her in the hallway. I asked if she was family, if she was going in. But she ran back down the hall. We didn't see her after that.*

Today, he was so sure a Soviet assassin or Nazi hunter had killed Marko Kovacs, but now he can't stop thinking of Zoya Kovacs.

He can almost see a young girl—only fourteen at the time—cowering outside her mother's hospital room, listening as her parents fought viciously. But something isn't adding up. Why did Zoya run away when Kay asked if she was going in? What was she afraid of? Her own father? Did she wait in the stairwell for him to leave and perhaps then saw him standing in Jeanie's doorway, and hit him over the head? If so, she could have run off in a state, perhaps when the Russian assassin happened along. He'd obviously finished the job. But how were the nurses involved?

Pat O'Dwyer had stated in the police report that a man came in after Marko Kovacs had been told to leave. And Kay confirmed this same man—with a foreign accent—had chased Kovacs down the back stairs. Had the nurses lied to the police?

Dan lets out a frustrated sigh. He's desperate for a look at the gun with strange initials engraved on it, but Jeanie refused to drug her old nurse, and Pat was apparently arriving on the first ferry tomorrow morning. Kay had rung Pat and told her of his visit, he's sure of it. The last time he'd seen O'Dwyer, she'd promised to call the police on him if he returned. If he stays to confront her, will she make good on her threat?

There's movement in the garden and he tenses, relaxing only when he sees Jeanie crossing the boardwalk, carrying a pile of white towels. He imagines his hands on her warm skin, losing himself in her . . . *Stop,* he thinks hopelessly. *These are useless fantasies. You are damaged and she is innocent. She can't be touched by your darkness.*

Dan survived those years with a stoic resolve that has never been broken; they broke other things. How strange that only here, in this free land, he feels unhinged, damaged beyond repair. Here he wakes out of nightmares in a cold sweat. His limbs tremble with the anticipation of violence.

Now Jeanie stands on the porch, her eyes gleaming in the moon's light. He stubs out his cigarette in a metal ashtray on the railing and takes the towels she holds out like an offering. "Guests don't come often," she says, "or . . . let's face it, *ever*—so I forgot these." Dan nods, afraid to say anything, afraid to break this tenuous enchantment that hangs in the air between them. "I did it," Jeanie suddenly admits. "I put one of my sleeping pills into her water."

Dan exhales in profound relief. Lantern light flickers through the window behind him, and he can feel Jeanie's eyes tracking the scars on his forearms. He rolls down his shirtsleeves, too raw to face her questions about the only tattoos that remain inked on the three middle fingers of his right hand—*Spasi, Otets, Syna*—*Save me, father, your son.*

Like two burglars, he and Jeanie make their way back along the boardwalk. Soon, they're standing in the living room, behind the couch where Kay reclines, listening to her snore. Certain that she's fast asleep, they steal up the stairs.

When they're in Pat's room, Dan quickly crosses to the bedside table and switches on the lamp. He searches the drawer but cannot find the gun. He's on his knees now, pawing through Pat's things, then he lowers his head, keeping his face immobile to hide his anger. "It's gone." He leaps to his feet, looks at Jeanie. "Kay came in here and took the gun."

Jeanie steps back, shocked. "But why would she need a gun?"

Dan doesn't answer. He'd rather the gun still be in Pat's possession instead of Kay's.

When they're back outside in the garden, he pauses a moment. He's too aware of his heartbeat—rogue waves surging on a deceptively calm sea. He and Jeanie stand only a few feet away from each other in a long-shadowed palm grove, spiked fronds rising in the moonlight. The sky is indigo blue, sprayed with stars and a mysterious, white-dusted galaxy that wheels over their heads. He can't see the expression on Jeanie's face in the near dark; he can only feel the celestial force of her, pulsating outward like a streaking comet.

"I'll see you in the morning?" she ventures.

A puff of wind rises from somewhere, and the palm fronds rattle like wind chimes. "I wish to show you something," he says, and turns on the path. When they climb the stairs to the guest cabin, he opens the door wide. The living space is expansive for a guest suite—a double bed against the far wall, a kitchen table and two chairs. Jeanie pauses in the doorway, the blood draining from her face at the sight of the kerosene lamp on the table.

He leaves her side to turn the flame lower and she finally ventures into the room. Her eyes land on his leather-bound notebook, open to a page filled with cryptic scribbles. Beside his notebook is an old photograph. He hands it to her, watching as she leans closer, one wary eye on the kerosene lamp.

"This was taken in 1938," he explains, hoping that seeing Marko Kovacs's face will jog her memory. "A year before Germany and the Soviets invaded Poland."

A few of the men's faces are blurred, as if they've been surprised by the photographer. She points to the unit commander at the far right, a revolver in a holster at his hip, fair hair cut short beneath a ragged cap, face stern and unmoving. "This is *him*, isn't it?" Suddenly, she utters a little cry. "He looks just like you . . ." Jeanie glances up at him, her eyes filled with sudden tears. "Marko Ivanets—Marko Kovacs. He's your father."

He stares back at her, astonished, then relieved. "Taras Ivanets," he says, holding out his hand formally, as if he's meeting her for the first time. "I am sorry to lie about who I am, but I had to fool Pat." He turns away. "I didn't want you to know my past as a convict. I wished to tell you sooner, but I didn't know how."

Jeanie lays a tentative hand on his arm. Through his shirt, he can feel her feverish touch flash through his blood. "A convict?" she repeats.

He glances at her. "I have been twenty-eight years in Siberian prisons."

"Oh, Dan," she gasps, her hand still on his arm. ". . . I mean, *Taras*! Tell me everything."

He begins to speak of it in a slow halting whisper, telling her how he was captured in a Ukrainian forest in 1944, after the Soviet Secret Police shot his mother. How the NKVD officer sent him to a prison in Moscow, then a work camp in Siberia. It's then that he's hit with a startling realization: Every day in the camps he thought of Lieutenant Belyakov. When Taras was finally set free, he assumed the monster was long gone, but what if he's wrong? Could the NKVD officer be the assassin who'd found Tato and Mama and Zoya in Vancouver? The Soviet had come to make his old victim give up her own husband. He thought of his pure, kind mother. What did the Russian hold over her? It was obviously Belyakov who had strangled his father—perhaps in Jeanie's hospital room—then disposed of the body and gone straight back to Moscow, robbing Taras of the chance for revenge.

Jeanie is still studying the photograph with a stricken expression, and he thinks back to nine months ago, when he'd turned up at Mama's door.

The police thought a thief might have surprised your father coming out of the hospital, a fight ensued, and the thief accidentally killed him, disposing of the body. How effortlessly Mama had tried to dissuade him from investigating his father's disappearance, when she knew exactly who had killed him. Taras looks at Jeanie, painfully aware of the awkward silence that has descended, as if they're circling each other, unsure of the next step. He thinks of Kay asleep in the living room of the house. Did Jeanie give her enough to keep her out?

"When your father opened my hospital room door," she ventures, "I think I was afraid."

"Why?"

"If he was curious, why didn't he just ask one of the nurses? Why go into another patient's room, at night?"

Without a good answer to that question, Taras broods silently. Jeanie's presence has transformed the room. The lamplight flows over her face, the curve of her neck, and delicate line of her jaw. She's studying him, too. "You see," he says, "I cannot hide my scars." Jeanie's gaze heats his blood, and he doesn't trust himself to read her intentions correctly. Or his own. There was one woman, a long time ago in the camps, a nurse, but she'd been killed by one of the thieves. Other than that, he has no experience with females. And certainly not a woman like this.

"You must have thought I was crazy," she says, shaking her head. "The day we met. It wasn't what it looked like."

Taras is silent for a moment. "I have seen it before in prisoners. One can rage against injustice for only so long. When I worked at the infirmary, I saw them come—they cut off their own fingers, smashed themselves with stones, swallowed nails and knives." He draws a deep breath, thinking this is not the way he hoped their conversation would go. "At first, I believe a man did such things to avoid work crews. But this is rage against the enslavers. Throw yourself on a sword to fight the beast."

A shadow passes over Jeanie's face. "The promise of suicide as a means of survival."

"In camps, the politicals—we whispered to each other. Mass suicide, this is what gives us hope—kill ourselves and we controlled our fate."

"You weren't a criminal," she says, edging closer to him around the table.

"But I became one."

Jeanie hands him the photograph. "An innocent, trapped with all those depraved souls."

"I'm sure the gun you found in Pat's drawer was my father's," he says. "Before he changed his last name from Ivanets to Kovacs, Tato carved his initials—*M.I.*—into the stock of a Luger he had in Ukraine." He traces his father's likeness with an index finger and suffers an image of Mama—an image he's endured so many times over the years—of her lying in the snow after she was shot in Ukraine. *Why was I taken by the NKVD, Mama,* he'd always wondered, *and you were left behind?*

Jeanie is staring at his damaged fingertip, tears hovering on her lashes. "Did you get frostbite from working in the cold?"

"Yes," he says, looking up to meet her measured gaze, feeling at once seen and stripped bare.

"You said you planned to escape," she breathes.

"One time I tried, a few months after I arrived."

"You were caught?"

He shakes his head. "You should not want to hear—"

"I do."

Taras carefully considers his response. "Forty days I spent in solitary. I never tried to escape again." He makes a bitter sound in his throat. "The guard comes to me, takes off his belt. 'Hang yourself,' he says, 'you are not worthy of this world'—" He stops short, afraid that he's gone too far.

"I hope you told him to fuck off," Jeanie says with a tremulous smile.

Taras laughs, a soft chuckle of relief. "I did not." He looks away, so she can't see the wound he carries with him. "In the camps," he says, "you trusted no one."

"You're no longer in the camps," she whispers, taking another step toward him. "And you're not shattered. I've never met a more genuine person in my life."

Taras is overwhelmed by an urge to take her in his arms, to kiss her, yet he stops himself and glances at the closed door. "You should go. Only a monster survives that place."

But his words have no effect, for she moves so close he can smell her freshly washed hair. It feels like a waft of loveliness, a gift. "Only a hero could live," she says.

He opens his mouth to protest but is mesmerized when she lifts her hand, like the supplicating statue of a goddess he once saw in a Kyiv museum. Taking it, he carefully places her palm against the scars on his cheek, where it cools his burning skin. "Frostbite," he says finally, his hand on top of hers. Her touch is so light, so exhilarating, he reaches out, his arm encircling her waist and draws her toward him.

"Before you arrived," Jeanie says softly, her voice muffled by his shirt, "I thought Gladsheim was no longer my home."

"Do you still think this?" he says, breathing in her intoxicating smell.

"You changed everything."

They sway like two trees that have grown together in the same forest, separate but now extending their branches. The top of her head fits neatly under his chin, and she must feel his heart beating wildly in his chest. His hand moves to her hair as she looks up at him.

He brushes her lips with his own. And instead of pushing him away, she stands on tiptoes, her arms around his neck. His hands entwine in her long, silky hair. Taras loses all sense of time as his mouth moves across her jaw, breathing softly into her ear. When she pulls away to take his hand, her eyes dazzling with invitation, he sweeps her up and carries her to the bed, lays her down gently.

She sits up, pulling him down to her. "The lamp," she whispers.

"I want to see you."

She shakes her head. Is she afraid he'll be repulsed by her scars when he has so many of his own? But he obliges her, turning the flame lower still. He draws his shirt over his head and removes his pants and socks, standing naked in the center of the room, daring her to witness his own injuries and his past, to know him completely. In the flickering light he lets her see him, the man he might have been and perhaps would be again. Her eyes travel over the unmistakable white of scars across his flanks, the tips of his toes that he lost to frostbite the first winter of his incarceration. The light in her eyes brings him to the verge of tears. Can a plant that has suffered without water and sun for too long ever come back to life?

The bed creaks under his weight and then he's in her arms in the near darkness. Long kisses and weightless hesitation. Her sweater comes off with some difficulty and a curse, both of them laughing, and then her slacks and undergarments, their held breaths. She pushes her hips up to him, and he hesitates. "Is it . . . all right?"

"Hell, *yes*," she whispers with a soft intake of breath as his hand moves slowly, questioningly, across her breasts and downward, until she quivers as a tuning fork might, struck against his palm, each cell shimmering to the key of C.

When he enters her, a sob escapes her lips, relief, or the body remembering this delicious falling, the buzz of thousands of bees in his ears and Jeanie a flower, so fragile he fears he might crush her beneath him. But her eyes shine upward in the shadowed dark, her body taut and hands fluttering across his skin, over his arms and back, the sacred ascending between them. Her rapturous incantations shake him to the core, they bring him to the edge of the waterfall and over it, cascading down into anguished release.

The lamp sends flickering shadows as he folds his knees into the back of hers, kissing the tip of her winged shoulder blade in this small bed they lie upon together, a boat on a calm sea. His hand travels over the scars on her back and he whispers, "How many operations for this?"

"I've lost count," she says. "Hundreds."

Taras turns her gently and traces the raised whorled scars over her breasts. "This is art," he says as tears roll down her cheeks and onto the pillow beneath her head.

40

SAVKA

Vancouver

DECEMBER II, 1972

ZOYA THREW HER SHEEPSKIN coat across a chair. "What's wrong?" she asked her mother in Polish.

Sometimes on Savka's day off, she met her daughter and son for breakfast at a diner in Richmond. These get-togethers often ended in an argument—always started by Zoya—before they even managed to order their food, so Savka forced a smile. "Nothing," she insisted.

"I know you, Mama—you're upset." Her daughter spread her arms and did a half turn before sitting down. "Is it what I'm wearing?" she said, setting her elbows on the table.

A distinct smell of skunk wafted from her daughters' clothes. *Marijuana*, Savka thought, wrinkling her nose. She did not approve of Zoya's casual and provocative state of dress—this morning it was a form-fitting white turtleneck, a pair of suede knee-high boots, and a miniskirt—nor did she approve of her long, dark hair: straightened with an iron and parted severely in the middle. But she always listened politely when her daughter ranted about feminism. Zoya followed Bella Abzug and Gloria Steinem, speaking of things like *the women's movement* and their right to *reproductive freedoms*.

Zoya looked at her watch. "Where's Taras?"

"Your brother won't be here this morning."

"He's busy?" A flippant smile. "Doing what?"

Savka refused to tell Zoya that Taras had not come home last night. He was a grown man, God knew, but she still felt protective of him. He'd taken a job washing cars and had finally earned enough to buy himself a used vehicle, which was a blessing and a curse. Taras had launched his own investigation based on Marko's missing person's report, which had led him to Salt Spring Island, where nurse O'Dwyer had ended up as a caregiver to the Fire Bride, who'd also been on Savka's ward.

"Pat threatened me," Taras had said when he returned from the island last week and thrown his car keys on the table, his face like thunder.

Savka was not surprised, remembering the sour look on the nurse's face as she told Marko to leave the hospital ward, and she couldn't help feeling dismayed at how good a detective her son had become. "How did you discover where they lived?" She'd listened with a fixed, uneasy smile as Taras recounted how he'd driven onto the ferry without knowing how he might find Pat O'Dwyer's address, when a man joined him at the railing. Taras said he was looking for an artist who had painted a picture for him years ago. The man had smiled—*The Fire Bride? Everyone knows where she lives*—and proceeded to tell him exactly how to get to Southey Point, which, ironically, was on the northern tip of the island.

Savka recalled what she'd read of Jeanie, whose tragic history was similar to her son's—two wounded soldiers who'd been alone far too long. Normally, Savka would have encouraged such an interest, but not with this woman, not with the Fire Bride. And Taras *had* been interested. Too much so, relating how he'd found Jeanie in a power struggle with Pat O'Dwyer.

Savka looked up at her daughter and smiled. "Your brother has been investigating your father's death."

"Why?" Zoya said, pretending to read the menu. As expected, the mention of Marko had set her teeth on edge.

"The thought of his father kept him alive in the camps. He wants to know what happened." Savka thought with discomfort of the phone conversation with Belyakov only a month ago.

"Why did your son go to the police?" he'd asked the second she'd answered the call. She had blanched, worrying—*Belyakov knows of Taras's return*—but Ilyin must have still watched the apartment periodically, hoping Marko might show up. He'd seen her son coming and going. "Taras wanted to see the missing person's report," she'd told him. "Wouldn't you be suspicious if you learned your father had disappeared from a hospital ward and was never seen again?"

"Tell him to stop," Belyakov had shouted, making her jump.

"I have," Savka said, heart thumping rebelliously. "He won't."

"He is asking too many questions."

"What my son does is no business of yours." She'd gloated at the new power she held over her Russian handler. "You no longer own him. Moscow let him out. They issued an exit visa—"

"This fucking country," he sputtered. "Letting in too many Ukrainians!"

"They let *you* in, didn't they?" she'd cried, slamming down the phone.

The diner waitress arrived with coffee and her notepad. After they'd ordered, Zoya smiled as she poured sugar into her cup. Savka's hope soared. Perhaps her daughter would act respectfully for once. Outside, a determined sun broke through the clouds and washed the diner and its occupants with golden light. Savka had been happily stirring cream into her coffee when she looked up. Her spoon stilled when she realized that Taras had entered the diner without her noticing and stood near the door, a lit cigarette between his fingers.

"Taras," she cried, still unable to get over that he was in Vancouver now, *safe*. He walked slowly toward them, wearing the western clothing he'd cobbled together from thrift stores, the style set firmly in the sixties, and more suited to an ageing professor than a man with the rest of his life ahead of him.

Taras kissed his mother's cheek and sat down beside Zoya. Savka took out a pack of cigarettes; after lighting one and taking a long first drag, she exhaled smoke slowly out of her lungs, studying her two children and the awkward silence that hung between them. It was strange that her son hadn't kissed his sister. She'd thought they were becoming close.

Taras, clearly agitated, had moved to the edge of his chair, and Zoya, oblivious, playfully ran her hand over the stubble growing like a shadow on his head. "There's no lice here. Grow your hair, man."

"I'm used to it short," he said, leaning away from her with a frown.

"Haven't you noticed?" Zoya teased. "The Canadians wear it long."

"I don't wish to look Canadian." The waitress brought him a coffee and took his order. Taras reached for the sugar and glanced at Zoya for the first time since he'd arrived, then back at his mother. "I've been out to see Jeanie," he said at last.

Jeanie. Two scarce meetings, and Taras spoke her name with a kind of reverence. And that starstruck look of his—why, he was a little in love with her. How could he not be? The girl not only summed up his very existence, she personified it. Savka tilted her head, waiting for him to continue.

"Jeanie's memories are coming back." Something sparked in his eyes, and Savka immediately knew that he'd been intimate with the artist. "Mama, do you remember a nurse named Kay?"

Savka nodded, waiting for her racing heart to slow. "The tall one, with an English accent." She'd underestimated the lengths her son would go to find out what had happened to his father. How had he learned so much about that time, about the hospital and the nurses?

The waitress came by to refill her and Zoya's coffee cups. As soon as she was gone, Taras looked at his sister. "Kay said you were 'skulking in the hallway,' and you didn't want to go in while Tato was visiting." He paused then studied her hair. "She described your dark curls."

Savka could feel her throat close. She looked at her daughter, and said, her voice strained, "You were there, the night Marko disappeared?"

Zoya lowered her eyes in resignation. "He'd come home earlier and packed his suitcase, as he always did before leaving on a trip," she admitted. "He was swearing and throwing things—freaking out. He shouted insults at me, said he was going to the hospital to see you, make you face what you'd done. Then he would leave us, forever."

Taras gave his sister such a mournful look, Savka wondered if he suspected that Zoya killed his father. "Men were following Marko," Savka said, anxious to steer his interest away from Zoya. "Bad men, who thought he had something they wanted."

But Taras was not to be deterred. "You followed him to the hospital," he said to his sister. "Why?"

"I was afraid he would hurt her, so I broke my piggy bank," Zoya replied, too calmly. "I got a taxi and went after him."

"Tato wouldn't hurt Mama—she'd just had an operation." Taras gave Zoya a searching look. "The nurse said she asked if you were going in to see her, and you ran away."

Savka's heart jumped a beat. The smell of fried food drifted to her from the diner kitchen, and it was everything she could do not to retch. She stared at her daughter, remembering what she'd shouted to Marko that day he told her she couldn't speak Polish under his roof.

I hate you so much, I wish you would die.

Then Marko was dead not one week later.

"I stood outside her room," Zoya said, stammering under her brother's relentless interrogation. "I heard them argue. When that nurse went in, Marko was shouting. Before he left her room, I ran down the hall and ducked into the stairwell, heading to the main floor, thinking I'd beat him to his car. I waited for him in the parking lot, but he didn't come down, so I left."

"Why would you wait for him?" Savka asked, finally breaking her silence.

"To finally tell him he destroyed our lives."

Taras tapped his fingers against his coffee cup, thinking. Savka had not seen him so despondent, so angry, and it frightened her.

"Did you see this man who came up," he finally asked his sister, "claiming to be Tato's brother?"

"What man?" Zoya stared angrily at him. "It was late when I left. The nurses had gone back to the main desk."

At that moment, the waitress delivered their eggs, and Taras waited while she arranged the plates on the table.

Zoya sat back in her chair. "You think I killed him and stuffed him in a laundry bin?" Her voice was shrill, and several other diners turned their heads. "Come on, Taras—this is getting trippy."

Taras began to eat with deliberation, as if he were still in the camps, desperate to nourish himself before the food was stolen. "Why didn't you tell us you were there?" he asked between bites.

Zoya ignored his question. "I'm glad he's dead, but I didn't kill him."

Savka couldn't touch her food, she couldn't speak. The only way to stop Taras from interrogating Zoya was to tell the truth. Not all of it, of course. But some part of what she'd come to realize that day with Lev at the Stanley Park Zoo. She put down her fork and leaned across the table to take her daughter's hand. "You wondered why Marko hated you. You don't resemble him . . . or me for that matter. He feared you were the child of another man."

Zoya pushed her plate away, her eyes blank and expressionless, as if this was information she'd always known would come. "*Am* I the child of another man?"

Savka sat back. If she opened her mouth again, she might scream. But there was no avoiding the truth now. "Your father is an NKVD agent."

Taras carefully placed his fork and knife on his empty plate. "I remember Belyakov sending Ilyin back . . . he told him to search you again, make sure they hadn't missed another *shtafeta*. Mama, if I'd known . . ." he trailed off, an odd, stunned expression on his face.

As realization dawned slowly over Zoya, her face crumpled. "My father was your rapist . . ." she whispered.

Savka gulped the last of her coffee, got herself under control, then told her two children, in halting words, some of what had happened that day in the forest, how she'd not remembered until shortly before Marko's disappearance, that an NKVD soldier had violated her while she was unconscious. "It came to me in pieces. But it was a long time ago," she said, more for her own benefit than Zoya's. "We must put it behind us."

Zoya's dark eyes were stormy. "So, I was conceived as a *fuck you* to Marko and the work he was doing with the SS," she said in her characteristically frank manner. "And he had the nerve to punish *me* for it." Other diner customers were now openly staring at them and Savka reddened.

Her daughter stood abruptly, sending her chair flying. "Maybe he got the death he deserved!" She stomped out of the diner and left Savka staring blankly after her.

Taras did not watch her go, for his eyes were now on his mother. "That day in the forest," he mused, "Lieutenant Belyakov ordered his men to take me up the hill. He spoke to you quietly. What was it he whispered?"

Savka regarded her son with defiance. Since he'd shown up at her door, Taras had treated her with deference, honor, not asking questions that he must have turned over in his head the entire time he was in prison.

But he was asking them now.

After a long pause, she said, "The officer told me that if the NKVD couldn't have Marko Ivanets or his wife, they would have his son."

A muscle twitched at the corner of his mouth. "Mama—"

"Taras, it was a long time ago and the worst day of my life." She hoped he would back off, but her son had a curious glint in his eye that told her he meant to see this through, regardless of how much pain it caused her.

"What did you agree to do?"

The implication hovered in the air. "I had been shot, Tarasyku, I was bleeding to death." She placed a tentative hand on his arm. "How could I remember everything he said?"

Taras gave her a long, loaded look. "I always wondered why Belyakov just left you there."

Savka stared down at her eggs, now congealing on the plate. "They thought I was dying."

"Kuzak found you and removed the bullet?" His voice was respectful, but she could hear the doubt there.

"Kuzak banished me."

"Why?"

"He . . . suspected that I'd been turned," she murmured, feeling drained by the burden of secrets she'd kept for so long.

"The nurse Kay said you had a Russian visitor before Tato came in, before he disappeared."

The hairs on the back of Savka's neck stood up with foreboding. Taras could never know that Belyakov was her Soviet handler, that he made her spy on his father and still ordered her out on useless assignments. She took out her pack of cigarettes and let Taras light one for her. Inhaling deeply, she waited for the smoke to soothe her nerves. "The nurse is lying. I can't remember a Russian visitor."

"Belyakov was here in 1959. Is he still here? Is he following me?"

Smoke from her cigarette curled up and around her spinning head. "No," she lied. Her arm went suddenly numb, just as it had the moments after she was shot twenty-eight years ago.

"I have something to tell you." Taras pushed his coffee cup away. "I went this morning to the Ukrainian Cultural Centre and found a man who knew Tato. He said my father went to New York several times before he disappeared, to work with Mykola Lebed." Taras leaned forward, his eyes dancing with excitement. "Tato left his car behind to throw off whoever was following him. Mama, all this time, he's been in New York . . . with Lebed."

4I

JEANIE

Salt Spring Island
DECEMBER 11, 1972

"JESUSCHRISTALMIGHTY, she really *is* here." Pat has just returned from Vancouver, reeking of hairspray from a fancy salon visit and wearing a new green wool coat that must have cost her—or me—a pretty penny. She stands in the living room, watching Kay swim back and forth in the bay. Pat looks as though she'd like to strangle her fellow nurse with her bare hands.

And I'd like to strangle her. *What the hell did you have to do with Taras's father's disappearance?* But I say nothing, because I won't let Pat's griping shake me off the cloud of love I'm floating upon. I flush at the memory of Taras's hands on my shoulders only a few hours ago, before he left, as he shared his plans to visit the Ukrainian émigré community in Vancouver and ask more about his father, then to question his mother and sister.

"Escape with me," Taras had said before getting into his car, the two of us standing close together, heads touching, still in our own private world.

"First, I need to fire Pat," I said, kissing his cheek. "Then you can return and stay . . ."

But Taras can only stay if Pat is gone. And I haven't quite figured out how to fire her. I don't want to look at her miserable face, or even acknowledge her reentry into my life this morning. I need Kay's help. "Kay has come to see *me*," I explain to my caregiver as the sun battles its way out of the haze. "All the way from Africa."

"By God," Pat fumes. "I'm not going to let her stay longer than a goddam week."

After the difficulties yesterday with Kay, I can't argue Pat's point. And Taras was wrong—besides Pat's call here yesterday, it's obvious that she hasn't spoken to Kay since the day she left for Africa. Clearly, there's no sinister plan between them to commit me. Kay will help me tell Pat she's fired and must leave immediately.

With an oblique glance, Pat hands over my morning medication cup. I reluctantly accept it, noticing as I do, that it contains *two* orange pills instead of one.

She's upped my dose of chlorpromazine.

Pat crosses her arms and looks at me, her face a guarded blank. Gazing down at the medication cup, my breath shallow with panic, I hash out a mad plan. One pill I can easily spit out without her noticing, but two will require a circus act in my mouth. She follows me into the kitchen and fetches a glass of water, watching as I dutifully swallow the contents of the cup under her stern gaze, pushing the two slick, round ones to the side of my cheek. When she slips out the back door, presumably for a furtive cigarette near the compost pile, I remove the pills, soggy and congealed, from my mouth. One of them still sports the faded number *SKF T76* on the side. But the sink is full of soapy dish water. The back door handle rattles and I let out a startled cry, yanking out the garbage can from under the sink. Hurriedly, I bury the two pills among the plastic wrap and coffee grounds.

Feeling brave—or very desperate—I snatch the percolator off the stove, despite the heat it emits. When Pat stomps back in, I'm standing at the counter, pouring coffee into my favorite cup.

"The last thing you need is more coffee," she says, face like a hurricane. "Your hands are shaking."

Silence and brooding. Later I'll be sorry, later I'll wish I'd played along, Jeanie the puppet, Jeanie the easily controlled prisoner. But without too many doses of chlorpromazine careening through my blood, I'm feeling confident, clear-headed. I can't resist turning to her. "I'll do what I like."

She watches, wild-eyed as I swan past her—coffee cup in hand—down the hallway and out the door without stopping to put on a coat. Free and easy, I march across the boardwalk and pause at the door of the guest suite, smiling to myself, remembering last night and Taras's tender words to me as he drifted a gentle finger across the scars on my breasts. *This is art.*

Tuna has followed me out of the house and climbs the stairs behind me, his old joints practically creaking. In the studio, I crank the blues station and pace, noticing that at some point after she arrived this morning, Pat had come in and placed the blank canvas she'd prepared for the Paris financier's commission firmly on my main easel. I'd much rather play with the abstract of Taras, but my work ethic whispers its obligation to Octavius Karbuz.

I regard Pat's substandard attempt at an underpainting, whilst plotting to call Aunt Suze's lawyer for a referral to an accountant, or someone who can investigate Pat's transactions with my art dealer. I'll finish this commission on time *and* get all the money for it.

I sketch in a half-hearted composition of sea, island, sky, and throw down my rag to pick up a flat brush, mixing titanium white pigment with a smidge of ultramarine blue, then apply burnt sienna to my palate, pulling in more white. After washing in sky, I take up a round, pointed brush and spend the next hour tapping in some clouds and daydreaming of Taras.

Before being released from the hospital, I often lay in bed, my skin on fire and silently asking, *who will ever love me?* At the time, the answer had been—*absolutely no one.* Now it's: *a man who was hurt just as profoundly.* Taras has awoken something in me I thought had died, and that part of me happens to be sick and tired of Pat. How can I live even one more day with her in my house? I don't have long to wait, for Kay will soon be finished her swim. Perhaps she'll fire Pat the moment she sees her.

I step back to let the paint dry a little before I go in with the tree line. Another memory of Taras sends tingles along my spine, and I turn to look at the abstract on the other easel, stopping short when I realize it's no longer there. With frantic gasps, I tear through the entire studio, but the painting of Taras is nowhere to be found. *Did she take it?* The idea that Pat could have destroyed it tips me over the edge.

I'm filled with rage, but also empowered by the fact that I have a *lover*, a handsome Ukrainian man who is quite possibly the best thing that's ever come down that drive. I charge to the window and glare down at the house. There's a blur of activity in the kitchen, so I grab the binoculars I keep to watch birds at the feeder near the waterfall, and adjust the focus. Pat's face comes into the room with me. She stands at the kitchen counter looking confused, unsettled. Does this calm, together version of Jeanie frighten her? I sincerely hope so.

What's she doing? Cleaning furiously, I see, swiping at the counters with a feverish energy one usually reserves for mold control. Pat turns and I notice Kay come into the room, wrapped in a towel, her hair still wet from her swim. How fortuitous that I'll witness their first confrontation. Thirteen years since they've seen each other and they're already speaking heatedly about something.

Lowering the binoculars, I mutter, "Fire her, *fire* her . . ." But the words die in my mouth when I remember Kay passing me in the hallway this morning, shortly after Taras left, on her way out for her swim. She stared impassively, her lips in a tight moue of disapproval. "I saw your friend leave. He certainly looked pleased with himself." Her voice had a knife-like edge.

I'd felt myself blush. In high school, I'd missed all the incessant gushing among girls over their boyfriends. I wanted to tell Kay I'd fallen in love with Taras the first time I'd seen him running up the headland to save me from myself. But something held me back.

As Kay watched my face turn what was surely an embarrassing shade of scarlet, her own expression morphed into one of distaste. "I hope you didn't throw yourself at him," she said and pushed past me to the door.

I'd stared after her, mortified, but put it off to her nerves at the prospect of facing Pat, after all the years they'd been adversaries. Lifting the binoculars again, I watch the two of them now in the kitchen. When Kay slowly approaches Pat, I hold my breath. Will there be fisticuffs?

Pat takes a single sheet of paper from the top of the fridge and holds it out to Kay, and I fiddle with the focus on the binoculars, sure that she's somehow got hold of my new last will and testament, but it can't be. That's four pages long. Kay accepts the paper, and, lifting it to her face, begins to read. Pat leans toward her, pointing out a certain passage. They're standing too close together for enemies, there's an easy familiarity and a kind of relief in their manner, as though the two of them are catching up after a long absence. But Kay despises Pat! And Pat has never mentioned her these past thirteen years.

My eyes are practically glued to the binoculars, watching Kay murmur something that must be disturbing, for Pat suddenly twists away from her. The two women glare at each other. Kay speaks to her and Pat stands there like a chastened schoolgirl. This is more like it. Then Kay hands Pat the document and turns, leaving the kitchen. Pat, clearly agitated, begins to obsessively line up the toaster with the bread box on the counter. She stops in mid-action, looking as if she's just figured out the solution to a complex mathematical equation. Her head jerks up, swiveling toward the window and I duck behind the curtain. What's she up to? Did Kay tell her that Taras has been here while she was away? She *wouldn't*.

Cautiously, I sneak out from behind the curtain and again train the binoculars at Pat, who's futzing about below counter level.

I move to the other window, where I have a clear view of her on her knees, going through the garbage bin that lives under the sink. My heart begins to thump dangerously in my chest. Is it possible she somehow saw me spit out the pills? What supremely rotten luck.

I throw down the binoculars and snatch up the French landscape. Tuna lowers his head and closes his eyes, as if he's decided that whatever this is, it's not worth him getting out of bed. I bump down the stairs with the canvas, my chest heaving. I'm not sure what I'm going to do, but it's going to be big. Fire Pat *big*.

As I gallop down the wooden walkway toward the pond and waterfall, Pat bursts out of the house. "What are you doing?" she cries when she sees I'm carrying her bread and butter, the precious painting she thinks means thousands of dollars in her bank account. She has an object in her hand, something small and cylindrical, which she attempts to hide by wrapping her palm tightly around it. I quicken my pace until I'm standing on the rocks at the edge of the waterfall, dangling the canvas precariously close to the spray.

Pat shouts some indecipherable sentence at me over the sound of the water, and I turn, holding my painting over the pond. "Isn't this a pretty picture?" I shout.

Pat angles close, holding up her hand to talk me down. "Don't throw away your work!"

"Don't throw away your paycheck, you mean! Do you think I'm stupid? I've noticed your new duds."

She idles even closer, and I balance on the edge of the pond, trying to keep my eye on whatever she's hiding in her hand.

"I promise things will change," she says, modulating her voice to a more respectful tone. "*I'll* change."

"Too late!"

"You're insane," Pat screams. "You should be in an asylum!"

And there it is. Proof that she's trying to commit me. We face each other across the pond. "That's what you want, isn't it? Send me to the crazy hospital." I raise the painting above my head. The koi are darting around, deranged at the appearance of a shadow, fearing they're about to become an eagle's lunch. "Don't come closer. I'll send it to the bottom." I'm truly enjoying the look on Pat's face. Are those tears in her eyes? I'm appalled when one tracks down her cheek. What a performance.

"Please," Pat entreats.

"I don't trust you." I glance past her toward the house. Surely Kay has heard us and will soon run out to save me from this monster. *Hurry, Kay.* "You drugged me with . . . with antipsychotics! Don't think I didn't know. Keeping me stupid so I won't remember."

Finally, I see Kay. She's changed out of her wet bathing suit and stands on the porch, hesitant.

"Kay," I scream, "Pat wants to commit me."

She sprints toward us, shouting something I can't hear over the sound of the waterfall.

I look smugly at Pat. Thankfully, Kay is here to protect me. But Pat isn't looking at Kay. Her eyes are trained on me. "Settle down, Jeanie," she says. "Settle down."

"You're fired," I shout to her. Finally. Finally I've uttered the words I've waited too many years to say. "Pack your things and get out."

Pat staggers forward, as if losing her bearings. She's about to topple into the pond and ruin her fabulous new coat. I lower the painting to get a better view, when Pat charges past the waterfall and grabs me by the straps of my overalls, tossing the canvas clear, where it lands on top of a cedar hedge.

I scream in outrage and flail at her, but Pat is bigger and stronger, and she kneels, turning me over her knee. With one quick motion, she yanks my overalls aside and jabs a needle into my back. Within seconds I stop struggling and my head droops. I fear I'm having a heart attack, it's beating so hard against my ribs, yet I instantly know what's happened.

She's injected me with an ampule of chlorpromazine. From the medicine cabinet.

I struggle to remain conscious, to fight. Then Kay's feet come into view. "Kay . . ." I gasp, straining my neck to look up. She also has something in her hand—a single sheet of paper. Is that the document I saw her discussing with Pat in the house? My vision is blurry; besides a legal seal on the top, I can't make out what it might be.

She gazes down at me and takes the empty ampule from Pat's hand. "We love you Jeanie, but you're an ungrateful bitch."

Horrified, I feel my body go limp and slither to the hard ground. Pat sits on her heels, trying to catch her breath, and Kay squats beside her, the mysterious document still in her hands. "Do you know how much time and effort we invested in you? How dare you turn against us—leaving Gladsheim to the Salt Spring Historical Society? After we made the ultimate sacrifice for you, after what we *did* to save your skin." She cradles my head in her hands and waits until my eyes cease swimming so I can focus on her face.

"You'll get such lovely drugs in Riverview, darling," she says, as if from very far away. "Lucky you."

42

SAVKA

Vancouver
DECEMBER II, 1972

TARAS DIDN'T SPEAK WHEN he drove Savka back to the apartment. As the sun disappeared behind a towering bank of dark cloud, her eyes filled with angry tears. Not one hour ago, during a harmless breakfast, one of the most damning of her secrets had come out. Zoya had learned she was the daughter of a Soviet rapist, and Taras now suspected her of being one of their spies. The wall of deception that Savka had built around her was crumbling, and she felt as though she were lying open and vulnerable beneath the thundering sky.

She glanced at her son. The excitement was gone from his eyes, but his single-minded focus scared her. "What are you thinking?"

"I'm sorry you were violated by the NKVD." His eyes had not left the road. "But I'm leaving tomorrow for New York. To find Tato."

Savka shook her head. "Tarasyku, can't you see? The Soviets couldn't get to Mykola Lebed, so they killed his right-hand man—your father. The nurses saw the assassin follow Marko down the back stairs. Your Tato left his car behind because he was taken somewhere else and killed." She knew her words would do nothing to dissuade Taras from continuing this ridiculous investigation—there was something in his eyes she hadn't seen since his return, a lost fragment of the determined, headstrong son she'd known long ago. The real Taras. Was it possible this search for his father had given him purpose? Or had the Fire Bride brought him back to life? Savka looked away and caught herself leaning forward to stare too long in the side passenger mirror, fearful that Belyakov and Ilyin might appear behind them in their black town car.

Her son's mouth was now set in determination. "You're expecting someone to follow us? Lieutenant Belyakov, who turned you in the Carpathians?"

For a split second, she thought of telling him everything, but her old secretive self kicked in again. Savka thought back to a recent phone conversation with Belyakov. "Your son knows someone is following him," he'd shouted. "He took Ilyin on a joy ride across the city and turned down an alley to lose him."

"Why do you continue to bother Taras?" she'd shouted back. "Leave him alone."

But Belyakov was persistent. "Why is your son going to Salt Spring Island?"

"He's fallen in love with a girl."

"Mama," Taras said, breaking into her thoughts. "The Soviet who visited you in the hospital—I know that he was Belyakov, the one who took me. And now he's following me. If this Russian killed Tato and you're still working for him, I . . ." He trailed off, unable to look at her.

"Where did you get such a ridiculous idea?" she said, her voice sharper than she intended.

At a stoplight, Taras turned his head to regard her. "Did Tato discover you were spying on him for the Soviets? Did you kill him yourself?"

Savka jolted in her seat at this reckless accusation from her son. Part of her wanted to rail against the insult, but he'd suffered enough. "Look at you, here with me—you survived. You've become a fine man—a hero—despite all the Soviets did to burn you in hell."

"I told Jeanie I'm not a hero for surviving the Gulag. I tell you that, too." There was a note of exasperation in his voice, but she also caught the reluctant smile that crept around the edges of his mouth.

"You're not getting involved with this girl," Savka said, still trying to protect him from hurt. "You hardly know her."

"I know her better than anyone in this life."

Savka turned her face to the windshield, wounded to her core. *Better than your own mother, who sacrificed everything to protect you?*

After he parked, she bolted from the car and started up the stairs to their apartment, feeling Taras's formidable silence behind her like an impending storm.

When he caught up with her on the stairs, he insisted his father was still alive. "Why can't you see that?" he said, trying to make her look at him.

Savka's hand shot out to the railing, fearing she might stumble and miss a step. What if he was right and Marko *had* been in New York all this time? As she climbed the stairs to the third floor, her heart ached, that persistent pain in her chest. She crossed the landing and headed down the hall toward their apartment, glancing up only when she heard someone say, "Try again." Her heart froze at the sight of two police officers, one about to knock at her door, the other frowning down at a notebook in his hands. Her first thought: *Belyakov has been arrested. And brought me down with him.* Now they would arrest her, send her to prison.

She shrank back, but they'd already seen her and Taras, who'd reached the landing behind her. "Mrs. Savka Kovacs?" one of the officers said. There was nothing for it but to accept that this was the end. She walked toward them as if to the gallows, then glanced over her shoulder at Taras. He'd stopped dead, his body a study in confusion and uncertainty. He had been back for only nine months, and now she would be the one dragged away to prison. *This is what you deserve.*

"Can we come in?' The officers were polite, but weren't they all when approaching a potential suspect? She'd seen enough detective shows on television to know.

She nodded and unlocked the door, opening it wide to let them pass, her stomach churning with anxiety. Taras followed, his face pale and bloodless, flinching at their every move, as if he expected violence. When the officers stood in the living room, Savka bent her head, waiting for the charges to be read, the handcuffs to come out. How might she defend herself? Tell them that Belyakov had forced her to spy on her husband? That he'd held her son captive to make her do things she never wanted to? "I had no choice . . ." she began.

The taller officer frowned. "It's about Marko Kovacs."

Taras's face was suddenly alive with hope. "You have found my father, in New York?"

The shorter officer cleared his throat. "He was discovered on a site near Maple Ridge, that was being bulldozed for a housing development."

Her son took a step back, his eyes wide and mouth working. "I don't understand . . ."

"Construction workers found his . . . remains . . . in October," the officer continued. "Forensics identified him by his dental records."

Savka lowered herself to the sofa, head in hand, vaguely aware of a strangled sound coming from Taras, a sound that made her feel strangely empty and alone. In her ears was the low insect buzz of shock and she only half listened as the officer asked them to come to the station in the morning, where a detective would provide more information. The door had hardly closed behind the police when Taras stumbled toward the kitchen. In a moment, she heard him dialing the phone. *He's calling Zoya,* she thought. *I will have my children with me to face this horrible news.*

A crash, as Taras slammed down the receiver. He came back into the living room, hands in tight fists at his side, his expression unreadable. "Pat and Kay aren't answering the phone," he said. "I must speak to Jeanie."

Savka felt an unnatural swell of rage and paused to let her breathing calm. "Your father's remains have just been dug up by a bulldozer and the first person you wish to speak with is the Fire Bride? You must honor him by coming with Zoya and me to see the detective tomorrow morning." Taras had become very still, so still it scared her. "Don't you want to find out what happened to him?" she cried.

Taras glowered at his wristwatch. "The last ferry has gone. I will catch the early one tomorrow." He went to his bedroom and closed the door. The apartment was silent as a grave and her blood chilled. What was he doing in there? Either grieving his father's death or obsessing over the Fire Bride, and the information locked in her memories of the night Marko disappeared.

43

JEANIE

Salt Spring Island
DECEMBER 11, 1972

MY HEAD FEELS LIKE a balloon filled with helium. I open my eyes to find myself slumped forward, my cheek against the kitchen table. When I try to raise my hand, it feels like it weighs a hundred pounds. Out of the corner of my eye, I see Pat, clearly agitated, as she races around the kitchen, digging out the fondue pot and fuel.

With a great deal of effort, I unfold myself to sit upright in the chair and take desperate stock of my situation: Every light in the house is on despite the fact the wall clock says it's not quite noon. My old nurses carried me in here only an hour ago.

Kay's words echo back at me, the last I heard before losing consciousness: *You're an ungrateful bitch. How dare you turn against us— leaving Gladsheim to the Salt Spring Historical Society?*

Then it hits me: This ungrateful bitch is being shipped off to an insane asylum.

Kay's voice floats across the room. "Sleeping Beauty's awake." I turn my head, eyes swimming, to find her standing near the back door. She's wearing my Cowichan sweater and nursing a cup of coffee, a cigarette between two fingers; she clamps her lips over it and sucks in a lungful of smoke before she manages to breathe again.

"You can't . . . smoke in the house," I remind her; the smell of smoke, and what it represents, makes me nauseous. But she no longer cares.

I frantically glance around the room and notice that, while I've been out, Pat and Kay have merrily decorated for Christmas. A poinsettia graces the center of the table, and I'm astonished at the sight of Aunt Suze's old, green construction paper chain draped across the kitchen doorway. The wall clock ticks loudly in my ear as I look down at the table, set with three plates, cutlery, napkins, and sharply pointed fondue forks. Are they hosting a celebratory, send-off meal? Pat and Kay exchange a look that's familiar and colluding. I crane my neck to get a better look at Kay. "You told me you hate Pat . . ."

"Pat and I will always be the very best of friends," she says, exhaling smoke like a dragon.

"What have you done?"

Pat whips around to stare at me, a block of cheese in her hand. "Sacrificed our lives to protect you, that's what." There's some kind of blockage in her nostrils—perhaps she caught a cold in Vancouver—for each breath comes as noisily as the last.

"Protect *me?*"

It's then that I notice Tuna, lying very still in his dog bed near the table. To my eyes, he's not breathing. "Tuna!" I cry. "You finally killed him." I'm starting to hyperventilate when Tuna opens one eye. To my profound relief, a whimper escapes him. Even he's afraid of these women. *In the presence of evil just go back to sleep, Tuna. It's safer.* But I can never go back to sleep, even if I want to. I think of the remains of the rabbit out on the headland—a few fluttering bits of fur left behind by a predatory eagle—on the day I met Taras. I should have climbed into his car this morning, when he asked me to escape with him.

Kay is staring at me impassively, some secreted emotion—guilt perhaps?—lurking at the corners of her mouth. "Pat and I have suffered to keep your secret. One day you'll thank us." She raises her eyes to Pat. "Did you have to give her an entire ampule?"

"Yes," Pat huffs, dragging the block of cheese over a grater.

"You lied to me," I cry, my voice a croak. Tuna climbs out of his bed to sit at my side, looking up with a concerned expression on his sweet face, only closing his eyes with relief when I scratch behind his ears.

Kay crosses to the fridge and takes out a bottle of wine. "Pat's right," she says, pouring herself a glass. "You have no idea what we've sacrificed for you."

Two against one. Desperately, I claw my way up through the blackness of Kay's deception. I blink and flex my fingers. Could I snatch up a fondue fork and stab Kay? Not before Pat dragged me off her. "Why did you drug me?" I ask. "Afraid that I'll leap at your throats?" In the impending silence, I realize they're terrified of what I represent. If I ever see Taras again, I'll trust his instincts. He was oh so right. "Or are you afraid I'll remember what really happened that night."

Another loaded glance is exchanged between them. "Trust me, you wouldn't want to remember," Kay says.

The block of cheese still in her hand, Pat slaps something down on the table in front of me. It's the one-page document I saw my old nurses discussing in the kitchen this morning, the same one Kay had in her hand before I lost consciousness only a few minutes later.

Tuna's sleek fur under my fingers is the only thing keeping me grounded as I gaze blankly at the paper. "What the hell is this?"

"The Salt Spring Historical Society will never get Gladsheim," Pat says darkly. "Your new so-called *will* means nothing."

"But Aunt Suze's lawyer made a special trip out here," I insist, shaking my head in frustration. What is Pat suggesting? "He had me sign my new will when you were in Vancouver . . ."

"A wasted trip," she declares. "He didn't know you'd earlier signed over your health care and property to *me*." When I blink rapidly, trying to understand, Pat smiles. "You obviously don't remember the local notary that I brought in shortly after you were discharged from the hospital."

I'm suddenly wide awake and rigid with shock, the effects of the drug completely gone. Lifting the paper with a trembling hand, I try to focus on the legalese.

In accordance with the Power of Attorney Act I declare that this power of attorney may be exercised during any subsequent mental infirmity on my part.

And my signature on the bottom. I look up at Pat. "But this . . . this says you can only exercise power of attorney if I'm deemed mentally infirm. It's obvious to anyone that I haven't lost my mind."

"Dr. Reisman would disagree," Pat says, touching her arm to remind me how I'd flown at her with the craft scissors.

Mental infirmity. My heart swings like a pendulum from shock to sick realization. Details are hazy, but now I remember the notary and Pat conferring over a pot of tea in the living room while I lay on the couch, wrapped in blankets. I'd been on stronger pain medications then and was so thankful that Pat had my best interests at heart, I hadn't bothered to read what I was signing. As soon as the notary left, the document had slipped from my memory. *Like so many other things.*

But the matter of whether I'm sane or insane can't be determined by Pat and Kay. I crumple the POA into a ball and pitch it against the stove. Even Tuna looks as if he'd like to destroy it. "You can't activate this until Dr. Reisman evaluates me. He won't rely on a story of me going after you with craft scissors," I say, holding my hands over Tuna's ears. "I'll tell him you threatened to kill my dog."

Kay is leaning against the fridge, drink in one hand, cigarette in the other, watching me with interest. Pat scoops up the POA and carefully smooths it on the table in front of me again. "Dr. Reisman was particularly dismayed at news of your latest suicide attempt, and the screwdriver you stole from the shed to kill me with. He prescribed chlorpromazine to see if you would improve. But you've gotten worse."

"When Reisman sees me, he'll know what you're up to," I say, gripping the edge of the kitchen table, where Aunt Suze used to sit with her morning coffee. What would she think to see her dream house on the ocean going to two criminals? It would kill her all over again. "Reisman will know I'm perfectly sane and you're the one who should be institutionalized."

"Good luck with that," Pat says so breezily, I must assume she's got Reisman in her back pocket. "He's already arranged a room for you at Riverview."

I turn my head and stare blindly out the kitchen window, my throat aching with unshed tears. Gladsheim is Aunt Suze's legacy. Gladsheim is my *life*. The thought of Pat and Kay ripping it away from me through devious plans, lies, and a POA I signed under the influence of serious medication, makes me livid with rage. Now I regret the suicide performance art and running at Pat with my craft scissors. Even stealing the screwdriver. All of it ammunition she needed to show Dr. Reisman that I was going insane.

Seething, I turn back to Pat. "This doesn't mean you can commit me." I itch to snatch up the POA and rip it into pieces, but she obviously has a copy somewhere.

Pat points to another clause, just above my signature, and I squint to read, barely able to breathe:

Without restricting the generality of the foregoing, I give the power and authority to do all acts necessary to transfer any and all property owned by me in the name of my Attorney.

"You can't steal Gladsheim," I cry in desperation.

Pat looks ready to slap me, but Kay intercedes, saying, "Let her have a strop. Fat lot of good it will do her." Then she smiles. "*Steal*," she tsks. "How gauche. We're selling Gladsheim and splitting the proceeds— along with what you've made on art sales—"

Pat's jaw drops as she turns to stare at Kay. "Hold your horses. Jeanie's art sales aren't in the bargain. You weren't in the trenches with her all these years, preparing canvases and putting up with her bullshit. That money is all *mine*."

"You were the one who asked me to come back," Kay says, meeting Pat's eyes with an explicit, unspoken warning. You couldn't do all this yourself."

"But I managed . . ." Pat sputters.

"Did you really?" Kay has taken a few steps closer to Pat, who shuffles away, her head down, like a puppy submitting to the alpha dog.

Pat's betrayal hurts, but Kay's? Devastating.

Kay drops her cigarette butt into the sink. "What if Danek Rys shows up?"

Pat throws down what remains of the cheese and slings the bottle of fondue fuel onto the counter, rubbing her forehead. "If he dares arrive tomorrow, we'll deal with him." She raises her eyes and throws a secretive look at Kay. "Just as we have everything else that's come our way."

44

SAVKA

ON THE LARGE PHOTOGRAPH Savka held in her trembling hands, the orbital bones of the skull yawned black; the few remaining molars left in the bleached and gaping jaw gave it the look of a Shakespearean stage prop. But a wife knew her husband's front teeth better than she knew her own.

Marko. "Were there any other bones found in the area?" Savka choked out. Just saying the words made her quake with loathing at whomever had murdered her husband.

The detective shook his head. "Nothing."

It felt as though an arrow had thunked deep into her chest. She couldn't breathe. It took everything in her to push the photograph across the desk of Detective Jaeger at the Vancouver Police Department headquarters. She hadn't expected a young man, with such startling blue eyes and athletic build. The cleft in his chin was so deep it cast a shadow.

She felt abandoned, out of her element. Zoya had refused to accompany her, claiming she had to cover a colleague's shift at the clinic. Savka must work, too, but she had called in sick. It seemed impossible to face this without help and she was still livid that, true to his word, Taras had obstinately left this morning for Salt Spring Island.

"You'd rather visit your girlfriend than find out what happened to your father?" she'd cried, grabbing his hand.

But Taras had charged out the door saying, "I must speak to Jeanie."

How would she tell her son the police had found only his father's skull?

Detective Jaeger's office was nothing more than a cubicle, windowless and stuffy with the unpleasant smell of stale coffee and cigarettes that had been crushed in a glass ashtray on the desk. She felt as though she were suffocating.

Savka clutched her purse and got up. "Thank you for letting me know—"

"Wait," the detective said. "Please look at the postmortem report."

He handed it to her, and she tried to focus on the words, her eyes swimming with tears.

Cause of death: *undetermined*

Manner of death: *undetermined*

Date and time of death: *unknown*

"When did you last see your husband?" the detective asked, watching her carefully.

His scrutiny unnerved her. "When he left my room that night."

"Did you see where he went?"

She was shocked at the suspicion in Detective Jaeger's hypnotically blue eyes. Surely he had reviewed what she'd told the detective investigating Marko's disappearance. Did he think she'd murdered her husband right after she'd had her womb removed, and dragged his body away? Savka took a handkerchief from her purse and dabbed at her eyes. "I had surgery that morning. It was impossible to get out of bed." She wouldn't tell the detective that Zoya might have run into Marko in the hallway that night. "My husband would be devastated to see his legacy reduced to a gap-toothed skull buried in a shallow grave," she blurted, then berated herself. What a thing for a widow to say. She handed back the report and composed herself, consciously lowering her shoulders, which were almost at her ears. Despite everything she'd gone through with Marko, she didn't wish him this kind of end. "My husband's assassin is still out there," she found herself saying.

Jaeger gestured at the chair. "Sit down, Mrs. Kovacs. There's more." Savka nodded, stricken, and reluctantly lowered herself into the chair. Jaeger cleared his throat. "The forensics report on your husband's skull has told us he suffered blunt force trauma."

Savka felt herself gasp for air. Somehow, she must summon her voice. "Someone . . . hit him?"

"Many times, it appears." Detective Jaeger frowned. "We've determined an instrument like a lead pipe was used. We'll need the rest of the body to know how he really died." He directed her attention to a close-up photograph of Marko's skull. "See this nick at the base of the occiput? It's a clean, sharp edge, which means it was made after death. At first, the coroner thought it might be damage from carnivores disturbing the site, but he confirmed the damage was made by a serrated instrument . . . possibly a saw."

Savka clapped a hand to her mouth, horrified. What kind of assassin would do such a thing?

Jaeger blinked a few times. "The body might have been dismembered as well as decapitated. A lot of thought and effort went into covering this up, burying the body." He paused, as if hoping she'd offer something else. "Do you have any idea who would have wanted your husband dead in 1959?"

Savka pressed her quivering lips together. As she'd suspected, a Nazi hunter had found Marko and instead of forcing him into a car and shooting him in the back of the head in a remote field outside of Vancouver, for what he might have done with the Waffen-SS, the assassin had beaten him to death in a fury of revenge. The Nazi hunter—and perhaps an accomplice—had savored the grisly act of dismemberment, and, like Set had done to Osiris, buried the pieces across Egypt.

"My husband was very . . . political," she finally managed. "There were Soviet operatives tracking him."

Detective Jaeger looked doubtful. "There are no Soviet operatives in Canada," he said with naïve confidence. "Any other ideas?"

She had *questions*, not ideas. Why had Taras insisted on going to Salt Spring Island this morning? What did it matter if Kay and Pat weren't answering the phone? They could have been outside. Savka remembered O'Dwyer as if it were yesterday, the look on the nurse's face when Marko had knocked her over on his way out of the room. She suddenly felt sick to her stomach, recalling the nurse springing up like a cat, as if she had revenge on her mind. And Pat was one of the last people to see Marko alive. Savka leaned toward Jaeger. "What of the two nurses on the ward where he was last seen? Can I see their statements?"

The detective leafed through the file and handed over the deposition, his forehead wrinkled in another frown.

Kay's interview was short and unremarkable, but Savka studied the original investigating detective's questions to Pat. And her answers. Savka's finger moved across the English words. They swam on the page, and she blinked hard to bring them back into focus.

DETECTIVE: You mentioned a man came up the elevator at 9:35 p.m. What did he look like?

PAT O'DWYER: He was foreign—had on a dark coat and hat—I couldn't see his face all that clearly. He said he was looking for his brother, Marko Kovacs. I told him visiting hours were over, and besides, Mr. Kovacs had left a few minutes before and probably went down the back stairs. The visitor had already pressed the elevator call button, but he suddenly dashed down the hallway when he thought we'd turned our backs.

DETECTIVE: You didn't try to stop him?

PAT O'DWYER: We are two nurses, detective. Alone on a ward, caring for helpless women confined to their beds. We were afraid if we tried to stop him, he would make a scene and wake our patients.

DETECTIVE: You didn't watch to make sure he'd really left?

PAT O'DWYER: We're not police officers. And it seemed harmless, a dispute between two brothers.

DETECTIVE: Did you hear anything? A fight perhaps?

PAT O'DWYER: A patient had a hemorrhage and Kay and I were busy with her for half an hour. We heard nothing.

Yet Taras had told her that Jeanie remembered seeing a man with a dark coat and hat in the doorway of her hospital room. Had the assassin discovered Marko in the Fire Bride's room and overpowered him, bundling him down the back stairs and into a waiting car? But something else concerned her more: Pat O'Dwyer hadn't mentioned stumbling upon Belyakov in Savka's hospital room earlier, nor had she said anything about being knocked down by Marko. Why had she lied to the police?

Savka handed back the deposition, and Detective Jaeger stood, offering his business card. "Call me if you remember anything," he said. "Anything at all."

After leaving the police headquarters, she stood outside in the cold wind coming off the ocean and lifted her hand to hail a cab. Her back ached and she yearned to curl up in her bed, take this rare second day off from work to rest. Savka thought of Taras, still on the ferry to Salt Spring Island. Perhaps seeing Marko's skull and hearing how it had been cut from his body with a serrated saw had made her paranoid, but she couldn't help but wonder if the Fire Bride had remembered something after her son left yesterday. Maybe it was a particular memory the nurses had found damning? Then it hit her: Taras hadn't gone to the island for another romantic tryst with Jeanie, he'd raced there out of concern for her safety. Savka's mouth was suddenly so dry, she could hardly swallow. Surely a man as big as Taras would not be in danger from two nurses, who must be in their forties by now.

A cab swerved out of traffic and pulled up at the curb. She leaned toward the open passenger side window, feeling the pull in her old hysterectomy scar. "Take me to the Tsawwassen ferry terminal," she told the driver, and got into the back seat, terrified and overwhelmed. As the cab headed south, the first vague, simple steps of a plan had begun to form out of every betrayal and loss, from the memory of Ewa, who could never believe Savka was a warrior, from Marko and Natalka, who had called her a coward, and Belyakov, who'd owned her for what seemed like a lifetime.

And finally, the two nurses, whose fate had somehow become inextricably linked with hers on a dark night fifteen years ago.

45

JEANIE

Salt Spring Island
' DECEMBER 12, 1972

IT'S ONE IN THE afternoon the day after my old nurses injected me with an antipsychotic, and yet the dark sky makes it seem closer to dusk. An hour ago, sun was shining through the skylight of my studio, but now thunderheads are building, casting a long shadow over Kay, who reclines on my velvet settee, casually flipping through a magazine.

"You and Pat have plotted all this time," I say, seething with resentment. "You waited until you could steal this place away."

She looks up at me where I stand in front of the French landscape, which was hauled in after Pat had rescued it from certain drowning. It must be finished, the paint dry, and shipped to Brussels before the new year, which seems a formidable task.

"Let's just say we have a shared interest in keeping you safe," Kay says, turning a page. "You have no idea what we've done for you," she adds. "What we *continue* to do."

I open my mouth to scream, but nothing comes out. This morning, a chlorpromazine tablet was back in my white cup and Pat examined my mouth after I took it, ensuring I didn't spit it out. Just enough antipsychotics to keep me groggy and bitter, but not so much that I can't work on this commission.

I mix some paint and, with delicate strokes, begin working in the trees along the shoreline of my composition. Prison warden Kay watches me out of the corner of her eye. The pressure in my chest is unbearable. All morning, I've been trying to figure out my game plan. If I engage Kay in civilized banter, perhaps she'll see I don't deserve to be committed to a mental hospital and have Gladsheim snatched from me. But those best-laid plans go to pieces the moment Kay takes out a pack of cigarettes and a book of matches.

My eyes widen with alarm. "You can't smoke in here. There's enough turpentine to blow the place sky high." Not to mention my absolute terror at the thought of a live flame in my sacred space. But she ignores me, striking a match with dramatic flair and letting it burn down before she lights her cigarette, while I die inside.

"What happened in Africa?" The gloves are off and I have to know who Kay really is.

She settles back for a smoke and turns another page of her magazine, shooting me a weighted look. Finally, she must have decided that there's nothing to lose. "I left."

"You were fired." My guess is close to the mark because Kay cringes slightly—imperceptible to any other eye but mine, the poor burn survivor who knows her so well.

She throws down the magazine and uncrosses her legs, moves to the edge of the settee, as if to get up. "I resigned."

"What did you *do*?" I'm afraid of the answer, afraid of Kay. Smoke mushroom clouds above her head, and her eyes, well, they look chillingly calm, which, I realize now, is some kind of psychosis. "You're the crazy one," I say. "Not me.

She sighs and takes another dramatic lungful of cigarette smoke. "If that's what you want to believe," she says, exhaling.

"You told Taras his mother had a Russian visitor just to upset him." I load a larger brush with paint and fight the desire to hurl it at her, anything to wipe that complacent look from her face. "Then you throw his sister under the bus. Admirable, Kay, really upstanding."

"Taras? I thought his name was Danek." She smiles into the middle distance. "Think what you like, love."

My paintbrush falters in midair. "Don't call me that. Ever again."

"I'm gutted," Kay says with a mock pout. She blows smoke in a volcanic plume toward me.

"You know what they say, don't hurt the hand that feeds you. And you can't keep me chained to this easel forever."

Kay stares down at the burning end of her cigarette. "Enjoy the process. Where you're going there are only crayons and coloring books."

My heart stops beating. "What do you mean?"

"You heard Pat, when you finish this, there's a room waiting for you at the Riverview Mental Hospital."

Even though I knew this was coming, my hands are numb with the shock of betrayal and with every dumb, slavish hope I once entertained, that my old nurse would return and be my caregiver. "You can't! Kay— this is *me*."

"I know."

"How can you be so cruel?" I pause at the sound of a car pulling into the driveway and rush to the window, Kay at my heels. She pushes me aside so she can see the beat-up gray Toyota Corolla. I close my eyes with relief. *Taras.* Then I remember what Pat said last night:

If he dares arrive tomorrow, we'll deal with him. Just as we have everything else that's come our way.

Kay throws down her cigarette, stamps on it, then leaps through the door. I follow her down the stairs. As we stand on the porch, Pat rockets out of the house. My old nurses can't hurt me any more than they already have. But Taras? Through the windshield, his handsome face has darkened like the clouds that amass overhead. How can I possibly protect him from these two evil souls?

46

TARAS

Salt Spring Island
DECEMBER 12, 1972

BEFORE TARAS CAN OPEN his car door, Pat charges toward him like a killer who had once tried to shank him in the mess hall at Black Eagle.

"I told you I'd call the police if you stepped foot on this property—"

Taras gets out of the car and stares her down. "Go and call them. I will wait." He glances toward the guest cabin porch, where Jeanie stands, Nurse Kay clutching her arm. A bitter wind has come up, bringing with it a sharp, briny smell of sea. Taras's leather coat flaps around him, lashing his body like a whip. "You have not hurt her," he warns. He's sure that the nurses have his father's gun, but hopefully they would never use it. His shiv is in the breast pocket of his coat, in case they try.

Jeanie attempts a desperate lunge forward. "Taras, they're taking Gladsheim from me . . . ," then she squeals in pain when Kay yanks her back.

Taras takes a few steps toward them, gravel crunching beneath his boots. "This is Jeanie's house. I leave when she tells me I leave." The nurses exchange a look. Taras fears what he might do to Pat and Kay, these women who possibly saw the assassin kill his father and have lied about it for years. "I lift a rock and maggots run, afraid of the light." His gaze lingers on Kay, certain that she's the ringleader of this nasty business. But her face reveals nothing.

Taras shouts, "Where did you find my father's gun?"

Kay smiles, and Taras must strain his ears to hear her over the wind. "It was the Russian who killed him. Not us."

The Russian.

Taras remembers driving to the Tsawwassen ferry terminal earlier, distracted with worry over Jeanie, going over every reason he could think of, wondering why the nurses weren't answering the phone, and fearing the worst. The wind had picked up, and he remained in his vehicle during the rough crossing, obsessing over what he might find at Gladsheim. At one point, he'd glanced up at his rearview mirror and glimpsed a black town car parked farther back on the ferry. Paranoid, he'd studied the car in his rearview mirror, finally determining, with relief, that it was an older model than the one that had followed him last week. There was no need for concern.

Taras turns to face Pat. "You did something that night," he says. "You know something. Only the police know he is dead."

"If you knew the truth you would hate Jeanie," Kay yells across to him, "not arrive here to save her."

Taras pauses. Does Kay mean to accuse his lover of killing Tato? Jeanie also seems stunned at this pronouncement, as she should be. "You will blame a woman confined to a hospital bed for your crimes?" he shouts.

"Confined to bed?" Pat steps toward him, stopping near the fender of his car. "Jeanie had relearned to walk, and her arms were like steel from hauling herself up with that blasted trapeze bar. Listen, if you go now, we won't press charges."

Taras backs away from her. "I'm staying here, with Jeanie."

"We found your father's gun on the floor of Jeanie's hospital room," Kay calls to him.

Taras finally strides toward the guesthouse, charges up the steps and pulls Jeanie from Kay's grasp. He wraps his arm around her thin shoulders and hurries her to the passenger door of his car. Jeanie stumbles and he pulls her close enough to feel her heart beating against his chest. He pushes Pat aside and bundles Jeanie in, quickly rounding the front of the car, his hand on the hood.

Jeanie locks the passenger door and looks up at him with frightened eyes. He doesn't notice that Kay has come up to him from behind. He turns, too late, to find her hand held high—*a knife*, he thinks—as she brings it down like a cobra's strike. There's a sting at the back of his neck and he collapses against the hood of the car, dragging himself toward the driver's door.

But the already dim light grows grayer, and he feels himself slump, sliding down the fender to the ground. Kay stands over him like a terrible statue, clutching an empty hypodermic needle, eyes glittering.

He can hear Pat banging on the passenger door, growling at Jeanie through the window. "Unlock it!"

Jeanie's voice comes muffled from within the car. "How dare you drug him!"

He can feel Pat rummage through his coat pockets. Taras watches numbly as she jumps up with a triumphant cry. *She's found the car keys,* he thinks, slipping into a dream haze. He raises a hand, and before losing consciousness, feels the hard outline in his breast pocket, where the shiv lies, waiting.

47

SAVKA

Salt Spring Island
DECEMBER 12, 1972

SEA SPRAY MISTING HER face, Savka leaned over the railing, staring down at the desolate ocean, cruel waves crashing against the prow of the ferry. She raised her eyes to the hulking shadow of Salt Spring Island as it drew closer, mountains rising into the fog. "How beautiful," she said to herself, for there was no one else on deck.

Although she could feel curious eyes on her back. Five lines of cars were parked behind her, each with the dimmed profile of its driver and passengers within. They sat and smoked as the ferry chugged forward, as if pulled by a string. She imagined their whispers. *Who's that crazy lady standing on the deck in December?*

She eyed the ominous clouds hovering over them. A storm was coming.

The ferry swung into the middle of the channel, and Savka gripped the rail. She was heading straight into the lion's den but needed to fit a few pieces together before forcing the nurses to admit their involvement. They knew something that would give Detective Jaeger a break in the cold case of her husband's disappearance and murder.

This trip across the Strait of Georgia to an isolated Gulf Island was so far out of her comfort zone she might as well be on a rocket ship to outer space. Yet by the end of this day, she'd learn the truth. Despite

Belyakov's insistence, she wasn't a real spy. She wasn't one to take risks. But she was here and had to muster the same courage that Taras showed the first time he'd stood at this very bow rail, waiting for someone to approach.

Wind had picked up, sending a blurred pattern across the waves. "Stay calm," she whispered to herself. "*Calm.*" At least she knew that the Fire Bride lived at the very northern tip of the island. She would find her way there if it meant keeping a taxi waiting and knocking on every door on Southey Point.

She was suddenly conscious that a woman had come to the rail to stand next to her. It was a hippy chick about Zoya's age, long auburn hair flying in the wind. She was dressed in a tie-dyed sweatshirt and a pair of embroidered bell-bottom jeans. A purple scarf was wound around her head and her feet were bare on the wet deck. Savka wanted to wrap her in a blanket. Wasn't she cold?

The woman turned her face to the wind. "Isn't it gorgeously *wild?*"

The ferry adjusted its course toward the island terminal, waves rolling and cresting against the bow. Savka widened her stance to avoid losing her balance, and she smiled briefly at the woman, who'd begun to twirl like a dervish.

"My boyfriend said I'd get blown over the railing," the woman said, dancing around her. "But then I saw my sister out here grooving with the elementals." She punched a fist into the air. "Strong women building a gentle world!" Laughing, she flashed a peace sign. "I'm Kali. After the goddess, dig?" Savka did not *dig*, but Kali blundered on, not expecting an answer. She glanced back at the line of cars. "I told him to sit on it. He can't lay a guilt trip on me."

Savka looked over her shoulder, afraid for Kali, expecting to see her boyfriend charge up behind them and grab her arm. "Didn't he try to stop you?"

"Fuck no," Kali said, stretching her arms above her head to feel the wind. "I can split anytime I want. Women's lib—that's where it's at!"

She felt unsettled, bothered. When Zoya spoke of the women's lib movement, Savka dismissed it as something for young women, not for her. Yet back in Ukraine, she *had* been a strong woman, trying to protect her family. Once, a teenage Zoya had shouted, "When did you get so uptight and *lost*?" At the time, Savka had disciplined her for disrespecting her mother. But now, watching Kali sway on the deck, she had an answer to that question:

I lost myself when Marko came back to Deremnytsia.

She thought of that night in February of 1944, how Marko had endangered her family, demanding that she escape with Taras and deliver the *shtafeta* to Kuzak. At first, she'd refused, her skin prickling with caution.

What if we run into Soviet partisans? It's winter . . .

We've driven the partisans off the mountain, he'd insisted.

And yet Belyakov had stolen her and Taras, forcing them into the underworld, where they still dwelled among the shadows of the dead. Her lip trembled as she thought of herself floating like a specter beneath the surface of a raging sea like this, while life went on without her in the world of men.

As the ferry approached the island, Kali leaned in, the coming storm forcing a strange intimacy between them. "I saw you walk on earlier," she said. "Recognized a fellow priestess of the light. Need a ride to the full-moon gathering? It's going to be rad."

48

JEANIE

Salt Spring Island
DECEMBER 12, 1972

"IF YOU'VE HURT HIM, I'll kill you!" I can hardly breathe at the sight of Taras, out cold and lying crumpled and helpless on the driveway. His dear head is turned at an awkward angle on the gravel, as if he broke his neck falling to the ground. The wind has changed direction since he arrived, and the palm tree fronds are rattling, the cedar and fir trees lining the bay lashing back and forth like mad ghouls. Numb with shock, I turn to Kay, who stands looking down at Taras, a serene smile on her face. In her element, one could say. She almost seems to be enjoying herself. "You'll never get away with this . . ." but my voice dies on a terrified whisper, as Pat begins to pace the driveway, looking pale and stunned. "Let Taras go. Let *me* go." I face my old nurses, fists determinedly clenched.

Pat pulled on her new green coat before she came out, but I'm shivering in my overalls and sweatshirt. She turns to Kay. "Get me another ampule—"

"No." Kay is still looking down at Taras, as if he's a lab rat she means to dissect. She folds her arms across her chest. "It's time she hears the truth." Her hair, normally combed flat over her ears, has been rearranged, courtesy of the wind. Her eyes are wild. My old nurse regards me with something akin to pity. "Do you want to go to prison?"

The sky above us seems to darken another impossible degree. I shake my head. "Why would I go to prison?"

"It was *you*, Jeanie."

I'm confused and glance at Taras again. *Wake up!* "I have no idea what you mean."

"*You* killed his father."

As though Taras has heard, his curled fingers twitch, and he groans in drugged oblivion. My guts twist into a knot. It's strange and terrible to be told you're guilty of a crime you don't remember committing. Most people would deny such an accusation immediately. But I'm not most people. My first instinct is to believe Kay. *Did* I kill the father of the man I love? The two of them regard me with expectation, waiting for me to confess, but I've gone rigid with shock and I'm speechless. Grief or guilt? I don't know.

"Of course, you can't remember, Jeanie," Kay says. "We came into your room that night and found Marko Kovacs laying on top of your bed, the trapeze bar bloodied. You were delirious."

Suddenly I'm back in my old hospital bed, exhausted from a long day working with a physiotherapist that Dr. Reisman had arranged, painfully learning to walk again. To strengthen my arms, an ancient trapeze bar had been attached to my bedframe—it seemed to have been made in the previous century—and I'd been getting stronger every day. How many times had I reached up to grab the cold, steel handle? My fingers would roam over the chain, ensuring it was clipped in before applying my weight. Despite this precaution, the bar would often come loose. I can still hear the grating sound of the chain links' clank and rattle, like a prisoner's shackles.

"You were helpless," Pat adds, her voice at a treble, "and high on morphine. Marko Kovacs must have been pawing at you." She points to Taras. "Trapped by *his* father. You had to make him stop."

"No," I croak, hand to my head. "He just stood in the doorway." I try to sound certain, but what if my brain has blocked the truth? I feel it somewhere inside me, like a flashing beacon warning of hazards at sea, showing me only fragments that shimmer and rise out of the fog, just out of my reach. A crippling doubt enters my mind. I'd completely blocked out entire months of my life. But Marko Kovacs disappeared just before Dr. Reisman had discharged me from the hospital. Had I been strong enough to break through a morphine haze to find someone "pawing at me," and murdered him?

There are too many missing pieces, I think, glancing up at Pat. "How did you come into possession of Marko Kovacs's gun?"

"After you beat him to death," she explains, "we held on to it for safekeeping."

I look at Taras, horrified. His eyes are still closed, but his lips move slightly, as if he's fighting his way back to consciousness. Did he somehow hear Pat's accusation, that *I'm* the one who killed his father? But if I'd committed such an abhorrent act, I would remember, wouldn't I?

"He already knows," Kay says, noticing my glance at Taras. "Why do you think he put you in his car? To take you to the police and turn you in."

"Wait," I say, holding up my hand in a vain attempt to halt the progression of this conversation. I don't like where it's going. "That night you'd given me my evening medications—my sleeping pill—how could I have moved after that?" With the pressure of accusation goading me forward, I close my eyes, make a concerted effort to climb the brick wall my brain has erected against me. To my surprise, the ghost images firm up, and I see the man standing against the wall near the door. Like a clip from a black-and-white movie, he walks slowly toward me in the shadows. "Marko Kovacs came toward my bed," I whisper. "It was dark. I thought it was one of *you*."

I open my eyes, not wanting to see the rest, and sink to my knees on the gravel drive beside Taras, placing a tentative hand on his arm. Is it possible I killed his father?

Suddenly Pat is behind me. "Don't do this to yourself. Kovacs did an awful, horrible thing to you. And *you* fought back." She sneezes violently, the cold she's been fighting finally taking hold. "The trapeze bar was unclipped from the chain, and you reached up in a panic as he lifted your sheets," she says, wiping her nose on her sleeve. "You hit him again and again, then blocked it out."

"I didn't kill him." My voice rises in sudden fury. I tear my hand off Taras's arm and leap up, turning on Pat. "How could I have had the strength?"

"You were filled with rage at Michael," Kay says quietly, "how he left you after you'd been burned so horribly, after you'd suffered the devastating loss of your baby. You were delirious, ready to take out your grief and anger on the next man who mistreated you. That man happened to be Taras's father."

"We found you in a dither and gave you more morphine," Pat adds. "You can't remember. How could you?"

"You *wanted* me to forget!"

And then Kay says something that chills me to the bone. "Your little friend has to go."

I spin to face her. "Go where?"

"Do you want him to tell the police? Jeanie, you'd be sent to prison for life."

Pat frowns briefly, seemingly unaware of Kay's plans. "What are we going to do with him?"

"That ampule held a dose meant for Jeanie," Kay says, her voice sharp, "not someone fifty pounds heavier. He won't be out for long. Grab him."

Taras groans as Pat takes his shoulders, and Kay his feet. When they hoist him, I notice his eyes flicker slightly and feel a rush of hope. "Where are you taking him?"

"Down to the ocean," Kay orders. "He's going for a little swim."

"No," I scream.

"We've protected you all these years," Pat shouts back. "We protected you from life in prison. Are we going to stop now?"

Crab-walking across the drive, Pat and Kay swing Taras around to the path that leads down to the beach, me stumbling desperately behind them. Kay walks backward, Taras's booted feet in her hands. Wind sweeps in from the sea, wrecking Pat's salon coiffure. I choose the moment to lunge at her, grabbing a good amount of her hair in my fist. "Let him go!" I shriek.

Pat scrambles to tighten her hold but drops Taras's upper body against her knees. "You bitch!" she cries, as I jerk her head back and Kay drops his feet, scrambling to pull me off Pat. Kay tries to get me into a headlock, but I twist away, too aware that I must stop them here. Taras won't have a chance in the water unconscious. He'll sink like a stone.

But Kay grabs my ear, wrenching it mercilessly. I yelp and lose my balance, sprawling across the dirt path behind them. Pat and Kay pick up Taras again and continue down, as if I'm merely a mosquito buzzing around their ears.

Kay's sweater has ridden up in the back and I see the handle of Taras's father's gun stuck in the waistband of her trousers. *Mollify Kay,* I plot, *pretend you agree with her plan, then snatch the gun.* Do I have the courage to use it?

I run ahead of them onto the beach and stand swaying in the wind, as if I can somehow stop them from drowning Taras in the rolling waves that crash against the rocks on the headland in plumes of white. Gusts of wind tear across the water and the air smells of fish and rotting seaweed, it smells of death.

"I remember hearing Russian words," I try to convince them. "Someone followed Marko Kovacs into my room. An assassin—you saw him yourself." I pause for a moment, my pulse quickening. "Why did you come into my room anyway? You'd already given me my medications."

Pat and Kay drop Taras onto the beach. "I went down the hall," Pat says, her nose red and congested. "Making sure Kovacs's Russian *brother* had gone down the back stairs—"

"She doesn't need a bleeding explanation." Kay's voice contains an ominous warning, but Pat takes no heed.

"I thought I'd check on you," Pat says, rummaging in her coat for a handkerchief. "When I opened the door, I found that bloody arsehole Kovacs lying across your bed, groaning and flailing about." She loudly blows her nose. "You can imagine how upset I was—a girl I'd looked after for two years beating a man half to death."

The nurses are facing the ocean and I have my back to it, looking up toward the house. "The Russian assassin did it, not me," I cry, fighting my way out of the dark to some kind of clarity.

I flinch at sudden movement from the driveway.

Two men have just come out of the trees and are running toward the beach path, guns in their hands.

49

TARAS

Salt Spring Island
DECEMBER 12, 1972

AS IF HE'S SURFACING from a deep dive, Taras floats up through consciousness.

Lying on his side, where the nurses have thrown him, he tries to move his arms and hands, but only his fingers answer his brain's command. He's trapped in his body and can't shift his head to dislodge a few crushed clamshells stuck to his cheek. His tongue feels like cotton in his mouth, incapable of speech. But he has heard everything. Jeanie killed his father? He doesn't believe it.

Yet Kay's threat is more worrisome. *Your little friend has to go.*

He opens his eyes to slits. Lightning strikes at the horizon, and the sky has visibly darkened by the arrival of threatening clouds. A great blueish-white bird skims the surface of the ocean, heading for the tree-tops, which sway in the wind like a lament. He yearns to leap up and grab Jeanie, but he must wait for the drug to wear off, wait until he can move, stand, walk, fight.

He stares at Kay through his lashes. She's looking up with dismay at the house. "Who the bloody hell is that?" she cries, reaching into the back of her slacks and drawing out a gun.

Taras tries again to move his head, but the muscles will not respond. Who could have arrived that made Kay pull out a gun? Which he's certain is his father's revolver. With a sinking feeling, he knows who has come: *Mama*. Did she catch the next ferry and follow him to Salt Spring?

Beckoning Pat to stand behind her, Kay levels the barrel of the gun at whomever is coming down the path. "You're trespassing," she shouts, backing away slowly. "Get out." Although the nurses might now be outnumbered and there's only a revolver for their protection, Kay's eyes—magnified behind a pair of plastic framed glasses—spark with anticipation.

Taras can hear the crunch of clamshells as one person, then another arrives on the beach.

"You have killed Taras Ivanets?" a man says just out of Taras's field of vision, calm and collected. "Give us the gun." A Russian accent. And a voice he recognizes. Taras's heart grows cold, and he's taken back to Siberia, remembering the aftermath of a mine explosion, shortly after he'd arrived in the camp. Late in the night, he'd jolted from a deep sleep in the infirmary, his ears still ringing, yet suddenly alert to clipped Russian voices unsettling the air around him.

"You were to keep him out of danger," one of the voices said.

"We didn't know the shaft would collapse," another answered.

A shadow morphed into a monster that coiled in the corner of the room as if at the gates of hell, waiting for Taras to weaken. That monster was Lieutenant Belyakov, whose gloved hand had been at his shoulder in the Carpathians. The same hand had pushed him onto a train that took him to Moscow, where other hands had shoved him into a black van, then a cattle car, and finally to a ship that carried him and thousands of other prisoners up Kolyma River and into the heart of darkness.

How long has he waited to find Comrade Lieutenant Belyakov? Twenty-eight years, fantasizing with great detail how many times he'd stab the man who he believed had killed his mother. And now Taras lies helpless before the Russian, with a shiv he'd made to do the job still in his breast pocket.

Belyakov has moved into his sightline, and Taras's eyes fasten on him, still seeing the look on Mama's face when he told her Kay mentioned a Russian had visited her after she'd had emergency surgery. Her panic. *The nurse is lying. I can't remember a Russian visitor.* And her frank denial when Taras asked if the Soviet was still here, if he was following him. When Mama *did* watch Tato for this beast.

"You are nurse from hospital," Belyakov says to either Kay or Pat. "What have you done with Taras Ivanets?" A pause. "Did you do something like this to his father?"

Taras forces the muscles of his neck into obedience and can turn his head slightly, enough to truly study, through eyes half-lidded, the small Soviet agent who'd sent him to purgatory. Belyakov, perhaps shorter than ever and spider-like, his thin, wiry frame clad in black leather jacket and slacks. With a pistol in his hand.

Kay's upper lip curls in disdain. She's pointing Taras's father's gun at the Russian. "I remember you," she says. "When I saw you leave after visiting Mrs. Kovacs, I thought—here is a sad, short little boy dressed up like a man."

Taras watches a dark cloud cross Belyakov's face. He nods to his accomplice, who appears and nudges Taras with a booted foot. He swallows a groan as the man says in Russian to his master. "He's out cold."

Ilyin. He'd memorized Belyakov's ruthless thugs' names, too, repeating them over and over in his mind in Siberia, until *Belyakov, Ilyin, and Yeleshev* had become a kind of desperate chant.

"Leave him alone," Jeanie shouts at Ilyin. She flies across the beach as if she's on a soccer pitch and kicks the Russian in the shins with her clogs. Jeanie shrieks when he shoots out a hand and grabs her. Taras's heart stutters as he watches Ilyin restrain her, while training his own gun on the nurses. Jeanie looks terrified, bent almost double, staring blindly down at the shell beach.

Then he hears the slow crunch of those shells as Belyakov approaches him with confident, cat-like steps. Up close, he looks different, older, his hair long and combed carefully over his forehead and ears. Taras panics as the KGB operative squats and leans close. "We wondered," he whispers in Russian. "Why would Taras Ivanets return to Salt Spring Island a day after he'd just come from there? This Fire Bride, does she have the list? We shall see." The Russian rests his pistol on one knee, his gold tooth gleaming in the low light. "You did not see us following you? We parked on the ferry, only three cars back." He cocks his ear, as if expecting Taras to respond. Belyakov clucks his tongue. "I am disappointed. You are like a son to me. A son—he would notice such things." Taras's body screams. *Criminal! I have never been your son*, but Belyakov is still smiling, absently stroking one of his carefully trimmed sideburns. "Perhaps you *did* notice our car, when you took off at the terminal, leaving us to scramble to find the Fire Bride's house." The Russian draws a thumb across Taras's lower lip, and he wants to retch. "Does she mean that much to you?" Belyakov frowns when a gust of wind tears into his helmet of hair. "I will always find you, little mule," he says, attempting to palm it back into shape. "You will always be mine."

Taras wants to crawl away, but he forces himself to meet the Russian's oddly affectionate gaze. *You never owned me. You never will.*

Belyakov straightens and brushes off his black leather coat. "Give me that gun," he says to Kay, "or my man kills the Fire Bride."

Jeanie's lovely features are contorted in an expression of horrified confusion, and Taras's heart races as he struggles to tame a paralyzing fear. What will the Russians do to her if Kay can't come up with this list they're after?

His eyes shift to Pat and Kay, who look at each other, weighing their choices. Kay turns back to the Russian and says with finality. "Do what you like with her. Jeanie is dead to us."

Belyakov cocks his gun and points it directly at Kay's head. "Where is the Rimini list?"

"I have no idea what you're talking about," she snaps back.

Taras notices Ilyin drag Jeanie sideways, in an attempt to edge closer to Kay, his weapon trained on her and his dark eyes not leaving the barrel of her gun. What was Belyakov talking about? Had he followed Taras's parents to Canada because Tato was in possession of a list?

Belyakov carefully studies Kay's weapon. "Where do you get this Webley—British issue?"

"It's . . . Taras's father's revolver," Jeanie tells him.

"You took it off Marko Kovacs's body," the Russian says, a light dawning in his eyes.

"Pat had it in her room," Jeanie adds, with a glance up at the house. Taras smiles inwardly. *Brave girl*, he thinks. *One less Soviet to deal with on the beach.*

And Belyakov takes the bait. "Ilyin," he shouts. His man releases Jeanie and turns, breaking into a run up the path, almost tripping over the wide flare of his blue jeans on his way to the house.

50

JEANIE

Salt Spring Island
DECEMBER 12, 1972

I CAN STILL FEEL Ilyin's rude hands on me as I watch him yank open the front door of Gladsheim and disappear inside. A few barks come from Tuna, still in the house, and then eerie silence. I freeze, expecting a gunshot. I wanted to get rid of him so I can help Taras, but would the Russian hurt my old, defenseless dog?

Kneeling beside Taras, I start rubbing his arms and legs, anything to bring blood back into his numb extremities. He looks up at me with pleading eyes that break my heart, and I remember him telling me about the NKVD agent who had turned his mother. "Is it *him?*" I breathe into Taras's ear.

"Belyakov," he whispers, nodding slightly, and I almost gasp with relief. The chlorpromazine is wearing off.

"Belyakov," I repeat to myself. "The bastard who took you from her. What should I do?"

Without moving his mouth, Taras says, "Run."

"I won't leave you," I tell him. Belyakov doesn't appear to have heard us. He shifts the hold on his gun and fixes his cold, dead eyes on Kay, who seems to flinch, as if she's seen something there that unnerves her. *Jeanie is dead to us.* The words still smart, even though I already knew yesterday that my old nurses were committing me to a slow death by mental institution. There's something about having it confirmed in this moment, when a gun is involved, that puts a finer point on the truth.

"What happened to Marko Kovacs in the hospital that night?" Belyakov demands of Kay.

Her skin has turned so pale, I can see every blue vein crawl over her cheek and neck. "What a shrimp." She laughs in his face. "I could squash you like a bug."

"Don't make him mad," Pat interjects. "Do you want him to shoot you?"

"Coward," Kay hisses at her.

I watch the two collaborators, now turning on each other, and decide to level the playing field even further. If Taras continues to recover and I can drive a wedge between Kay and Pat, we might stand a chance against this Soviet. I get to my feet, leaving Taras briefly, and face Pat. "Kay told me about your little crime at the hospital." She starts violently, and I try on a disdainful smile. "The terrible thing you did, that got you fired."

There's a long silence as Pat grapples with this new, surprising bit of information. Overhead the clouds are murky, dark, yet muted light still moves like the hand of God far out to sea. In the damp, cold air even the silhouette of Vancouver Island seems very near. A storm cloud has opened up in the distance, and it pours a curtain of rain upon the ocean, joining heaven to earth. I shiver and hug myself as Pat recovers and levels a glassy stare at Kay.

"Why would you tell her, Kay? Why?" she says, her voice subdued, hurt. Then she turns back to me. "You always got your proper morphine dose, Jeanie. Nobody missed the little extra." Pat sends Kay another insolent glare. "You should tell this Ruskie just what you were up to in the surgery ward at the hospital. Before you convinced me to transfer with you to Gynecology." Kay sends her a warning look, which seems to make Pat more incensed. "You had to work in a place without male patients to tempt you into yielding to your *dark urges*."

Her pronouncement sends shockwaves through my body. Is she saying that Kay *preyed* on men in some way?

"Shut up," Belyakov shouts at Pat, waving his gun in the air. Even he looks uneasy at what she's suggesting. He glances up at the house, as if he regrets sending his man away to face these two alone.

"You lie." Kay's eyes have not left Pat. "You were the one seeking revenge after Kovacs knocked you down before leaving his wife's room."

Pat is speechless for a moment. Finally, she finds her words and shouts, "You bitch!"

Belyakov shifts nervously on his feet, seemingly frustrated at this disturbing sidebar, and I falter, remembering the day Kay arrived at Gladsheim. When I asked what Africa had done to her, she'd said something that only made my pulse leap in the moment, but somehow seems like a huge red flag now: *Africa did not appreciate the lengths to which my duty drove me . . .* And all that bullshit about me being the only one to understand her genius. Why didn't I send her away when she started following Taras and me, like she meant to off us both?

Despite Belyakov's warning to shut up, Pat isn't done with Kay. "I kept the letter you wrote me, when you were hauled before an African tribunal." Pat has a hand at the small of her back, as if she threw it out dragging Taras to the beach. "*Angel of Death* they called you. But you managed to pin it on someone else. Only escaping a few years later when it got too hot for you."

Kay adjusts her grip on the gun. "I came back because you wrote that Jeanie changed her will."

"That's right, you have a big dream for this place, don't you? And for Jeanie." Pat turns to me. "Kay had me tell Dr. Reisman you were losing it. It was Kay that suggested chlorpromazine. She got the idea to declare you insane and snatch this place out of your hands."

Breath heaving, I charge at Kay, but the Russian shoves me back and takes a few steps toward Pat. "Stop," he yells. "Or I'll shoot."

Kay has let the barrel of her gun droop slightly as she glares at Pat. "I seem to remember *you* enthusiastic about that plan. No more working as a slave for Jeanie in this gorgeous place."

A muffled bark comes from inside the house, and I let out a relieved gasp. My dog might be unsettled by Ilyin's rampage, but he sounds okay.

"What happened to Marko Kovacs?" Belyakov demands.

Kay stares through a curtain of hair at me, in a cold rage, livid to have her dirty laundry aired in front of so many people. "Why don't you ask Jeanie?" she says, a shred of reluctance sneaking into her tone. "She's the one you want."

I reel back as though she's struck me. Does Kay still think she can blame *me*? Whitecaps frost the surface of the ocean, the waves crashing at our feet like a thousand voices of accusation. I have the sensation of floating, as if I teeter at the very razor's edge. Despite Kay's betrayal—learning of her and Pat's deliberate plans to take Gladsheim from me and send me to a mental hospital—I still held out some small hope that she's simply misunderstood, that all of this hasn't really happened. But seeing her standing there, a look of rabid hostility on her face, I finally awaken from the long enchantment I fell into on the day of my wedding, like Sleeping Beauty shaking off the witch's evil spell. "All those eight-hour shifts you spent as my vigil nurse in those early days," I say to Kay. "When I was discharged, you told me you loved me. When you're *incapable* of love." Suddenly Pat's words return to me, after she'd injected Taras and he lay at our feet.

I found that bloody arsehole Kovacs lying across your bed, groaning and flailing around.

I turn to regard Pat, who's sniveling, her nose running like a faucet. "How could I have killed Marko Kovacs if he was still alive when you came into my room?"

Pat looks like a little girl caught in a lie. "When I . . . found Kovacs, he was alive, yes. I left to get a stretcher, take him to emergency, but

Kay came along, pushed me back into your room and closed the door behind us."

Kay directs her words to Belyakov, her eyes resolute, believing her own lies. "And we found Jeanie with her hand on the trapeze bar, arm raised to make the final blow."

51

SAVKA

Salt Spring Island
DECEMBER 12, 1972

SAVKA STOOD AT THE end of a long driveway that disappeared into a forest of massive trees that rose on either side of the track like sentinels. An old engine revved behind her, and she turned to watch Kali's boyfriend back up their Volkswagen camper van into a turnabout and spin his tires, mud flying into the air.

Kali leaned out of the passenger side window. "You sure you won't come worship grandmother moon?"

When Savka smiled and shook her head, Kali raised a fist. "Stick it to the *man*, sister," she shouted, as they sped away.

Savka could still smell marijuana on her clothes and almost regretted accepting Kali's offer of a ride to the north island. Their van had followed other cars disembarking at the ferry terminal, and from there it had been surprisingly easy to find the Fire Bride's house. Not twenty minutes from the terminal, Kali—who'd been to the island before—ordered her boyfriend onto Southey Point Road, then Arbutus Road, where six mailboxes were dispersed along the dirt track, each with the last name of the occupant painted on its side. Patches of ocean had shimmered through the trees to their left as the point of land narrowed. When Savka feared they might run out of road, she spotted a mailbox with *O'Dwyer* painted on it in block lettering.

Savka skirted that mailbox now and started down the driveway with determination, russet-brown cedar needles crunching softly beneath her feet. Storm clouds had piled up overhead, and she thought she could hear the sea. Within moments she was swallowed up by a rainforest. Large boulders loomed among the trees, carpeted with verdant green moss and lichen. It was quiet. Too quiet. What had Taras discovered when he arrived here earlier today?

Then she stumbled, almost falling. A black town car was parked at the edge of the drive, still inside the tree line, hidden from anyone who might be in the house, which she could see now through the trees as the driveway ended in a large gravel clearing, open to the ocean. A Jeep was parked near a small guesthouse. Taras's Toyota was nearby, the driver's door open wide. Savka's pulse quickened. Why hadn't her son shut his car door?

As she ducked across a wood plank boardwalk, crouched her way through a series of lush shrubs and skirted the main house like a thief, a dog barked inside, as if it sensed her there. Here was a grove of strange and beautiful trees with red, peeling bark, and, miraculously, a stand of mature palms.

Where was Taras? Savka imagined what terrible things might have befallen her son. She would not entertain the idea of his death at the hands of Belyakov and Ilyin, not after all he'd been through. Was he in the house? And where were the nurses and the Fire Bride? Her eyes darted over the property. To the right of the house and drive, a rocky point of land was surrounded on three sides by churning ocean. The sound of waves crashing at the rocks below sent her into a panic of claustrophobia. The driveway and thick forest behind the house and beyond the rocky point were the only means of escape if things went wrong. She glanced back at Taras's open car door. And things had already gone horribly wrong.

Wind whistled through the trees, and she thought she heard the faint sound of shouting. Rounding the side of the house, she stopped dead at the sight of four people standing on a beach at the foot of the point. She sighed with relief that her son was not there, but it took several moments for her to register what she *was* seeing. The young woman kneeling beside a dark humped object near the water appeared to be the only one who noticed her. It had to be the Fire Bride, who looked up with wide, startled eyes to see Savka. The other three figures stood facing each other, engaged in what looked like a shouting match. Pat and Kay were thirteen years older now, wrinkled, their hair flying out around them like they were witches. Kay and a short man were pointing guns at each other, in a standoff. Savka's heart stuttered to a stop in her chest when she recognized him.

Belyakov.

Savka started down the path, raw ocean wind slicing through her coat. Pat was shouting at the Fire Bride. "I was sick, sick to my stomach to see you with that bloody trapeze bar in your hand. You were right to beat him. Bastards like that don't deserve to live."

Savka tripped, anxiety clutching at her stomach. Where was her son? Then she knew. The crumpled object lying on the beach . . . Taras. Her knees buckled. Was he dead? She'd underestimated her Russian handler yet again. He'd followed her son here and shot him or knocked him out cold. Why hadn't she admitted to Taras yesterday that she was still this man's possession? And warned him to watch his back?

It would take only a turn of the head for either the nurses or Belyakov to see her flying down the path, eyes locked on her son. She caught a flutter of movement. Taras was alive!

Kay was shouting at Belyakov. "Marko Kovacs was almost unrecognizable. Jeanie beat his head in."

Savka now stood at the edge of the beach, awash with panic, her breath coming in gasps.

"Jeanie didn't beat him," she shouted. "It was *me*."

Kay swung the gun at her, this new arrival to a bizarre gathering on a remote island in the Pacific Ocean. Ignoring the weapon, Savka ran across the beach and skidded to her knees beside Taras, bellowing, "What have you done to him?" Her hands traveled over her son's legs, his arms, checking for injuries. He groaned and looked up at her, his pupils dilated. Yet he seemed more conscious than he appeared. Savka turned to glare up at the nurses. "I beat my husband. But I didn't kill him. What did you do to him?"

Jeanie reached out a hand to grip hers. "They drugged Taras," she said, and the two of them helped him sit upright.

"Wake up, Tarasyku, wake up." Savka felt him stir in her arms, and he lifted his head, blinking rapidly. Her son could move his hand, his fingers. But he was in no shape to face this trial.

"What are you doing here?" Belyakov shouted at her.

A distant, brooding rumble of thunder issued far out to sea, and she briefly raised her eyes to look at her Russian handler, standing only meters away, looking anxious as a border collie trying to herd sheep. It took her back to the Carpathian Forest to see him with a gun in his hand, and he seemed ill at ease training it on Kay and Pat, then on her, Jeanie, and Taras. His dark hair looked as though the sea wind had ripped through it like a tornado, rearranging it into a nest that perched on top of his head like a dead animal. He seemed worn and jaded in his uniform of black turtleneck, slacks, and a leather coat—a sixty-year-old KGB agent who was still searching for the Holy Grail.

"Leave Taras," he said, waving his gun at Savka and Jeanie. "Both of you, stand over there." His eyes were bloodshot, his voice unsteady. Savka rubbed her son's back and glanced around, hardly able to believe Ilyin had not come with Belyakov. "You're done telling me what to do with my son," she shouted in Ukrainian, wondering if there was a chance to overpower Belyakov as he stood there, alone against four women.

A long wolf-like howl sounded from the house and Savka suddenly knew what had set the dog off.

Sirens. Wailing in the distance.

"It's just a fire truck," Pat said, noticing Belyakov glance nervously toward the forest, and the road beyond. "Or an ambulance."

Savka's hand stilled on her son's back. The police. Earlier, at the Tsawwassen ferry terminal, it had occurred to her that she and Taras could very well need help questioning the nurses, who might deny any wrongdoing, or perhaps become hostile. As a precaution, she'd found a payphone and called Detective Jaeger, asking him to contact the Salt Spring Island police detachment and dispatch a unit. He was unable to guarantee action, but it appeared the island police would arrive in time to stop Belyakov and Kay from hurting anyone. A brief flash of panic. Savka hadn't remembered Jeanie's last name, just "Southey Point." There were several other houses on the road. With Pat O'Dwyer's name on the mailbox, how would they know where Jeanie lived?

Jeanie held onto Taras's arm, as if she were infusing him with life force, and he rubbed his face with a trembling hand. Savka helped him to stand. He swayed briefly, but all of his years in the Gulag had given him a kind of toughness the nurses hadn't bargained for.

"I don't believe it was *you*," Kay was saying to Savka. She still trained her gun at Belyakov, yet she had a cool, disturbing look in her eyes. Kay, the nurse who'd stood at her bedside when she and Marko were in the middle of their last fight. Kay, who had told Marko about the Russian visitor coming to see his wife earlier that night, obviously knowing that he would lose his temper.

"It *was* me," Savka said to her, anxious to clear Jeanie of blame. "Marko threatened to kill me and insisted that Taras was dead."

She watched comprehension flicker across the nurse's plain, horsey face. "You beat your husband to protect Jeanie."

Savka turned reluctantly and held out her shaking hands. After thirteen years of hiding the truth, she finally faced the Fire Bride. Jeanie stared back at her, mouth open, trying to take in yet another shock. Hadn't she suffered enough? The time had finally arrived to tell her what really happened that night in her hospital room. And to come clean to her son—that she'd been the one to beat his father. "Marko left my room in a rage," she began. "I was afraid he would go home, take it out on Zoya. I got out of bed and watched as he went down the hall. I willed a nurse to come." Her hands dropped in a gesture of defeat, still holding Jeanie's frightened gaze. "I see him stop at your door. He opened it and stood there looking at you. When he goes in your room, I followed in the hallway," she said, now glancing at Pat and Kay, "looking for one of you, but you were at nurse's station, on other side of the ward. I fear what Marko will do. So I follow him into Jeanie's room. He goes too close, and her eyes were open, terrified. She couldn't move. I only meant to hit him once."

"But you got carried away," Kay said, a fascinated voyeuristic look on her face. "And left Jeanie to deal with your mess."

Pat stood with her arms wrapped around her waist, shivering as the sirens grew louder, obviously traveling up the point. "It's only a fire truck," she insisted again, as though trying to convince herself.

Savka could see that Belyakov was also agitated, looking up at the house again and again. Did he care who really killed her husband? He only wanted the list. The wind was picking up and Savka held her blowing hair back with one hand. The sirens emboldened her. "I hit Marko over and over again. He was alive when I left him there. I went back to my room, waiting for you to discover him in Jeanie's room, waiting for police to come. But nothing happens."

"*That's* how your stitches opened up," Pat said, with a disapproving look. "The surgeon had to come in and repair them."

Jeanie stared back at Savka, wringing her hands. "If Pat found him still alive," she said, "who killed Marko Kovacs?"

Savka felt dizzy. "The same person who cut off his head, dismembered his body," she paused, unable to get a full breath, "and buried the pieces in unmarked graves."

Taras stumbled and Jeanie braced her body against his to prevent him from falling. Anger rolled off him in waves. He rubbed his eyes again, trying to dispel the drug in his system. "Tato . . ." he trailed off.

"Kay did it," Pat shouted, her face flushed with emotion. "There was a length of rubber IV tubing on Jeanie's tray. Kay took it and slipped it around Kovacs's neck, strangled him to death."

Belyakov had been aiming the barrel of his gun at whoever was speaking, but now it rested sharply on Kay. All eyes went back to the nurse, as if they were watching a horror film and could not look away. There was an odd expression on her face, a cease and desist look, directed at Pat. "You have no right."

"I have no right to do what?" Pat said, her voice quavering. "Mention that every man you ever met was just another version of your father? You enjoyed strangling him," she cried. "And he fought hard. There was still life in him."

Ignoring an agonized shout from Taras, Kay turned on her fellow nurse. "Don't piss me about. I can't seem to remember *you* having a better idea. We were in it together."

Pat narrowed her eyes. "*I* seem to remember only one person strangle him to death."

Finally, Kay broke. "Men are vile creatures. They should be wiped from the face of the earth."

"So you took it upon yourself to do that," Pat said. "Doesn't God decide who lives or dies?"

"God?" Kay scoffed. "God was not in the Congo."

"And God obviously wasn't on our ward." Pat jabbed a finger at her. "When Marko Kovacs showed up, you had a certain look in your eyes."

"Why did you kill him?" It was Taras, hobbling a few steps forward on the beach, one hand on Jeanie's arm, the other clenching and unclenching, as though he were a boxer warming up for a fight. "Tato could have recovered from his wounds."

"Kay was raging as she strangled him," Pat offered. "She enjoyed cutting Kovacs into manageable pieces with a surgical saw in the hospital basement. And made me help her smuggle the parts out in garbage bags."

Jeanie stalked up the beach toward Kay. "You!" she said, almost spitting with anger. "You murdered Taras's father and . . . *dismembered* him. And you have the nerve to blame me for your crime?"

The sirens were louder now, and Jeanie's mention of the police seemed to galvanize Belyakov, who glanced back up toward the house at the same moment Ilyin flung open the front door and ran down the path toward them.

Belyakov looked at him hopefully. "The list?"

Ilyin shook his head. "*Nyet.*"

Savka's rapist landed with both feet on the beach and, in a lunging movement that took them all by surprise, launched himself at Kay. The nurse panicked and squeezed off a shot. It went above their heads, narrowly missing Pat, who ducked in reaction, screaming.

The sirens floated urgently over the trees and Taras surprised her, running clumsily toward Belyakov, who bolted for the water, followed by Ilyin, who had knocked the gun out of Kay's hand. She struggled to her feet in the shallows, pants soaked, and glanced at Pat, who stood there, numb and panting, before turning with a few frantic lunges and diving headfirst into the surf.

52

JEANIE

Salt Spring Island
DECEMBER 12, 1972

"NO!" PAT SHOUTS AFTER KAY, her voice whipped away by the blustering wind. Pat staggers up and down the beach like a caged animal, not sure what she'll do now that the brains of *Operation Commit Jeanie* has abandoned her.

Savka and I find ourselves in a huddle, our eyes on Taras, who stands at the water's edge. He's scooped up his father's gun, and there's a look on his face I've not seen before, riveted in this earth-shaking instant. He aims the gun at Ilyin and Belyakov, who don't seem to care that Kay has escaped, swimming now out into the bay. The two Russians are up to their knees in the ocean, pointing their pistols at Taras while they struggle to stay upright in the rolling waves. Savka and I clutch each other, shivering, powerless to help Taras. I imagine the emotions coursing through him as he ventures into the ocean, his pants wet in the surf, finding himself in one of the most anticipated moments of his life.

Desperation is writ large on the Russian's faces. They've obviously left their car up on Arbutus Road, and have few avenues of escape—the headland and forest to our right, the water itself, as Kay chose, or the beach to our left, with the boats . . .

Belyakov appears to notice the kayak and old rowboat and yells something, pointing them out to Ilyin.

Take the rowboat, I think, *take the colander.*

The Russians look like cornered rats, thinking only of a way out of this trap. I fear what they might do to Taras. My muscles cramp in sudden shock as he advances toward Ilyin.

"My son has handled worse than this in the Gulag," Savka whispers in my ear and hugs me closer. She's wearing a coat over her sweater and skirt, and I regret not wearing something warmer; my teeth are chattering in the increasing wind.

In the water, Belyakov and Ilyin are wading toward the kayak and rowboat, but Taras lunges after them. Ilyin spins, firing two quick shots. Taras falls back, disappearing beneath the surface.

"Was he hit?" Savka screams. We're watching the ocean, breath held, and gasp with relief when Taras's head emerges close to Ilyin, who panics and squeezes off another few shots. Savka and I pitch backwards, out of the range of fire, but a wave knocks Ilyin off kilter, and he drops his gun, not expecting Taras to reach out a long arm, his hand on top of the Russian's head, dunking him as he struggles to stay above the surface.

Savka takes my hand. "I will not lose my son again," she says, just as terrified as I am that Taras won't survive this.

Oblivious, Pat paces the beach like a jungle cat, tracking Kay's progress out in the bay, swimming as if someone is right behind her, heading for the Secretary Islands, a destination she might reach if the incoming tide doesn't sweep her away. Pat takes a few steps toward the ocean's edge and falters, glowering at a dark cloud mass the color of a bruise surging overhead. She seems to remember that she's a poor swimmer and thinks better of entering these menacing waves as the light fades perceptibly. It might very well be dusk.

As Taras and Ilyin grapple in the sea, Pat suddenly rounds on me. "I've been trying to protect you all these years," she says, her eyes swinging wildly. "I had your best interests at heart. And you fought me every step of the way." She gestures at the ocean. "The Fire Bride should be out there trying to escape, the woman who immolated herself on her husband's stupidity. Jeanie Esterhazy, the deluded romantic, a sacrificial victim to love."

Shaking, I feel myself cycle back unwillingly through the past thirteen years, so many wretched moments flaring and fizzing like dying stars. "All those times I stupidly accepted medicine cups from you," I cry, vaguely aware that Savka has let go of my hand and stares silently at Belyakov, who's now wading back to shore. I take a few steps toward Pat. I don't want her to miss a word. "Medicine cups filled with uppers, downers, antipsychotics," I stutter in outrage, conscious that Belyakov is now closer to Savka, as Ilyin and Taras wrestle behind them in the deeper water. Pat has poor timing, but I can't resist this last chance to tell her what I really feel. "You haven't protected me. You did everything you could to *fight* me. When I'd spent two years in the hospital. If anyone should know, it was you and Kay—I'd already gone through the fight of my life!"

Pat looks momentarily cowed at my unexpected outburst, then a crazed smile breaks across her face. She flies at me like a deranged bird and grabs my arm, dragging me toward the water. I struggle against her, scratching and fighting with every ounce of my strength.

"You want a fight?" she says through clenched teeth. "I'll give you one." Pat outweighs me, and her hands feel impossibly strong on my arm. If she can't beat me, she'll kill me. Has it come to this, after thirteen years of unjust treatment? Is she really going to win?

The police sirens set up a piercing wail as they make the turn on Arbutus Road, and Pat falters, letting me go. My old nurse lingers in a moment of indecision, finally breaking with a violent howl and plunging away across the beach.

53

SAVKA

Salt Spring Island
DECEMBER 12, 1972

AS BELYAKOV WADED TOWARD SAVKA, the police sirens inexplicably stopped in the near distance. Savka stood rigid as a board, her body frozen with fear. And a chilling certainty: The police didn't know which long driveway led to Jeanie's house.

Belyakov lifted his gun and aimed it at Savka, his face strangely animated. Everything else disappeared from her awareness. *Finally, it has come,* she thought, *Belyakov will put a bullet in my head, as he's longed to do all along.* She had dared rise against him and must be dispensed with at once. A scream threatened to burst from her lungs and suddenly Ewa's voice resounded in her memory:

I would never have believed you were a warrior.

Belyakov gripped his gun with both hands as he struggled through the waves, even as a much larger swell rolled close behind him. Savka felt her throat go dry. The rogue wave knocked Belyakov to his hands and knees, leaving him gasping and spitting sea water. He stared down at his now empty hand, stupefied to have lost his gun. Reluctantly he plunged his hands into the water up to his armpits, frantically feeling for the pistol, but quickly abandoned the search.

Savka tensed as Belyakov emerged from the water like a sea monster.

Somehow, she found the courage to stumble forward. "You think you will survive?" she shouted at him. "Like a cockroach?"

Her heart beat staccato against her ribcage as she shoved Belyakov, but her hands slid off his slick leather coat and he squirmed away, leaving her on all fours, soaking wet and gasping in the surf. He bolted toward the headland, and Jeanie rushed to her side, dragging her out of the waves. Savka crouched with her at the water's edge, trying to get her breath back, aware that in the shallows of the bay, Taras had grabbed Ilyin by the coat, throwing him out and away from him. The Russian went under for a moment—the water too deep for him to get his footing. He flailed his arms as a boy would and Savka watched him struggle. "He doesn't know how to swim," she said to Jeanie, in wonderment. Could it really be that simple—Ilyin following her thousands of miles from Ukraine to Canada, only to drown in the Pacific Ocean?

Taras swung around, wiping salt out of his eyes to search for his old enemy. He thundered out of the sea and hovered for a moment to look Jeanie and Savka over. Convinced they were unhurt, he lifted his head to find Belyakov, who was scrambling up the headland, slipping on the rocks and moss. The cold sea water had revived her son. To Savka's surprise, he dropped his father's gun on the beach; the long barrel stuck up menacingly among the broken clam shells, gleaming in the dull light. She watched, astonished, as Taras fumbled in his breast coat pocket and took out the leather sheath containing his small, thin knife—the shiv he'd made to kill Belyakov.

Her Russian handler had climbed to the top of the headland. He looked back once, then turned, heading for the tree line on the other side. Taras sprinted after him, the shiv hard and glinting in his hand.

Savka broke away from Jeanie and stood, her coat sleeves dripping sea water. She couldn't take her eyes off Ilyin, who was still struggling in the sea. Finally, he seemed to give up and his head sank from view. This was the end, she thought, a fitting demise for the Russian soldier who, on Belyakov's orders, had shot her, then returned to rape her while she lay unconscious and bleeding in the snow.

Jeanie took a few steps into the frigid water, as if she meant to help the man she had no idea had violated Savka in such a horrific way. "We can't let him—"

Her words were cut off by a sudden, cascading spout, and Ilyin broke the surface of the ocean like a whale and somehow thrashed his way to shallower water. Savka stared in horror as Ilyin found his feet on the rocks. Why wouldn't he sink into oblivion? But he waded toward her, now waist-deep in the surf, his eyes searching out Taras who climbed the headland path, racing after Belyakov. Ilyin would never let her son catch the man who'd stolen his life.

Ilyin spotted Marko's old Webley on the beach at the same time Savka did. As if in a daze, she reached down and picked up her husband's gun. Then, everything seemed to slow. The wind died suddenly, as though holding its breath. When Ilyin noticed Savka raise the gun and point it directly at his chest, he paused, water lapping at his ankles.

From behind her, Jeanie said, "Wait, the police are coming . . ."

Savka took another step forward, her finger finding the trigger of Marko's revolver. *Could* she wait? The police were obviously up on Arbutus Road, unsure which driveway was Jeanie's. If Ilyin remained at a distance, she thought she might let the police handle this, but he waded slowly toward her, hand up as if he meant to talk her down. His eyes again flicked to Taras on the headland, and he smiled, his white teeth gleaming. "Savka," he said. "I could have killed you that day—in '44. I aimed for your shoulder. I could have aimed for your heart."

"My *heart*?" She stood rock still, her arms straight out and the gun foreign in her hand. A jolt of pain traveled down her arm and into her finger, tensed against the trigger, and her rage was there, too, the hopeless anger she'd kept hidden in her body for too long. She tightened her grip on the gun and adjusted her feet under her on the beach. "You wounded a little bird," she shouted at him, her voice surprisingly assured. "And put her in a cage—so you could *play* with her."

Ilyin's smile broadened, and her anger sharpened to a point. He found this, her, *amusing*. "We let you live."

He took several steps closer and Savka swallowed hard. In a moment, he would lunge at her and take the gun, then follow Taras. He'd shoot her son, probably kill him to save Belyakov. "Pretty bird," she said, lifting her thumb to pull down the hammer on the revolver. "Why don't you fly away?"

Then Savka squeezed the trigger with chilling determination, recoiling only at the surprisingly innocuous *pop* and a puff of smoke erupting from the barrel of the gun. Ilyin's eyes widened and he stared at Savka in disbelief as a blotch of red bloomed like a rose in the middle of his chest.

Savka backed away, watching silently as her rapist fell like a tree into the water, floating only for a moment before half sinking below the waves. Then it grew eerily quiet. She was vaguely aware of Jeanie prying the gun out of her hands as the police sirens suddenly started up again, fracturing the trance she'd been in. The sirens grew louder, they were almost here, and without a word Jeanie took a few running jumps on the beach, then threw the revolver far out into the ocean, where it could never be found.

54

TARAS

Salt Spring Island
DECEMBER 12, 1972

SHIV IN ONE HAND and his wet coat almost hanging off him, Taras
stands tall in the cool of the forest. He can see Belyakov running, his
head down, gasping with effort as he dodges among the trees. Taras
flinches at the crack of a single gunshot from the beach behind him. In
the ominous silence that follows, he turns his head. When he left Ilyin
in the water, the man had been drowning and weaponless. The shot
couldn't have come from him.

Taras hesitates, worried for his mother and Jeanie. Is it possible that
Ilyin recovered and came out of the ocean? He has to believe it's true,
that his mother has picked up Tato's gun and dispatched the man who
violated her in a Ukrainian forest so long ago.

He shakes his head to dispel the last vestiges of the drug, and to
catch his breath. Belyakov's figure is getting smaller, almost disappearing among the trees ahead. Taras hovers in a moment of indecision. If
he returns to the beach, the Russian will get away. The sirens are now
ear-splittingly close. He decides to go after Belyakov. The police will be
here soon to help his mother and Jeanie.

Taras bursts into a run, weaving and jumping over thick under-
growth. He spots Belyakov, resting with his hand on a tree, believing

he's escaped. Taras's old nemesis looks more like a drowned rat than a dangerous criminal.

With a few long strides, he closes the gap and sends the Russian sprawling, his pant legs peeling up his ridiculous legs to reveal a pair of drenched socks that reach all the way to his knees.

"Fuck your mother," Belyakov spits, his teeth bared and eyes on Taras's shiv, as though he has plans to lunge for it.

Taras blinks away the vile Russian curse and shifts the handle of the knife in his palm, its blade sharpened to a razor's edge. "Not the one my father gave me—not the knife you took from me in Ukraine," he says in Russian. He wants this man to understand every word. "I made this in the camp infirmary, for one purpose—to kill *you*." His voice calm even as his heart beats out of his chest. How many years he has fantasized about this moment, one he thought would never come. Face to face with the man who sent him to hell.

Belyakov crouches low, his dark eyes agleam. "You should never have been released from Black Eagle. A mistake. If I'd been camp commandant, you would die there."

Grief hits Taras like a hammer. He blinks rapidly to clear his head. "You're a petty grunt to the KGB. Only good enough for shit jobs." Taras inches slowly toward him. Since he found Mama in Vancouver, he's untangled countless mysteries swirling around the disappearance of his father. But there are still too many questions left unanswered. "Why were you following me? Why did you force my mother to spy for you, why follow her and Tato to Canada?"

Belyakov crawls backwards on his hands and feet, looking past Taras toward the headland, as if hoping Ilyin might appear to save him. He glances up at Taras and smiles. "Your mother didn't tell you about the Rimini list? Ukrainian men who fought against the motherland. Your father stole it." Belyakov's dark eyes flit desperately. "When I interrogated him at Rimini, I offered him a deal. Do you know what he said to me? *I would not trade my wife and son for eight thousand Ukrainian men.* He could have saved you, saved your mother from her fate, if he'd wanted to. But he chose his compatriots over you."

Taras glances at his hand—holding the shiv—and the tattoos inked on his middle fingers like a desperate prayer. *Spasi, Otets, Syna—Save me, father, your son.* A life-long obsession with his father had culminated in a fruitless search to find him again. But he's had it all wrong. Tato chose to save his men, not his own son. It's his mother who kept him in her heart for twenty-eight years, his mother who has sacrificed so much. "You used me as a bargaining chip to make Mama spy on her husband for this list?" He takes another menacing step toward Belyakov. "I once dreamed of running this knife across your throat, but death is too good for you."

Belyakov's escape has been blocked by a large tree. He presses his back against it with a look of shrewd desperation. Like all bullies, he doesn't enjoy having the tables turned on him.

Taras slips his shiv back into its leather sheath and circles the tree, circles his nemesis. "I'm handing you over to the Canadian police. Moscow will repatriate you. What I wouldn't do to see you in Black Eagle."

Belyakov cowers, raising his hands in front of his face, as if to ward off a blow. "Why don't you kill me?" He jumps to his feet, but Taras clamps a hand around his neck before he can bolt away. The Russian fights like a fish on a line, slashing and scratching at him with long nails that seem sharpened to a point. Taras yanks Belyakov's hands behind his back and he cries out in pain.

"These hands will soon beg your fellow prisoners—the worst serial murderers in the Soviet Union—not to kill you," Taras says in his ear. He kicks him in the back of the knees, and Belyakov sprawls forward, whimpering, his face pressed against the moss. Taras pulls out his blade again and drags him by his coat collar. The Russian twists, still fighting, his booted heels leaving wild drag marks in the moss and pine needles as he moans and roars in protest. The house and headland come into view and Taras flips Belyakov like a turtle, then pauses in the trees, his shiv drawing a prick of blood at the Russian's throat.

His eyes travel past the headland, where he can just see a sliver of beach, and a police officer wading out into the ocean to a body that's floating face up in the waves offshore.

Belyakov struggles to stand. "Ilyin," he cries, snot running down over his lip. He's spotted the body in the water, and Jeanie leading Mama up the path to the house. "*She* killed him." Belyakov cried. Taras's pulse leaps. After Mama exacted revenge on her rapist, did she have the sense to throw the gun into the ocean before the police arrived?

There's a burst of frantic activity at the far end of the beach, near the rowboat and kayak, where two police officers are dragging Pat out of a thicket of dense and thorny bushes. Another officer comes up over the headland path and spots Taras and Belyakov. He pulls his service revolver when Taras shoves the Russian forward. "KGB—high up," he tells the officer. "A prize."

Belyakov is snatched by the officer and pushed toward the waiting squad cars. He glances back at Taras, his eyes wild and uncomprehending, as if he can't believe he's been caught by Marko Ivanets's son, the one he sent to purgatory so long ago.

Bedraggled and dazed, Taras trails down the path from the headland. He's still soaking wet and bone tired, but he won't rest until he sees Belyakov in the back of a police car.

Jeanie leaves his mother and runs up the path toward him. She lifts Taras's hand. "No," she stammers, inspecting his bloody knuckles. "You could have been killed." She stops short of yanking up his sodden shirt to check for hidden injuries, then peers up into his face. "I could get used to that ecstatic look of victory."

He pulls Jeanie into his arms. *Victory.* Yes, that's what this is. Taras finds himself fighting tears, then he feels a warm flush of euphoria. The pressure in his chest eases, as if a shaft of light has burst out of the clouds and cracked him wide open. His hand in Jeanie's, they make their way down the path toward his mother, who draws him into a ferocious hug.

"My son," she says into his coat, still trembling after her confrontation with Ilyin.

Taras knows the Russian was her brutal rapist, a thug who made it possible for Belyakov to operate with ease, but killing a man, even an enemy, was not so easy. "I want to know every part of your story now, Mama," he says past a lump in his throat at the thought of the injustices and betrayals she has suffered, what she's sacrificed to keep him safe. "Don't leave anything out."

She releases him with a tentative smile and slides an arm around Jeanie's waist. "I will tell both of you." As the three of them make their way up the path toward the driveway, they don't look back, where two officers have pulled Ilyin's body out of the ocean. His mother's eyes are on the house and several officers who are struggling to handcuff a reluctant Belyakov. "I will never see him again," she says, her voice breaking.

At this moment, the clouds open up, and rain begins to pelt down, plastering Belyakov's hair to his forehead. "Don't touch me," he shouts, fighting the police officers' attempt to handcuff him. "I am important person—Stalin himself would tell you—"

He's cut off when an officer pushes him roughly into the back of one of the three police cruisers parked in the drive. "Stalin?" the officer says, slamming the door. "Stalin is dead."

A tall, rumpled plainclothes officer has come out of the house, a notebook in hand. He glances between Mama, Taras, and Jeanie. "Staff Sergeant Rumboli," he says, scratching his head. "Care to tell me what the hell happened here?"

"There's a woman swimming out in the waters of Houston Passage—" Jeanie's interrupted when two of Rumboli's officers pass them, dragging a reluctant Pat. "Kay strangled Marko Kovacs," she continues.

"And both nurses . . . violated his body." The sergeant frowns and uses his walkie-talkie, directing someone to call the coast guard.

"Lies," Pat shouts. "Jeanie murdered Marko Kovacs." She rears away as an officer claps a pair of handcuffs around her wrists. "You're making a mistake!" When the officer begins reading her her rights, Pat glances back at Gladsheim, the house she'd already considered her own. "You're arresting the wrong person," she insists. "Jeanie's insane."

Jeanie reaches for Taras's hand, but the officer has already wrestled Pat into the backseat of another police car. When two of the cruisers pull out and disappear in the trees, Jeanie takes a deep breath and turns to Sergeant Rumboli.

"The body in the water," she tells him. "Kay shot him before she dove into the sea."

Rumboli's eyes rest on Savka, who seems to hesitate.

"That's right," Taras adds. "I saw her do it." Kay admitted murdering his father, and men in Africa, what does it matter if another body, a Russian monster, is added to her list of crimes?

Rumboli nods and seems more concerned that the three of them will be inconvenienced by the presence of two officers on the beach, who, he tells them, will remain until the coroner collects Ilyin's body. He scratches something in his notebook, then flips to a fresh page. "Now which one of you wants to make a statement first?"

Mama leads him into the house, sending a small, brave smile at them over her shoulder, passing Tuna, who has ambled down the hallway to investigate.

"There's a body on my beach," Jeanie says, running a grateful hand over Tuna's dark coat. "Yet he's still smiling."

Taras laughs and scratches behind the dog's ears. "Tuna knows this was our last fight."

Jeanie turns her face to the sky, where a patch of pure blue opens like a window into another world. The rain has stopped as quickly as it began, the clouds scudding off to the west.

"We might fight over who gets the Sunday comics first," she says, leaning her head on his shoulder, "or if we should finally retire Aunt Suze's old rowboat."

"Aunt Suze's boat definitely must go," he insists with a grin, feeling as if he's come to the end of a long road on which he's been walking his entire existence, a road that led him to Salt Spring Island and the woman who lived in a bright and radiant house by the sea.

55

JEANIE

Salt Spring Island
MAY 1973

"HOW DIVINE," OCTAVIUS KARBUZ breathes over my finished French landscape. He turns to regard me like a father would a daughter—with pride and gratification. "It's an honor to finally meet you, my dear. I was stunned that you answered my call."

My art dealer wears a smart herringbone suit and square-shaped tinted glasses. His salt-and-pepper beard contrasts with an almost bald head that catches a ray of spring light blazing down through the skylight high above us. I took a long break after the events before Christmas, but finally returned to my studio to paint more abstracts and to face the French landscape. Better late than never. When Octavius hadn't heard from Pat about the commission, he called last week from the gallery in Brussels. He was so thrilled to finally speak to me in person that he'd gotten on a plane and arrived two days later.

"Pat told me you wouldn't let me come here." He adjusts his glasses, that keep sliding down the bridge of his nose. "She swore you were a recluse."

I steam a little, not surprised at Pat's lie. She not only kept thrill seekers at bay, but also the rest of the world—for her own benefit—and made me feel like I was a recluse by choice. It was Pat who ate away at my self-esteem, reducing me to a drugged puppet she could control, churning out art for her to sell and profit from. Pat who locked me in my own room at night and accused me of insanity.

Pat, who's now wearing prison overalls, denied bail and awaiting trial.

Octavius has wandered over to the stacks and is flipping through the abstracts I've painted for fun in the past five months. He makes a high-pitched noise of excitement. "Darling, why have you been hiding *these*?"

"Hiding what?"

"The most *remarkable* abstracts!"

I look at him in amazement. "Pat said you hated them."

He gazes at me, puzzled. "When Pat sent me one, years ago, I begged her—when is Jeanie going to do more? She said it was a one-off piece."

"Pat always told me I was an unremarkable artist who painted unremarkable landscapes," I say, surprised. "She said you refused to sell it— that you'd thrown it in the garbage."

"Well, I did sell it—for an unprecedented amount."

I'm stunned. "I find that hard to believe."

"Would I lie to you? Jeanie Esterhazy is one of my top earners."

This explains the substantial amount found in Pat's bank account. Apparently, she'd been skimming from the very beginning of the career I didn't know I had. Pat had been amassing a tidy little nest egg. With me out of the way in a sanatorium, she and Kay planned to live off the proceeds of the sale of Gladsheim.

But Pat isn't the worst culprit in my story. It was Kay who murdered Marko Kovacs, then escaped to Africa in the guise of nurse, angel, and savior. The coast guard found her—hypothermic and exhausted—on North Secretary Island, where she'd swam ashore. Canadian authorities reported Kay's admission of misdeeds in her clinic to the World Health Organization and the Congolese government, but the crimes she committed there could not be pursued because of her two convictions in Canada—strangling Marko Kovacs and shooting a Soviet spy.

I tune back in to what Octavius is saying. "Your landscapes fetch a decent price—better than decent—but you could have made more money with your abstracts. I never understood why Pat insisted you only paint landscapes and seascapes."

The answer hits me like a hammer. "Because it made me miserable. She didn't want me to be happy."

After Octavius leaves—wrapping up and taking the French landscape and every abstract except the one I'd done of Taras—I crank up some blues and start on a new work I've been planning, slashing away memories of the many years I painted ocean and mountain scenes, so that Pat could keep me in servitude. Late afternoon sun is filtering through the skylight when I suddenly realize that I've never started a single abstract with the fear I'll get it wrong.

There's a knock at the door and a voice, "I saw Octavius leave. Are you ready for lunch?"

"I'm always ready for lunch." I turn to find my husband standing in the door to my studio. "You don't have to knock, you know."

Taras grins. "I didn't wish to bother you."

I pat my growing belly. "I think you've already done that, Taras Ivanets."

He comes into the room bearing a sandwich and a cup of tea. After drawing me in for a kiss, he hands over the plate and peers at the new canvas. "Beautiful." As Taras studies my new work, realization, and then tears come to his eyes. "You have captured her."

"I've been sketching her for days."

He crosses to the window. "She's been out there since first light, come and look."

I follow him, munching on my sandwich, and we gaze down, the *three* of us, at Savka on her knees in the old vegetable bed near the house. After she weeded it out, a local gardening center trucked in soil and she planted every seed under the sun, getting her hands into verdant earth again.

Taras smiles. "She's in heaven."

"We'll have a harvest for the first time since Aunt Suze built this place."

Taras steps closer and slips his arms around me from behind. "In more ways than one."

I'm five months pregnant, due in September. *A harvest baby.* Taras has not left my side since the nurses and Belyakov were arrested. I think of how much my life has changed. No more deadlines, no more dodgy medication combinations, and Pat and Kay telling me what to do so they could live off the proceeds of my slavery. Less than a year ago, I was drugged with antipsychotics, and desperate enough to mount suicidal gestures. I once felt trapped here, unloved and unwelcome in my own house, sure that I owned it only in deed alone. Now it's *mine* for the first time. My "burn family" have left Gladsheim for good.

The day Taras came into my life I stood here in front of a dreaded blank canvas, feeling trapped, isolated, and sure that I was nothing to no one.

Now I'm a wife, about to become a mother, and I've inherited a mother-in-law and a sister-in-law. A true family. Gladsheim was once my prison, but now it's my refuge, where Taras, Savka, and I live in peace and safety, a place to grow. And a place for my husband to write anti-Soviet missives in Pat's old room, which we've converted to his office.

I put down my brushes for the day, and Taras and I leave the studio. We convinced Savka that she *must* move into the guest cabin, and that at age fifty-nine she never had to work again. She's in the process of clearing out her apartment in Vancouver and Taras and I are urging her on, but she's still traveling back and forth, complaining that it's a massive task to sort through a lifetime of junk—Marko's and hers—and it will take time.

Taras and I are heading toward the house, Tuna ambling along behind us, when a car comes down the driveway. Savka straightens in the garden, waving. Zoya parks and leaps out, laughing and running her hands over my belly. "The baby has grown, *matką być*."

I laugh with her. "This baby will speak many languages."

Savka joins us, brushing dirt off her hands. She puts her arm around me when Zoya turns, speaking to Taras in either Polish or Ukrainian.

"English please," he says, smiling at me. He's doing a lot more of this in the past five months. I lost count after the first few grins—when he said we would no longer have to fight anyone for our right to survive, when I told him I was pregnant, and again when we were married in a simple ceremony on the headland, under the Garry oak tree where we'd first met. With a nod to Aunt Suze, I wore her white Japanese kimono and a beautiful, beaded necklace that Savka had brought all the way from Ukraine.

I've learned a few words of Ukrainian from Taras and Savka. *Doro-hotsinnyy*, for one—precious—a word they use when referring to my pregnant belly. I watch them laugh together. My baby is *someone* to these beautiful people. *I* am someone. Although I lost many things to fire, although I lived so long a victim, although Taras and Savka and Zoya were born half a world away, into war and abuse and famine, I've found my love, I've found my family.

56

SAVKA

Vancouver
MAY 1973

SAVKA KNELT ON THE shag carpet in her Vancouver apartment, thumbing through family photographs. She was here to clean up and go through the last boxes that had been in the downstairs storage locker for decades. It was impossible to resist turning the album pages—the few old snapshots she'd had of Zoya as a child, and more recently, of Taras and Jeanie's wedding and their honeymoon in Italy.

She gazed around the rooms where she'd lived with Marko when they'd first come to Canada in 1949, where Zoya had grown up, the home where Taras had recovered from twenty-eight years in Siberia. The old furniture was gone—donated to Goodwill or taken to the dump. Nails protruded from the walls, the cheap framed pictures gone, too, leaving ghost-like squares from where she'd hung them long ago. Savka hadn't been happy here, so why was it difficult to finally say goodbye? Jeanie and Taras had made the guest cabin her own and Savka loved being on Salt Spring Island, spending every waking moment in the garden, her first one since the house in Deremnytsia.

Her life in Ukraine was a distant memory and so vastly different from the life she'd made here. Each beet and cabbage seed she'd planted in her new garden was in homage to her family—Mama and Lilia, her father, and Andriy, lost to the war and Belyakov's violence.

There was movement at the door and Savka flinched. It had been five months since the police had taken Belyakov away. Detective Jaeger had told her he'd been extradited to Russia and they'd lost track of his fate in a complicated tangle of Soviet red tape. Over the years, Belyakov had appeared so many times when she thought she'd escaped him. Was it possible that he was finally gone from her life?

"Your storage locker is now *empty*!"

Savka carefully placed the photo album into a box marked "Salt Spring Island" and smiled up at Lev Podolyan's shining face. "What are those?" she asked, glancing at the boxes he held in his arms.

"They were buried in the back of the locker. Looks like they haven't seen the light of day in years." He set them down in front of her. Lev pulled the yellowed tape sealing a box labeled "Tax Records" and began flipping through its contents. "Why did Marko keep every one of your tax returns?"

"Oh?" she said, lifting her head. "How many are there?"

"Some go back to the Middle Ages," he laughed, emptying the box of files onto the carpet. "They should all go in the garbage."

She sighed at the sight of folders labeled by year. Marko had done their taxes before he disappeared, and she'd only had her own to bother with since then. "We should go through them; some might be important."

Lev raised an eyebrow. "Tax records from the fifties?"

He got on his knees, his leg companionably against hers. She felt herself color like a schoolgirl. In the months after the events on the beach, she found herself struggling with her decision to shoot Ilyin. If anything, the man had haunted her dreams with that last look he'd given her, daring to smile. A few weeks ago, she'd finally screwed up the courage to call Lev, fearing he'd moved on with another woman in the fourteen years they'd been apart, but he'd come over immediately after hanging up the phone. They'd been circling each other—brushing hands and sharing looks of secret yearning—but had yet to take it further.

"Are you ready?" Lev grinned as he surveyed the mess of files and old receipts on the carpet. They dove in and soon had a mountain of papers destined for the basement garbage bin. Lev ran a hand through his now silver hair. "Will our children care to keep anything when we are gone? That is what I want to know."

He went downstairs to pull his car up to the front of the building, and Savka stood, surveying the remains of her old life. Her eyes lighted on the pile of papers and brightly colored tax files. A document had slid loose from one of the folders, and it now lay face up on the rug, yellowed with age and decidedly out of place. She stooped to slip it back into the file, and suddenly she was back in 1947. Savka's hand reached for the nearest wall before her legs gave way beneath her. Fingers shaking, she brought the document closer, shocked tears blurring her vision.

It didn't seem like anything much, this ten-page typewritten military document of names in alphabetical order, validating birthdates of each soldier in the Fourteenth Waffen-SS Division, and the villages in Ukraine where they'd been born. The list felt like fragile parchment in Savka's hand, the names of men the KGB still wanted dead for taking up arms against the Soviet Union. She held it against her pounding heart, the list she'd spent half a lifetime looking for, this testament to the fight against oppression and tyranny that still raged on the far side of the world. The document was watermarked and worn by twenty-seven years of devotion, and it bore signs of the long journey it had taken—stolen from a British commander's desk in the Rimini prisoner of war camp, and stashed, most likely in the lining of her husband's coat, sailing on the troop ship through the Mediterranean and across the English Channel, then brought to Canada, hidden by Marko in places that had eluded her and three KGB operatives tasked to find it by Stalin himself over continents and decades, only to land here, in an old tax folder.

The Rimini list.

Marko had hidden it so well it had taken a move for her to find it.

Heart in her mouth, she went into the kitchen, to the old stove where she'd cooked thousands of meals for Marko and Zoya. Where she had stood for so many years of her life, tired and aching, grieving for things known and unknown.

Turning the large front element on high, she waited while it heated up, finally glowing red as a poker. Touching the edge of the Rimini list to the burner, she watched it smoke, then catch fire before she tossed it into the sink, where it blackened, the names obliterated as it burned to cinders.

She heard the door open again and Lev's voice from the hall. "Where are you?" He popped his head into the kitchen. "What's burning?"

Savka turned and smiled. "I'll tell you later," she said, and picked up the remaining box that constituted the best memories of her life.

Lev threw the files into a large green garbage bag and opened the door. He wedged the bag against his hip, lifting a hand to smooth her hair. "When you wouldn't take my calls, I thought I'd done something wrong."

"Far from it." She gazed up at him, her eyes brimming with tears. "Come out to the island," she said. "I'll show you my garden."

Lev touched her arm, bending to kiss her, and she felt her heart race with possibilities. He drew away after a delicious moment and smiled. "I've never seen you so . . ."

"Happy?" Savka laughed, a little breathless at the sweet burn of his lips on hers, and at the sight of his face, wavering in reflection, as though he looked down at her in the underworld and all she must do was finally emerge from the shadows of the dead, breaking the surface with a stunned cry for all that she had missed.

It wasn't too late.

AUTHOR'S NOTE

Jeanie's voice has haunted me my whole life. Jeanie is loosely based on a burn survivor whom my mother took care of after graduating from nursing school. Mom kept the newspaper clippings about her tragic accident and photographs of her in the hospital, where she remained for two years. This burn survivor was moved to Mom's gynecology ward only because a big enough room was available there to house her Stryker frame.

As I was growing up, I often studied these news articles, wondering what had happened to this burn survivor after she was released from the hospital. When I was thinking of my next historical novel, I knew I wanted to respectfully base a character on her and dream a story where "Jeanie" found her own perfect place in the world.

When plotting this book, I imagined being in a hospital ward for two years. And what "Jeanie" might have heard or seen sequestered in her universe of four walls. My mom remembered a nurse on that ward who was accused of stealing a patient's morphine, which inspired me to create Pat O'Dwyer, and I began searching for another female character who would also be admitted to the ward and whose story would parallel Jeanie's, linking them forever. I asked my mother about the other patients at that time, and she said there were women newly arrived from Eastern Europe. In the late fifties, when my mother was on that gynecology ward, many of these women were having hysterectomies. Why? I started to research, some kind of vague horror driving me forward. Where was this quest going to take me?

I started to look at women's experiences in WWII in Eastern Europe. I came across articles by four remarkable female academics and daughters of Ukraine (listed below). Because the Eastern Front rolled through Ukraine many times during the war, there were often mentions of Ukrainian women's experiences of sexual violence. These stories triggered a raw secret I still held in my own body and a startling realization. The Ukrainian and Hungarian women my mother treated in a Canadian gynecology ward in the late 1950s could possibly have been there because they'd experienced horrific sexual violence during WWII.

I did this research in the fall of 2019, not knowing that Russia was readying itself to invade Ukraine yet again. I realize now that it was my own past trauma that drew me to the Ukrainian female OUN insurgents these academics wrote about, and I felt compelled to pull their forgotten stories out of the historical record. The character of Savka Ivanets emerged as a composite of the brave female insurgents who served in the underground during and after WWII. And whose roles were not adequately reflected in history. I should mention: these stories only seem "forgotten" to most of the world, but not to the Ukrainian academics who first told them, and not to the ancestors of these women, who still carry centuries of Russian abuses in their DNA and are faced with the same dangers their mothers and grandmothers had suffered in WWII.

In an earlier draft of *The Last Secret*, my editor (thank you for your sensitivity and keen insight, dear Bhavna Chauhan) asked me why Savka didn't react to injustices or say much in her scenes. I hesitated to answer, having only told therapists and my trusted friends my "terrible secret" over the past forty-two years. Taking a breath, I told Bhavna, "In 1981, I was drugged and raped by three men. Because I also experienced sexual violence, I thought Savka would be numb, like me." My editor said, "You're a survivor, and Savka's a survivor. You're going to give her a voice." That was a pivotal moment for me. A voice? I was a writer. Supposedly I gave voices to underdog characters, but some traumatized part of me still felt I didn't have one. The voice you hear in Savka is me trying to heal an experience of sexual violence and get past the need to keep it hidden from view for fear of pity, shame, or judgment. Perhaps the last secret I tell in this story is my own.

I was inspired by the following four remarkable female academics and daughters of Ukraine to write Savka Ivanets and the brave Ukrainian female insurgents who served in the underground during and after WWII.

Dr. Olena Petrenko: *Among Men: Women in the Ukrainian Nationalist Underground 1944–1954*; "Intermediate Positions: Women in the Ukrainian Armed Underground of the 1940s and 1950s"; and "Anatomy of the Unsaid: Along the Taboo Lines of Female Participation in the Ukrainian Nationalistic Underground."

Dr. Marta Havryshko: "Illegitimate Sexual Practices in the OUN Underground and UPA in Western Ukraine in the 1940s and 1950s"; "Love and Sex in Wartime: Controlling Women's Sexuality in the Ukrainian Nationalist Underground"; and "Women's Body as Battlefield: Sexual Violence during Soviet Counterinsurgency in Western Ukraine in 1944–1953."

Dr. Olesya Khromeychuk: "Militarizing Women in the Ukrainian Nationalist Movement from the 1930s to the 1950s."

Dr. Oksana Kis, author of the article "National Femininity Used and Contested: Women's Participation in the Nationalist Underground in Western Ukraine during the 1940s–50s."

Maria Savchyn Pyskir's book, *Thousands of Roads*, and Luba Komar's wartime memoir, *Scratches on a Prison Wall*, gave me a glimpse into the lives of women in the Ukrainian underground during WWII and beyond. And other women's experiences in Eastern Europe during and after WWII with Agate Nesaule's *A Woman in Amber* and *Eine Frau in Berlin* by Marta Hillers.

Taras Ivanets is a fictional composite of Ukrainian intellectuals who were arrested, tortured, and sent to Siberia in the 1930s and 1940s. I am indebted to Aleksandr Solzhenitsyn's *The Gulag Archipelago*, Eugenia Ginzburg's *Journey into the Whirlwind*, Varlam Shalamov's *Kolyma Tales*, and Danylo Shumuk's *Life Sentence: Memoirs of a Ukrainian Political Prisoner* for helping me understand a political prisoner's life in the Gulag.

The character of Lieutenant Belyakov is based on Nikolai Yezhov, the 5'1" head of Stalin's Secret Police from 1936 to 1939. He often threatened his prisoners by making the sound of a man strangling at the end of a rope and saying, "I may be small, but I have hands of steel, because these are Stalin's hands." The quote in the prologue: "Do you understand how far you have fallen? I'm disgusted to look at you . . . a monster, a filthy person, a pervert . . ." was verbatim from Yezhov's interrogator before he was executed in 1940 for "unfounded arrests," during Stalin's purges. Yezhov was obviously a psychopath, and I wondered, if he had lived after being denounced, what evil he might have gotten up to if assigned to look for something so valuable and elusive to the Soviets as the Rimini List. A roster of the Ukrainian soldiers who were incarcerated in the Rimini, Italy, prisoner of war camp from 1945 to 1947, this list also served as inspiration for *The Last Secret..* In this story, I took creative license and had Marko steal the list to keep it from the Soviets, but in reality, the Rimini List was classified and kept by the British government at the Public Records Office (now called the National Archives) in London from 1947 until it was declassified in 2014.

The character of Marko Ivanets/Kovacs is a fictional composite of several real-life Ukrainian underground leaders who joined the Fourteenth Waffen-SS Division to fight the Soviets in WWII, eight thousand of whom spent two years in a POW camp in Rimini, Italy, before the British government moved them to the United Kingdom. Some of these men continued to fight Russia for an independent Ukraine during the Cold War, sponsored by both the SIS (MI6) in England and the CIA in North America. I found valuable information in Timothy Snyder's *Bloodlands*, and in *Harvest of Despair: Life and Death in Ukraine under Nazi Rule* by Karel Berkhoff. For more insight into the Fourteenth Waffen-SS Division, I read Per Anders Rudling's article, "'They Defended Ukraine': The 14. Waffen-Grenadier-Division Der SS (Galizische Nr. 1) Revisited," and Michael James Melnyk's books *The History of the Galician Division of the Waffen-SS, Volume 1: On the Eastern Front: April 1943 to July 1944* and *The History of the Galician Division of the Waffen-SS, Volume 2: Stalin's Nemesis*. Also Terry Goldsworthy's book *Valhalla's Warriors: A History of the Waffen-SS on the Eastern Front 1941–1945*, and *Searching in Secret Ukraine*, Wasyl Nimenko.

Wasyl Nimenko, author of *Searching in Secret Ukraine*, helped me understand how Britain failed the Fourteenth Division in its early days at the Rimini POW camp. Nimenko wrote: "Fundamentally, the British were a little slow in realising that if they kept to the conditions agreed at Yalta, every 'Soviet' they sent back would be executed by Stalin's unspoken directives or sent to Siberia as traitors who fought with the Germans against the Russians." It was only when Eleanor Roosevelt and the Pope got involved that Britain began to protect the remaining members of the Fourteenth Division at Rimini and moved them to England to keep them out of Soviet hands.

The quote in chapter 7, "The olden times were not like the days we live in. In the old days, all manner of evil powers walked among us," is from an old Ukrainian folk tale, "The Tsar of the Forest," in *Cossack Fairy Tales and Folk Tales*, translated by R. Nisbet Bain.

Historical novelists generally stick to the historical record, but sometimes we bend facts to serve our stories. Salt Spring Islanders who lived there in the seventies will notice that I took artistic license with the ferry service to their island. In 1972, there were only two sailings each day.

I set Savka's story in Western Ukraine. Although her family village, Deremnytsia, is fictional, what happened in so many Ukrainian villages during WWII was abominable. Ukrainian women and children suffered first under German occupation, then under Soviet reprisal when the Germans were driven out. In this story, I took artistic license in mentioning that some members of Savka's and Marko's families starved to death during the great famine, Stalin's genocidal starvation of Ukraine from 1932 to 1933, which is now referred to as the Holodomor. After WWI, lands previously held by the Russian and Austrian empires became the Republic of Poland from 1918 until 1939, when Hitler and the Soviet Union invaded Poland. The Carpathian Mountains are in the Southwestern corner of Ukraine and were included in the Republic of Poland. As a result, this historic part of Ukraine narrowly missed experiencing the Holodomor.

It would be an oversight not to mention such a horrendously criminal act as the Holodomor in Savka's story set in wartime Ukraine. The hardship and suffering wrought by this horrific genocide is in every Ukrainian's DNA. And it is not such a difficult thing to understand why Ukrainian men joined with Germany to fight their common enemy during WWII.

I also briefly mention the Nazi forced labor transports in this book. Savka's and Lilia's husbands were in Waffen-SS and Schuma battalions, so they were exempt from forced labor transports, where Ukrainian children as young as ten years old were stolen from villages to work in Germany under horrendous conditions. Erin Litteken's *The Memory Keeper of Kyiv* and *The Lost Daughters of Ukraine* are powerfully moving historical novels about how Ukrainians suffered and found ways to survive the Holodomor, and the forced labor transports in Ukraine during WWII. I highly recommend reading her novels to learn more about these harrowingly pivotal times in Ukraine.

ACKNOWLEDGEMENTS

Bhavna Chauhan, editor extraordinaire, you elevated this story and brought out the best in me as a writer. I raise my grateful hands to you. Thank you, thank you to my stellar agent Carolyn Forde, who first championed *The Last Secret* and has been so supportive during the editing process. I'm very grateful for the team at Doubleday Canada and Penguin Random House Canada, in particular, for Maria Golikova, Megan Kwan, and for Kelly Hill for the gorgeous cover and interior design. And a gushing, fangirl thanks to Gil Adamson, an author I've long revered, for her brilliant copyedit.

Thank you to Canada Council for the Arts for their support in the writing of this book. I extend continued gratitude for inspiration and soul nourishment from the unceded territories of the Snuneymuxw First Nation and Coast Salish peoples of Salt Spring Island and Vancouver Island, upon which I wrote this story.

Thank you to beta readers Sandra Coldwell, Maria Peck, and Kristina Birkhans. So much gratitude to Ken Koshgarian for his fine beta read, unwavering support, and for consulting with legal issues in the text. Thank you to Dorrie Ferster for helping me with Salt Spring information and whose beautiful house on Southey Point served as inspiration for Gladsheim. Gratitude to Katja Geiger, who helped me with German words/phrases. My thanks to talented painter and friend, J.D. Hawk, who provided valuable information on painting techniques. Any remaining errors are mine alone.

A special thank you to Bogdana Varvaruk, daughter of Ukraine, whose insight into the story was invaluable to me.

My gratitude to Dr. Jeffrey Burds, whose article "Sexual Violence in Europe in World War II" was so helpful to me. Jeffrey has been very supportive of this book, keeping me supplied with articles, and patiently answering my weird research questions.

My beloved daughter Shasta—thank you for support while I was in the chair, researching, writing, and editing for four and a half years, and for not rolling your eyes too much when I hashed out plot issues with you on our walks.

I am blessed to have dear friends like Sandra Coldwell, Heather MacTaggart, Patricia Fortner, and Helen Murray, who listened to me talk about Russian submachine guns one too many times and whose support was a lifeline for me while writing this story.

My biggest thank you goes to bestselling author Lilian Nattel, who I blind emailed four years ago while plotting this book, asking a big question in regard to writing about women and sexual violence on the Eastern Front in WWII. I'd decided that if Lilian answered in a certain way (or did not answer at all!), I would take it as a sign I should abandon this story. But Lilian took a strange writer under her wing and became not only a mentor but a dear friend. You've read this story because of her.

QUESTIONS AND TOPICS
FOR DISCUSSION

1. *The Last Secret* is largely told from Savka and Jeanie's perspectives. How do their alternating points of view enrich the narrative?

2. Secrets play a pivotal role in this story. Of all the secrets kept and revealed throughout the novel, which did you find the most impactful?

3. The primary settings of the novel—war-torn Europe and Salt Spring Island—are dramatically different. In what ways did the contrast between these two settings affect your reading experience?

4. The frailty of memory appears as a recurring motif throughout *The Last Secret*. How do Jeanie's memory issues influence her reliability as a narrator?

5. Savka is faced with an impossible choice: to spy on her husband to get her son back or to kill her Russian handler to prove she is not a spy. What would you have done if you were in her situation?

6. Jeanie is frequently made to feel like a monster by those around her. Who do you think are the real monsters in the novel, if anyone?

7. Both Savka and Ewa must make moral compromises to survive the war. How do their choices differ? Could you see yourself betraying a friend to protect your family?

8. At different points throughout the story, both Savka and Jeanie admit that they feel like marionette dolls, and at the mercy of puppeteers pulling the strings. How do Savka and Jeanie's experiences mirror each other?

9. Imagery of caged animals appears throughout the novel, with Jeanie even referring to Pat as her "zookeeper." To what effect do you think Maia Caron uses this imagery?

10. As a Ukrainian woman facing a Soviet Counterinsurgency, Savka is treated as if "her body [is] nothing but a hilltop in war, [with] the conqueror taking his spoils." Why do you think women's bodies are so often used as battlegrounds during periods of war and instability?

11. While under the thumb of Belyakov, Savka is forced to make countless sacrifices to protect her son. Was there ever a time when you didn't agree with a choice that Savka made?

12. Who would you cast in the screen adaptation of *The Last Secret*?

13. While Marko values his duty to his country over his duty to his family, Savka values the opposite. How do their differing values fundamentally shape their relationship?

14. How do Jeanie and Taras—two people who have been profoundly hurt and betrayed throughout their lives—learn to trust in each other? Could you see yourself trusting in a stranger after everything that they have endured?

MAIA CARON is an Indigenous writer and author of *Song of Batoche*. She swapped her dream home in Toronto for a dream life in the Pacific Northwest, where she researches and writes women's untold stories of the past. She can often be found hiking the wild, mossy trails of Vancouver Island with her family and a fierce little pug called Scout.